NO LEMONS IN MOSCOW

HELEN WHITTEN

Matador
Unit E2 Airfield Business Park,
Harrison Road, Market Harborough,
Leicestershire. LE16 7UL
Tel: 0116 2792299
Email: books@troubador.co.uk
Web: www.troubador.co.uk/matador
Twitter: @matadorbooks

ISBN 978 1805141 570

British Library Cataloguing in Publication Data.
A catalogue record for this book is available from the British Library.

Printed and bound in Great Britain by 4edge Limited
Typeset in 11pt Minion Pro by Troubador Publishing Ltd, Leicester, UK

Matador is an imprint of Troubador Publishing Ltd

To my sons
Rupert, Oliver and Daniel

and my grandchildren
Emmeline, Max, Ivy and Eliza

May they live in a peaceful world
and
may they always be able to speak their minds

She would never forget him
Never forget Russia
There would always be some dusty corner
In her heart where he stood
In the shadows of the Kremlin

PROLOGUE

Russia, 2000

From the cold confinement of his hidden compartment near the chassis of the battered Lada, Valentin can sense the driver, Andrey, brake and park. He hears Andrey open his door quietly, leaving it on the latch so as not to disturb the sleeping neighbours, then walk to the back passenger door. He undoes the catch above Valentin's head, lifting up the back seats, and helps Valentin to extricate himself from the mesh cage below, in which he had been travelling, curled up like a foetus. Valentin pulls his long legs out and manoeuvres himself onto the darkness of the pavement. He hesitates. Then, as an afterthought, he grabs his laptop from the car, not wanting to leave it with Andrey, and quickly slides into the shadows at the back entrance to his apartment block. He lets himself in.

Once in the hallway, he starts to climb the dimly lit stairs. The grey light of dawn seeps through the landing window. He stops for a moment, leaning his back against the wall, exhausted, cursing the fact that there is no lift in the apartment block. The laptop is heavy on his shoulder, but he's grateful that his old army colleague Lev has sourced it for him after his last was stolen. Reaching the fifth floor, he puts the laptop down beside his front door. Flicking his dark hair from his eyes, he pulls the key from his trouser pocket but, as he fits it in the lock, the door swings open. He stiffens.

Silently, he inches himself through the wooden door, his body taut. He pushes open the kitchen door to his right with his foot, then the bathroom door. No sign of anyone. The small studio room, that doubles as a workspace and bedroom, is ahead of him, and he suddenly sees a flicker of light. He backs himself against the wall, his heart pounding. What to do, run, or risk being killed?

Taking control of himself, he pulls his body up to his full height, feeling his strength as he does so. *Remember, Valentin, you were a soldier, you fought in Afghanistan*, he thinks to himself. *You can tackle this.*

As he moves forward, a man, short, stocky in a black anorak, barges like a streak through the door, throwing Valentin back against the wall so hard that he bangs his head. The man runs down the short hallway and out onto the landing. It takes Valentin a moment to right himself, then he chases after him, but the man is quick as a bullet, already several floors below on the stairs and out of sight.

Valentin follows, jumping over the banisters to the next landing. He wants to see the man's face, be sure he would recognise him, but he is out of practice. Those army days were many years ago now and the intruder has vanished out of the apartment block and halfway down the street by the time Valentin reaches the door. He sighs, gasping for breath. He'll never catch him now.

Wearily he runs up the stairs for a second time. He knows Andrey won't wait for long. At his doorway, he stops to collect his laptop. It's gone. He and Lev had spent most of the night downloading his articles and research. All gone. Again. He punches the wall in fury.

"How could I have been so stupid?" he curses himself, but he didn't know Andrey, couldn't trust him, so he couldn't have left it in the car.

He runs to his desk in the studio and sees that the drawers have been rifled. His research papers are everywhere. He's worked hard to hide away in recent months, to move from one place to another, but they have found him again. Taken everything. He gathers up what he can, but he can't afford to keep Andrey waiting. His fellow journalist, Alina, had been shot outside her apartment block last month. He knows he could be the next target. His mind works fast. He reaches for his mobile phone and dials London.

"Kate," he whispers her name with urgency, "I need your help."

PART ONE

1990

ONE

Russia, 1990

Kate leans towards the window as the plane starts its descent into Moscow Sheremetyevo International Airport. She can see little through the dense October clouds. The wings dip and dive, then the plane lands and skids along the wet runway.

Moscow. The place she has dreamt of visiting since her teenage years. As the engines switch off, she grabs her bag from under the seat and follows the slow shuffle of passengers down the aisle towards the exit, down the steps and onto the tarmac. She stops a moment to experience the sense of finally being here, in Russia, remembering how she had written to her mother from school, in a melodramatic teenage sort of way, that she had wanted to die in Russia. *What drama queens teenagers are*, she thinks to herself, as she decides she definitely does not want to die here.

"I hope you made the most of the British Airways' offerings on board?" Harry, a man Kate had met briefly at Heathrow as they had boarded the flight, is in the passport queue ahead of her. He has a pleasant face, a little worn with life, thinning blond hair and smiling blue eyes. He's wearing a dark navy fleece coat and brown cords, and she estimates that he's a few years older than her, perhaps around forty. She notices that he doesn't wear a wedding ring and clocks that this is the kind of thing she may be looking out for now when she meets men. "I've heard that there are food shortages and no lemons in Moscow," he says, "so I guess we'll have to drink our G&Ts without."

Kate laughs. "Yes, but surely, we'll be drinking vodka from now on?"

Harry nods, with a rueful expression. "Of course. I'll have to get used to that. It's not my favourite tipple."

The terminal building is dimly lit, and although it is early afternoon, it feels like dusk. Kate hands her documents to the unsmiling passport officer. He looks at every page, slowly, as if it might hold threatening secrets. Eventually, after several long minutes, he refers to a large book, and then, almost reluctantly, stamps the visa and hands her back the passport.

The smell of tobacco in the baggage claim area is choking. Armed guards in uniform line the beige concrete walls. Harry wanders off to get his case and Kate looks around her. She's a small figure, neat, in jeans and a cream polo neck under a sheepskin coat. She fidgets with her shoulder-length red hair, which defiantly escapes any attempt she makes to keep it tidy behind her ears.

Spotting her black suitcase, she sighs with relief, picks

it off the carousel and makes her way towards Customs. Newly divorced, it's the first time that she has travelled abroad alone in all her thirty-five years. She tries to disguise her anxiety. She's used to her ex-husband, Simon, taking control of organising their holidays. He runs an art gallery and frequently flies to visit artists in their studios abroad to check out whether he will represent them. Kate, on the other hand, has travelled little and has certainly never travelled without a parent, friend or husband to accompany her. Now she is alone, in Moscow, with twenty-two strangers, all with an interest in Russian literature.

"Thank God we're out of that," a pink-faced lady with a Scottish accent exclaims as they walk out into the Arrivals Hall, dragging their cases behind them.

"Yes, indeed," Kate agrees, turning towards her, in relief. "My name's Kate."

"Gillian," the older woman responds with a smile. "Is this your first time in Russia?"

"Yes. And you?"

"No, I came here as a student, in Cold War times. Mind you, despite Gorbachev and his Perestroika, it doesn't feel as if it has changed that much!"

A short woman with curly grey hair, wearing a dark coat and sensible brown walking shoes is holding a placard up: 'Russian Literary Tour'.

"Oh look," Kate points, "she must be our guide."

The two women walk over to hear the guide introduce herself as Olga. She speaks good English and tells the group to get into the waiting coach and that if they have any requests or interests, they should come to her and not go off anywhere alone.

The coach driver picks up the cases and throws them into the baggage compartment as Kate and Gillian climb the steps to take their seats. As they enter, Kate notices a handsome young man with thick dark hair sitting next to the driving seat. She finds her eyes pulled back towards him as she makes her way down the coach. Gillian finds a place near the front and Kate moves down the aisle to sit in one of the last available seats, next to a large man she estimates to be in his fifties.

"Hi, I'm Mike." He extends a pudgy hand towards her. "Pleased to meet you'all."

Kate smiles at him, finding his Southern accent endearing.

"I'm Kate."

"You travelling alone?" he asks.

"Yes, and you?"

"Yeah, my wife ain't interested in books. She's a musician, plays the saxophone. That's her game."

The coach moves off down wide boulevards and streets full of dreary Communist-era concrete blocks. Large black limousines career around the streets with no consideration for other cars.

"Hey, you can bet they're the communist officials," Mike comments, looking out of the window. "Whatever the political system, people always create a hierarchy, don't they?"

Kate nods.

"Did you hear, the Reunification of Germany was signed yesterday?" he carries on. "It's nearly a year since the Berlin Wall fell. All those years of division and suddenly it went down in an evening. How crazy is that?"

"Yes, there's so much change since then, isn't there," Kate replies. "Where do you live?"

"London. We have an apartment near Tower Bridge overlooking the river. I work for an American bank – as you may have guessed, I'm originally from the Nashville area." Mike grins as he says this. "So, where're you from, Kate?" he asks.

"London too, but I'm just moving house, so rather betwixt and between."

"Oh hell, really?" Mike looks at her with a concerned expression. "I hear from your voice that this is a difficult move?"

"That's perceptive. Yes, I'm in the middle of divorcing and so my son Tom and I are moving. He's not that happy about it."

"And where's he now?"

"With my best friend Eve, in Hampstead. She's his godmother, and they adore each other. I almost didn't come as I feel so bad about leaving him at this point. My mum really disapproved of the whole thing, but she's not well enough to look after him herself." Kate's hands knit firmly together as she speaks.

"Don't fret too much, Kate," Mike says. "It's not always as bad as you think. It can be a great moment. I'm divorced. I'm much happier now, and so is my ex-wife. My kids went through a hard time, but they're good now."

"Oh, thanks, that's a nice response. It does feel horribly difficult and sad when you're going through it." Kate raises her eyebrows and gives him a forced smile.

"Yes, it is," he agrees. "You have to put your armour on until you get to the other side."

"So, it's your second wife who plays the saxophone?" Kate asks.

"Yeah – that's not something our London neighbours appreciate very much! Hey look, it's the Kremlin," he says with excitement, peering out of the murky window.

The coach trundles over the Moskva River and the architecture changes. Kate recognises the red walls of the Kremlin – gold domes, green roofs – from all the pictures she has studied before the visit. Then, all of a sudden, they pull up in front of a hideous monolithic block of concrete. The Rossiya Hotel.

"It's one of the largest hotels in the world," Kate says. "Around three thousand rooms!"

"Wow, let's hope we don't lose one another then," Mike jokes, smiling.

Kate walks along an endless, brown-carpeted corridor to find her room. She passes a formidable lady with a samovar who looks at her over thick-lensed glasses, then lets herself in and lifts her case onto the bed. She looks around. Her first impression is of a dingy room with battered furniture, dim yellow light bulbs and a narrow bed that looks more like a camp bed, its mattress thin as paper as she sits on it. She unpacks, then investigates the bathroom to wash her hands. There is no soap, so she's glad she has brought a bar of Imperial Leather. The water is tinged brown as it runs from the taps, and the towel she wipes her hands on is as threadbare as a teacloth. She had wanted a bath, but there is no plug.

She notices a television set in the corner of the bedroom. It's an old brown set and she tries the knobs.

It doesn't work. There is no hairdryer in the room so no hope of taming her hair. "I look like some bloody flame-haired Medusa," she mutters to herself as she changes and goes down to join the others for supper.

The hotel restaurant is enormous, like some giant school canteen. The smells are similarly of boiled cabbage. There's a table set aside for the Russian Literary Tour group. Kate sits down next to Olga.

"I haven't a clue what I'm eating," a man who introduces himself as Desmond whispers in her ear when Olga is distracted talking to the person on the other side of her. "I think the first course was some kind of fish? And I don't know if this is veal, or chicken? What do you think? It's the worst food I've ever eaten!"

Kate looks at him and agrees conspiratorially.

"Let's go for a walk across Red Square," he suggests as supper comes to an end.

"That sounds fun. I just need to get my coat from upstairs."

"I'll meet you by the front door in ten minutes. Mike wants to come too," Desmond says.

The two men are waiting for her when she comes out of the lift, and the three of them walk out across the cobbled stones. It's a crisp, clear night and St Basil's rooftop shines reflected colours in the moonlight. Kate stops to take it in.

"Isn't that beautiful? I can't believe I am here. It's so wonderful," she says dreamily, "though I wish I didn't miss Tom so much."

"Just enjoy yourself, Kate," Mike advises her, patting her shoulder. "Let go. Guilt gets you nowhere. Live in the moment."

He is interrupted by a couple of young street vendors who approach them, offering fur hats and alcohol. Desmond delights in bartering cigarettes, biros and chewing gum for a bottle of vodka and a tin of caviar, which had been hidden in the young boys' backpacks.

"Everything costs $5." He laughs. "Hold on, I'll just get another bottle of vodka, then let's go back to the bar and drink it!"

"Sure," Mike says and does a deal to buy two more tins of caviar. Kate watches with admiration. She has always felt awkward bartering in street markets.

Back at the bar they battle with a Swiss Army penknife to open the tins of caviar, with the men competing to be the one who succeeds. Eventually, with the help of some nail scissors, the juicy black balls of caviar are revealed and enjoyed as they pass them around, using the penknife to scoop them out. They slug the vodka straight from the bottle.

"Oh God," Kate exclaims after some time as she looks at her watch. "It's nearly two o'clock. I must go to bed. I feel exhausted."

She rises and says goodbye to her new friends, making her way to the hotel lift. As she walks past reception, she sees Harry chatting to a brunette. He waves to Kate.

"Goodnight! Mind you, don't get kidnapped by some Russian," he calls.

Kate shakes her head. "Of course I won't!" she replies irritably, wondering, as she walks on, whether her irritability came from a sense of jealousy that Harry was talking to another woman and hadn't joined them on their walk.

The lift takes forever to arrive, and just as the doors open, the tall young man she had noticed in the coach arrives and walks in behind her.

"Hello. Which floor?" he asks, and she delights at the sound of his Russian accent.

"Fourth, *spasebo*."

"So, you speak some Russian? But you need to say *pozhaluyshta* if you want to say please." There's an arrogance about him, she notices. He says something more in Russian, and she gets the feeling that he's deliberately trying to discomfort her.

"No," she says firmly. "I don't speak Russian. I was just trying to be polite."

"Ah," he replies, and smiles. Or is it a smirk? "My name is Valentin Kotov." He holds out his hand, but at that moment the lift arrives at the fourth floor and Kate gets out, calling 'goodnight' to him as she walks away.

"You might think you're some kind of Casanova, Mr Russian Valentin," she says under her breath, "and I have to admit you are the most incredibly handsome man I have ever met, but right now I just want to get to bed."

TWO

Russia, 1990

The alarm rings and Kate sits up in bed. She reaches over to the small photo of Tom on her bedside table, kisses it and slides it into the purse in her handbag. Getting up, she tears a piece of paper off her notepad and writes a short fax to Eve and Tom: 'I have arrived in Moscow! Love and miss you, Mum xxx'. Then, remembering that Tom had been worried about her safety, she adds a PS: 'I am safe and well looked after'. She drops the fax at reception as she goes down to breakfast.

"Kate! Come and sit here," Harry calls to her as she enters the restaurant. "We're talking about literature, whether there's a particular author that drew you towards the trip?"

"Yes, certainly – Boris Pasternak," Kate replies as she takes a seat and helps herself to a bread roll. "I read *Doctor Zhivago* as a teenager, and I think it's fair to say that it changed my life. Then went on to read other Russian authors. I bought all Pasternak's books of poetry and even tried to learn Russian to read them in the original, but that was one goal too far!"

Harry laughs. "Yes, that would be a stretch. I'm particularly interested to see Tolstoy's estate. Like you, I read the Russian novels in my teens and student years. It will be interesting to see whether all these places are anything like we imagined when we read about them."

"Yes, I wish we were able to visit Pasternak's home at Peredelkino, but I think he's still persona non grata."

"Well, it's not a good thing to be a writer on the wrong side of a brutal regime." Harry frowns, twisting his lip.

"True. But it was Pasternak's lover who had the hardest time. The Julie Christie character in the film," Kate points out. "She was put in prison, lost his baby."

"Careful who you fall in love with then," Harry says slowly, with a wink.

The group are taken by coach to the Palace of Kuskovo, built on a lake for Count Sheremetev, a field marshal under Peter the Great, who led the Russian army into victory over the Swedes. Sheremetev, Olga tells them, became one of the richest men in Russia and ordered the palace to be more beautiful than any other building.

"Gold, gold gold," Harry notes. "Not surprising they had a revolution."

"Just what I was thinking," Kate agrees. "And makes me wonder how the Russian people will adapt now to the changes Gorbachev has in mind for them. Will the idea of opening up to the West feel too alien for them?"

"I fear it won't be straightforward," Harry muses, and they stop to listen as Olga points out a fresco on the ceiling, depicting Innocence at the crossroads between Love and Wisdom.

"Oh God, that makes me think." Harry sighs. "How many times have I been caught in that trap, and wisdom has flown out of the window!"

Kate laughs with him. "I don't think I have a wise cell in my body."

"Well, you were wise enough to come on this trip. That says something. But without mistakes we can't become wise, can we? Maybe the more mistakes we make the wiser we become?"

"In that case I should be some kind of wizard by now!" Kate laughs, as Olga moves them on to look at the palace gardens, dotted with pavilions, and tells the group how the servants used to perform sea battles on the lake.

They return to the hotel to eat another meagre meal for lunch and Olga recommends that they have a restful afternoon, as they will go to see *The Snow Maiden* at the Bolshoi that evening. Gillian suggests to Kate that they take a walk down the Arbat. Kate is delighted to have company and they saunter past the stalls of paintings, bric-a-brac and Russian Matryoshka nesting dolls, some painted with the faces of Russian presidents, from Lenin to Gorbachev. Kate decides to buy one for Tom and negotiates with a vendor, a man with a chipped front tooth and dressed in an old khaki army jumper with holes in the elbows, who asks her, in broken English, to pass him the dollars in a handshake, then returns to slide the doll into her handbag.

"They can get five years in jail if they're caught taking dollars," Gillian tells her. "But they're pretty desperate so they take the risk. There's so little food in the shops."

As they walk back towards the hotel, they turn a corner and come across a young man on a soapbox. He has straggly dark hair, wears a battered-looking leather bomber jacket and is reciting what sounds like poetry in Russian. A group of people have congregated around him, and Gillian and Kate join them. Neither understand what he is saying but are drawn in by the passion in his voice.

"Americans?" asks an elderly man, bent with age, with watery blue eyes and a pale wrinkled face, standing beside them.

"No, British," Gillian tells him.

"Political poet," the man says, rather breathlessly, pointing to the speaker. "Criticising the government, talking of the days of Marxism. Wants to turn back the clock."

"Do many people want to go back to Communism?" Kate asks.

"Old people, yes. But young people want to buy jeans." He shrugs. "No food, no medicine. Just want jeans." He shakes his head.

Suddenly they become aware of the sound of shouting. The crowd starts to move and separate. There's a scuffle behind them. Kate can't see what's happening but then two policemen in black helmets with rifles in their hands appear out of nowhere. They push through the small audience, who quickly disperse. One of the policemen tries to grab the poet but the young man pushes them aside, leaps high in the air, jumps from his box and runs like a cheetah across the square and out of sight. The policemen run after him, shouting.

"What happened?" Gillian asks, turning to where the old man had been, but he has gone. "Come on, Kate. We should get out of here."

They turn back towards the hotel and Kate starts to run, but Gillian catches her hand. "Walk," she whispers firmly. "We don't want to attract attention. We could be arrested just for being here, for watching."

"Christ! This is a different world," murmurs Kate, as they slow down and walk purposefully back to the hotel, where they go straight to the bar and order shots of vodka to calm their nerves.

After a short rest, Kate slips on a black velvet dress and pats her hair down, then walks down to reception to join Olga, who will take them to the ballet. As the group assembles, Kate notices the tall Russian from the lift last night. Valentin. He's standing next to Olga and bending down to talk to her. He glances over at Kate and smiles. Quite a genuine smile this time, she thinks. He is absurdly handsome.

"I have an announcement to make!" Olga calls them all to attention. "I want to introduce you to Valentin. He's my cousin. He's a journalist and is joining us for the ballet tonight. He will tell you a little about the Bolshoi and the story of *The Snow Maiden*. He's also interested in talking to you about what brought you here to Moscow, as he may write an article about this group of British with a passion for Russian literature."

Valentin steps forward. He looks young and, in this

context, rather nervous, brushing his dark hair frequently off his forehead. His suit could have belonged to his grandfather and has definitely seen better days. He's tied a red scarf loosely around his neck.

"Good evening. Tonight we will see Tchaikovsky's *Snow Maiden*," he says in excellent English. "He wrote it in 1873, finished it in a month. So, he was a fast worker." Valentin pauses and looks around. "It's a Russian folk tale. The Snow Maiden is beautiful. She has snow-white skin, deep sky-blue eyes and curly fair hair." For a second his eyes land on Kate. She shifts awkwardly under his gaze, her lips moving stiffly into a smile. "The Snow Maiden is the daughter of Father Frost and Mother Spring, the immortal Gods, and goes to live with an elderly couple who have no children. She sees a young man, but her heart is made of ice and unable to know love. But Mother Spring takes pity on her and creates a spell that allows her to fall in love. The trouble is that as soon as she falls in love, her heart warms her body, and she melts. So, it's a tragedy. We're good at being melancholy here in Russia."

"That's very true," Desmond whispers to no one in particular, and several of the group murmur and nod in agreement.

"Off we must go now," Olga interrupts and leads them all on a swift walk to the Bolshoi, where they take their seats in the magnificent auditorium, surrounded by lush gold and red velvet decor, to watch the ballet.

"How did you find it?" Valentin approaches Kate at the end of the performance.

"Fantastic!" she replies, after a moment's hesitation.

"It's not quite The Royal Ballet in London, is it?" he probes.

"No, I will admit that I have seen more polished performances, and more beautiful sets, but it's wonderful to be here, in Russia, seeing the Bolshoi. I've waited for this for such a long time."

"Have you? Then I hope we shall make your trip memorable."

He helps her with her coat and leads the group out onto the cold street.

"Wow, it's freezing," Kate exclaims, and Valentin spontaneously takes off his fur cap and places it on her head. "You won't have time to get used to Russian weather in ten days. But you would need to be here in January or February to experience real cold."

"Well, I'll have to come back and test it out for myself then, won't I?" Kate replies.

"Olga," Valentin calls to his cousin. "Let's take them to a bar."

Olga nods and they walk to the next street and enter a noisy bar where people stand talking and smoking. "Vodka for everyone!" Valentin says to the barman in Russian and then in English, as he settles the group down in two tables of twelve at the back of the room, then takes a seat next to Kate. A chipped glass carafe of vodka is placed down on the table, with a variety of small shot glasses. He pours some into Kate's glass, then his own and passes it around the table. "*No Zdorovie!*" he says, clinking her glass.

"*Nostrovia,*" she responds, taking a gulp and gagging as the fiery liquid hits her throat.

"You'll get used to it!" he says, laughing.

"Tell me, how did you get such a good English accent?" Kate asks him.

"I went to an English college here, before I went to fight in Afghanistan."

"You fought there? That must have been ghastly."

"Yes, it was cold, and hard, and I learnt that it is difficult to change things in another country. The longer I was there, the more I felt that really only the Afghans can change their own lives. We weren't popular, of course."

"No, I can imagine that," Kate replies, then pauses. "So, what are you doing now, apart from guiding us?"

"I earn a pittance working as a journalist on a local paper in Orel, where my sister Anya lives. She looks after my daughter, Lara. She's nine."

"You have a daughter?" Kate nearly chokes as she hears this, as he doesn't look old enough to have any child, let alone a daughter of nine.

"Yes," he says with a slightly sheepish look. "All a bit of a mistake. But she's beautiful."

"Good. I have a son, Tom. He's only seven. I love him to bits."

"Of course you do," Valentin's voice softens as he speaks, and Kate's shoulders relax as this beautiful young man pays her attention. "So," he continues, "you have longed to come to Russia, and I long to go to England, but it's expensive and very difficult to get visas."

"Is it?" she asks, surprised. "I thought everything was opening up now?"

"Only if you have money. For most of us we have no food, no jobs; people who have degrees are doing menial work. I can't see an end to it."

Kate notices Harry looking at her from the other table. He smiles and she smiles back.

"Well, despite all that, Valentin, you are living my dream," she says. "I always wanted to be a journalist when I was young."

"You're still young, not much older than me, for sure." He's flattering her. "But why didn't you?"

"My mother put me off!" Kate laughs. "She told me I would meet nicer people in libraries. She meant a suitable husband, of course. So, I worked at the London Library for a while, then set up an events consultancy when I had Tom."

"She wouldn't have considered me to be a 'nice' person then?" Valentin looks at Kate teasingly, his brown eyes flashing. He's definitely flirting, his leg touching her thigh, his hand occasionally caressing her arm.

"Obviously not," Kate replies. The vodka was relaxing her reserve and she told him about her wish to become a foreign correspondent, someone like Kate Adie, covering Tiananmen Square. "But I didn't have the guts," she confesses.

"I want to set up my own press agency," Valentin states. "Where I can publish news without the interference of the Kremlin or the government. I think your newspapers are free of this meddling by governments and the elites?"

Kate shrugs. "Mainly, yes, but editors have their own views and can shape what is printed. But we do have a free press."

"I'd like you to tell me about it. I am beginning to build up some good stories here, stories that need to be told, but I don't think I can print them in Russia." His voice dips as he speaks, and then his attention is alerted to two men who have just entered the bar and taken their seats at a table nearby. *They look like clones of the gangsters one might see in a Mafia film*, Kate thinks, thick-set, dark-haired, in black jackets, with the shadow of a beard around their chins. Kate notices Valentin watching them, and them watching him.

Mike asks Olga whether the guides are allowed to tell tourists everything or have to edit the information they give the group, as they used to in Cold War times.

Olga looks uncomfortable. "No, of course we can tell you what we like, answer any of your questions."

"Maybe," Valentin interjects, with some reservation in his voice, and perhaps a little too much vodka in his system. "But, Mike, you should hear my mother. She's always telling me to stop blabbing, to keep my mouth shut. 'You'll get yourself into trouble, son' she says to me. That generation, you know, they have fear in the blood, from times gone by."

Olga coughs and Kate notices that she seems to try to signal something to him, her eyes darting to the two men who have recently arrived, then back to Valentin. There's a pause and his words freeze on his tongue, like a hesitation, within the hubbub of noise. There's an awkward silence, then, as if to repair a mistake, Olga starts to tell the group what they will be doing the next day. Conversation gradually revives and the moment passes, in which time Olga moves towards Valentin, and Kate hears her whisper something angrily in his ear. She gets the impression that Olga is accusing Valentin of being responsible for the presence of the two men.

Valentin frowns and stands up. "Let's go back to the hotel," he says to the group. He takes Kate's hand to help her up, placing himself between her and the two men, his muscular body like a protective shield, sheltering her from the sinister energy of the two watchdogs.

THREE

Russia, 1990

Kate awakes with a start in the night, restless, calling for help. As she pulls herself upright, she shakes herself, knowing the nightmare scenes all too well. The birth of her first son, William. Her experience of being left in a small room while in pain and haemorrhaging. Blood soaking the sheets. No one coming to her aid. William born floppy, being sent home as he recovered but dying a week later. She wipes the sweat from her forehead and, as she recalls the shock and sadness, remembers that today would have been his ninth birthday.

She can't get back to sleep. It's five o'clock, so she rises, pulls back the heavy curtains and looks out onto Moscow. It's a grey morning and she feels alone and far from anyone who knows or loves her. She thinks of Tom sleeping quietly in Eve's house, can almost smell the scent of him, the sense of stroking his skin, ruffling his dark curly hair. It leaves a deep hole in her stomach to feel so distant.

Yet she is finding that travelling alone is also liberating, a moment to experiment with who she is. After years of caring for Simon and Tom she has noticed that she had almost forgotten even what she likes to eat herself. Being here, surrounded by new scenes, tastes and smells, and people with similar interests to her own, is reawakening her taste buds and her senses, remembering the parts of her she felt she had lost.

Her mind drifts back over the experiences of the last couple of days, how she has learnt to hide dollars in teapots and napkins, in *cafés* or restaurants, doing deals to buy tins of caviar and bottles of champagne. How the maid working in the ladies' toilet in the hotel had offered her a bottle of vodka, signalling that she had a bottle secreted under her overall. Kate had slipped $5 into the maid's pocket then tucked the bottle under her jumper as she exited. She is learning that everything is hidden. Everything is $5.

Yet, in the midst of the black-market deals, yesterday she had experienced a transformative moment on a visit to the Zagorsk Monastery, as she stood under the golden frescoes of the vaulted ceilings. Harvest offerings had been scattered around the altar and the scent of incense pervaded the air. The priests, in long, dark robes, were chanting incantations in deep voices. She'd felt moved to tears by the moment, in a place that felt truly spiritual. Walking out in a daze she had joined Harry, who exclaimed, "Extraordinary atmosphere," and he talked of feeling something eternal inside the walls, though confessing to not being a particularly religious man.

He had continued by musing, "I'm intrigued by the monastic life, though. I've often speculated on the fact that it is necessary for monks to be celibate."

His comment surprised her. "Why?" she'd asked.

"Because falling in love and keeping love strong is so all-encompassing. I'm not sure I'd have time for Jesus and for prayer as well. I'm just a bloke, you know, as we are, one thing at a time!"

She'd laughed, and thought about it, but remarked that maybe the monks and priests weren't necessarily as pure and celibate as they might appear.

Harry had nodded. "You're probably right. One day I hope I shall mature enough to find that warm thread of love that will burn quietly, like the coal in my Aga at home, gently heating the heart, rather than completely overwhelming me. Mixed metaphors, sorry. But do you know what I mean? I haven't managed it yet. It's all too dramatic, somehow."

He'd surprised her again. She hadn't taken Harry as someone who would be overtaken by his passions. On the outside he seemed so much to be the reserved Englishman. He'd gone on to tell her how, in his work as a financial advisor, he had noticed that couples sometimes come together later in life, 'when the passions of the ego have dissipated a bit', how he had noticed they were able to be more authentic and honest. "I've spent half my life pretending to be someone else when I'm in love, fearful that they won't like the real thing."

Kate had listened to him quietly, then told him how lost she was feeling at the uncertainty of her future after fifteen years of marriage. He had stopped and taken her hand.

"The only advice I would give you, Kate, is to take your time. Don't rush. Get the divorce over and have a break. Regroup." Then Olga had called them back to the coach.

Kate turns away from her reverie at the window and remembers that today they are leaving Moscow to go to Orel and Tula. They will visit Tolstoy's and Chekhov's estates. She must pack.

As they leave Moscow, Kate watches the countryside change. Flat fields where people are working on their hands and knees picking vegetables, digging potatoes. She sees little farm machinery, just back-breaking work, as if turning the clock back several decades. Even the main roads are full of potholes and covered in mud from the fields.

She finds herself sitting next to Margot, a woman of around forty who is always dressed pristinely, her blonde hair perfectly curled, her clothes fresh and uncreased despite the days of excursions. Kate feels rather daunted by her as she sits next to her, but Margot turns and chats in a friendly manner about her life running a PR agency, and they share their experiences of the tour.

"Do you know anything about fundraising?" Kate blurts out after a while, as the coach goes around a corner, its wheels sliding through the sludge at the side of the road.

Margot turns her cool grey eyes towards Kate, quizzically. "No, not exactly," she replies. "What are you thinking of?"

Kate explains to her that she wants to set up a charity, to create a maternity home where babies can be born in safety in a peaceful environment that doesn't feel clinical, where mothers can feel held. "Rather like a hospice, I suppose, a small centre, with staff trained not only medically but also to support the emotional needs of patients."

Margot's eyebrows rise as she listens. "It will be hard work, Kate, for sure," she says, frowning. "And it's not my experience. I've never had kids, so I don't know what's involved, really, other than what I have read about and the stories of my friends. It would be a major project but a worthwhile one, of course. You will need several million to make that happen, I would have thought, plus, of course, the ongoing income to keep covering the cost of running it."

"Yes." Kate nods slowly. "I haven't done the detailed calculations yet. It may all be quite impossible."

"I wouldn't give up on it that easily. I am sure people told Cicely Saunders that her ideas were a pipe dream originally when she was setting up the hospice movement, and now it is a crucial part of end-of-life care, so no reason why you can't start something similar for beginning-of-life care!"

Kate smiles. "Thanks for being so encouraging. My mother thinks I'm barmy to think of it."

"No, don't let that get to you," Margot muses. "There's no logical reason why you can't do it. We certainly raise money for corporate sponsorship. Companies are beginning to think more about corporate responsibility – you know, giving to their community and that kind of thing. Let's keep in touch and I shall put my thinking cap on for you."

"That's incredibly kind, Margot, thanks."

Valentin's voice interrupts them over the Tannoy. "We are arriving at Chekhov's country house." He comes to stand beside Kate and Margot, microphone in hand. "Please get your things together for our visit," he says, giving Kate a smile that sends a current down her body.

FOUR

Russia, 1990

It's a tranquil estate. Chekhov's house has a pretty veranda overlooking the cottage garden. Here, Kate reflects, Chekhov had practised as a doctor and written *The Seagull* and *Uncle Vanya*. There's a gentleness in the autumn air, a humming of bees, a dragonfly that hovers close. Kate breathes it in, thinking of the writer, a man who tended the lines of vegetables and fruit trees, a man who observed the intricate and often complex relationships between families and within families. She enjoys soaking up the soft scents of harvest time, her feet sinking into moist earth and fallen apples.

She's happy to wander alone for a moment, away from the chatter of her fellow companions. Enjoying the solitude of this quiet place, she notices a bench at the edge of the vegetable garden and sits down, allowing her mind to drift.

A little while later she sees Harry approaching. He has some wild flowers in his hand.

"Do you mind if I sit beside you, or did you want to be alone?" he asks quietly.

"Of course you can," Kate replies, smiling and happy to see him. She is finding his presence comforting in the midst of so much activity.

"Here," he says, handing her the little bouquet of pink, purple and yellow flowers, "you have these. They won't last long but I couldn't resist picking them."

"How lovely, thanks." Kate is touched by the softness of the little flowers, and by his gesture, and the thought that he is the kind of man to notice such tiny petals in the midst of the woodland bordering the garden.

"D'you know, I have been reading Pushkin at night when I go to bed. The last few days have been such a turmoil of experiences and conversations. They've become all mixed up with scenes and memories of my life," he says softly. "I feel I have been put in a tumble dryer and totally shaken up. Do you?" He looks at her.

"Absolutely." Kate finds it a relief to express this. "It's been so full on. New people, new places, learning about Russia, yet not really understanding the people, I think."

"It's such a rich history but so full of conflict. But having you on the tour, Kate, has stirred something up in me too. I'm not sure what, but I wanted to share this poem with you, if that's OK?"

"Of course," Kate says, bemused.
And he recites, quietly and slowly:

"A magic moment I remember:
I raised my eyes and you were there,
A fleeting vision, the quintessence
Of all that's beautiful and rare
I pray to mute despair and anguish,
To vain the pursuits world esteems,
Long did I hear your soothing accents,
Long did your features haunt my dreams.
Time passed. A rebel storm-blast scattered
The reveries that once were mine
And I forgot your soothing accents,
Your features gracefully divine.
In dark days of enforced retirement
I gazed upon grey skies above
With no ideals to inspire me
No one to cry for, live for, love.
Then came a moment of renaissance,
I looked up – you again are there
A fleeting vision, the quintessence
Of all that's beautiful and rare."[1]

He has a melodic voice, with a slight drawl, old-style British, but not plummy.

"I read this to my wife many moons ago," he says gravely, running a hand through his smooth grey-blond hair. "It's still true of her today and, when I think of her, I can still remember the magic moments of times gone by, of when Isabelle, our daughter, was little, how a new baby in the house brings that absolute quietness of a new life.

---

1   Alexander Pushkin, 1799–1837, 'A Magic Moment I Remember'

Do you know what I mean?"

"Well, I'd hardly say quietness was the word I'd use, when they scream all the time!" Kate laughs. "But yes, I think I know what you mean. It's an extraordinary moment when a new life enters the home. Thanks for sharing the poem. It's beautiful. And this is a beautiful environment in which to hear it."

Kate would like to say something meaningful but is lost for words.

"When I looked at you yesterday, as we walked around Moscow, it came to my mind again. Those words, 'beautiful and rare'," he says. "So, that's it."

He stands up abruptly, puts a hand on her shoulder, then walks away. She sits there, watching his retreating figure. The ground feels like jelly beneath her feet as she tries to grasp what has just happened. He seemed to want to share some message, but she can't make out what. Perhaps, she thinks, as she stands and straightens her skirt, it had nothing to do with her. Perhaps he was just feeling sentimental about his ex-wife?

She shrugs her shoulders and walks back to join the group. The battered coach rumbles back into action and off they go again. She sees miles of flat countryside, fields edged by walls of pine and birch trees, standing like soldiers to attention, as if ready to march. She dozes, confused after her encounter with Harry, worrying about how she will make money when she returns to London, relieved that Margot has said she might be able to help her raise funds for the charity.

Kate wakes suddenly, her neck cricked at an awkward angle, her head leaning against the coach window. She's waking from another nightmare, this time about the men in the bar in Moscow after the ballet. The ones she thought might be KGB. There was snow all around and they were chasing her. They threw her into a basement room, with no windows. She didn't know where Tom was and felt completely isolated and helpless. She shudders.

"Are you OK?" Alison, sitting next to her, asks. "You were jumping around in your sleep as if you were fighting someone off," she says, frowning as if in disapproval.

"Just a bad dream," Kate brushes her off, aware that she's not being particularly friendly.

"The coach driver keeps losing his way," Alison goes on. "He doesn't even have a map, so he has to keep stopping to ask the route. We've had to turn around several times, in the middle of these narrow country lanes, then his wheels got stuck in the ditches. You've slept through it all!"

"Well, it doesn't sound like I have missed much," Kate replies stiffly, embarrassed that she had let her guard down in her sleep.

"We saw brides, all dressed up, disappearing into the darkness of the woods," Alison burbles on. "I asked that man, the tour guide, Valentin, what they were doing. He explained there are chapels in the woods where young couples like to marry. Brides are too poor to buy new wedding dresses, so they borrow or hire one for the day. Sad, isn't it?"

"Sounds quite sensible to me," Kate murmurs, thinking of her dress lying scrunched at the bottom of her wardrobe.

Looking out of the window again, Kate is aware that the shortages are obvious here in the countryside too.

There are queues of cars and trucks lined up at garages, due to the shortage of petrol, queues of people outside butchers where she can see only one or two chickens visible in the windows.

"Terrible, isn't it," Alison comments, pointing at the queues. "Olga tells us that the price of meat is rising daily. And there are no lemons or oranges!"

Harry, sitting on the other side of the aisle, hears Alison's comment and waves to Kate. "Told you so!" he mouths.

The coach brakes and comes to a stop in a country lane. They get out and buy some apples from pink-faced and jolly Russian ladies selling a variety of apples from buckets beside the road. They stand in front of a row of small colourful wooden houses set in modest gardens, surrounded by white picket fences. The women have scarves around their heads and, a little further away, Kate notices a group of women heaving weighty bags across the muddy fields, their clothes old, their shoes tattered and covered in earth. But they are chatting animatedly amongst themselves and at least, she thinks to herself, they can barter butter, milk or vegetables between them here.

They climb back into the coach, munching their apples, and reach the motel at around seven in the evening. It's dark, and the air is cold. The ladies on reception greet them eagerly with cups of hot tea.

It's a low two-storey concrete building, more modern and comfortable than the Rossiya. Kate's room has a simple bed, chair and plywood wardrobe and looks out over a scrubby lawn and some trees. She has a shower and hears music coming from somewhere down below. A thud, thud of drums. She pulls on a green wool dress, brushes her hair, touches up her make-up and goes downstairs for supper.

The music is coming from a party of Russians sitting at a large table at one end of the restaurant. The women in the party are in garish dresses and have badly dyed hair of various red, auburn and peroxide colours. The men are sweaty, drunk and raucous. They call out a greeting to the British group as they assemble at the tables set aside for their tour.

"Dance! Dance!" they shout as Kate and her companions sit down and are served with watery soup.

"Here," an elderly man totters over to the table, "have some champagne." He passes the bottles over.

"It's an anniversary celebration," explains Valentin. "They are telling you to enjoy yourselves too, and join in. It's unusual for them to have a tourist group from Europe here."

Alison and Desmond join in the dancing. Mike seizes Kate's hand and pulls her up, deftly drawing her into a jive. She's impressed by his footwork, considering what a large man he is, and realises she hasn't danced for years. The music, champagne and exuberant Russians are a heady mix.

Two women from the Russian group bring over slices of an enormous chocolate cake. They invite the Englishmen to dance. A large peroxide-blonde woman in a tight-fitting pink satin dress pulls Desmond to her breast, a buxom girl in a silver lamé dress pushes between Kate and Mike and takes him into her fleshy arms. Liz, Margot's mother, a plump woman in her mid-sixties who is the antithesis of her daughter, always rather dishevelled, looks drunk as she dances. Her lips are smeared with red lipstick as she clings to a sleazy-looking silver-haired Russian with wandering hands. Margot looks horrified. "Mum! For goodness sake, sit down!"

Kate notices Harry dancing close with the Spanish brunette, Lucia, on the tour, who, Kate believes, has been trying to monopolise him. She feels a pang of jealousy that he isn't dancing with her and drifts off to the bar. As she enters, she notices Valentin sitting on a stool at the counter.

"Hello, Kate," he calls. "Have a drink."

The bar is full of smoke. Men stand around talking loudly amongst themselves. She takes the stool next to his and looks at him. He's wearing a white shirt and black trousers. The shirt is unbuttoned at the top and she can see the dark hairs of his chest, the line of his broad shoulders. Her body responds spontaneously to the closeness of him as he hands her a glass of champagne.

"That's a pretty good way to party," Kate remarks, laughing.

"Yes, work hard, then play hard. That's what we have to do in this country." His voice is disconsolate, angry even.

"Is everyone fed up with the government?" Kate asks. "I thought Gorbachev was opening up opportunities for you?"

"Pah! No. It's all talk. No one understands what he is trying to do. I trained as an engineer, but I would only get 160 rubles a month if I practised. Rubles – just paper money. Worthless! You can't buy anything. You will have seen that. There's nothing in the shops."

"But journalism can't be better paid than engineering?" she questions.

"No, but at least I am doing something I believe in, and if I have to work doing guiding or waiting in bars, then I shall make time to write." He's a little drunk, she notices. "I told you, it's my dream to start my own press agency. I have stories to tell the world." His brown eyes flash, his jaw juts forward as he speaks, although his lips are having a little trouble in articulating the words. "It's all impossible."

"But it won't always be. Not if the banks understand private enterprise. You will get a loan, pay it back as you start to make money," she says, trying to help him see a different perspective.

He shakes his head, strands of thick, dark hair falling across his forehead. She has an impulse to touch them, to smooth them back in place.

"I have to write, Kate. I have to tell people how hopeless it is here."

There's something Byronic in his despair, in his passion and his good looks. Kate watches his lips and wants to kiss them, to taste his tongue, touch him. She keeps her hands safely on her glass.

"That's a great aim, Valentin. Don't lose sight of it. I'm sure you will be able to make it happen."

"Perhaps with your help, Kate?" His hand touches hers as he speaks. Their conversation stops as the chemistry sends a charge from one to another.

"Of course," Kate replies. "If I can help you, then I will."

He places a hand gently on the side of her face. "That's kind," he says. His beauty overwhelms her, his brown eyes consuming her, and she feels his breath on her cheek. She feels like a novice as he leans forward and kisses her lips. He tastes delicious to her, of tobacco and vodka, and at his touch, she is on fire. The champagne slips through the pathways of her mind, she has a fleeting image of Harry dancing with Lucia, of Simon in his new relationship in London, of Tom miles away. Nothing is clear. Then Valentin's hand is on her leg, sliding slowly up her thigh and she loses touch with where she ends and he begins.

He takes her hand and helps her off the stool, leading her down a corridor. It's dark and he stops and kisses her hungrily. She hardly notices where they are going until she is dimly aware of a small bedroom. Nothing matters or registers as he pulls her to him, his hands lifting her dress over her head. He draws her to the bed in his strong arms and, despite a voice somewhere deep inside her shouting that this is not a good idea, she is overwhelmed with longing as they weave their bodies into one.

FIVE

Russia, 1990

In the first shadows of the morning, Kate wakes to find Valentin deep in sleep, his long eyelashes dark against his pale skin. His legs are heavy, entwined with hers. She feels embarrassed, wanting to get back to her room before the others wake up, fretting about how she will manage this situation.

Yet her body feels alive in a way it hasn't felt for years as she slowly moves herself from under his limbs and climbs out of bed. She steps to a corner of the room to dress, then creeps out of the door and back along the corridor towards her room. As she crosses the reception area, she sees Liz coming back through the main door, with the sleazy silver-haired man she had danced with the night before. They kiss, and Kate scuttles up the stairs to her room, hoping she hasn't been seen.

The sun is just beginning to come up as she showers, then makes her way down to the restaurant.

"Hi there, Kate, come sit with us," Mike calls to her, waving his beefy arm, a broad smile on his face.

"Thanks," she replies, grateful for the easy ability some Americans have to make conversation.

"Margot tells me that you're hoping to set up a charity, some maternity homes?"

"Yes, well, just one to start with anyway." Kate explains her idea to him.

"Hmm," he says as he finishes chewing on the stale bread roll, "that's some ambitious dream, Kate, but maybe my bank can help you raise some money. Who knows? Let's keep in touch when we get back. It sounds a worthwhile cause."

"That would be fantastic," Kate responds, feeling uplifted that the two people to whom she has mentioned her charity idea have responded so positively. Then, at the entrance to the dining room, Kate notices Margot having an argument with her mother, Liz. She presumes Margot was not impressed with her mother's antics the night before and hopes that Liz didn't see her creeping through the reception area in the early hours of the morning.

Her attention is distracted as Olga summons them to the coach to head for Tolstoy's estate at Yasnaya Polyana.

"Good morning, Kate," Harry calls as she climbs up the steps of the coach. He pats the seat next to him. "Let's talk a little of *War and Peace*."

Kate sits beside him on the faded, brown seat and hopes she can get her brain to work to say something intelligent.

"The question Tolstoy posed, or one of them, as I understand it, was whether peasants are the noble race. Personally, I don't see that nobility of soul is restricted to any one race or class, do you? Surely this is a quality available to any human being, peasant or king, don't you think?" Harry turns towards her, his blue eyes questioning.

Kate gulps. This all seems a little heavy for first thing in the morning, especially after the night she has just enjoyed. Then, summoning her brain into action, she says, "I read that Dostoyevsky came to understand just that, when he was sentenced to hard labour. He started off by being horrified by the savagery of his fellow prisoners – murderers, rapists, thieves. Then, as time went by, as he received some kindness from them, he came to understand that they had been the victims of brutality themselves so, basically, that barbarity creates barbarity. So, he argued, there's such deep complexity within us all that there is the potential for compassion within even a barbarous murderer."

Harry pauses and looks out of the window for a moment, considering her words.

"I am a great believer in human development," Kate continues, "that we can turn our lives around, have become more understanding of diverse ways of living, different perspectives."

"Ah, now there I agree. At least we don't sentence people to hard labour, nor eviscerate criminals in the village square anymore. Our society is way more tolerant and compassionate than it used to be in our parents' time, let alone in the middle ages."

"What did your parents do?" Kate asks him, hoping to move the subject to a simpler topic.

"My mum was a housewife and my dad ran a boat-building company on the Dorset coast. I still live not far away."

"But you didn't carry on in his business?"

"No, sadly the company went bust when his partner fiddled the books and took all the money. It killed him." Harry sighs, sadness clouding his eyes. "So, I became a financial advisor. Some people think it's boring, but I know I can help people provide for a good quality of life and hopefully not get ripped off the way he did." He pauses and lifts his left arm, drawing back his cuff. "This is my dad's watch. I think of him every time I look at it."

"That's lovely," Kate replies. "It's a beautiful watch. And your mum?"

"She died shortly after he did. About ten years ago now, when I was thirty-one. I thought I was a grown-up, but I felt bereft when I had to sell the family home. My sister lives in the States, so it fell on me to do the organising. What about you, Kate? Where were you brought up?"

"In Ealing, London, not far from the common. My mum worked in the local library and my dad was a dentist. He was a workaholic, spent every hour in his surgery. It gave me a lot of freedom. My best friend Eve – she's looking after Tom – and I used to have teenage parties in the house in the afternoon because both Mum and Dad were out. But then he died. Just like that. He collapsed one afternoon at the surgery. I was at school, but my mum rushed to the hospital, so she was with him when he died that evening. I was told to go home with Eve, so I didn't know anything about it until she got back from the hospital and picked me up from Eve's house."

"How terrible for you," Harry says softly.

"Yes, I was just seventeen. He'd started to help me understand the world, begun to help me feel like a woman. My mum had always been quite hard on me, and he softened that – complimented me when I was going out to a party, encouraged me with my studies. His death left a huge hole in my life."

"How did your mother cope?"

"Basically, she didn't. She spoke over and over about how she didn't tell him she loved him in those last moments of his life. She felt that if she said those words, they would both start to cry and never stop. But tears aren't like that, are they? They do stop eventually. But she went into a depression and became really quite abusive to me, very critical. Then she became an alcoholic. Her first bout started when I was at uni. I didn't know how to cope, so Eve and I moved into a flat together."

Harry whistles and nods pensively.

"I think that's why I was so nervous of coming on this trip, leaving Tom behind. I thought, *what if anything happens to me?*"

"But he has his dad?"

"Yes, he does, but Simon's so busy with his gallery. You know, he's quite an arty-farty type, obsessed with his artists, not very organised about home life. I just can't imagine him looking after all the small things that matter to Tom at this age, the things that make his life good."

"Well, he won't have to, will he. You will get home safely to look after him," Harry says firmly. "But, Kate, if there's one thing I would advise you, from my own experience, do keep on good terms with Simon. You know, there's no one else in the world who will love Tom as much as the two of you do, and it has made a huge difference to my daughter Isabelle that Lillian and I are still friends. We chat if we're worried about her. Lillian's a great mum. We may live separately, but we parent together."

Kate is touched at the way he speaks of his ex-wife with such affection. "Thanks, that sounds wise advice."

"We're arriving at Tolstoy's estate." Valentin walks up to where they are sitting. There's something quite domineering about his manner as he stands over them. "Time to get out," he almost barks at them.

Harry looks taken aback. "Yes," he says irritably. "We're just coming."

They gather up their coats. "That was a bit odd, wasn't it?" Harry comments. "He didn't need to be that imperious, standing over us like that?"

Kate blushes as she wonders whether Valentin could have been jealous of her spending the time deep in conversation with Harry. She realises that Valentin may feel as confused about last night as she does.

It's a dazzling morning as they walk down to Tolstoy's grave. The gentle grass is damp with dew, the trees golden, the sky blue. A hush descends on the group as they approach the tomb, a single raised area covered in grass and leaves. The freshness of the morning enhanced by the beauty of the natural surroundings, the birdsong. They stand in silence, a sense of awe pervading the atmosphere. Kate breathes in the moment, to be here in Russia, to stand at the grave of this great writer. She senses Harry standing next to her, quiet in his own reflection.

As the group starts to move away, Kate feels rooted to the spot, as if the inner turmoil of her life prevents her moving in any one direction. Then Valentin is by her side, his hand brushing hers, but with some force. "Come," he says, almost pulling her with him, shaking her out of her reverie. He leads her up to the house but says nothing until he has the group assembled in Tolstoy's study.

"Tolstoy's wife redrafted his work every night," Valentin tells them. "She handed the clean copy to him for his next draft in the morning. It took five or six drafts of each chapter for him to finish both *War and Peace* and *Anna Karenina*. That's what I call devotion," he jokes.

"Poor woman," Margot says to Kate as they walk across the hall to the next room. "He treated her abysmally apparently."

"It seems artists and writers often do make dreadful husbands. It's a huge house, too, isn't it?" Kate adds. "Quite a way to live. I guess they had lots of servants, but I think she made the curtains and carpets as well as bringing up ten children. Domestic Goddess or Domestic Slave?"

Margot laughs. "Yes, certainly not a bad way for him to live. Easier to feel inspired to write great works in an environment like this than in some suburban semi looking out on a dual carriageway!"

"He was a great writer, for sure, though," Kate says. "And now I'm interested in the ambivalence that the Russians seem to have towards freedom, towards the reforms that Gorbachev seems to be wanting to introduce, turning Russia towards the West. I understand that Peter the Great had similar intentions, but it doesn't sit easily with the Russian people."

"Yes, I've been talking with Valentin about it," Margot replies. "He's incredibly handsome, isn't he – I can't quite believe any man can be made that perfectly!" She exchanges a wink with Kate. "With Russia, if people have never had freedom, they don't know what to do with it. And who are we to say what is right for them? It feels right to us that they should become more Western because we're so used to our way of life, to capitalism, democracy, but there's much we don't get right, and democracy can lead to endless delays in making decisions. We can't sit on a pedestal and tell the world they have to do the same."

"No," Kate replies as they walk into the next room, "but I can't imagine living in any other system but a democracy, can you?"

"No, I can't. But Valentin is not at all sure about it," Margot continues, and Kate finds herself bristling a little with jealousy that he has been talking with her about such subjects. "He seems genuinely interested in how our government runs, our institutions of law, freedom of speech, et cetera."

"It must be awful to have so little information about the wider world. What did you tell him?" Kate decides that she will not duplicate whatever Margot has told him but endeavour to give him some tangible and useful snippets of her own, to help him build his career.

"Oh, about Maggie, the Queen, the House of Commons, Lords, the elections. You name it. I told him about lobby groups and how my business promotes certain policies in order to lobby and build up a client's business."

Kate says nothing, biting down the feeling that she wants to go to Valentin right now and take him in her arms again, claim him as hers, not Margot's, feel his strong body next to her.

"He really wants to visit England," Margot continues. "Says he plans to do so at the earliest moment once he has raised some money for the flight and worked out how to get a visa"

"Hmm," Kate muses, her mind suddenly illuminated by potential scenes of times together in London. She finds the idea both exciting, yet terrifying.

SIX

Russia, 1990

Back in Moscow before catching the night train to Leningrad, Kate longs to find a moment to connect with Valentin but has failed to get any chance to be alone with him all day. She longs to touch him, be touched by him, feel his tongue caress hers, be held in his muscular arms. She can think of little else as they journey back after another night in the motel. Harry has sat next to Lucia, and Kate finds herself alone and confused. It's so many years since she's been at the start of a relationship, and can she even call it a relationship, she wonders? But for sure she doesn't want to believe it was only a one-night stand.

She diverts herself by finding a currency exchange desk in the hotel to cash some traveller's cheques. She writes out the cheques and hands them to a large woman behind the screen, who handles the rubles in great wadges, without bothering to count individual notes, then hands her a large bundle. Kate hasn't a clue whether she has been given the correct amount, but doesn't feel like questioning the fearsome-looking bank teller, so gathers up the notes and stuffs them in her handbag.

They go for an early supper at the Hotel Prague. It's old Russia, plush curtains, chandeliers, white tablecloths laid with antique-looking crystal glasses. A faded elegance. For $10 they enjoy the best meal they have eaten so far, an hors d'oeuvre of generous quantities of caviar, salmon eggs, salami, beef, vodka, squid, mushrooms, accompanied by delicious Georgian wine. Followed by steak and chips and ice cream.

"That's set us up for our train ride," Mike says over coffee. "But did you hear that Ukraine is seeking independence?"

"The Russians won't like that," Margot comments. "After all, the old guard like the states to remain within the USSR."

"How could Ukraine afford to live independently of Russia anyway?" Desmond asks.

"It's nonsense!" Valentin chips in angrily. "Gorbachev wants to create a new federation of states. He has no respect for history, the Motherland. We need to be united!"

"So much change for you," Kate says quietly, looking at Valentin across the table. "I hope it works out for you."

"It will never work under Gorbachev," Valentin snaps, and Kate is surprised to see tears in his eyes as he abruptly rises from his chair and strides out of the restaurant.

"Oh dear." Desmond sighs. "He wasn't happy about that news, was he?"

Kate feels glued to the floor, watching the retreating figure of her lover disappear. She tries to smile at Desmond, but her stomach feels heavy and her feet like lead. "Come along everyone," Olga picks up the initiative and looks displeased at her young nephew's outburst. "We need to get to the train station."

The train to Leningrad is comfortable. There are twin bunk beds, clean sheets, well-equipped bathrooms and a lady who brings tea from the samovar. Kate is sharing with Gillian, the painter from Scotland.

"I feel sad to be leaving Moscow, and I do wish Leningrad was still called St Petersburg," Gillian comments. "It's so much more romantic."

"I agree. Let's go find some vodka," Kate suggests, feeling restless.

They find some in Mike and Harry's compartment, and caviar too. Kate looks at Harry somewhat tentatively, uncertain what he meant by the Pushkin poem, aware that he is spending more time with Lucia, and wondering, too, whether he has picked up her connection to Valentin. Nonetheless, he is generous with his offerings, and they all agree that they will have a reunion in London on their return.

Leningrad is cold as they walk along the station platform in the grey of the morning. They get a coach from the station and pass by tall buildings bordering canals, to arrive at their hotel, the Hotel Leningrad, overlooking the Neva river. Kate notices that the elegant buildings have seen better days but that there are more foreign cars here

– Volvos, BMWs, Mercedes – and the women look more fashionable, in shorter skirts and brighter colours.

They check in then go on a tour of the Hermitage Museum. Kate is entranced by the Rembrandt portraits, thinking how she might well walk straight past one of the elderly men or women were she to pass them on the pavement, yet here they are made beautiful and sensitive at the hand of a great artist. The lighting is dim, a far distance from visiting the Tate or National Gallery in London, but their eyes shine through, and the skin seems almost alive in its perfection.

Lunch is a disgusting mix of hard-boiled eggs swilling around in some kind of liquid, followed by red jelly, served in a restaurant as large as a municipal cafeteria. Kate declines the jelly and takes the lift to go up to her room. As the lift doors are shutting, Valentin slips through and, without a word, puts his arms around her and draws her towards him.

The afternoon passes in hours of passion, and they lie, exhausted, on the bed, a sheet wrapped around their bodies like a shroud.

"Did you call your daughter Lara after Zhivago's Lara?" Kate asks as she lies against his shoulder.

"Certainly not," Valentin says forcefully. "Lara means cheerful in Russian. Anya, my sister, she chose it."

"Pasternak had a hard time," Kate carries on. "So did Solzhenitsyn."

Valentin shrugs. "They were on the wrong side of history. But sometimes there are causes worth suffering for, even losing your life for."

Kate looks at him, wondering whether she could

imagine having a cause worth losing her life for. "I guess we don't know what we are capable of until we are placed in a specific situation," she ponders. "I nearly didn't come on this tour as I felt bad about leaving Tom."

"Then maybe you wouldn't have met me," he says, with a grin, twisting her hair around his finger.

"Maybe not indeed," she replies, not totally sure how she feels about this.

"I hope we can stay in touch," Valentin says, his breath warm on her neck. "I plan to come to London as soon as possible."

"I hope you can get a visa. I heard this morning that there are long queues outside the British Embassy every day and only twenty visas a day being processed. It's the same at the US Embassy. They say that they get two hundred applications but only ten per cent are processed. It won't be easy for you, will it?"

"No it won't but don't be so negative, Kate. Of course, it will be difficult, but I know people. I am checking out my contacts. That's how things work in a system like ours. Under Communism it looked as if you couldn't get anything, but if you knew the right people, you usually could."

"But people can't even get food today…" Kate wonders why she's raising every hurdle.

"No!" he explodes. "But that's because the supply chains are sabotaged in this 'new' Perestroika."

Kate looks at him, shocked at how quickly he can change from being soft and loving one moment to a smouldering ball of fury the next. His whole body becomes enlarged and puffed up with anger. Just as quickly, he relaxes himself back on the pillow and turns towards her, his tongue licking and moving around her body as they make love again.

"Kate," Valentin says slowly, as they begin to rise. "Would you do me a favour?"

"Yes, of course," she replies, flattered to be asked. "What is it?"

"I need you to take an envelope to London to keep it safe for me, please. Until I come and see you."

Kate hesitates. She knows this is not advisable and has seen enough spy films to know that this is not what people are supposed to do.

"I don't think I can do that, Valentin. We are told definitely not to do this. What is in it anyway?"

"Oh, it's nothing for you to worry about, Kate. Just something I have written. A few papers."

"But what? Why can't you keep it here?" Kate challenges him.

He pauses, and she notices a flicker of irritation slide across his face. She can feel her heart race and her stomach churn with discomfort as she sits naked on the bed, with him standing above her. She grasps the sheet around her again, as she builds herself up to stand up to him if necessary.

He sits down beside her. "It's safer with you, Kate." He pauses and looks out of the window for a moment, as if to choose his words. "Let me explain it to you. I know you wanted to be a journalist when you were young, so you will understand that a good journalist must get their story out into the world, into print. Yes?"

Kate nods grudgingly.

"The story must get out, especially if it involves bad people. I've been following a very evil man, someone who is corrupt but has also murdered people. I can't get it in print here in Russia at the moment, but I may be able to get it printed in London. At least I want to make sure that the evidence I have collected doesn't get taken here. That it's safely stored until I can print it."

Kate feels increasingly uncomfortable. "What's this man done exactly?"

"It's better for you not to know too much, but let me just say he's made himself rich and deprived other people of money that was theirs, as well as committing two murders. He needs to be exposed."

Kate doesn't reply. He moves closer to her, putting his arm around her waist, stroking her. But the pressure is tight.

"Please, Kate. It's nothing to put you in danger. Just a few words on a page. No one will suspect anything of you, an English tourist, a woman. But you will be playing your part like the journalist you told me you wanted to be, like, who did you say, Kate Adie? On the side of the angels, I think you call it. Please?"

With his impossibly handsome face so close and pleading, Kate can hold out no longer. "OK, I suppose if you are exposing a villain, that is good."

"Thank you. I will come and see you in London, or you come back to Russia. We can stay friends, lovers?"

He slides a small package under the sheet and Kate lifts her face to his for a kiss, but he stands up and walks across the room to his clothes and hastily puts them back on.

"Good girl," he says. "Bye," and with that he kisses the top of her tousled hair and walks out of the hotel bedroom. The door shuts and Kate is left alone. Suddenly the room feels several degrees cooler.

She picks up the package and is glad it is, indeed, small and flat. She looks at her suitcase, ready for the flight home the next day, and wonders where she can secrete it. As she feels the case, she is delighted to find a small tear in the outer lining, where the hem has torn, on the underside of the case. She is able to slide the envelope down between the suitcase material and the frame, pushing it right down to the far end. As she turns the case upside down and shakes it around, the envelope seems to stick well in position and there's no shape detectable from the outside. She seals it closed with her clear nail varnish. She feels rather pleased with herself. *John le Carré would be proud of me*, she thinks, although she notices her heart is pounding and her hands are shaking.

She takes the lift down to the restaurant for supper. "We missed you this afternoon," Harry says as she walks out of the lift. "Where did you skip off to?"

"I was tired. What did you do?"

"Oh," Harry shrugs, "Mike and I walked along beside the river and there was a young couple getting married. Their parents couldn't be there because you need local ID, so they asked us to toast them. It was fun. They gave us each a glass of champagne and the young husband spoke quite good English, told us that the shortages are catastrophic for the average family. He says a lot of people are leaving the country."

"How sad," Kate says, as they walk to the restaurant for their last supper in Russia.

"Then when I got back to the hotel," Harry continues, "I heard on the World Service that the medical records of the Chernobyl victims have been wiped from computers. I wonder if we shall ever get to know the whole truth about what happened?"

"It felt pretty scary at the time, didn't it?" Kate agrees. "I remember being out in the rain in our garden with Tom and wondering whether it could be radioactive."

"Olga says there's a major cover-up. She encourages the children she guides on school trips to find the opportunity to interpret the truth for themselves. The history books are full of false information." Harry stops a moment as they reach their table for supper. "Keep in touch, won't you, Kate. Let's have that reunion?"

"Yes," she replies warmly. Then he turns and walks to the table where Lucia is waving to him. Kate looks around, wondering awkwardly where to sit, then sees Margot.

The sky casts a silver light over the river as Kate prepares for her journey home the next morning. A swirl of images and memories chase through her mind as she walks through reception to board the transfer bus to the airport. She notices the security guard who was on duty yesterday standing beside the coach, speaking into a walkie-talkie. Thinking of her package, she tries to look relaxed and tells herself that there is nothing to fear.

At the airport, they take their bags through to check in. As Kate reaches the desk, she offers her ticket and passport to the British Airways clerk. As he looks at the passport, a guard standing next to him leans forward and looks over his shoulder at Kate's papers. He nods to another guard standing nearby and they come up to her.

"Come this way," the taller one says, hauling her case off the baggage check-in.

PART TWO

1990-91

SEVEN

Russia, 1990

Anya's fingers are turning blue, even inside her mittens. And winter is only just beginning. She's standing in a street in her home town of Orel, queuing for food. Again. As she does every day. The wind is whistling down the street. She's so far down the pavement from the store that she doesn't even know if there's any food left for her to buy. She's got up early, before going to work, to see if she can be ahead of the crowd, but everyone else has had the same idea. *It would be helpful if someone would come down the line to tell us whether there's any food there, whether there's any point in staying. But no one does. That's asking too much in today's Russia*, she thinks bitterly.

She chats with Silvana, who lives in a nearby block. Silvana's retired now, a widow. She has a pale face, lined and with dark rings under her eyes. Her grey and black checked coat is threadbare, but Anya notices that she has darned some patches since she saw her last week. Sometimes Silvana babysits Valentin's daughter, Lara, who lives with Anya. Silvana needs the money, but it has become more complicated since Lara was diagnosed with diabetes. That's Type 1 diabetes – insulin injections – and it makes Silvana nervous of taking care of her. "It's too much responsibility," she tells Anya. "It's a life-threatening condition for a little girl of nine. I can't cope."

"But I have to work," Anya tells her. "Someone must look after her after school. Her grandmother helps, but she's getting old now, and I have to watch over her too."

"Where's that no-good goat of a brother of yours then, Anya?" Silvana asks as they walk a couple of paces up the road.

Anya bristles. She knows Valentin is a no-good father but does not want to admit it to her, or anyone outside the family.

"He's working. He's helping our cousin Olga guide tourists around Moscow and Leningrad. It's good work for him."

"Yes, we are getting tourists now. I suppose that's meant to be a good thing? But can't Valentin even spare the time to come and see his daughter?" Silvana's tone is sarcastic, derisive.

"No. He's away," Anya repeats. "But I am sure he will visit soon."

"Ah, the queue is moving more now," Silvana pushes forward.

They start to move up the pavement and there is a noise ahead of them. Women are coming back down the street towards them, scarves around their heads, coats buttoned up against the wind. But their baskets are empty.

"There's no bread."

"No bread."

"No bread, nothing," they hear from the passers-by, some with tears in their eyes, desperation in their voices.

Anya sighs. "I've got to go, Silvana. I have to clock on at the factory now." And she hurries down the street, her legs walking mechanically, her aching back bent over with weariness. She's plump, the buttons on her coat straining a little as she walks, and her dark hair has strands of grey. She feels older than her thirty-nine years and tired after a night of watching over Lara again. The girl nearly fainted with low blood sugar, her eyes rolling, her body shaking. Anya fed her glucose but couldn't get back to sleep again, fearful she might go into a coma. And now she feels dejected for not being able to find food for her. Lara is hungry as a wolf, growing taller every week.

Anya reaches the factory gate and clocks in. She goes to her locker, leaves her coat scrunched up inside and steps into her overalls. The factory manufactures machinery, vehicles, defence tools. Anya doesn't know how they are used. She doesn't want to know. She can't stand the place. Same routine every day, and everyone smokes. It chokes her. Today, like most days, the conversation is of lack of food. No chickens, no bread. Same old, same old. They are tired and hungry. They talk of Russia, her history, and they grumble. It's something they feel they excel at, grumbling, and here in this factory, they are top of the class.

"You had a bad night?" her colleague Pavel asks on seeing her.

"Yes." Anya takes her place next to him. "Lara wasn't well, and I'm finding it difficult to get insulin for her."

"I'm sorry. But you know, Anya, I'm still hopeful," Pavel continues. "I think Gorbachev could turn things around for us. I tuned into the BBC World Service in my kitchen again last night and it's clear that they have plentiful food, clothes, medicines in the West. What's not to like?"

"I agree." Anya nods. "But we're in the minority here still, aren't we? We're the ones who want to go forward to a new era, but so many others are slow to change. They're like Valentin – they want to go back to Communism, the old ways. I worry that this division could start a revolution, and what's the point of that? Just more bloodshed."

"Get to work! Stop nattering!" their boss calls from his desk.

Mama, Lara's grandmother, is with Lara when Anya gets home after her shift. They're sitting in the tiny kitchen, playing cards. Mama signals to her daughter that Lara has been upset. While Lara looks at her cards, Anya raises her arms to question why. Mama shrugs.

Anya kisses Lara's cheek and sits down to watch their game for a while, resting her legs, then gets up to make tea and soup from the potatoes and leeks she has left in the cupboard.

"Good day at school, kitten?" Anya asks Lara. Lara's silent, her shoulders hunched.

Anya sits next to her again and puts her hand on her arm. "Tell me, my little bluebell. Did something go wrong?"

A silence, then a sob. "They teased me again, told me I was sick, to keep away from them, that they might catch my disease if they come near. Even my friend Sofia."

"She just wants to be in the crowd, Lara. You know she's your friend really," Anya soothes her.

"Yes, but it hasn't been the same since I got diabetes, Auntie."

"They will come to understand. You will have to keep explaining to them that you aren't infectious, that diabetes means that your pancreas isn't working properly, the chemicals inside don't function correctly. Nothing they can catch. They will come to understand this, my little sunshine, I promise you. Now let's have supper."

Halfway through serving the meal, there's a knock on the door. Anya puts down the spoon and opens the door, her hands covered in flour, a teacloth in one hand. "Ah, Valentin, where've you come from? I didn't expect you, but you're in time for a little supper." Anya forces a smile. "Mama's here. Nice that you deigned to visit." She walks back into the kitchen. Lara is sitting on a stool in the corner, a schoolbook perched on the kitchen top. Their mother, a small round figure with a heart-shaped face, short curly grey hair and piercing blue eyes, sits at the kitchen table, a cup of tea in front of her. She waves a hand to her son, and he gives her a hug.

Lara rushes up to him. "Papa!" she cries in delight, jumping up to kiss his cheek. He takes off his coat. He's wearing an old blue jumper and dark trousers; his shoes are scuffed.

"You look terrible," his mother says, in the way mothers

do. "What have you been up to now?" She shares a wink with Anya as she directs this question to Valentin, as if he is some naughty schoolboy.

"I've been up to Leningrad with Olga. It was a literary tour. Mainly British. I told you about it, Mama. They were very interesting. We visited the houses of the Russian authors."

"But you didn't come to see us last week when you were in Orel?"

"No, I didn't get time," Valentin says in an offhand way.

"Was it the tour or was it some woman that kept you from us?" his mother interrupts.

"You may scoff, Mama, but there was a woman, Kate, who will be helpful to my career."

"I knew there would be some fancy woman," Mama murmurs, looking rather proudly at her son. "He always finds one."

"It's because he's so handsome," Lara pipes up in defence of her father, looking up and smiling at him.

"Well, I have plans now to start my press agency. I know more about the free press in the West, how they can expose governments and business corruption. It's what I shall do."

"Oh, Valentin, for goodness sake, my boy, I've told you so many times before, be careful." His mother stands up, gripping the edge of the table. Automatically, she turns to switch up the volume of the small radio behind her so that music blares. "That might be all very well in England, but it's dangerous here, my son. Walls have ears. People are always looking out for those who are anti-government."

"It's my time, not yours, Mama. It's a pivotal time in our Russian history. I can make a difference. I know it. I can write about what is really happening here. No jobs, no food. We were more secure before."

"He's on his pulpit again!" Anya counters, exasperated at her brother's self-righteousness. "You're talking rubbish. There was hardly any food then either and really badly paid jobs. We can't keep living the old ways – we need change, and we can learn from the West. Look how we're living here. We may not have to share our homes with other families in the way we used to, but we still have cramped spaces, damp walls, no lifts. Do you know that I am finding it difficult to get insulin for your daughter, Valentin? Do you know how much energy it takes to run our lives?"

"Of course I do," he replies irritably. "You always did like to play the victim, the burdened older sister."

"Come next door." Anya points to Valentin.

"Yes, ma'am," he says, saluting rudely to her, as if she is some army general.

They move into the small bedroom Anya shares with Lara. Anya stands by the window next to her bed, covered in a homemade patterned quilt.

"You have no idea, Valentin, how much work it is to take care of your daughter."

"Yes, I do," he replies coldly. "That's exactly why I wanted her adopted, because even though I was young, I knew precisely how much work it would be and how much responsibility. We were just teenagers. Yulia was only fifteen. I wasn't ready for it, nor was Yulia, and I am not now either. We didn't force you to become Lara's guardian. No one forced you. It was your idea. I would have been happy enough for her to be adopted by another family. You know that."

The words slice through Anya as she thinks of the innocent girl next door, the child she loves, and her hand automatically goes to her lips as she hears him. "I can't believe you said that, Valentin, not when you know how lovely she is."

He looks a little ashamed. "She is, I know. But I say it again, it was your decision to take care of her. You got the baby you were wanting so much, didn't you? We gave you that."

"I had imagined, when I did so, that you would be more helpful than you are being. That you would be here more often to share her care, the babysitting, the school duties. I can't ask Mama to do so much these days. She's getting old and frail."

"I have to make my way, Anya. I can't keep coming here. I have to make contacts, research stories, write articles. I am beginning to get a reputation locally, you know."

"Oh, good for you," Anya says, resenting his cockiness. "She misses you. Whatever we decided all those years ago, you are her father, and I need your help."

"Just hear these words again, Anya. She is your responsibility, and if I help at all, I do so out of the generosity of my heart." He turns his back and walks back into the kitchen, leaving her there shell-shocked at the coldness of his response.

"I must be going," Anya hears Valentin announce to Lara and their mother as she walks into the kitchen behind him. Lara stands up from her stool and comes towards him. She's tall for her nine years and like him, her skin pale, with his dark eyes, dark hair. She puts her arms around his waist.

"Papa, please don't do anything dangerous," she pleads.

He squeezes her shoulder and hugs her.

"Don't you worry, my little one." He kisses the top of her head. "Don't you listen to your auntie's or babushka's tales. Your father, he knows how to look after himself. I was a soldier, remember. I'll be OK."

Anya's fist is tight as she closes the door behind him.

EIGHT

Russia, 1990

Valentin walks slowly down the stairs, his shoulders tense, angry at his sister for trying to make him feel guilty about not taking more care of Lara. He continues their conversation in his head, justifying his absence and his decision that she should have been given up for adoption. *There are so many families in Russia who would have been glad to take her,* he thinks. But no, his stubborn sister decided she would take the baby on and yet, even at that young age of sixteen, Valentin had known that this arrangement would be more complicated than any formal adoption. But he was outnumbered by Anya and Mama and was too young to argue them out of it.

As he exits the block, he is greeted by the cool night air and feels free. The call of the wide world and his future invigorates his mind; he files the domestic situation he has just left behind in a compartment of his brain and hops on a bus back to his tiny room across town. Tomorrow he will take the train to Moscow. He hasn't dared broach his move to Moscow with Anya yet as he knows she will give him more grief about not being there for Lara.

But to follow the story he is writing, he has to follow the man he is writing about, Igor Novikoff. Valentin is building evidence that, in his role in local government, Novikoff has taken bribes for deals done on local infrastructure contracts. He's known Novikoff personally, from his army days in Afghanistan. He had been a brutal leader, cruel and prone to humiliate the young recruits, including Valentin.

Novikoff has become a wealthy and powerful man, and Valentin has information that he is moving to Moscow from Orel. Valentin senses he has richer pickings in mind there, including the potential privatisation of nationalised industries. Valentin is determined to expose any wrongdoings, starting with his suspicion that Novikoff has committed murder.

Across town, Anya wakes in the night. There are gunshots in the street below. It's becoming a common occurrence these days, where vigilante groups roam the streets, ready to kill for a few rubles. She buries her head in her pillow as she hears a cry, then a car speed off somewhere not so far away. Lara sleeps deeply next to her, her dark hair splayed across her pillow, her threadbare teddy bear clutched to her chest. Anya puts a protective hand on her shoulder and tries to rest.

She rises as the sun comes up, shakes her shoulders and tries to feel optimistic about the future. But her mood deteriorates when, at the end of a long day at the factory, she is summoned by her boss. He has received a call from Lara's school to say that Lara has been taken unwell. Anya runs down to her locker, pulls off her overalls as fast as she can, thrusting her arms into her coat as she runs out of the building.

It's dark outside and her nose freezes in the cold winter air. Rushing up the street towards Lara's school she finds herself behind two men, one short and bulky, the other skinnier, taller. They are straddling the pavement and as Anya tries to pass them, she can't help hearing their conversation.

"The city is filling up with scum," the short one says. "Moslems, foreigners, blacks, homosexuals. Where's the old Russia?"

"Gone! It's all changing," the tall one stoops as he replies, spitting in the street so that Anya has to veer to one side to miss its trajectory.

"Anton had some fun last night," says the burly one. "He went down to that bar, you know, where the queer filth hang out, gave two of them a real beating. Black eyes, broken noses. That was his idea of fun, Anton said to me."

"Good for him," the tall one sneered, nodding his head. "We need more independent action like that. The police and the government are doing nothing."

Anya can stand it no longer and barges between them, muttering her disapproval, disgusted by their sentiments. She knows that these are the kind of men who are prowling the streets at night, looking for trouble. She wishes she had the guts to argue with them but knows it would get her nowhere. She carries on up the road, feeling sick.

Lara is in the staff room at her school when Anya arrives. She's very pale. One of the teachers is supporting her, stroking her hair and holding her hand. Anya rushes towards her. She needs glucose or sugar urgently. Noone has told her that the school has had trouble finding sugar. She runs home and returns with some sugar and mixes it into a glass of water for Lara to drink.

After an hour Lara is recovering and feeling well enough to go home. They walk up the road slowly, Anya supporting her niece, holding her steady.

Mama is waiting for them in the kitchen and has made a warm soup. They sit around the table, not saying much but lapping up the sustenance of the broth until gradually they all feel better and go next door to Natalya's flat to watch television.

"I'm running low on insulin, Mama," Anya whispers to her mother as Lara settles into a chair near the television. "I don't know what to do. It's hard to get hold of. Can you ask around? I'll ask Natalya, too, and see if the chemist she works at has got any more stock in this week."

There's a group of six other neighbours sitting and perching on chairs and on the floor, watching a news bulletin and talking at the same time.

"What kind of communists are these?" Arseny, an elderly neighbour, says as he puffs his cigarette.

"They're consumers, not communists, making thousands of dollars, buying apartments in London and Monaco, but you'll never hear about that on the news," interrupts Irina, who lives on the floor below.

"But have you heard?" Natalya takes up the conversation, looking at Mama. "A gang burgled the shop below our building in the middle of the day today."

Mama places a finger to her lips, indicating not to speak too loud, not to frighten Lara. Natalya nods in understanding but carries on in a whisper, "And a young girl was raped outside the school. Take care of Lara."

Anya groans. She can't watch Lara all day and can't bear to think of anything bad happening to her.

"I was in that shop this morning," Mama says. "Before they raided it. There was an old man in there counting the change in his wallet. He could only buy two eggs and a slice of the cheapest dog meat. I've known him all my life, he was a teacher, and now he's almost starving. The young seem to be able to buy things for a few kopeks and sell them for a few more, but we old folk, we can't begin to know how to live in this new way – it's beyond us."

Anya moves over and puts her arm around her mother's shoulders to comfort her. "Don't worry," she says. "You won't ever have to do that. We'll look after you." Although, with all the old customs and ways of life fragmenting, Anya could not be sure that she could protect her mother. People were making up new rules as they went along, and Anya was not sure that her mother knew how to play by them. But the concern that preyed most on her mind was how, in this new Russia, to find insulin for Lara when her doctor seemed unable to provide it for her.

NINE

England, 1990

It's Christmas morning 1990. The first Christmas morning on which Kate has woken up alone, in all her thirty-five years. It's London but the house has a deadly hush about it, and she is finding it difficult to raise her head from the pillow. Tom is with Simon in Chiswick. The day stretches ahead of her, with the single promise that Eve will come for a visit early evening after spending Christmas lunch with her brother and his family.

Bardot, her tabby cat with white paws and chest, climbs up onto the bed and sits on her stomach. Kate is warmed, stroking her sleek fur, her whole body vibrating as she purrs. The cat's dribble is less attractive, but Kate is happy to tickle her ears as the cat's enigmatic gold eyes survey her.

"It's just you and me today, Bardot, so you'd better not

go out catching too many mice for your Christmas dinner! I need you here with me."

She stays tucked under the sheets until Bardot jumps off the bed and disappears downstairs. Kate hears her go out of the cat flap.

"I'd better get up," she says to herself, stretching and noticing that it is already ten-thirty in the morning.

As she goes downstairs, she looks around her new home. There are still a couple of packing cases to unload, but the sitting room and kitchen-diner are in reasonable order now, and she and Tom have settled into their new house in Notting Hill pretty well over the last three months. She had noticed that Tom was nervous at first. He would go around making sure all the doors were locked at night and the window in his bedroom properly shut. Kate watched as he adopted the 'man of the house' role, yet detected, with a little sadness, that he obviously felt too young to be given this responsibility.

The discussions over the divorce are now over. Once the financial arrangements had been agreed, Simon and Kate had talked over the situation with Tom easily and without friction. She has thought often of Harry's advice to maintain that good parental relationship with Simon and is grateful that Harry took the time to share his own experiences with her.

Kate wanders into the kitchen, is glad that she has chosen to cook herself a roast pheasant for lunch. Something to look forward to. She pulls a bottle of Bordeaux from the cupboard. No reason not to treat herself just because she is alone, she thinks. Then she makes herself a cup of tea and goes into the sitting room.

She and Tom decorated their large tree together, and it is scattered with multicoloured lights and hung with many of the small decorations that Tom has made over the years in his nursery and primary school. There's a delicious smell of pine, and Kate puts her nose into the branches and takes a sniff, gently touching the wooden Father Christmas that is a legacy from her own childhood. It's as if the pace of the day suddenly slows down. There's no rush, nothing to do, no Christmas meal to prepare for anyone else, no one coming to see her and, in some ways, she realises that this feels like a luxury.

She walks to the CD player and puts on Vivaldi's 'Gloria', then sits on the carpet beside the tree and begins to open one or two presents from friends and cousins. As she opens the packages of books, scented candles, bath salts, she becomes transported by the music. Time seems to stop as the notes and choral voices play around her in a way she hasn't experienced before. She feels a sense of connection to everything and everyone, despite being alone.

Her reverie is interrupted by the ring of the phone on the mahogany table by the door. She jumps up to answer it.

"Hi, Kate, Happy Christmas, shall I come round at sixish?" Eve asks.

"Yes, that would be fantastic. Thanks. I'll have a bottle of bubbly in the fridge."

"You bet!" Eve pauses. "And how are you doing?" Her voice becomes gentle.

"Actually, so far it isn't as bad as I thought it would be. And Bardot started by being very loving, though she's bummed off now."

"That's good." Eve sounds relieved. "What's your mum doing?"

"Oh God, Eve, she's back in some rehab. I just can't cope with her. I feel racked with guilt that I haven't invited her over, but I haven't got it in me."

"I understand. She has her own nightmares to resolve, and you can't do it for her. You know that."

"No, I know, and it's easy to say but so much harder to do."

"I'll see you later and we can chat about it. Must go now. Bye, sweetheart, and have a good day."

The mood broken, Kate goes upstairs to get dressed, then takes herself for a walk in Holland Park before making her lunch.

Eve is prompt, which is unusual for her. She walks in, leans down and gives Kate a bear hug, the batwing sleeves of her dark wool coat almost suffocating Kate as she puts her arms around her shoulders.

"Now, how are you? How's it been, Kate?" she asks.

Kate leads her into the kitchen and takes the bottle of champagne out of the fridge. She struggles a little to open the cork and they laugh as it pops and flies across the room. She pours them both a glass and then, bottle in hand, they walk to the sitting room and sit on the oriental rug in front of the gas log fire.

"It's been OK," Kate says. "Not as bad as I thought it would be. I now know that I can do this. I can be alone but not feel lonely, and I can make the day good, with a nice home, music, good food, fresh air, a large glass of wine and the knowledge that I have a very good friend coming to see me and that Tom will be back tomorrow."

"Yea, a survivor!" Eve whoops in a rather exaggerated way.

"Have you been drinking already?" Kate asks her, smiling.

"Of course, my dear. My brother opened some rather good claret with the turkey. I've walked here from the King's Road to try to sober myself up." Eve giggles.

"Not highly successful, that, then!" Kate remarks as they clink their glasses together and share presents. Eve talks of her day, her nieces and nephews, and they chat about family and start to think of the year ahead.

"1991, then, Kate. What's it to be? A new man?"

Kate blanches. Eve's question feels intrusive, even though she is her oldest and best friend. She doesn't feel ready for the prying questions of friends about her love life.

"I don't know," she replies awkwardly.

Eve looks at her, a suspicious glint in her eye.

"I know you, Kate, and I know that there has been something you just haven't been telling me these weeks since you got back from Russia. You've been different. Cagey, distracted. I keep asking you why, but you fiddle-faddle and don't tell me. I know you're keeping something from me. In fact, I am absolutely sure you are."

Kate raises her eyebrows, sighs and looks out of the window. On her third glass of champagne, she is beginning to relax, but she has never found it easy to share her emotional secrets, even with Eve. So, Eve has learnt to ferret out the truth.

There's a silence. Then Eve says again, "Come on, Kate, my love. I've known you all these years. If you can't tell me, then you aren't telling anyone, and that isn't wise. A problem shared and all that. You get to understand it better as you talk. You know you do."

"OK," Kate says slowly, reluctantly. "Yes, there was a man in Moscow. A Russian, Valentin."

"Wow! How exciting." Eve is impressed.

"He's extraordinarily handsome. A journalist, you know, one of those investigative types, wanting to expose corruption, or wrongdoing in politics or whatever. He seemed to like me. He made me feel alive."

Eve listens carefully, her cool eyes watching her friend. She says nothing while Kate gabbles on about him.

"Sounds wonderful. He obviously found you very attractive, and I'm not surprised," Eve says when Kate stops talking. "So, what now? Is he going to come here?" Eve asks.

"Yes, he wants to come over. He was very interested in everything I was able to tell him about the press in the West. He wants to build a press agency independent of the influence of the Kremlin."

"Wow," Eve says again. "That's pretty ambitious, I would have thought. And risky?"

"Yes, he can't publish his stories there yet. He wants me to help him."

"In what way? What has he asked?"

"Well," Kate hesitates, "he did ask me to bring an envelope back to the UK with me and it gave me goosebumps going through customs and—"

"He what? You did what?" Eve interrupts, horrified.

"Yes, I know, it was really stupid of me to agree, but I couldn't refuse him. He's after some corrupt politician with a long Russian name, and he wants to expose him. Says it's impossible to print the story in Russia so wanted me to have a copy to keep safe."

"I cannot believe you did something so utterly stupid, Kate!" Eve exclaims, looking at her friend as if she's deranged.

Kate looks down, bites the edge of her finger and says nothing.

"What happened at the airport, then?" Eve asks, more quietly, after a while.

"It was terrifying, actually, and I realised what a fool I had been to agree to bring it back. There was a guard beside the British Airways check-in counter. He told me to bring the suitcase to another room. I honestly think we must have been watched, or someone must have tipped him off. There was no other reason why he should have suspected me of anything. I had to stand in this small room while he looked through my case, turned everything over. Amazingly he didn't find the package – it was very small. Flat. I'd hidden it in the lining of the case. I was sure he would find it. But he didn't." Kate speaks as if she still can't believe her own luck. "Perhaps they just wanted to frighten me."

"That was so dangerous, you stupid woman," Eve says, but gently.

"I know. I can't tell you the relief when he gave me back my case, but I didn't feel safe until the plane had taken off from Moscow airport."

"I bet you didn't. Kate, this is madness. I always had a bad feeling about that trip. Turns out I was right."

"But, Eve, it was also wonderful. I felt I could be myself, whomever that is because I've rather forgotten. I was with a bunch of strangers, but really interesting people, who shared my love of Russian literature. We had such fun, drinking vodka and caviar, talking. I felt liberated. And Valentin… well, it was some kind of awakening, I suppose, or a reawakening. And when he asked me to bring the package – I don't want to know what is in it, I've hidden it upstairs – I felt as if I was doing something useful, helping him with a good cause, exposing corruption. Doing my bit. It felt exciting, meaningful, a bit of an adventure. Can you understand?"

Eve raised her eyebrows and sighed. "I just worry about which part of you it woke up? And where that part might take you next year, Kate?"

TEN

England, 1991

Kate lugs a packing case into the kitchen, fed up with falling over it in the hallway. She's determined to finish putting things away after the move to their new home. She lifts casserole dishes from the reams of paper in which they are wrapped and tries to find places for them in the cupboards. She is on her hands and knees pushing the Christmas turkey plate to the back of a corner cupboard when the phone rings. She hits her head on the shelf above as she raises herself up from kneeling and runs to lift the kitchen phone from its bracket on the side of the wall near the window.

"Hello?" she says, slightly out of breath from the effort.

"Kate," she hears her name spoken in a deep English drawl. There's both warmth and sensuality in the tone.

"Harry," she says, recognising his distinctive voice immediately.

"Well done. Yes, I was just wondering how you are, dear girl? It was kind of you to send me your new address."

"Oh, I'm still unpacking." Kate sighs. "It takes forever. Other than that, Tom and I are settling in OK, thanks."

"How's the charity going, that maternity home you were talking about when we were in Russia?"

"Well, I have a meeting with a potential sponsor tomorrow, so think of me. My friend Freddie has told me about him. He's called Edward Babbington. I gather he has made a fortune and Freddie felt that he might want to gift some money to good causes. I hope so! I am terrified as I have never had to do this kind of thing before. I used to run an events company, and I'm just getting it going again, but I have never had to ask someone to give me lots of money!" She laughs nervously.

"I am sure you will do brilliantly," Harry says, and she can sense a genuine kindness in his voice.

"Have you got over your dramas at Moscow airport? Did you ever understand why that guard took such an interest in your case? It intrigued us all!"

Kate hesitates. "No, I don't know what he was on about," she replies guardedly. "How was your Christmas?" she asks, changing the subject.

"Good. Quiet. Isabelle came down and we walked beside the sea. How about you?"

"Yes, quiet. Tom was with his dad, but he and I had a fun time when he came back on Boxing Day. He's back at school now."

"Talking of walking by the sea, I was wondering whether you might like to meet up some time? No one seems to have arranged that reunion we all promised ourselves, so maybe we could meet for a meal in London? Or a trip on my boat as the spring comes?"

"That sounds lovely," Kate replies. "Are you going to contact the others to join?"

"No, it's you I'd like to see." He pauses. "I'll be in touch then, when I know if I shall be up in London. Or when the sun starts shining and we can set sail. I shall look forward to it. Now you can get back to those packing cases."

Kate puts the phone back on its cradle and stands looking out of the window for a moment, trying to work out Harry's motives and feelings towards her. Whenever she is with him, she ends up confused, yet his call has lifted her mood.

She finishes off placing the last items in various cupboards and stuffs the packaging paper in the dustbin, flattening the packing case and putting it out by the dustbin, then moves into her study. Her desk, of battered pine, stands in the bay window overlooking the garden and the backs of the Victorian terraced houses beyond. A large bookcase lines one wall. Bardot is curled up on the easy chair in front of the slate fireplace.

Kate takes a moment to look at her books. In moving from Shepherd's Bush to Notting Hill, she has brought with her only those books she loves, the ones that told a story that intrigued her, the ones she could remember buying, or who had given it to her, or where she had read it. The rest she has given to charity. As she stands in the room, she realises that they make her feel at home, that they represent who she was, who she is now, who she might become. They give her inspiration and a feeling that, with them by her side, so to speak, the future could be good.

She rips open the last packing case and her fingers pull out some photos in their silver frames. Her wedding day, herself and Simon, youthful faces, full of hope, optimism, naivety. Simon, fresh from art school, handsome with his dark bushy beard and black curls. She feels a lump in her throat as she remembers how in love she had been with Simon when they married, how both William and Tom were conceived in a loving space, even if things went wrong afterwards. She looks at Simon for several minutes, holding the photo up to the light. She nods her head in appreciation. "I didn't choose badly," she whispers to herself. "It was simply that we grew apart," as she wonders whether to place the photo on a shelf. Somehow, through the divorce proceedings, she has had to put aside the memories of joy, intimacy, any closeness they had shared. They had no place in a lawyer's office. She stretches up and puts the photo on a high shelf.

Next, a pottery dinosaur reveals itself from the packing paper, made by Tom at nursery. She places it carefully on the shelf next to a photo of him on his first day at school, proud in his red cap, tie a little askew, school blazer too big for him. He's built like Simon, chunky and muscular.

Then there's a photo of William, tiny and fragile, on the first day of his birth, wrapped in a white blanket, eyes shut to the new world into which he has arrived. She brings the photo to her lips and kisses it, then turns, as if sensing a presence behind her, as she holds the photo. She smiles to herself, kisses the photo again and places it on a shelf near her desk. She moves a photo of her parents on their silver wedding anniversary next to it, as if to watch over the tiny baby. Her mum, frozen forever in her green silk dress and her dad, the English gentleman in his jacket and tie. "You died too young, Dad," she says as she looks at it. "You would be so sad at what's happened to Mum."

William's death had changed her life and it had changed her marriage, too, as the pain of William's loss left a chasm between them. She and Simon had grieved in different ways, as can often happen. Simon buried his grief in his work. She sat alone at home and sobbed.

Bardot jumps down from the chair and brushes herself against Kate's legs, purring. *It's all beginning to look, and feel, like home*, Kate thinks. But now she must prepare for her meeting with Edward Babbington and rehearse how she might ask him for money for her charity. As she starts to jot a few notes down on her pad at her desk, the fax machine beeps. She leaps up. This is her main route of communication with Valentin. She tears the flimsy paper from the machine and reads: 'Dear Kate, please send comment from Western press on opinion of Gorbachev. Valentin'.

She stands frozen for a moment. *Well perhaps he wrote it at work*, she thinks to herself as she returns to her desk, *and could not put anything personal*.

ELEVEN

England, 1991

"Tom!" Kate shouts, "please get downstairs now! I have an important meeting today and I can't be late. Have you got your sports gear?"

"Yes, Mum," Tom says wearily as he stomps down the stairs, dragging his school backpack behind him.

"Great, thanks, darling. Right, into the car – spit spot!" Kate opens the front door for him, and he runs towards her car, a pale blue Renault Clio, parked in the road outside. She locks up the house, opens the car doors and they drive down the road towards his school.

"Are you picking me up today?"

"No, do you remember, I am going out of London for this meeting about the charity, so Ben's mum is picking you up. You'll go back to their house, and I'll come as soon as I can."

"OK." Tom looks at her with a frown and, after a few minutes, says quietly, "D'you know, there's something different about you since you came back from that trip to Russia?"

"What do you mean?" Kate asks, a little defensively.

"You forget things – like which day I play football or whatever. You're late to pick me up. You never used to be."

"Am I? I don't think so, sweetheart, but maybe I have had a lot to think about since we moved house. I'm sorry, I'll try to get my brain back in gear." Kate ruffles the dark curls on the top of his head as she parks outside his school, and he gets out. "Bye," she calls as she watches his figure walk through the school gate and disappear into a crowd of boys and red blazers.

"Oh dear," she says to herself as she puts the car in gear. "He's probably right." She sighs and stretches her arms above her head to get herself to focus on the day ahead.

Kate has bought a new navy-blue trouser suit for the meeting with Edward Babbington and last night printed out a short summary of her vision for the maternity home, a home that will have good clinical care but also sofas, and fountains, and natural daylight, where women will feel safe and held and where babies can enter the world within a peaceful environment. Everything she did not experience herself when she gave birth to William.

Edward Babbington has made his fortune in commercial property. Freddie, a friend Kate trusts absolutely, worked as a consultant with him for a period and has made the introduction. Babbington lives in the Wirral and so, as Kate turns the ignition, she readies herself for a long drive ahead. She listens to Radio Four as she travels, but after listening to much discussion of the IRA mortar attack on Downing Street, she turns to Radio Three to soothe her nerves with classical music.

As she drives, she practises her lines, the things she wants to tell Babbington. An actor friend of hers has advised her to 'rehearse, rehearse, rehearse, get your lips used to saying the words you want to say'. He also told her not to focus on her anxiety but to focus on why she wants to create the home, to be less concerned about getting it all 'right' but tune into her passion within the meaning of the words. And as she practises, she notices that she is becoming more fluent.

And then she is in Oxford, and there's a long traffic jam. Bumper to bumper. And so, the nerves return and, as she stops for petrol near Bicester, it starts to snow. The traffic slows down to a standstill of stop start, stop start. She's surrounded by huge lorries on the motorway. They slip and slide around her small car. Suddenly she wishes, for a moment, that she was back in her kitchen with Simon and Tom, but here she is, and she must plough on through the fear and the snow.

Finally, at around three o'clock in the afternoon, she pulls into a manicured driveway and is faced with a dauntingly large and elegant red-brick house with tall chimneys and leaded windows. It's a house that had been built by a wealthy industrialist in the nineteenth century. There are beautiful mature trees around a large lawn, with fields beyond rows of iron fencing. Everything is covered with a fine layer of snow. She parks her car to the left of the front door, straightens her jacket, tucks her hair behind her ears and hopes she looks professional as she rings the doorbell.

A slim, grey-haired woman in her fifties opens the large oak front door.

"You must be Kate," she says with a smile. "I'm Annabel. Edward is expecting you. I'll take you to him and make you a cup of tea. You must have had a long journey. Would you like to use the bathroom first?"

Kate is touched by her warmth and apologises profusely for being late. Her kind manner is easing her nerves. Annabel, an elegant woman dressed in a plain black wool dress with a polo neck, leads her across the black and white tiled hallway to a toilet so basic that it reminds Kate of her childhood. The towel is threadbare, and the room is freezing cold, a draft billowing through an open window. She shivers, makes herself comfortable, tidies her face and hair and finally feels ready to brave the meeting.

Annabel is waiting for her in the hall and takes her to some double oak doors and knocks. "Darling, Kate has arrived. Shall I bring her straight in?"

A gruff voice behind the door replies in the affirmative and Kate walks into a large study, lined with books. She sees a rotund man with a ruddy complexion sitting at a desk in the square bay window, from which there is a vista of the grounds and distant hills. He is balding, with glasses, and is wearing a brown tweed jacket and a red waistcoat. He has a cravat tucked into his cream and blue checked shirt.

Kate walks across the dark green carpet and stretches out her hand to shake his. He takes no notice and indicates that she should sit down in the chair on the other side of the sizeable desk. "You're late," he says.

Annabel nods encouragingly at Kate as she sits down, saying, "I'll bring you both some tea. Kate has had a long journey." Then she disappears out of the door.

Kate starts to apologise about the traffic and the snow, but Edward gives no sign of having heard her.

"So, Miss Chisholm, Kate, why are you here? What have you to say to me?" Edward Babbington adjusts his chair and looks at her with shrewd hazel eyes.

"Because I believe I have a good idea that could help women, and I believe your money could make it happen." Kate sits upright in her chair, looking him straight in the eye to deliver the message she has been practising in the car.

"Hmm," he almost snorts as he looks quite taken aback by her directness. He says nothing for a moment, then picks up his fountain pen in his thick fingers and slides a pad in front of him. Kate takes this as an encouragement and so carries on to explain her plan to set up the maternity home. She outlines some of the problems women have when things go wrong at birth and tells him that she would like to be able to offer places to women who have experienced a stillbirth, or previous loss of a baby, and would not usually be able to afford personalised care.

Annabel brings in a tray of tea and shortbread biscuits and places it on the desk beside her husband. He doesn't acknowledge her, and she leaves as quietly as she had arrived. As he does not move to offer Kate some tea, she rises and offers to be mother, pouring them both a cup of tea and handing him a biscuit, which he takes and demolishes in a couple of mouthfuls, a few crumbs landing on the front of his waistcoat.

Kate sits down again, cup in hand, and continues to tell him her plans for the charity. She shows him a sheet of information, with figures and a chart tracking the future time-plan for the project.

Across the desk, Edward scribbles a few words down on his pad, looking up every so often but giving nothing away. Kate hesitates, not knowing whether he is listening, bored, or interested. Eventually, her words run out and there is silence.

"Hmm," Edward murmurs after some time. "This is the first time you have managed this kind of project, isn't it?"

"Yes," Kate replies with a sigh. "I started off as an archivist at the London Library but changed direction when I had my second son, Tom, and set up an events planning business, so I have to admit that I don't have experience of creating an enterprise as big as this one."

"No. That's obvious. There's a lot of detail missing here, Kate. Figures. The projected differential cost between a new build or a conversion, how much it would cost to run with alternative figures depending on the number of beds, and all that detail."

"But I did give you those approximate figures," Kate interrupts him.

"Vague, vague, vague," he counters. "Just not good enough. You can't expect me to put money into something that could be a bottomless pit."

"It won't be a bottomless pit, though, Mr Babbington. It's just that we have to start with some projections and the numbers will add up more specifically once we have explored the building work."

"I fear it's a pipe dream," Edward rises from his desk. "Sorry, Miss Chisholm, but don't waste my time with dreams. I need something far more tangible. As it is, I can't help you." He moves towards the door and Kate finds herself gabbling that she does have a team, that it will be like the hospice movement that Cicely Saunders set up, that she will provide him with more figures, but before she knows it, she is at the open door, and he is holding out his hand.

"Off you go back to London," he says brusquely. "Annabel will see you out."

He shuts the study door behind him, and Kate stands shell-shocked in the hallway, with Annabel beckoning her towards the front door. She puts her hand consolingly on Kate's shoulder as she sees her out and wishes her a safe journey. As Kate walks out to the car, her shoes sink into several inches of snow. She starts the engine and drives down the dark driveway. She feels the car skid a little as she reaches the lane beyond. There she stops and bursts into tears.

The snow thuds down in large flakes onto the windscreen and the windscreen wipers struggle to clear it. She lays her head on the steering wheel. "Oh, William, I have failed you horribly," she sobs.

TWELVE

England, 1991

The bar in the King's Road is busy. Young men straddle the pavement enjoying an after-work beer, even though it is a cold night. Eve is waiting near the doorway and waves to Kate as she enters. They hug and make their way to a small table by a window.

"Wow, unbelievable – you're first here!" Kate teases her friend. "I'll get your usual. You keep the table." She pushes her way through the crowd to the bar and orders them both a gin and tonic and some crisps, then carries them back.

"How are you then, Kate?" Eve asks as they settle down.

"Fine."

Eve raises an eyebrow. "Oh yeah? Pull the other one. What's going on?"

"Oh God, well I had this disastrous meeting with that man that Freddie put me in touch with for sponsorship, Edward Babbington. And I have had a few more like that, though not as bad, thank heaven. I just don't know if I can convince people that this idea of a maternity home is viable as a charity."

"You have chosen quite a complicated project, dear friend, haven't you? What is the pushback you are getting from the people you talk to?"

Kate sighs and takes a gulp of gin. "Like you say, it's going to take a lot to get it going – the building, for example. Do we convert an old building or start a new one? Then there's the equipment, beds, medical equipment, the clinical staff and admin, and I really want to make it different – you know the fountains, birthing pools, and all that."

"Big thinking," Eve agrees. "Nothing but the best for your prospective mums…" she pauses, and in the silence adds softly, "but you know that it won't bring William back, don't you?"

Kate sighs. "Yes, of course." She looks at her friend with a sense of exhaustion as she says, "But I do so want to make sure others don't have my experience. I'd love to set up a best-practice model for childbirth."

"And so you should," Eve says emphatically. "You just have to chunk it down. Don't see it all as one huge leap into the dark. Start at the beginning with the building. Have you spoken to that architect Freddie mentioned to you?"

"Yes, I have a meeting tomorrow."

"You'll have to manage that meeting. Architects inevitably want to build something dramatic that will make their name and change the landscape, so you will have to keep impressing on them that this is a charitable enterprise and get them to be honest as to whether it will be more efficient to build a new place or convert an old. They're likely to want to build something new, and it could be that this would be more cost-effective than a renovation, but be prepared to be tough with them."

Kate nods, in gratitude at the advice. "Thanks for that. Yes, you're right. I'm finding there's so much more to think about on every level now that I'm living alone – the move, managing my finances and heaven knows what else."

"And now you really have set yourself a huge task. You know, it might be worth considering whether you can reshape your vision in a way that's simpler to achieve? But enough of that, what's happening in the rest of your life – any good sex?" Eve teases her. "What about that handsome Russian? Has he been in touch?"

"Yes," Kate says slowly, running her finger around her glass. "I'm going to go back to Russia in a couple of months, probably."

"Really?" Eve looks quizzical. "Is that wise? There's quite a lot of disturbance going on out there at the moment, isn't there?"

"I'm sure I shall be fine," Kate replies. "I can't leave it as it is. I can't stop thinking about him. It's terrible, ridiculous really, but I just long to be with him."

"Lust or love?"

Kate laughs and shrugs her shoulders. "Certainly lust! More than that, I don't know yet."

"Where will Tom go? Do you want me to have him to stay again? He was such a dream last time."

"No, but thanks. Simon says he will take him away, depending on the time of year, but he will definitely have him to stay, either way. He's being quite helpful, and we don't have a problem sorting out dates, thank heaven."

"Do you think he wants you back?" Eve asks, giving Kate a searching look.

"I doubt it. I think I probably just drove him mad – I didn't know enough about art. I loved the paintings he exhibited but I could never remember the details about the style or the artists. It annoyed him."

"But he did love you in his way."

"True, and I loved him, but it's gone too far now, and I can't imagine we could make a go of it – we're on different paths. He's loving spending more time with his artistic types, and after William died, I became a bit of a hermit."

"Yes, you were in a state. Are you still having those nightmares?"

"Sometimes. I have them when things are going wrong – sometimes about the birth but also anxiety dreams where I lose Tom and can't get to him. They're like panic attacks, as if my mind is too busy in the daytime, when I am trying to convince myself that I can get my life in order, so at night my unconscious goes berserk, reminding me of all my fears."

Eve takes Kate's hand. "You're in the midst of a major change. Divorce is a loss of all you knew or thought you wanted, those expectations of getting old together and all of that. You're doing fine. No one gets a venture off the ground without a struggle. But it's worth it, isn't it, and I can see you're getting stronger every day."

"Thanks, Eve. I don't feel stronger. But you're right, I shouldn't expect it to be easy. And Tom seems fine, luckily, happy that he is still at his old school with all his friends, and he likes the new place, especially as he has the largest room in the house!"

"Are you doing OK for money? Presumably you can't get any income from a charity that hasn't formed yet, so what are you doing?"

"Simon's art gallery is doing well, so he covers Tom's expenses, then I am trying to grow the events business to make ends meet. Plus, of course, I still have my dad's legacy, remember? Though I'm getting through that in having to pay for Mum's care when she gets into trouble."

"Oh dear, that's sad. I have such happy memories of times together with your parents, when we were at school," Eve reminisces.

"Yes, we were quite a pair, weren't we? It was lucky that Dad worked so hard at his surgery. He didn't notice what we were doing half the time!"

"But your dad died too young, didn't he?"

"Yes." Kate takes a deep breath. "It was a horrendous time, and I remember feeling so angry that I was seventeen and should have been out partying but instead I felt so lonely, feeling I had to keep Mum company. I don't know what I would have done without you. Mum just couldn't hack living without Dad. It was so hard being with her. She couldn't handle her grief. She became so irritable, do you remember? Critical and really quite nasty to me. I think she just wanted to die, so it wasn't totally surprising, when I think back on it, that she took to drink. You were a rock, Eve."

"Well, if I am totally honest, I was dead chuffed that it meant that we could share a flat together!" Eve grinned.

"Yes, those were good days – do you remember how we used to sing the Kinks' 'Waterloo Sunset' and then shout 'London Here We Come!'?"

"Yes! It must be tough, though, having to support your mum."

"It is. I watch other grandmothers being so loving and helpful with their grandchildren, but Tom hardly knows her because she is either drunk, or missing somewhere, or in rehab. It's ghastly. And yet all she ever does is criticise me for all the decisions I've made in my life. She even seems to suggest that losing William was my fault, not the fault of the bloody overstretched NHS maternity team."

"No! Well, you mustn't listen to her. See her for what she is – a deeply troubled woman." Eve touches Kate's arm in sympathy. "Oh but, Kate, are you really sure about going back to Moscow? Is it a good idea? It doesn't feel like it to me."

"I think I've got to get it out of my system, try to understand what these feelings are all about. Maybe I will come to my senses," Kate replies thoughtfully. "But what about you, now. Who's the latest lover?"

"A painter, Irish, does wonderful watercolours. We met at a wedding. He's full of the blarney, recounts endless stories, and great fun to be with."

"So, no plans for your own wedding then?"

"God no, Kate. You know I'm not the marrying kind. You say you drove Simon mad. Believe me I would drive a man to killing himself – or me! I love my independence. But now I must go home to bed. I'm knackered after work. A new client expecting the world of me. A Russian, actually, Stepan," Eve says as they pay the bill and walk out into the night.

"Really?" Kate asks, surprised.

"Yes," Eve says as they walk towards the tube. "But this man is not handsome like your Valentin. He's fat, old, but very rich, and our company is converting a massive house in Knightsbridge for him."

THIRTEEN

Russia, 1991

"A woman was shot on the street near my mother's home in Orel yesterday," Valentin tells his colleague Mikhail. "They wanted her watch. She wouldn't give it to them. So they shot her. Can you believe it? She had a small child with her."

Mikhail, a seasoned journalist, some fifty years of age, with greying dark hair and a paunch, takes a puff of his cigarette and sighs. "Yes, this isn't like Western capitalism," he says thoughtfully. "It's becoming more like the Wild West – it's as if people can just steal money rather than make it."

"I think Gorbachev is like a man pulled in two directions, the left hand communism, the right hand capitalism." Valentin takes a slug of black coffee from his mug. "Yeltsin is every bit as bad as Gorbachev. What is the future? We've castigated capitalism for a century but now we chase it blindly without any understanding of what it will mean for us."

"Yes, we need to take this up as a story, dig up what is happening in the provinces as well as Moscow. You're still following your reports digging up dirt on Novikoff, aren't you?"

"Certainly!" Valentin replies with force. "Scum. Taking money out of the mouths of those who deserve it."

"Well, next I would like you to make a list of prominent people to give us their opinions on this, Valentin. Go talk to writers and influential people. See whether we can get a group of opinion-makers together. The intelligentsia don't pander to the wealth-grabbers. Make a list and get talking to them. I have a plan that we can publish an important piece to bring the government down." Mikhail clicks his pen against his yellowing front teeth.

"You mean a call to action? For revolution?"

"Maybe, yes. A letter to the Russian people. To wake them up. We have the remit on this newspaper. Now go and get on with it." Mikhail signals to Valentin with his hand, dismissing him from the room.

Valentin walks out, shutting the door behind him. His eyes are bright with excitement.

'Kate, can you get me a list of the Russians in London? Bring it to Moscow with you when you come? V'.

Valera sends the fax to Kate from his office and within a few seconds has received a response "Yes, will ask Eve. She has a new Russian client, Stepan, who knows many of the Russians in London. Will do my best. Kx"

It's a bright spring day when Kate boards her flight to Moscow. She tries to read and sleep on the journey, but adrenalin paces through her body as she thinks of Valentin and of another adventure in Moscow. Simon is taking Tom on a camping trip to the Lake District for half-term, so she feels free to enjoy herself, knowing he will have a good time with his dad.

And then she's back in the glooming of Moscow airport. Her hand shakes a little as she goes through passport control, remembering the last time she was here and the fear she felt as the guard searched her suitcase. The unsmiling border controller takes an inordinately long time pouring over her papers. Her heart races as the minutes tick by. Then he looks at her, stamps her passport and she's through.

She collects her case, and there is Valentin at the entrance to the Arrivals Hall. He walks towards her, handsome in a faded leather jacket and jeans, takes her in his arms and kisses her lips. "So, you couldn't keep away from Mother Russia, then!" He smiles down at her, as she lights up at his touch, the fears that he would not be there to meet her evaporating.

They take a bus into the centre, and he helps her check into her hotel, the Ukraina, explaining again that his room is too small for her to stay with him. The hotel is enormous, decorated with paintings by Russian artists, with an elaborate ceiling in the reception area: 'The Feast of Labour and Harvest in the Hospitable Ukraine'. It was definitely a step up from the Rossiya.

"I have to work now," he says, "but I shall come back at the end of the day, and we can go out for supper."

He kisses her and is gone. She looks around the room. A large bed, mahogany furniture and a marble-lined bathroom that speaks of a grander era. She unpacks, undresses and runs a bath, remembering her previous visit to the Rossiya and its lack of a bath plug. The water is warm, if still tinged with brown, and she tries to relax.

After a walk around the Kremlin, she passes the GUM department store and watches smartly dressed women being dropped off by chauffeur-driven limousines. There are more tourists than before, yet she notices many of the people standing at a bus stop look tired and pinched.

When she gets back to the hotel, she asks if there are any messages or visitors for her. A young woman at reception shakes her head dismissively in the negative. Kate goes up to her room and waits. And waits.

Eventually, she is so hungry that she takes herself down to the hotel restaurant. A waiter shows her to a table and gives her a menu. "Vodka, *pozhaluysta*."

She understands little of what is on offer on the menu. "*Sbasibo*," she thanks the waiter when he returns with her vodka, and she orders a borsch followed by chicken, as these are the only items she can easily translate.

She eats alone and slowly, looking around her at the besuited men at other tables. She seems to be the only woman eating, certainly the only woman dining alone, and she is aware of some strange looks from the men as they pass her by.

As she is eating her chicken, the restaurant door opens and Valentin walks in. He comes to her table and pats her shoulder, taking the seat next to her.

"Kate, sorry. I got held up writing a report."

"No problem," she replies awkwardly, trying to give him a genuine smile. "Do you want something to eat?"

"No. I've already eaten."

"Oh!" Kate struggles for words.

He doesn't offer any conversation as he sits and watches her finish her meal.

"How's Lara?" she asks.

"Ah, Lara and Anya, my sister, are coming down from Orel to see me on Sunday, so you'll be able to meet them. They're very excited about meeting a real-life English woman from London!"

Kate laughs. "It will be lovely to meet them." She begins to relax and feels that he must have feelings for her if he is to introduce her to his daughter and sister.

They order coffees and he brings his chair closer to hers, putting his hand on her knee, his fingers stroking her thigh very gently. She looks at him, trying to discern his thoughts, then he moves forward and slowly, so slowly, kisses her lips. "Come on," he whispers, "let's go upstairs and make love."

She feels his hand take hers and they rise as one and move towards the lift. As soon as the doors close, they come together in a passionate embrace and, arriving at her floor, they move along the corridor to her room. As she fiddles with the key to open her bedroom door, he stands behind her, the strength of his muscular body against hers, his arms around her, his lips nuzzling into her neck. And then they are alone together, and he deftly undoes her buttons and slides her clothes off, drawing her to the bed. His need excites her, and she gives herself to him hungrily, moulding herself to his movements and reaching the pleasure she has been waiting for all these months.

Later, when she wakes and turns over in bed to touch him, her hand slides across an empty space. He has gone.

It's Sunday, and Valentin has told Kate to meet him at two o'clock by the main entrance to Gorky Park. He will go there with Anya and Lara. She catches the metro and nervously walks towards the park, unsure how Lara will feel about meeting her and unsure what he will have told them about her. She spots him as she reaches the edge of the park. He looms over his sister in stature and, as Kate approaches, she can see that Lara is very like her father, with long, dark hair and deep brown eyes.

They shake hands as Valentin introduces them. Kate feels Anya's eyes on her, as if she is trying to work out what she is doing with her brother. It puts her on edge, and she slides closer to Valentin as they start to walk across the park towards the lake.

"So, Kate, what you do here?" Anya asks in halting English.

"Just a tourist visit," Kate replies. "And you have come up from Orel? Is it far? Valentin tells me you want to set up a health food shop one day? Do you have plans?" She's aware she's gabbling and asking too many questions at once.

"Sorry, Kate, my English not good. Slowly, please," Anya says, putting her hand up.

"Sorry," Kate says, embarrassed. "Valentin tells me you look after Lara?"

"Yes. She lovely girl. Hard work, though, when I at factory all day."

"Yes, I understand. I have a son, Tom. He's eight. I know how non-stop it is."

"Ah, but your Tom not have diabetes? Valentin, he not understand how Lara has special needs," Anya says, and Kate detects a tiredness in her voice.

"He's young, I guess," Kate replies, in Valentin's defence. "Good luck with your shop, though. There are people in England who have started a business from their kitchen. Have you heard of the perfumes of Jo Malone? She began her business last year, I think, mixing fragrances in her kitchen. Now I hear she's hoping to open a shop in London."

"I not do fragrances. I do health product, I hope. Herbs, mixtures, you know?" Anya smiles at Kate as Lara, who has been skipping along beside her father, moves towards them.

"So, you live in London?" she asks shyly, in good English. "I really want to come and see it."

"Well, and so you shall," Kate replies. "You can see the black taxis, red telephone boxes and Buckingham Palace all for yourself one day. Come and stay."

"Wonderful!" Lara says excitedly.

Then suddenly they find themselves surrounded by three men who have approached them quickly from behind a row of trees. One grabs hold of Valentin's arms behind his back, the other two jump on Kate and Anya, pulling them close in a lock, leaving Lara standing stock still in the middle of them, looking from face to face, shock paling her skin.

"So, these are all your ladies are they, Kotov? Now we know what they look like. Your friend Igor asked us just to pay his compliments today and tell you that he doesn't appreciate the lies you are spreading about him," the older man, with grey hair and a pockmarked face, growls into Valentin's ear.

"Let them go!" Valentin shouts. The walkers around them stop and stare but know not to get involved.

Kate looks at them, not understanding what is being said or what is happening. Her wrists are being held tightly in front of her by a young man with pale blond hair and cold grey eyes. He brushes his body close to hers and she can feel him getting a kick from frightening her, hurting her. She tries to push him away, but he brings his face even closer to hers. She can smell his foul breath.

"Don't say you haven't been warned," the older man says to Valentin, lifting his arm up behind his back until Valentin screams in pain. Then he lets go, moves to Kate and says in broken English, "And, Miss Kate, Mr Novikoff knows about you. Don't think he doesn't."

With this, the three of them let go of their hostages and run away across the park, scattering people out of their way as they barge through the Sunday walkers.

The group stands in shock. Lara looks traumatised and breaks down in tears. Anya hugs her to her chest, looking with fury at Valentin.

"What the hell was that all about?" Kate asks Valentin, through chattering teeth.

FOURTEEN

Russia, 1991

Valentin bundles them all into a taxi and they head back to the Ukraina Hotel. Kate invites them up to her room, and they sit in a silent heap of shock, Lara sobbing and Anya with her on Kate's bed, trying to soothe her. She is beside herself.

Valentin looks grim and strides around the room, fists clenched, wearing a track in the already quite threadbare carpet. Every so often, he mutters something to Anya, Anya hisses back at him and there is another long silence. Kate sits alone and isolated on a chair, her whole body shaking uncontrollably.

"We must speak English, Valentin," Anya says, looking at Kate.

"Shouldn't we tell the police?" Kate asks, eventually. "Or perhaps I should notify the British Embassy what has happened?"

"No!" Valentin says forcefully. "The police will be bribed by Novikoff, you can be sure. That would get us all into trouble; they would find some way to make life difficult for us. That's the system here."

"You need give explanation, Valentin. What happened?" Anya asks her brother.

Valentin looks at her angrily, as if this were something she had arranged herself. He turns on the television, which blasts away loudly in Russian in a corner of the room as he speaks.

"I don't know what to say," he says, in an aggressive tone. "You know that I am investigating Igor Novikoff. I told you both about this." He says this as if it alleviates him of any responsibility for what has just happened. "He's corrupt, and I am convinced he has murdered the wife of one of his colleagues in local government who wouldn't play ball with him. So, I exposed this. I wrote an article about it."

"And presumably he isn't amused by that?" Kate points out drily, calming down gradually.

"Obviously not!" Valentin barks. Kate is taken aback by the way he is projecting his anger onto her and Anya. She starts to say something but retreats, fearful of his response.

"Look," Valentin says in a steadier voice. "He's an evil man and he should be stopped. He's taking money from everyday Russians. If people don't do what he wants, he is likely to kill them. He's dangerous. He's building himself an empire, and I believe he should be stopped."

"I can't argue with that," Kate says slowly, in a monotone. "But presumably that puts you at risk and, potentially, if he's willing to kill the wife of an enemy, that puts Anya and Lara at risk too. If he wants to silence you, then he threatens your family. Right?"

Valentin stops pacing and stands near where Anya has Lara on her lap. He takes a deep breath. "Yes," he mumbles the word, as if not wanting to accept the truth.

Kate and Anya exchange glances. Kate notices Anya's face looks worn, almost white against her dark and greying hair. She's only a few years older than Kate, but the age gap feels larger.

"Valentin," Anya says. "You do good work. Yes. But go too far. Must keep Lara safe." There's a long silence. "I need take Lara back to bed, Valentin. She needs rest," Anya says, sounding exhausted.

"But will those men follow us?" Lara asks in a small voice. "Won't you come with us, Papa?"

"No, my little Lara, you will be safe, my rabbit." Valentin comforts her, though Kate and Anya exchange frowns. "I'm sure they don't know where my room is, and I shall be back home later. Don't you worry."

Anya looks at her brother in disbelief. "Surely? You come with us?" she asks, raising her shoulders to communicate that she expects him to leave with them. He takes no notice and continues to stand beside the window, close to Kate. Kate turns to him.

"You should go with them, Valentin."

He just stands there, as if he hasn't heard. Anya wraps Lara in her plump arms and leads her towards the door.

"Papa!" Lara whispers, with anguish.

"Ssh, ssh, sweet kitten," Anya is saying as their voices drift down the corridor and the heavy, polished wood bedroom door swings shut behind them.

Left in the room with Valentin, Kate sits awkwardly, a frown on her face. She longs for a drink but there is nothing in the room, no minibar to alleviate her nerves.

He turns to look at her. "So, Kate, we have some time," he says slowly, and his deep voice runs through her like a masseuse stroking a track through her body.

"Yes," she says doubtfully, fighting a craving for his touch. "But I need to know how we will protect ourselves now from this Novikoff man. It's frightening."

"Oh, it's just bluster." Valentin shrugs it off.

"No, Valentin, it isn't, is it. He kills people. He's angry about you exposing his wrongdoings. I'm frightened."

"Kate, really. It will be me he is after, but I am not going to let this go now. Surely you can see that? It's the right thing to do, to expose him."

Kate sighs and wrings her hands together. "Yes, yes. I can see that, and of course I admire you for what you are doing, but I worry for myself… and for Lara, for Anya. You must protect them."

"The sooner we are able to get Novikoff arrested, the sooner we shall be safe," Valentin says, putting his hand on Kate's shoulder, playing with her hair with his fingers.

She pauses. "But will we?"

"I'm building a really good reputation here as a journalist, Kate. It's beginning to give me a voice to speak of the things I want to tell the world. And we all have to suffer a little for the truth," he says emphatically.

Kate thinks it all sounds a little grandiose but reflects that he is a young man, and his fire excites her as much as it frightens her. He comes and kneels before her, putting his hands on her shoulders.

"I know you understand what I am doing, really, in your heart, Kate. You wanted to be a journalist. You know how much the truth matters. It's what pulls us together, you and me."

"Mm," she says doubtfully. "I guess so."

"Please keep those papers safe for me. I need to give you some more. There's more evidence about Novikoff now. Transactions, letters, deals he's done. If anything happens to me, or to the material I am working on here, you can give them to Mikhail." He stops and looks at her with his deep brown eyes so close to her, raking his fingers through his dark hair as it falls across his forehead. "Please, Kate."

She sighs again. "OK. For now, just once more."

He takes her face in his hands and pulls her towards him, his tongue seeking hers. She responds for a second but then pushes him away.

"No, Valentin," she says, in a shaky voice. "You must go to Lara and Anya tonight. Lara is frightened. She needs her father. You must go and help her feel safe."

"She's fine. She has Anya with her. Igor has never been to my address."

Kate knows he is bluffing. "He found you today, Valentin. I don't know how but he did. Go to them," she says, rising from her chair. "I'm a mother. I know that your daughter needs you."

He holds her hand. She can feel his desire, smell it. "Go back home," she says firmly.

He releases her hand, and the tension softens from his shoulders. "OK, Kate, I give up. I will go home. We have two more nights before you fly home, yes?"

She nods. He turns his back, walks out of the door, and lets it shut automatically behind him. Then he's gone. As the door clicks, Kate sits back down on the chair and puts her head in her hands.

FIFTEEN

Russia, 1991

"You do have that list of Russians living in London, don't you? They could be really helpful, to get many more names to sign our petition," Valentin says. They're lying in bed together in Kate's hotel room, having spent the afternoon making love. Kate can sense the pressure as he speaks.

"Well," she says somewhat reluctantly, "yes, I managed to get some of the names, but I am sure there are many more. They don't always want to be visible to the authorities or the media, but there's certainly a network. My friend, Eve, has an interior design consultancy that is doing up some of their homes in the London area. One of her clients helped me to put the list together." She gets up and walks naked to her suitcase. She unzips the case and pulls a piece of paper out from under her shoe bag and hands it to him.

"Good," he says, looking at it briefly. "It's a good start, though I'm sure there are many more names. Can I rely on you to keep looking? This is so important – it's a turning point in history. It could mean revolution. The people's revolution against this corrupt government. Do you see how exciting this is?"

Kate grimaces and shakes her head as she stands beside him. "I have images of Lenin, of bloodshed. It's not a good vision," she says.

"We're bringing together a huge group of important people – writers, generals, politicians, scientists. It's a call to arms. And Kate," he pauses and puts his hands around her waist, bringing her back towards him, "I so appreciate how you are helping me here."

Two days later, back in Orel, Anya and Lara are preparing a small celebration in their flat, for Anya's birthday. Anya wants to make it a special time to compensate for the shock of their experience in Gorky Park. Mama is due to arrive, and Valentin has promised to join them, getting the train after seeing Kate off at the airport. Anya teaches Lara how to chop the onions and make the potato salad while she prepares the fish.

There's a knock at the door.

"Natalya!" Anya greets her neighbour warmly. "I'm so glad you can join us."

"It's not far for me to travel!" Natalya laughs as she says this, looking back across the corridor to her front door. The two women are old friends, of similar age, and have known one another from the days when Anya's grandmother lived in the rooms Anya and Lara now occupy.

"I'm exhausted. There's never a dull moment at the pharmacy," Natalya says. "And it's hard when we can't always get the medicines." She glances over towards Lara, knowing that, although she is supposed to be able to receive insulin from her doctor, Anya frequently has to go to the black market to source the insulin for her. "You look beautiful, Lara," she tells the young girl.

"Ha, she grabbed the lipstick from my drawer!" Anya laughs.

Lara blushes. "I love the pale blue of this dress, Auntie," she says to Anya. "You're so clever to have made your dress fit me."

"Little does she know how long it took me to get the seams in the right place and the hem straight," Anya whispers to Natalya. "It really suits you," she says as she looks at her niece's dark hair tumbling over her shoulders and the way her young body is beginning to blossom. A shadow flits across Anya's eyes as she thinks of the challenges of the years ahead, to manage not only puberty but diabetes also.

Mama bursts through the door, carrying a box. "Here, Anya my love. This is the cake I baked this morning."

Anya kisses her mother and takes the box, placing it carefully on the small worktop behind her. Moments later the door opens again, and Valentin arrives and places a bottle of vodka and two tins of caviar on the table. "There, my sister," he says. "The best of Moscow's black market. Now you can't tell me I don't do anything for you!"

"Ah, my boy, my boy." Mama purrs.

Mama hugs him, and Anya turns away, muttering to Natalya, "Sons, they're always the favourites, even if they do little to deserve it."

Natalya nods, raising her eyes to the ceiling in agreement.

"By the way," Natalya says to Anya. "There may be a job going at the pharmacy."

"Really? What? When?"

"It's just at the counter," Natalya carries on, picking up a fork from the table and polishing it on a napkin. "But I know you're interested in health, and I think you could learn a lot and maybe even do some night study, take a qualification? The money isn't great, but it's only a little less than you get at the factory. I've mentioned you to my boss."

"That could be a wonderful birthday present." Anya hugs her friend. "Thank you. That news gives me a feeling the year ahead will be a good one! Now, let's eat."

There's a clatter of chairs scraping the floor, of cutlery, as everyone settles into their meal in the tiny kitchen.

"I've been watching the news," Mama says. "It's depressing! I want us to be united again as a country, but look what's happening – Latvia, Ukraine and these other states pushing for independence. Look at us old folk, reduced to scrabbling around in the bins for food. There's no security for us."

"Well not you, Mama," Anya challenges her, with a laugh. "You're not scrabbling in bins. You don't starve. We look after you."

"No, I don't starve," says the old woman, "but I have plenty of neighbours in my block who don't have family, so they don't have food."

"She's right. Things have to change," Valentin says as he stretches his arm across the table to help himself to more potatoes.

"I don't want more change," Natalya argues. "It could mean civil war, and that's no good for any of us."

"I like what Gorbachev is doing, anyway," Anya says firmly. "We begin to see more about how people in the West are living, how they can say what they want, do what they want, buy what they want. They don't have to resort to bribes, corruption. They can just go to a shop and buy things, buy services, medicine. You can see why the young want this."

Valentin looks at his sister. "You wait and see. Things will change. And soon."

"That reminds me of that joke," Anya says. "*A communist is someone who's read Marx; an anti-communist is someone who's understood him.*"

"What rubbish!" Valentin explodes.

"Shh!" Mama gets up and turns up the volume of the radio. "We can't have this kind of conversation!"

"You just did," Valentin points out.

"There's something you're not telling us," Anya challenges her brother, knowing he's holding something back.

Valentin looks irritated. "Now's not the time." Then he adds, "After all, it's your birthday celebration."

There's a pause, and Mama starts to sing 'Happy Birthday' and Lara joins in happily. Anya turns her attention back to the cake, and they all enjoy a slice and talk of other things.

As they are clearing the plates away, Anya can't resist pushing her brother for answers. "Go on, Valentin. What are you up to?"

"I can't tell you that. Everything I am doing at the

moment is confidential. But I shall have to be less available to you in the next few months. There's an important project we're working on at the newspaper."

"What's that supposed to mean, then? To us?" Anya prods him.

"I won't be visiting you. I may not be available at all for a while."

"You can't be serious, can you, Valentin?" Anya says, incredulous that he can think of being even less accessible to Lara and the family. *It can take over six hours to reach Moscow anyway*, she thinks, *and it sounds as if he means that he will hardly ever see us.*

"I am serious, Anya, yes. It's a great opportunity. It's just that I can't tell you more. But I hope I'll be able to send more money home to you."

"Money isn't everything, Valentin. Love and attention mean more, you know." Anya feels torn as to whether to have this conversation in private, but her blood pressure is up now, and she carries on. "What about Lara? Your daughter?"

Lara looks at them with wide eyes. "I'm OK, Auntie. I'm OK with you."

Anya bites her lip, thinking that Lara always defends her father, makes him out to be right and her wrong. She's the one who looks after Lara. He doesn't.

"You will look after her, Anya. You know you do such a good job. We can all rely on you. I will give you the office number, and they can contact me if there's an emergency." He puts on his placatory voice, trying to smooth Anya's anger with charm, but there's a patronising firmness in his tone.

Natalya pushes her chair back from the table and takes Lara by the hand. "Come, sweet girl, let's go next door and play some cards." She hustles Lara from the room and out of the kitchen. As Natalya closes the door and turns towards her apartment, Anya hears Lara ask, "What will happen if Auntie and Papa don't want to look after me?" and Anya feels as if her insides have been scrunched up and wrung through a mangle.

"You're a bastard, Valentin, you know that, don't you? I helped you out when you got into trouble. That was for Lara's sake, not yours. You know perfectly well that when I signed the papers and agreed to take care of Lara, you promised me – promised me – that you would be here as her father, helping me out."

"We've had this conversation before, Anya," Valentin flares up at her. "That was years ago, and I was a teenager. What did I know about life? And if you're regretting your decision to care for Lara, that's your problem not mine."

"No, Valentin," Anya replies coolly. "I've had several weeks to think since our last conversation, and I don't regret my decision to care for Lara for one moment. I love her deeply, but I do feel heartbroken that I shall never have a child of my own now. What man will want to take on my brother's child?"

Valentin looks at his sister, and she notices his dark eyes are cold. She continues, "But what I do know, Brother, is that I am not impressed with you, that I am disenchanted by the man that you have become. You may be doing important work in Moscow, I don't know. But I'm not impressed with how you choose to flit in and out of Lara's life, playing with her emotions. It's unforgiveable."

"I don't care what you think. I need to do this for Russia, for the Motherland."

"For Russia!" Anya stands up and shouts at him. "Don't give me that rubbish again, Valentin, like you are doing me and our country some favour or being some kind of saviour. This single-minded focus of yours, always on changing the world out there but not bothering with those who love you, is cruel. You're not doing it 'for Russia'. You're doing this because you want to – for your own sake, your own interests, your own career. And Lara can go to pot for all you care."

"That's not true!" Valentin protests. "Of course, I love her, but in order to keep looking after her, paying you for her upkeep, I have got to work hard, and this paper gives me the opportunity to mix with very important people. It's better than working for that crummy local paper and doing odd jobs for Olga. I've got a degree, Anya, this kind of life is not what I studied for."

"But you don't give me money. You never give me a kopeck! And loads of people with college degrees are in this situation. Look at me – I'm working in a factory. My doctor friends are having to drive taxis in their spare time to make money. You could do with a little humility and acceptance."

"But I have actually got this job as a journalist, Anya. There's nothing you can do about it. I signed the contract weeks ago. And I have to take it seriously, you know that. I have to fulfil my role on this project."

Mama shifts in her chair. Anya turns towards her, aware she has said nothing, just sat silently watching her two children shout at one another.

"He has to go and work on this, Anya," she now says firmly. "Valentin tells us he is doing important work, work that might be good for Russia. I worry for him, but I can see he must go."

Yet again, the son is the hero. This is Russia. Women don't count. *He's been spoilt*, Anya thinks. *He's had two mothers, me and Mama.* She turns away from him in disgust, feeling that she has failed Lara.

Suddenly the year ahead doesn't hold the promise it did a couple of hours ago.

SIXTEEN

Russia, 1991

A few days later, Anya reaches into her pocket for the key to the door of her apartment. It's the end of the day, and she's tired. Her shopping basket is full of vegetables, and her arm aches from carrying it up the stairs. Her hands, even in their gloves, are stiff and frozen from the cold outside. As she puts the key in the lock, the door creaks open. She stops. She's not expecting anyone. She puts her basket down, stands in the doorway and calls, "Mama? Lara? Valentin?"

There's no response, and she can sense an emptiness, a quiet, in the space, that tells her no one is home. She walks on into the kitchen and gasps. Everything is turned upside down; the contents of the kitchen cupboards have been emptied and strewn all over the lino. Looking into the bedroom, she sees the sheets pulled off the bed, mattress upended, books over the floor. She sits down on a chair in the kitchen, her heart racing.

Who has done this? she wonders. Looking around her, she knows it can't be any ordinary thief as they would have known there is nothing of value in her flat. *Has someone done this to frighten me?* she asks herself. But why? The police? She is a model citizen, has never done anything wrong, nothing to upset anyone as far as she knows. She suddenly jumps up from the chair and rushes to the fridge in panic. Her fingers reach to the compartment where she keeps Lara's insulin and she collapses in tears of relief as she sees that it is still there, hidden in a tin with a wrapped pat of butter to keep it cold.

She sits on the floor beside the fridge for a few minutes, shivering, her limbs stiff with shock. She looks around the devastation, idly picking up a bit of rice off the floor, wondering why it was necessary to break open her bags of rice and spill them. Were they just vandals who did this? What were they looking for? Did they just trash the place out of malevolence, or were they looking for something specific? Drugs?

"I'm a nobody," she says out loud, as tears fall down her cheeks. "I just mind my own business, my own small life."

Then she stands, as she realises that Lara will soon be home from school. "I can't let her see the place like this," she mutters to herself. Then stops and looks around her, wondering whether she should tell someone, but she knows it is pointless telling the police, and she wouldn't want to worry her Mama. Natalya, next door, is still at work. She goes towards the bedroom and starts to heave the mattress back onto the beds. She tucks the sheets in and tries to restore some order.

She moves over to Lara's side of the bedroom and tidies her book onto the bedside cabinet and then, half showing under the bed, she spots a wooden box out of the corner of her eye. She's never seen it before. It's quite a large rectangular box, made of pale wood, and it's been wrenched open, the padlock broken and thrown against the wall. As she picks it up, she notices a patch of brown damp on the white wall near the skirting. Yet another problem to fix.

She looks under the bed and sees papers strewn around the box, others left, creased and scrunched inside. Whoever looked at these was in a hurry. She sits on her knees and wonders whether they found what they were looking for. Still puzzled, she takes a closer look and suddenly sees Valentin's handwriting on some of the pages, clipped together with newspaper clippings where he has circled articles, some names scribbled down in the margin of what looks like bank statements and business letters. Is this the reason she has been raided? If so, was there information in that box that someone didn't want Valentin, or anyone else, to have?

She picks up the papers, skims them and then tidies them away. If Valentin left it there, he was putting her and Lara in danger from whomever it is who is so anxious that the information should not be released. She stands and straightens her skirt, smooths the pillowcase that Lara will lay her head on later and walks back into the kitchen to get the dustpan and brush to clear up the worst of the debris before Lara arrives home.

Mama brings Lara home from school. Anya is relieved that she has managed to tidy the majority of the mess away by the time they arrive. They don't seem to notice the packs of food that still need to be put back in the cupboards. Lara is hungry and needs something sweet to eat. She cuts a small slice of the cake Mama had made at the weekend, and which had been stored safely in a tin at the back of the top shelf of the cupboard. The raiders must have found what they wanted before they got to this area.

After a while, Anya beckons to Lara. "Sweetheart, come with me a moment."

Lara gets up and they leave Mama at the kitchen table and go to the bedroom. Anya shows Lara the box, which she has closed again.

"Have you seen this before, little kitten?" she asks her.

Lara goes quiet and looks at the floor.

"It's OK," Anya coaxes her. "I won't be cross, but please tell me what you know about it."

"Papa put it there," she says after a few moments, biting her lip, her big brown eyes looking anxiously at her aunt.

"When?" Anya's eyes rise to the ceiling and a wave of fury passes through her body.

"When he came for your birthday," Lara replies quietly.

"Did he say anything about it? Why he wanted you to have it? What it contained? Why he couldn't look after it himself?" The questions come in torrents and Anya digs her nails into the palms of her hand to control herself. How could her brother possibly leave this explosive material with his daughter?

"No," Lara replies. "He didn't say anything about it. He just said it would be safe here and would I take care of it for him, because he trusted me. He suggested putting it under my bed."

"Yes, of course, he did. Where I wouldn't see it!" Anya turns from her niece, her face puce with fury.

"Don't be cross with him, Auntie Anya," Lara pleads. "I'm sure he didn't mean to upset you."

"I'm sorry, my love, but I'm sure he knew exactly what he was doing." Anya takes Lara's hand, and they sit down together on the bed.

"Sweet girl," Anya starts, haltingly, "please never do something Valentin asks of you without asking me first."

"Why not?" She looks at her aunt, confused. "He's my papa. I should do what he tells me to do."

"Well, in normal family circumstances, yes, that may be true but, to be honest, there are certain things that your particular papa does that I question, and I think you know that. And I want to keep you safe and out of trouble. Your father was always getting into trouble when he was at school, and as a very young man, so I don't want you to follow suit. Do you understand?"

"I think so," Lara says and shares a knowing look with her aunt. "He can be a bit troublesome, can't he," she says, squeezing Anya's hand.

"That's an understatement," Anya replies. "Now I must try to phone him. He tells me he is unreachable at the moment because of all this 'important work' he is doing, but he needs to know what I think of this little hidey-hole of his, that's for sure."

Anya gets up and goes to the phone, while Lara returns to sit beside her grandmother; she pulls her schoolbooks out and places them on the table to do her homework.

Anya dials the emergency number that Valentin gave her on his visit for her birthday. "Can I speak to Valentin Kotov, please?" she asks the switchboard girl who answers the phone at his Moscow newspaper office. There's a pause and some clicks on the line.

After a few minutes, the girl comes back to her and says, "Sorry, I am afraid he's not here. He's working on a project in Orel."

Anya's shoulders tense with anger that Valentin is still here, in their hometown, and has not once been to meet Lara from school. She is more furious that he has put both her and Lara in danger hiding this box in their bedroom. She stands up and scans her options in her mind.

"Mama," she says after a few moments, "can you stay a little longer and put Lara to bed after supper, please? I need to go on an errand."

"Has something happened, Anya?" Mama looks anxious. "Something I should know about?"

Anya looks at Lara and knows that there is an unspoken agreement between them that they shall not mention the box.

"No, Mama, nothing. I just have to go and do something," and with that, Anya grabs her coat from the hook beside the front door, wraps her blue scarf several times around her neck, shoves her fur hat down over her hair and picks up her gloves. She walks over to Lara and gives her a hug. "Sorry, I need to go out. I shall be back as soon as I can," and Anya turns and walks through the front door, which is hanging off one of the hinges.

"I'll fix this when I get back," she calls behind her as she runs down the stairs.

"What happened?" asks her mother.

"I tripped as I was coming home today and broke the hinge," Anya calls behind her.

Anya isn't sure whether Valentin will still be in the room he had rented previously but thinks it's worth a try. It takes her nearly an hour to cross town by two buses, and she gets to Valentin's apartment block at around seven o'clock in the evening. It's one of several identical concrete blocks, all around ten storeys high. She rings the bell, the one she thinks she remembers is his. There's no answer. She looks around her, ringing again, several times.

Then a man approaches from the street and lets himself in, so Anya slips in behind him and climbs the stairs to the sixth floor. She reaches the room she believes is Valentin's and can see a shadowy light coming from under the door. She knocks softly.

"Valentin? Valentin? Are you there?"

She hears a brief movement the other side of the door and hopes that the people who have raided her flat are not already here. She stands still a moment, breathing slowly to calm herself. There's a silence. She can detect no movement, so she tries again.

"Valentin?" she calls, louder this time, and knocks again. "Valentin, it's me. Anya. I need to speak to you." She pauses. "It's me. Your sister. Please let me in. It's important I speak with you. I wouldn't disturb you if it wasn't urgent."

This time she hears a movement and steps towards the door as it is opened slowly. She sees Valentin, in a dark polo neck jumper and dark trousers, as he opens the door wider and looks around the corridor.

"Come in, quick," he says and pulls her into the small room.

She has only visited his room twice before. It's tiny and dark, and there's only one chair and a plastic table. There's a dank smell of man, damp and stale air.

"What do you want?" he asks, pointing her towards the chair and leaning up against the wall to look at her.

"Well, thanks for asking how I am, taking my coat, offering me some tea," Anya retorts. "What I want, Valentin, is to know what was in the box you asked Lara to store for you. Because today my rooms were raided by someone and completely wrecked. So, I want an explanation, because I have spent the last hours cleaning it up, and all roads to this disaster zone lead to you."

He sighs in a rather bored way, running his fingers through his hair, then goes to the sink and turns on the cold tap so that the sound of their conversation will be drowned out by the noise of gushing water.

"For goodness' sake, Valentin, answer me. You have put me and your daughter in danger twice now."

Valentin looks at her, and she notices that there's a small smirk on his face, a twitch of a grin. Then he gets up and starts walking around the cramped area of the room.

"I'm onto this story. It will make my reputation, Anya. That guy whose men approached us in Gorky Park, you remember?"

"They attacked us, Valentin. They didn't just approach us."

"Well, their boss, Igor Novikoff. I was in Afghanistan with him. He's older than me. A dreadful guy, as I told you, a nasty piece of work, treated people really badly. He's been in local government here in Orel, and I had information that he took bribes here and had various businesses on the side, some links to the local factory. Well, now he is getting involved in the oil refinery—"

"Are you telling me," Anya interrupts him, "that you kept information on this man in our flat, under your own daughter's bed?"

"Well, I thought it was the last place they would look. It was safe. My room here was far more likely to be raided than yours, Anya." He says this angrily, turning his body towards her, his shoulders broadening with aggression, as if it is all her fault.

"I can't believe you, Valentin," Anya says. "Each time I think maybe you are beginning to mature and become responsible, you do something even more stupid, and not just stupid, dangerous. Dangerous to Lara and to me."

"I thought it would be safe," Valentin says again, slowly, slightly sheepish now.

"Well, it wasn't. My rooms have been wrecked. It's taken me hours to clean up after a hard day's work. It was lucky we weren't home because heaven knows what might have happened. And now we are all on this man's radar because he knows where we live and knows that you store your 'explosive' information at our place."

"Obviously I won't be doing that again."

"No, you absolutely will not be doing that again. Keep your own dirty business to yourself, Valentin." Anya picks up her bag and walks towards the door, then turns to him.

"Am I safe? Is Lara safe?"

Valentin stands and looks down at his sister. "I don't know," he says slowly.

Anya shakes her head, then lets herself out of the door, checking that there is no sinister shadow of a figure waiting for her in the hallway. As the door clicks behind her, she hears Valentin whisper, "I'm sorry."

SEVENTEEN

England, 1991

Kate drags herself out of bed as the alarm goes off. The June sunshine filters through her blinds but inside she feels gutted, lost and bewildered. Since her return to London from Moscow, she has felt thrown back into the reality of not knowing how she is going to manage her future, or Tom's. She is also deeply conscious of the threat left with her by the incident in Gorky Park. Might Novikoff's people know where she lives?

Leaving Valentin in Moscow had felt isolating, and confusing not to know when she would see him again, or whether he had any real feelings for her. She despises herself for yearning for his attention, his touch, her rational mind telling her the whole relationship is a bad idea. Then, as she gets dressed, she hears the fax machine beep downstairs.

She runs down to her study and tears off the sheet of fax paper. It reads: 'Kate, those last articles you sent are old comments about Gorbachev. I need more recent ones. V'.

She freezes, stung by the coldness of his words. She had spent hours on her return going through the local library for more comment in the Western press about Russian politics. She thought he would be pleased. She looks out in the garden and sees Bardot prowling around the flower bed, sniffing for prey, and wishes her life could be as simple.

"Mum! Come on, we're late!" Tom shouts at her from the hallway.

Kate throws the piece of fax paper onto her desk, as if it would burn her hand if she held it any longer, walks into the hallway and grabs her car keys.

"Come on then," she says, in a voice that is more brittle than she would like.

She can't summon any words of conversation on their short trip to school. Tom turns and looks at her as he gets out of the car.

"Have I done something wrong?" he asks, in a tone that is half a question, half defiant.

Kate shakes her head. "Oh, darling, no, no, of course not. I've just got lots to think about this morning. I'm sorry. Have a good day at school."

"Oh, by the way," Tom says, stopping as he starts to shut the door. "Grandma rang while you were in the shower."

Kate's heart sinks. Returning home after the school run, she throws the keys back on the side table. She tidies the breakfast dishes as if she is on automatic, her head buzzing, her heart heavy. She wanders around the house, picking up Tom's sneakers here or his Lego pieces there. Then throws the sheets in the washing machine, sits down at the kitchen table and looks at her watch.

The day stretches ahead of her. Tom has a playdate after school, so she isn't needed until later. Eve is at work on a major project for some palatial house she is doing up for one of her Russian clients in Belgravia. Bardot comes into Kate's study and purrs around her legs, then jumps up on her lap, digging her claws into her knees as she stretches and settles.

Kate strokes her, appreciating her company. "You're my friend, old girl, aren't you. But you're an old lady now. Don't know what I'll do when you die. Hopefully your nine lives will keep you going a little longer. Please," she says pleadingly, kissing her fur. "I'd better try to get some work done now, though." She gently lifts the cat off her knee and places her on a kitchen chair.

Kate walks to her desk and sits down, opening her blue-covered A4 notepad. She looks at the list she has made of potential sponsors for her charity maternity home, notices how the crosses of rejection on the page outnumber the ticks for acceptance and sighs. Despondent, she picks up the phone to call her mother before making the fundraising calls.

"At last, Kate!" Her mother's voice is tense, slurred. "Where have you been? I've been waiting for your call."

"I've been taking Tom to school, Mum. You know what time it is."

"Don't you have other friends who can do that when I need you? I always used to have a school run with other mums and dads when you were little."

"Yes, I know. You were very well organised." Kate tries to keep the impatience from her voice. "What do you need anyway?"

"For you to come and see me, of course. You haven't been to see me for ages. What kind of daughter are you?"

"But, Mum, we came last weekend when I got back from my trip. You must remember. Tom brought you that nice painting of Bardot."

Her mother grunts at the other end of the phone. "And what about now?"

"I'm working, Mum. I have to ring fundraisers about the maternity home."

"Stupid idea. You'll never make it work. Loads of women have difficult births. It's part of life."

"Well, I care about it, and I'm going to make it work, so I need to get on now."

"You should have stayed with Simon, then you wouldn't have had to work—"

"I have to go now," Kate interrupts her, "bye." Her hand is shaking as she puts the phone down.

By lunchtime, her notepad has even more rejection crosses on the list. She knows she shouldn't have made these calls on a day when she feels so low and despondent. Her negativity would inevitably have filtered through and hardly inspired confidence in the person to whom she was talking. She berates herself as she makes a salad, forcing herself to eat something healthy, then tries to imagine where she might find any more information for Valentin. She decides to go back to the library in Kensington and spend more time going through newspaper articles on their system.

Sitting at a desk in the large reference library, she works her way through pages of coverage on Russia during the afternoon but finds little that would be of any real value to Valentin. She makes copious notes as she works, hoping that there might be something he can find useful, but her mind works against her, putting doubts in her way, that she knows nothing, that surely he would know about a piece of information anyway and fearing that she will not provide him with enough to win his gratitude.

It's late afternoon when she gets home. The house is empty. She longs to talk to someone adult, but there's no one there. Tom will be dropped off later. She looks around for Bardot but can't find her. She makes a sauce of Tom's favourite pasta dish for when he comes home for supper.

Then she goes to her desk and starts to compile a fax of notes for Valentin from her research at the library. As she pauses and looks out at the garden, she sees a shape in the flower bed that she doesn't recognise. It's dusk, so she can't be sure, but an ice dread grips her heart as she opens the French windows and walks across the small lawn. Her breath shortens as she approaches. Bardot. Her body is lying among the base of the forsythia, its yellow blossom an eerie halo above her in the grey light, a lone love-in-a-mist is tangled between her legs.

Kate's breath takes a sharp inwards gasp. "Oh no! God, this day couldn't get any worse if it tried!" The tears fall down her cheeks as she lifts the cat into her arms and carries her into the kitchen. She is already a little stiff. Kate gently places her on the table, perplexed that she has died so suddenly when she had seemed well this morning. Her fingers gently stroke the matted fur, looking for signs of illness or a wound.

And then she sees it. A deep wound across the back of her neck. "Oh dear, yes, you did get bashed, didn't you?" She smooths the wound, drawing the fur in its natural route to try to hide it. "You're usually so careful. What happened to you today? Did you get into a fight, my darling?" she whispers as her tears fall into the fur. "Or didn't you see a car when you walked across the road?"

Kate sighs. "I'd better bury you, my sweet girl. I shall miss you so much, so very much, and I only told you this morning not to leave me."

Kate carries Bardot out into the garden again and lays her on the patio table while she finds the spade from the tiny shed next to the kitchen. She looks around the small garden to work out where to bury her, wanting to get this done before Tom comes home. Then she spots a small area under a young Acer tree.

It's surprisingly hard work, digging. It hasn't rained for a while, and the earth is dry and crusted. Kate tries not to disturb the pansies that are providing the bed with some colour. Eventually, when she thinks the hole is large enough, she decides to go upstairs and find one of her scarves to wrap around the cat's body. She pushes off her garden boots at the back door and runs upstairs. There she finds a beautiful turquoise pashmina that she had bought on a trip to Southern India. It had looked wonderful in the light of the Indian sun but somehow looked ridiculous when she had tried to wear it in England.

She takes it downstairs, puts her boots back on and carefully wraps Bardot's body in the silk, then lays her in the earth. "Bless you," she whispers as she gradually pushes the earth back over her body. "You'll always be with me."

She puts the spade back in the shed and goes to the bathroom to wash the tears off her face, hoping she does not look too dishevelled when Tom's friend's mother drops him back. The phone rings. She wipes her face and eyes with the towel quickly, then walks into her bedroom to pick up the cream phone on the bedside table.

"Hello?"

"Kate."

"Harry, how are you?" Kate responds, immediately recognising his voice and trying to disguise her sadness.

"Are you OK?" he questions her, his words slowing as he picks up her tension.

"No, I'm really not OK," and Kate tells him about Bardot, sobbing between her words.

"Oh, my dear girl, I am sorry. I was just ringing as I was wondering whether you'd like to come down to Dorset for a sail? Maybe on Saturday?"

Kate's heart lifts at the thought of someone thinking of her and of having something to look forward to.

"That would be wonderful, thank you."

Harry tells her to get a pen and write down the address and instructions to find the boat. When she puts the phone down, there is a lighter sense within her.

Tom is devastated at the loss of Bardot. He sobs angry tears on her shoulder, as if there had been something she could have done about it.

"Darling, she must have been run over by one of the

cars. I don't think either of us could have done anything to save her."

"But she's always so sensible," he says, cheese sauce and spaghetti dribbling down his chin as he speaks. "She hardly ever goes on the road. Why would she now? I don't understand."

Kate's hand stops as she is about to put a forkful of pasta into her mouth. She looks at her son for a moment and then out into the garden.

"Yes," she says thoughtfully. "I don't understand that either."

EIGHTEEN

England, 1991

The drive to Wareham goes smoothly for Kate. It's a beautiful day and she listens to Abba, singing along happily, the AA map perched on her knee, the instructions Harry has given her jotted down on a piece of paper on the passenger seat.

There's a car park near the quay, and she pulls her backpack out of the car and walks down towards the boats. She spots Harry immediately, on the deck of a traditional wooden yacht. He's wearing jeans and a navy polo shirt. He waves and Kate makes her way over to him, glad that she has decided to wear flat shoes as she steps on board.

"Kate!" he welcomes her warmly, holding out his arms and giving her a hug. Then, holding her at a little distance, he says, "You are looking splendid, dear girl. The star you are." He leans forward and kisses her lightly on the lips.

She feels a tingle, like a question, run through her body. "Those sparkling eyes," he says, and she notices the fresh smell on his skin, blond hairs on his tanned arms.

"So, show me around your boat," she says, unsure quite how to respond to his greeting. "It's all a little frightening for a Londoner like me. I did tell you I am a landlubber, didn't I?"

He laughs. "You did. Have no fear; you're in safe hands." He takes her hand and helps her as they walk down a couple of steps into a small galley. "As you can see, it won't take you long to know where things are. It isn't the *Queen Mary*!"

The saloon has a settee around a dropleaf table. Sunshine shines through the windows and the place feels warm and light. There's a cabin with double berths, a tiny loo and basin. Everything is neat and clear, and Kate notices that it looks well loved and cared for.

"It's a yacht made in Woodbridge in the 1960s. I've had her for ten years."

Kate suspects that the boat, *Reflection*, could tell her a history of its own.

"Why don't you put your things in that hold." Harry points to a storage cupboard. Kate shoves her backpack into it, and Harry locks the door.

"Right now, if you help me cast off, I shall get the engine going," he says. Kate nods, and they climb back on the deck.

He shows her how to release the ropes and step safely back on board. "We don't want you falling in!"

His calm manner makes her feel at ease and she is pleased with herself as she manages to cast off the ropes without a hitch and take her place on Harry's left, close to where he is standing, his hands on the wheel.

Soon the water is lapping along the bows as they make their way along the river towards the open sea. Kate sits back, takes a long, deep breath and enjoys the view as they catch up with news since they met last month for dinner in London.

"Do you know, I am still finding it so hard to adjust after Russia, the first trip and this recent one," she confides. "It's a place so full of different experiences. I am not sleeping well, finding it really difficult to concentrate on life. I'm only half here. I feel I keep leaving a part of me in Moscow. Does that sound mad?"

"Do you now?" Harry looks at her quizzically. She picks up that he seems to be wanting to say or ask something but then thinks the better of it and says, "Yes, I think we're both still experiencing this, consumed with all those images and memories, gold domes and $5 deals."

"How's Isabelle?"

"Good, thanks. She's thinking of studying Russian at university. Got all excited when I told her about it. It's such a fascinating country, especially at the moment. I hadn't realised until we were there how unpopular Gorbachev is. Apparently, the locals think he can't speak Russian properly, looks too Mongolian or something, and they think his wife Raisa is even worse – 'arrogant and bigoted' it said in this article I read yesterday. What d'you know? We Westerners often have a completely different perspective. To us it seems that Gorbachev is moving the country towards the Western way of operating, and that feels like a good thing."

"Yes, one can be blind to these different ways of seeing things," Kate agrees.

"I wouldn't have missed that trip for the world. Sacred moments," Harry reflects as he shuts down the engine, raises the sails and guides the boat out onto the open sea. "Let's hope this transition from Communism is a peaceful one. There's been so much cruelty inflicted on the Russian people."

"I sometimes wonder whether certain geographical spaces haven't got some kind of energy that draws one conflict after another. Look at the Middle East," Kate suggests.

"I believe it's the people, not the land, who cause the trouble," Harry says firmly.

They sink into a peaceful reverie as the wind catches the sails and the sun glints on the rippling waves. The boat skims along, and Kate understands why Harry always looks so tanned.

"Look at your hair," Harry says, smiling. "It's like the flames of the sun now the wind is in it." Kate self-consciously tries to tidy it behind her ears, but it has a will of its own.

"Leave it, Kate," he prompts. "It looks wonderful. Let it go wild."

After a while, Harry points to the shore. "We'll moor in there and have a picnic on board."

He draws the boat gently into a bay. The cliffs loom above them and there's a small beach below. "She's got a shallow draft so we can go in further than other boats, perhaps even have a swim ashore if we feel like it after lunch."

He puts the sails down and lowers the anchor. It all seems very easy, and Kate appreciates the fact that he has not been bossy or patronising in the way she has previously experienced men in boats.

Once they are safely positioned, Harry pulls a cold box out of the galley and passes her a couple of glasses as he lifts out a bottle of champagne and pops the cork.

"Cheers, Kate. Wonderful to see you," he says as he pours the golden liquid into the glasses.

"*Nostrovia!*" she laughs as they take their first sips. "This is such a treat for me. A whole day out of London. Tom is with his dad. The sun is shining. What could be nicer?"

They chat, and he offers her smoked salmon sandwiches on plastic plates. There are no other boats in sight, and the beach nearby is deserted. Kate can see the odd dog-walker striding along the cliff-top path above them.

"So, how is the new house? Has Tom settled after the divorce?"

Kate sighs. "I don't know. You know what young boys are like. They tell you nothing."

"Well, I don't think old men give away much either." He laughs.

"Too true! But I think he's OK, and Simon and I are getting along fine, sharing the pickups and weekends. Your advice about keeping that relationship harmonious was invaluable. It can take some effort on both our parts, but it is really worthwhile."

"Did you think about having more children?" he asks as he takes her empty plate and digs some strawberries out from the bottom of the box. "We couldn't after Isabelle, sadly."

Kate is slightly taken aback by the intimacy of the question. She pauses, wondering what to tell him, then says, "We did have a son before Tom, but he died. Do you remember, I mentioned it as the reason for starting the maternity home project?"

"I'm sorry, how stupid of me," he says gently, and there's a silence for a moment as a seagull swoops over them, eyeing the crumbs of their sandwiches.

"Yes, it was terrible. I'd been so excited to be pregnant, but I had begun to feel something wasn't quite right a few days before he was due. There was less movement. I asked the hospital whether I should come in early, but they said not to worry, so I stayed at home. Then my waters broke, so Simon drove me in. The hospital was incredibly busy, and I was put in a little cubicle, but no one came and checked me out for ages. Simon went home to feed the dog, and suddenly I was in such pain. I knew something was wrong. It was excruciating. I called for help, but no one seemed to hear me. It was like a nightmare."

"How awful. Did Simon come back?"

"Oh yes, but I didn't see him, as the next thing I knew there was a doctor with me, then alarms ringing, lights flashing, and I was being rushed along a corridor. My hand, hanging outside the stretcher, was being scraped along the pebbledash wall. No one noticed. When we got into theatre, I heard a doctor questioning whether there was a heartbeat. I'd never seen the man before; he didn't know me, didn't know my history. All I heard was 'put her out' and then nothing."

Harry waits, saying nothing as Kate takes a deep breath.

"I don't know why I'm telling you all this," she says through a constricted throat.

"Perhaps because I asked. Perhaps I shouldn't have?"

"No, it's not your fault. The trouble is I keep reliving it in dreams. Seeing William all floppy after the caesarean. Something didn't seem right, but I was a new mother, so what did I know? They put him in an incubator for the night, then the next morning they brought him to me to breastfeed. He couldn't get much of a grip, but they sent me home the next day. Said they needed the bed. Five days later I went to his cot, picked him up, and he was like a rag doll. He was dead. We thought about suing the hospital, but I couldn't face it as it would keep it all alive in my mind, yet I wish I had, if only to point out lessons for other mothers."

As fast as the words had tumbled from Kate's lips, they suddenly dry up. "Oh, Harry. I am so sorry. This was supposed to be such a happy day out."

He leans over and takes her hand. "It must have been heartbreaking for you," he says quietly, drawing her head to his shoulder as her tears fall.

After some minutes, she sits up and he kisses the tip of her nose. They both laugh, slightly awkwardly but also with relief.

"I fully understand why you are so intent on this charity now," he says. "I shall support you in any way I can."

"But, Harry, how is life for you?" Kate asks, feeling she has had far too much focus on her own life.

"I'm just a boring country bumpkin, that's what Isabelle tells me. I love my time with her though; as I told you, she lives mainly with her mother. Let's tidy up the picnic. Do you feel like a swim?" he asks.

"No. It's so lovely just sitting here on deck. I feel so relaxed. I feel we can talk about anything and everything."

"Yes, I agree," says Harry as he tidies the plates back into the cold box. "I feel we have known each other far longer than we have – a bit like Terry and June!"

"Huh, I hope not!" Kate retorts, laughing, yet she knows what he means.

"Now I must get you back to dry land so that you can reach London before too late. You take the helm on the way back."

"Oh no," Kate protests. "I'll probably crash your boat."

"No, you won't. She's easy to handle and I am here." He raises the sails again and shows her how to guide the boat back towards the harbour. "Just let yourself relax into it. Feel the water and the wind. Flow with it."

And she does; she feels at one with the boat as it cuts through the small waves. She feels exhilarated, cheeks pink from the sun and wind, as she jumps off the boat at the end of the afternoon, to help him tie the ropes.

They pack up the boat and Harry walks Kate back to her car, helping her put the backpack in the boot. They both hesitate as they say goodbye, then Harry bends down and kisses her cheek.

"What happened to that Russian fellow you were in touch with? Valentin?" he asks.

"We are still in touch, writing to one another. I saw him when I went back to Russia last month. A bit of an eventful trip!"

"Did you now?" Harry asks, and Kate notices his voice change. "What happened?" he asks.

"Oh, nothing really." She wants to change the subject, get back to where they were. "Do you see anyone from the tour?"

"I meet up with Lucia every so often, for the odd film or a walk," he says, opening the car door for her.

"That's nice," Kate says awkwardly. "Thank you so much for a wonderful day."

But suddenly it feels like they are strangers.

"It's been my pleasure," he says briefly, looking around, distracted. "Really. See you soon. I'll be in touch."

And the warmth of the day chills as Kate drives back to London, wondering what just happened.

NINETEEN

England, 1991

Returning, on a hot summer's day, from running a conference for an IT company, Kate sees the light flashing on the answerphone. There is a voicemail from Margot, the PR consultant she met in Russia, who has taken an unexpected but helpful interest in Kate's charity.

"You'll never believe it, Kate." Margot's voice on the message is uncharacteristically enthusiastic. "An old client of ours, a wealthy woman called Edith Carter, died recently. I had mentioned your project to her," there is a pause, "and she's left her house to charity and named me as the executor who can choose how it is used. Can you believe it?" she repeats. "It's Margot. Ring me as soon as possible!"

Kate stops. She takes a moment to take in the news, then looks up Margot's number in her address book and calls her.

"It is true," Margot enthuses. "I can choose the charity, and I think this house of hers could be perfect to convert for your maternity home. She inherited a lot of wealth and ran a charitable trust, gifting money to many charities. My consultancy helped her publicise events. But we are talking about her house, her whole house – I know it well. It's big, and it's not far from London."

"What happens next?" Kate asks.

"I guess there will be legal stuff to deal with, probate and all that kind of thing. That will give us some time to pull a team together to look at the house and see what we can do with it. Edith lost two babies herself, obviously many moons ago, but I guess that is why she was fired up by your idea, though she left it to me to make the final decision."

"I can't thank you enough, Margot," Kate says, her mind reeling at the news.

"No need to do that. This is a win for us all. Let's talk when I know some more."

Kate puts the phone down and walks out into the garden. It's dark, and there's the scent of blossom in the air. The night is clear and, even under the diffused light of the London sky, she can see the stars and the crescent of a new moon. She remembers how her father would stand out in the garden and change his silver coins from one side pocket to another, believing it brought good luck. She had often stood beside him, as a small child, as they both looked up and thought of wishes they wanted to come true. She runs back inside to pull a few silver coins out of her wallet and put them in the left-side pocket of her jeans, then walks outside, looks at the moon and transfers the coins to her right pocket, wishing fervently for good luck with this wonderful piece of news. Perhaps this is a sign that her charity will work after all.

She stretches her arms up towards the heavens and tries to imagine the project happening as she has envisioned. She looks at her watch and goes inside to make herself supper, which she eats on a tray in the sitting room, to watch the news. Gorbachev is in London, in discussion with John Major and the G7. She watches a summary of the joint press conference they hold after the summit.

"We're building a world partnership... a landmark moment between the East and West," Gorbachev is saying. There's talk of new divisions of power and responsibilities within the Soviet Union, which Kate feels is optimistic for a closer cooperation between Russia and the UK, an end to the Cold War.

Kate pours herself another glass of white wine and toasts the television, as she watches Brian Hanrahan and other journalists from around the world challenge Major and Gorbachev to give their views.

As she goes to her desk after the news, she switches on her new Amstrad computer. She's not confident about making it work but is finding it helpful in sending out letters about the charity and also to send emails to Valentin from her CompuServe account to his work, though she can't include any personal information as she knows his boss reads what she writes.

She sits down and writes an email to him now.

'V, just watching Gorbachev being interviewed in London. He's talking about an integration of the Soviet Union into the world economy, improved trade access to markets for Soviet goods and services. He's impressive – says he has rejected the methods of the Cold War and is working towards a united civilisation where everyone moves from confrontation to cooperation. People here are inspired by all this and like the idea of a closer alliance between the UK and Russia. It's exciting, isn't it – our two countries coming closer together. K xx'.

Kate turns off the computer and heads upstairs to bed and then, an hour later, as she closes her book and turns over to turn out the light, she suddenly remembers how much Valentin hates Gorbachev and realises that her enthusiasm may make him very angry at her views. "How stupid can I be? How can I have forgotten this?" she asks herself. She runs downstairs to see if she can delete the email, but it has already been sent.

She hears nothing from Valentin in response, but only a few days later, she catches news of a pushback against Gorbachev in Russia. She watches news bulletins of protests on the streets. Worrying that this activity will interrupt any visit she might make to Moscow, she goes to Kensington Library again the next day to see what she can track down about what is happening. She finds an article about an open letter, *A Word to the People*, calling for rebellion against Gorbachev's reforms. As she reads it, she suddenly sees Valentin's name on the list of signatures. The letter he has signed is supported by a group of committed communists.

She walks home in a daze, her mood having swung from the hope that Russia would open up and make it easier for her to travel to and from Moscow in future, to the thought that there might be a revolution about to take place, and it could herald a return to Communism.

Tom returns with Simon that evening.

"We watched Arsenal, Mum. It was awesome. Dad and I had a great time. He bought me a T-shirt."

"How lovely, darling," Kate responds, almost automatically, delighted to see him happy though experiencing a twinge of envy that he is so enthusiastic about his time with his father. They eat supper and play a game of cards together then, as he goes upstairs to his room, she walks out into the garden.

Surveying the flowers and shrubs she sees, out of the corner of her eye, something glinting in the flower bed. She wonders whether she might have dropped a coin when she transferred them on the night of the new moon, but she had stood in a completely different part of the garden, so this would not have been possible.

She bends down over the earth and sees a silver coin. It is not far from the acer and is covered with a few small purply blue blossoms that have fallen from the irises above. She digs into the loose earth and picks it up. To her amazement, it is a five ruble coin. Russian. She looks at it, confused. She knows she never brought any Russian coins back from Moscow – she had changed the notes at Heathrow and donated what coins she had to a collection for charity at the airport.

She turns it over in her hand, looking at the floral ornaments, the double-headed eagle. the Bank of Russia. She walks back into her study and puts it on the mantelpiece, her mind tracking back over recent events to glean a clue as to how it might have got there.

TWENTY

England, 1991

Margot and Kate drive out to the ramshackle old house that this kind old lady, Edith Carter, has left to charity. It's a hot summer's day, and the lawn is looking a little parched as Margot drives her car up the drive and parks in front of the house.

The house is near Marlow, not far from the river. It's red brick, built on four floors, with gabled roofs, and there's a courtyard at the back with stables, a barn and outbuildings. It has large and well kept parkland surrounding it. *Perfect for the mothers to walk in*, Kate thinks, as she starts to look around.

"Access is good," Margot tells Kate. "Wycombe Hospital is ten minutes away should there be a medical emergency."

"That's good, but I really want to provide all medical services in the maternity home if possible. Build whatever facilities we might need," Kate replies.

Margot's eyebrows rise as she says, "Nothing but the best for our Kate!"

"Sorry," Kate says. "I just think it's so important."

"Fair enough," Margot says. "Now here's Elizabeth and her business partner, Chris, so we can talk about the architectural designs with them. I think you'll find Elizabeth is a great mix of pragmatism and innovation."

"Perfect. Is the obstetrician coming along too?" Kate asks.

"Yes, Dev. He'll be here in about thirty minutes."

Kate's delighted that Margot has become so passionate about getting the venture up and running. She walks around the building with Elizabeth Sparkes, the architect, a lively woman in her fifties, and her colleague Chris, an Australian who has previously worked in Sydney.

They investigate the space available on the different floors of the house, observing and discussing possibilities, and end up in the outbuildings. Dev joins them. He has recently come to the UK from Bombay and has finished an international research study on best practice in maternity care.

"Do you think we can convert these stables and outbuildings into birthing units and use the main house for rooms and accommodation for mothers and babies?" Kate asks the team. "I don't want mums to be chucked out of here the minute they have had their babies, unless they want to go. My cousin had her first baby at five o'clock in the morning and was sent back home by nine o'clock the same day. Luckily, she has a wonderful, loving and practical husband, but many women would be completely on their own trying to cope. I don't want them to feel the pressure to leave."

"OK," Elizabeth says, "and I hear you would like sitting areas, fountains and maybe tranquil spaces that mothers can sit alone with their baby to breastfeed and bond?"

"Yes," Kate says and, as she talks through the conversion needs and medical requirements, she realises that she is speaking with greater authority than she could have imagined only a few months ago.

"And I would like an operating suite for emergency caesareans on the premises too please."

"You'll need to insulate the stables well," Chris points out. "They haven't been designed for human habitation."

"I'm wondering about skylights in the roofs of the birthing suites," Kate suggests. "Usually, giving birth, one is in a room with no outdoor view, and obviously one couldn't have windows at low levels as people could see in, but I think it could be a good focus for mothers to look at the clouds, look at the stars or the moon as they give birth. What do you think?"

"Why not?" Elizabeth replies. "Of course, this is England, so they could just as easily be looking at rain, but it would be easy to fit double-glazed windows in the ceilings and insulate the roof space. No problem." Chris scribbles notes on his pad.

"I just can't believe our luck that Edith suddenly gave us this house," Kate exclaims, as she looks around, returning to the big hallway as they prepare to leave. "It's beyond amazing to have found someone who had lost her own babies and therefore cared about the charity and had no descendants. It would have cost us a bomb to buy or build something this size."

"Sure," Margot agrees. "Though it will still cost a considerable sum to convert, don't forget, Kate."

"No, no, I won't forget that. We must keep our eye on the ball for fundraising. It seems my friend Eve now thinks her Russian client Grigory might give us some money and might even have other contacts here in the UK who could be interested. I gather the Russians want to establish a role in society here. You know, do good works, give to charity. They can see that helps them meet people, build their networks."

Margot stops in her tracks. She nods. "That sounds exciting. We will need to know where the money comes from, of course, for governance. Did you ever think of going back to that fellow in the Wirral, Edward Babbington? I don't know why, but his name keeps popping up in the financial press, and I just wonder whether you couldn't give him another go? We still have a long way to go before we can give the project the full go-ahead."

Kate sighs and makes a face. "I must say, I'd written him off," she replies. "He was so horrible. That meeting set me back months in lost confidence. I'm only just getting it back. I'm not sure I could face approaching him again."

"You did say his wife was quite kind when you visited," Margot presses Kate. "Perhaps a phone call to her to test out the waters?"

There are butterflies in Kate's stomach as she thinks of ringing Annabel Babbington.

"Nothing ventured, nothing gained," Margot pushes Kate, who raises her eyes to the sky.

"I'll think about it, Margot. I'll probably need several G&Ts before and certainly several more after any phone call like that!"

Margot laughs. Dev has joined them and is leaning on the mantlepiece in the main hallway, poring over sets of figures, plans and lists of medical equipment as he considers what might be needed. He writes with a fountain pen and has beautiful handwriting, Kate notices, watching the way he reflects before writing the carefully crafted words down on the sheet.

Kate shakes herself and returns her attention to the subject of the meeting. Elizabeth summarises the intentions they have discussed and tells Kate that Chris will draw up preliminary plans and get some quotes for her so that she will gain some idea about the investment sums she will need. Dev shares his thoughts and promises to send an initial list of medical requirements, as well as calculating the number of staff required to service Kate's vision.

"Let us give you a lift back to London," Margot suggests to Dev, who had taken the train out to Marlow.

"That would be great," he says gratefully.

The three of them chatter all the way down the M4 and share ideas about the landscape, the windows and how to make the place beautiful.

"It's a spiritual experience," Dev reflects, "to have a baby, to bring a new life into the world. Yet most of the time the focus is on the effort of it, the surgical equipment in the room and ghastly clinical surroundings."

"True. Let's think about that more," Kate agrees, moved by the thought of how they could enhance that sense of the spiritual in the maternity home, without making it follow any specific religion.

"That's set all our minds going on some kind of

celestial journey," Margot says softly, as Dev gets out of the car in Maida Vale.

"It's a spiritual moment, too, sadly, when a baby dies," Kate remarks to Margot once Dev has shut the car door. "We can do our very best to support a safe birth, but we shall never be able to guarantee it."

"No, indeed, but we can provide a compassionate environment for all eventualities, I believe. That's our aim, isn't it, Kate?" Margot looks at Kate as she stops at a red light on the flyover.

"Absolutely," Kate replies.

And as Kate says farewell to Margot and walks back into her study at home, she feels that familiar prod on her back, the prod that tells her that William's spirit is with her and that all this effort and energy is worthwhile.

TWENTY-ONE

Russia, 1991

Since the raid on her flat, Anya hasn't been able to sleep. She listens to every knock or creak, wondering if someone is breaking in. Out on the street, and on the way to her new work at the pharmacy, she sees imaginary figures coming out of doorways, around corners, stepping off buses, intent on harming her or, worse, Lara.

Anya spreads the newspaper across her kitchen table, smoothing out the pages. In front of her she sees a photo of a man, the man Valentin had been talking to her about. Igor Novikoff. It's a long article about how he has bought into one of the oil refineries that had previously been state-owned. There is no journalist mentioned to identify who has written the article, but Anya feels sure that it was Valentin.

As she reads on, she is shocked to realise that it is accusing Novikoff of obtaining this refinery for a fraction of what it was worth and questioning how he could have afforded it when he had previously been a fairly lowly paid public servant. The insinuation being that Novikoff is linked to people at the top of the Kremlin.

Anya looks up and her gaze goes out of the window to the grey skies, where clouds drift slowly in a breeze. She fears for her brother, thinking that history has never shown itself to be kind to writers who expose corruption in elites or governments. Although Valentin's name is not on the article, she knows that Novikoff will be able to identify the source of the information.

She gets up and busies herself around the kitchen, not wanting to think about the danger her brother is in and knowing full well that nothing she nor her mother, nor Lara, were to say to him would stop him researching and writing these articles.

There are plots afoot in Moscow. She has heard about them, through whispers between neighbours. The possibility of civil war. People don't seem to want Gorbachev's policies to open up Russia to more Western trade and ideas. There's an agitation for rebellion, and Anya has a pretty strong idea that Valentin is playing some part in it. On the rare occasion that he has visited, he has spoken of a major article that he has produced, a call to action for the Russian people. When he talks about it, he leaps around the room like a tiger. All revolutionary zeal. It scares her to death.

"Who wants civil war, Valentin? Blood on the streets? Uncertainty, division? Most of us just want a quiet life and to be able to eat and go to work. I'd like to travel through Europe, go to Paris," she tells him.

But the reality of her life is far from this. Her evenings are quiet, lonely. She longs for a man and misses touch, adult conversation. She feels sure that no man will want to take her and Lara on, but since the raid on the flat she would love to feel the protection of a man, a man with the muscles to fight back.

One evening, as she has her hands in the sink, washing up, she hears Lara's voice behind her.

"Auntie Anya?" Lara's voice breaks through, in constricted pauses. "Can we go and visit Papa please? I miss him."

Anya stops washing up the pans, wipes the dripping suds from her hands and turns to look at her. She sees Lara has been crying, her eyes red, a drip still running under her nose. She walks to the young girl and cuddles her thin frame, her school shirt coarse against Anya's hand. Lara's dark hair hangs in fine strands, still damp from her walk home in the rain.

"I miss him so much," she sobs. "It feels like ages. I hate it when you two argue, and I worry about him doing something stupid, like you said he might and—"

"Shhh," Anya whispers in her ear, wiping a tear from her cheek. "Just because I told you that he was a bit crazy at school doesn't mean he will do anything stupid now, so don't you worry. He's told you, hasn't he, he was a soldier. He knows how to look after himself."

"Mm." Lara sniffs. Then, after a pause, she repeats, "But can I go and visit him? Please?"

Anya feels a heavy weight of frustration at her request. She doesn't know where Valentin is living, nor what he is doing, whether he would want Lara to come up. Nor how she can afford the train trip.

"Let me see what I can do," Anya says.

"Your brother is doing good work," her neighbour Kristina tells Anya a few days later. "That letter, *A Word to the People*, that his paper wrote, was brilliant. It's a real manifesto for communism, for patriotism, criticising Perestroika. "'We have to do this through our own tears and blood to prevent the grinding of the bones of the people, breaking the backbone of Russia'[2]," Kristina says with fervour. "I even learnt it by heart. It's brilliant."

The words disturb Anya. "Let me see that piece again," she asks Kristina and reads how many prominent writers, politicians, scientists and singers have signed the letter. She can't help being a little impressed that her young brother has got himself involved with the calibre of this group. She reads about how the group want to transform Russia into a genuine people's power, not 'some manger for the hungry nouveaux riches, who are ready to sell off everything for the sake of their insatiable appetites...'[2], and Anya thinks of Novikoff and his machinations with the oil refinery.

"So the main problem people are having is the break-up of the Soviet Union, one state after another becoming independent. That makes me sad too," Anya says to Kristina.

"Come and watch the news," Kristina says. "Natalya has her television on."

Anya watches and sees protests and hears cries of

---

2   Quote from *A Word to the People*, Sovetskaya Rossiya newspaper, 23 July 1991

'the Motherland is dying!'. She watches Gorbachev be interviewed and ridicule his opponents. Yeltsin is in Washington.

"That creep, Dick Cheney, is there. Yeltsin is cosying up to George Bush."

Natalya's tiny sitting room is full of smoke, and the chatter around the television is of the old days, the days Anya's neighbours remember, of sitting in their kitchens drinking tea, of toasting Fidel with Cuban rum in the 1970s, the sense of revolution, the arguments about Stalin and Solzhenitsyn, the way people would halt mid-conversation, wondering whether they were being listened to.

"Do you remember, we would point to the ceiling light, turn the radio up even louder?" an old man perching on a stool was saying.

An elderly woman, with grey-green eyes, a little multicoloured scarf over the long grey hair, her hands on her worn wool skirt, laughs and says, "Yes, we were the 'kitchen dissidents', never brave enough to speak out or resist on the streets. We were all living crammed together. All those squabbles between families, whose food was whose, why hadn't someone cleaned up the kitchen. But there was a lot of love in those kitchens too."

"It's all over." Kiril, a short man with slicked grey hair combed to hide his balding head, stands up. "Our rubles are worth nothing now. All those words, all that talk, in our homes, was based on myth. It didn't exist. What exists now is hardship. It doesn't matter if we have top degrees in philosophy or economics. All that matters is that we have money. We're nothing without it..."

Kiril stops and paces around the cramped space like

a caged animal, beads of sweat on his forehead. "We don't know who we are anymore. This letter, this *Word to the People*, it's a call for us to do something."

"But what can we do?" Kristina asks. They all look at her, and around the room at one another, and shrug. "I'm too old. I feel helpless and frightened. It's up to the young."

"Don't get your hopes up, old woman," another woman, sitting on the arm of Natalya's chair, says. "The young men are just out there doing deals, getting rich. They won't save you. They couldn't care less about you. They'll shoot you for your wedding ring if you're not careful."

Anya watches and listens but feels alienated from much of what they are saying. She doesn't want this, doesn't want conflict. Quietly, she takes her leave, waving to Kristina and Natalya as she goes. She creeps back next door to her bedroom, where Lara lies softly sleeping. There's a cold feeling of dread in her stomach as she looks at the sleeping child and feels helpless to protect her.

TWENTY-TWO

Russia, 1991

"I have to go and cover a story," Valentin tells Lara, who, after much persuasion, is staying with him for some days of her summer school holiday. "It's an exciting time. The country is in a State of Emergency, Lara. I need you to stay here. My neighbour will take care of you."

"I want to come with you!"

"No. You are safer here. I have to go. They're going to boot Gorbachev out!"

"But I thought he was a good thing. Auntie Anya likes him – says he will make it possible for me to travel to London or Paris."

"My sister has some strange ideas." Valentin shrugs, tucking his documents into his pocket. "Now, I want you to promise me you will stay inside. I shall be back as soon as I can, but it probably won't be until this evening or tomorrow."

Lara pouts as his neighbour, Marina, walks into their room, and Valentin strides off down the stairs.

"The army will take Moscow," Mikhail, Valentin's boss, briefs his team on that hot August day in Moscow, 1991. "A delegation will go to Gorbachev's dacha to ask him to resign. We will cover the story. I'll stay here, with Kiril and Ilya. Valentin, you will go down to Foros and cover Gorbachev's response to the demand that he resign. Go with Maxim and Dmitry. You'll need to keep a low profile, not upset anyone. Just take notes, OK?"

"Great," Valentin responds, delighted to be given this opportunity. "Gorbachev will get what he deserves."

It's 18 August when Valentin and his colleagues arrive at Foros, following Boldin, Shenin, Baklanov and Varennikov, who are part of the rebel group disillusioned with Gorbachev. They walk up to the door of Gorbachev's dacha. The bodyguard, Medvedev, notifies Gorbachev of their arrival. Valentin knows that the KGB has cut the telephone wires. Without waiting for permission, the group walk straight up to Gorbachev's office on the third floor. They make themselves comfortable and wait.

A little while later, Gorbachev walks into the room and is taken aback to find them all there, sitting on his chairs, leaning against his furniture.

"This is outrageous! Disrespectful!" he rages at them. Valentin stands in a corner and watches, pen in hand, taking down what Gorbachev is saying.

"We represent the State Committee on the State of Emergency," Boldin tells him firmly. "The country is breaking up. Emergency action is the only way to prevent catastrophe. Either you declare a state of emergency, or you resign and declare Yanayev as acting president. This allows us, members of the GKChP, to restore order to the country."

"Fuck that, you bastards!" Gorbachev swears, his face flushed. "You turncoats. I trusted you."

"Yeltsin will be arrested. You're expected to resign now, while we're here," Boldin continues, his voice a little hesitant, seemingly nervous at challenging his boss, Valentin notices.

"Shut up, you arsehole! Who are you to lecture me on what's going on? There's no way I am going to resign, so get out!"

Valentin watches this quietly from his corner, as the stand-off continues. When it becomes clear that Gorbachev will not comply with their demands, and the delegation stand and start to leave the room, he puts his notebook in his pocket and follows them out.

"Damn you!" Gorbachev yells at Varennikov and, looking at Valentin, "Damn you! Do what you want. But report my opinion!"

"Boldin didn't fight enough, he gave in too easily," Valentin mutters to Maxim, who just shrugs and walks down the stairs to leave.

"I've just been told that the KGB general at the dacha will keep Gorbachev, his wife and all those still here on house arrest," Dmitry says in excitement, coming up to Valentin and Maxim. "They have blockaded the helipad with fire trucks and street-cleaning machines and closed the main road. KGB are surrounding the area."

Valentin listens and they hasten to follow the

delegation away. As he walks down the path, one of the security staff approaches him.

"Hey, you, you're a journalist, yes?"

"Yes," Valentin affirms.

"Be careful what you write, understand? Say something we don't like, and we can finish your career very quickly," the man sneers at him. He's tall, thin, athletic, Valentin observes. But what he notices most are his cold green eyes, which send a tremor of fear running through his body, as he remembers that he has heard rumours that the KGB have arranged for some quarter of a million extra pairs of handcuffs and arrest forms to be sent to Moscow and that the Lefortovo Prison has been emptied to receive prisoners caught up in the coup. "We'll be watching you," the guard whispers in Valentin's ear, then abruptly walks away.

TWENTY-THREE

Russia, 1991

"Where is Lara?" Anya storms into Valentin's small room in Moscow. It's late afternoon, and she has just arrived by train from Orel to collect Lara and take her home.

"She's fine," Valentin says dismissively as he lets her in. "She's with my neighbour, Marina. She's probably taken her out for a walk."

"Today is a day to be inside, Valentin. You know that. And I can't believe that you allowed her to come down to stay with you when you knew, you absolutely knew, that there was going to be trouble in Moscow. You're right on the inside of it all. How could you? And now we don't know where she is!"

"Calm down, Sister. I'm sure she's safe, with Marina. She looked after her yesterday and today. And anyway, it was you who kept telling me how much Lara was missing me, how much she wanted to come down and see me."

"Yes, but I didn't know that there was about to be a coup, with soldiers on the streets. Or that you'd leave her with a stranger."

"She's not a stranger! She's my neighbour."

"She's a stranger to Lara, and you can bet she doesn't understand diabetes."

Valentin looks at Anya as if she is a thorough nuisance. "I'm going out," he announces. "You stay here and wait for her." And without further word, he stands and leaves, banging the door behind him.

Anya is left on her own, the minutes ticking by, her heart racing with fear for Lara. There are noises on the street below from time to time, and she tries to see out of the dormer window but can see little. She makes herself a tea on the small gas ring and tries to read a book. Every so often, she wonders whether she should go down and look for Lara herself, but she doesn't have a key to the room and wouldn't know where to begin.

Eventually, as it is beginning to get dark, she hears the sound of footsteps climbing the stairs and recognises Lara's voice. She opens the door to see Lara with a skinny, middle-aged woman with dyed red streaks in her grey hair.

"There've been tanks on the street, Auntie! Auntie Anya, there were tanks on the street! We saw it all," Lara says excitedly. "I waved to them."

"Hello, I'm Anya, Valentin's sister," Anya introduces herself. "You must be Marina?"

"Yes," the woman replies, in a not particularly friendly manner.

"We saw Yeltsin. He was standing up on a tank. At a place called the White House," Lara gabbles on, then stops a moment, moves towards her aunt and lays her head on Anya's shoulder, her arm around her waist. "But it was so noisy, Auntie. I was a little frightened. There were so many people in the crowd, and soldiers."

"I can't believe you took a child to these protests," Anya addresses Marina. "It was dangerous. You didn't know what might happen. You shouldn't have done that." Her voice gets louder as the anger rises in her. She feels Lara pulling her sleeve, trying to calm her down. She puts her arm around her shoulder.

"What you should be doing, Miss Auntie lady, is thanking me," Marina replies. "Your brother would just have dumped her alone in his room if I hadn't been here. He left his daughter with me so that he could cover the story. It's a moment in our history and I wasn't going to let the presence of a young girl stop me going to watch what was going on, believe me. So, I am sorry, Miss Self-Righteous, if you don't approve, but there we go. It was my decision. And here she is, perfectly well."

"We did get separated for a while, though, Auntie. I couldn't see Marina, and all these men were shouting around me."

Anya looks at Marina. "But I found her, didn't I. Here she is," Marina hisses through half-closed lips.

"And the soldiers were taking care of us in the streets, Auntie. They were kind to us."

"Yes, they were looking out for vulnerable people," Marina adds. "There was this old man trying to push to the front of the crowd, saying he didn't mind dying, 'after all, the Communists stole my life ages ago'. Stupid man, he's got it all wrong. But a soldier put his arm around him and led him to a safer place."

"Ah well, why not stay for a tea?" Anya concedes that it is important to be on good terms with Marina, in case Lara comes to stay with Valentin again. She washes the cups in the sink, which she now notices is filthy, while Marina and Lara look out of the window at the night sky. They sit down on the rickety old sofa and put their cups on a box on the floor that acts as a table.

"Tell me, then, Marina, what is happening here in Moscow? I have only heard rumours."

"There's been an attempt to overthrow Gorbachev. The word is that a delegation went down to his dacha at Foros to try to persuade him to resign. I believe your brother went down with the delegation to cover the story. Meanwhile, the army were stamping all over our city here, but many of the soldiers didn't have their hearts in it, so it failed," Marina told her.

"Papa is doing very important work, you know," Lara pipes up, and at that moment Valentin returns, barging through the door. He looks around the room and is obviously relieved to see Lara sitting between the two women.

"So, what's the latest?" Marina asks him. "The word on the street is that Gorbachev is 'ill and resting.'"

Valentin laughs. "Ha, he isn't ill. He's just stuck where he is."

They sit in the cramped space for a while until Marina goes to bed, then Lara and Anya settle into Valentin's bed, and he sleeps on the floor.

They spend the next two days walking around as Valentin observes the aftermath of the coup, gathering notes from people on the street. On 21 August, before returning to Orel, they walk down near the White House and Valentin draws out a pencil and notebook from his pocket and approaches members of the crowd who are still there, and pedestrians walking nearby, to find out what they think of the events. Some brush him away, nervously, but others are happy to share their views with him. They wander around, taking in the detritus left by the protests. The street cleaners are out on the streets and members of the public are helping to clear up.

As Valentin returns to Lara and Anya, who have stood aside to let him approach people, he repeats what they have told him, "The ringleaders didn't have it in them to cause bloodshed," he says despondently. "It's too late, some of them think, to hold the USSR together. Estonia and Latvia are stating they want independence. Three people have been killed. That's terrible. One was shot, another crushed by a tank. It's shocked people. There isn't the stomach to carry on after that. Yazov ordered the tanks to pull out. They just retreated."

"Oh, Papa, all that effort." Lara puts her hand on his.

"I can't believe they let the crowd topple the KGB statue." Valentin sighs. "Let's go back home."

"What I can't understand, Valentin," Anya looks up to her brother, "is how you have become so close to the centre of all this movement. You only moved to Moscow a short while ago. How have you managed this?"

Valentin pauses. Anya can see he is unsure whether to tell her the truth about this, or not. Then he says, "I had some information about the head of the movement. Information he didn't want spread around Moscow. So, let's say I put a little pressure on him."

Anya raises her eyebrows. "So, you're not averse to a little blackmail yourself, then?"

"It's not blackmail. There's no money involved. I just threatened to expose him. That's different."

"Not so different…" Anya murmurs, as they head back towards his block.

As they arrive back at Valentin's building, there are two men leaning up against his front door, smoking. "See you later," he says to Anya, handing her the key, and walks away with them, without a backwards glance.

PART THREE

1992

TWENTY-FOUR

England, 1992

Kate and Eve meet up at the Patisserie Valerie in Knightsbridge. They find a table and order cappuccinos. Kate has never seen Eve so excited. Her normally cool demeanour is transformed as she eulogises about the house she and her team are doing up for her Russian client nearby.

"So, what's the secret, Eve?" Kate asks. "You look amazing. I mean, you always do, but you are sparkling today."

"You wouldn't believe what my Russian client Grigory is doing to his house, Kate. It's like a palace in the middle of London. Gold-leaf, oak panelling, chandeliers, a swimming pool, a barber salon, gym, sauna, spa…"

"Yes, I get it, Eve. It sounds amazing. It must be great money for your business?"

"I can't tell you what a relief it is. With the recession here, our business had gone horribly quiet. You know, people are into negative equity; things look thoroughly depressing, but for the Russians coming to London, it all seems cheap. They're rolling in money, and they want to invest it in property. It makes them feel their money is safe."

"What does your guy do, this Grigory? How did he make his money?" Kate asks.

"Some kind of state media organisation. He doesn't say more than that."

"It must be fantastic to design a home when there's no budget problems. It's great that his rubles are providing you not only with good income but also with fun."

"It is. Really exciting. But how are things with you? How's the charity coming on? And are you getting more events and conferences in your consultancy to manage your income and everything?"

"Yes, thank heaven. The event business is putting food on the table for sure, and it's also giving me contacts. I've been running quite a few events for financial institutions thanks to Mike – you know, the American I met in Russia?"

"Brilliant. That sounds just what you need – to be able to take your time building the charity and let it run itself with the trustees and the teams they are hiring to make it happen, now you have more money in. And that house that's been donated– what a dream come true."

"Yes, I am coming to believe in visions and dreams coming true, to be honest." Kate smiles as she says this. "They do say 'believe it and you will see it', don't they?"

"Sure do. I went to that Tony Robbins workshop, walked on the coals to prove mind over matter and came up with lots of goals that I have started to realise," Eve says thoughtfully, as if her mind is tracking back. "In fact, that's making me remember all the things that have come my way since. It's quite spooky, a bit like magic!"

"Well, you were so full of it when you came out, it was inspiring," Kate replies. "And thinking about facing your fears and doing it anyway, Margot has persuaded me to try to tap Edward Babbington again, try to get him on board to donate money for the charity. Persuade him to be on the Board of Trustees. I was dreading it, but I spoke to his wife and she was encouraging, so I've made another date. I'm going to go up there with Freddie this time." Kate pauses and takes a sip of coffee. "Freddie is such a chum. It's a shame he and Veronica moved to the country, but they seem very happy with sheep at the bottom of the garden and the farmer up the road. But I miss them."

"Yes, they have been good friends to you, haven't they. And I am glad he's able to go with you. Edward B sounds ghastly. I'm not sure I would have the balls to go and visit him again myself," Eve says.

Kate looks at her, the bravest, gutsiest friend she has, and says, "You're kidding! Eve, you are the friend with the biggest balls of anyone I know!" They laugh together. "It can't be that easy dealing with the Russian, Grigory whatshisname, can it? I imagine if he's spending this much money, he must be pretty demanding?"

"Yes, he is, but he is so courteous and kind. He has these terrifying-looking henchmen, though, who drive him around in what looks like a bulletproof Mercedes with darkened windows. I think they have guns tucked into their jackets." Eve frowns as she says this.

"Really? Well, my own experience of Russia, as you know, is that it is a pretty edgy place. Apart from that experience in Gorky Park I told you about, I get the impression that there's a lot of street crime and that the wealthy hire their own bodyguards and vigilantes to look after them."

"Yes, a ghastly way to live. It does unsettle me, I must admit. But I feel I have to take this opportunity while it is here. Otherwise, my consultancy might just die a death, as the economy here is floundering," Eve says.

"Yep, go for it. It's what we have to do."

"Speaking of which, what's happening with your man in Moscow? Isn't it time you started dating someone more accessible here?"

"You sound like my dad would have done! Believe me, I have tried one or two. I've gone on *The Times* dating ads and met a few blokes for a drink, but there's no one like Valentin. The trouble is that he has set such a high standard for me now. It's really hard to get excited about the men I have been meeting here, both in looks but also in the fact that what Valentin is doing with his career is really important work."

"Hmm," Eve shrugs, "but I don't think he's good for you. What about that fellow Harry?" Eve scrutinises Kate as she asks her.

"He rings from time to time. We have a nice chat and I wonder if he is going to suggest meeting up but, since that nice day on his boat, he always asks about Russia, about Valentin and whether I am in touch with him, and then the call seems to go from warm to cold. It's as if we both take a step backwards, so I haven't seen him for ages."

"Perhaps you should call him? And, Kate, for God's sake, just don't mention Valentin. Be vague if he asks. Give him a chance to see that you are free? You've been a bit slow on this, if I may say so! Either way, I think you should keep at it here in London. It can't possibly work for you and Valentin in the long term. It's some kind of stupid romantic fantasy, and I can't see that it is doing you any good to be so much in his thrall."

Kate looks irritated. "Leave me be, Eve. Words aren't going to get me out of this one, and for now it feels right to be in it, and in some ways having a distant fantasy is just what I need at the moment, when I have so much on my plate in London. If I had a man in the house, I would never have the time or energy to launch this charity. I know that. You know what they're like – wanting attention, competitive with your success, wanting you to wash their bloody socks!"

Eve laughs. "Yes, I know only too well, which is why I never want to get into that position, married or not. But that's me, and you're not the same as me. Not all men are like that, and I could see that you enjoyed aspects of your married life with Simon."

Kate shrugs. "Yes, I did. Of course I did." She catches sight of her watch on her wrist and jumps up, signalling the waitress for the bill. "I must get going to pick up Tom – I'm late again!"

They pay the bill. It's raining as they leave the café.

"Look after yourself with Grigory, Eve, won't you? Walk on the side of the angels," Kate calls over her shoulder to Eve as they go in different directions. Eve waves, then walks on, pulling the collar of her smart black mac up around her neck, her black bob smoothly in place despite the summer rain, looking, Kate notices, like the ultimate designer model.

When Tom and Kate return to the house, Kate finds a fax waiting for her from Valentin: 'Coming for a visit to London'.

TWENTY-FIVE

England, 1992

Kate parks in the terminal car park at Heathrow. She is early, an hour before Valentin's flight is due to arrive. She goes to the cafeteria and tries to read a newspaper, but she can't concentrate. Time ticks slowly by, and she keeps watching the announcement boards. Eventually, after what feels like an eternity, she sees that Valentin's flight has landed. Although her rational brain tells her that it will take him at least half an hour to clear customs and baggage control, she walks to the Arrivals gate, in some agitation.

After nearly an hour of standing waiting, and peering at the double doors as passengers come through, Kate notices a man who was sitting next to her in the café. He's standing reading a newspaper, leaning against a pillar, but watching the double doors. There's something about him that makes her question what he's doing. Then she begins to see people coming through with luggage tags showing SVO and she knows this is the Moscow flight. And there he is, Valentin, walking through the doors, a tall figure in a blue anorak and jeans, his dark hair thick and flopping over his forehead. It's months since she has seen him and her body fills with adrenalin as she calls to him. He waves and walks towards her, pulling his case behind him.

Valentin takes Kate in a strong grasp and kisses her lips.

"Wonderful to see you, Kate." His deep voice and Russian accent vibrate through her as he continues to hold her close, drawing her long, red hair back from her face with his fingers and tucking it behind her ear.

"You too," she replies awkwardly. "I've got the car in the car park," and they separate as she leads him away from the Arrivals. They go up in the lift and walk to her car. He slings his case in the boot and climbs in, adjusting his long legs to slide into the passenger seat of the Clio. As she passes her ticket to pay at the kiosk she notices the man she had seen earlier in the café then reading a newspaper by the Arrivals door. He is putting on a helmet and climbing on to a motor bike.

"Take your change," the car park attendant calls, his hand out, and Kate refocuses her attention to drive down the exit ramp.

Valentin and Kate make rather stilted conversation about the flight, the weather. Kate becomes aware that there are few landmarks to point out to him until they pass the Russian Orthodox Church off the A4 flyover and then turn up Ladbroke Grove and pass the large houses of Holland Park.

She turns into her road and parks in a residents' bay. She feels proud of her home as she opens the front door and shows him in.

"The whole house is yours?" Valentin asks, looking around.

"Yes, and there's Tom, of course. He's with his dad for the next couple of days."

"It's still a lot of space for two people," Valentin comments, and she wonders if she picks up a hint of disapproval in his voice.

"Well, it's just an ordinary three-bedroom London Victorian terraced house. Most of London is made up of houses like this."

He raises his eyes to the ceiling in surprise, or displeasure. She is not sure which.

"It's beautiful, though," he concedes. "I love the stained-glass windows. And all those books in your study!"

"Yes, they are precious, each and every one," she tells him.

"Where shall I put my suitcase?" he asks as they go upstairs. Kate hesitates, unsure whether to put him in her room or the spare room.

"Dump it in the spare room, there," she suggests, opening the door for him onto the small bedroom the other end of the house to her and Tom's rooms.

He puts his case down on the spare bed, and they go downstairs to the kitchen. She hands him a bottle of champagne to open and makes him a plate of smoked salmon and scrambled eggs, with a side salad of avocado and tomatoes. She slices a French baguette and puts it all on the table, with the brown pottery butter dish.

They clink their glasses. She wishes she didn't feel so awkward. It feels different now he is in London, and she is the hostess. She feels responsible for giving him a good stay.

As the champagne hits their systems they begin to relax and talk more easily.

"Lara has passed her exams," he says when Kate asks about her. "I can really see her growing up."

"Marvellous. You must be proud. And Anya?"

"She's working in the chemist shop," he tells her through mouthfuls. He wolfs the meal down as if he hasn't eaten for months. "You know, she wants to start her own health food shop, so she's studying at night and at weekends."

"But I guess you're too busy to see much of them?" She prods a little, on Anya's behalf.

He just shrugs. "It was a big year last year, with the coup to cover in the summer, then protests in the autumn. The country is still upside down, halfway between one system and another, and no one understanding any of it.

"The coup wasn't a success. I realise that," he continues. "You helped me see what we should have done when you told me how your BBC reporter – Bridget Kendall, I think you said – had been so scathing about our plans, how she said that the conspirators didn't understand how to control the media, the messages that got out. And that we should have closed the airport, taken control of the streets. It kills me that she said it all looked 'amateur.'" He punches the table with his fist as he says this. "We're so restricted in Russia, in what we can do, what we can learn about the way other people do things."

"You said that the soldiers weren't fully committed?" Kate ventures. "And I guess I am used to watching generals walk into television studios and make announcements when I see coups in other parts of the world. But it really isn't an area of my expertise."

"No one's in charge now. That's why it's so important that I build this network of journalists who are outside the influence of the Kremlin propaganda machine. We need to open minds, influence minds. But it's been good for my career. I'm getting good commissions, and I have written some exposés."

"That can't make you popular! How is that man who sent his heavies to attack us in Gorky Park that day?"

"Oh, he hates me. I have written several articles about him. He keeps trying to frighten me. And his son is even worse. A nasty man if ever there was one. And there are plenty more where they come from."

Kate stacks their plates in the dishwasher. As she bends over, he comes up behind her and puts his hands on her hips, gently turning her around and lifting her face up to kiss him. She tastes the champagne and smoked salmon on his lips. He takes her hand and leads her up the stairs to the spare room, throwing his case off the bed and falling onto the cover, his hands around her waist so that she falls with him, beside him, their bodies moulding as they kiss passionately. He skilfully removes her defences, and her body responds hungrily to his desire as he enters her and they meld together, knowing they have the long afternoon ahead of them.

"Where is that package I gave you all those years ago?" Valentin asks Kate as they have breakfast in the kitchen the next morning.

"In the spare room, under some pillowcases."

"Right. I need to review it all later. There's an important document in there, and I don't want Novikoff to get hold of it. Can I use your computer?"

"He doesn't know where the document is, does he?" Kate asks, rather shocked that Valentin thinks the package might be something Novikoff is still looking for, after all this time.

"I don't know, to be honest, Kate. His men follow me around. They try to frighten me sometimes, but I go into hiding, publish the articles under other names. I have given them the runaround, that's for sure."

"Do you think they know where I live, then? That you're staying with me?"

Valentin shrugs his broad shoulders and looks down at her. "I don't know. But it's quite likely."

Kate stops suddenly, her mind piecing his news together as she finishes clearing the breakfast plates. "I didn't tell you, but I found a ruble coin in my garden a few months ago."

Valentin's hand hovers as he is about to hand her his mug, a frown crossing his forehead.

"Really?"

"Yes, it was a little while after I found my old cat, Bardot, dead in the garden. I was outside enjoying the night sky, then I saw something glinting. I've got it here." She ran off to the study and took the coin off the mantlepiece.

Valentin raised his eyebrows. "Just this?" he asks, looking disturbed.

"Yes, as far as I know."

"It looks like a calling card to me," he says. "Your cat died, you say?"

"Yes," Kate replies. "I found her in the garden; she had a wound on her neck, and I think she was run over in the street and made her way back to our garden to die."

Valentin turns the coin over in his hand but says nothing.

"OK, let's go on a tour of London." Kate doesn't want to think about Novikoff. It's a bright spring day. She wants time with her lover to show off her city.

"Sure," he says, and she drives him around, showing him the Tower of London, Trafalgar Square, Buckingham Palace, the Houses of Parliament and Big Ben. Then she shows him the houses in Chelsea, Belgravia and Knightsbridge, where Eve is doing up her Russian clients' houses. He is particularly interested to learn about the way the Russians are establishing themselves in London and makes some notes in his notebook as they drive by.

When they return, in the evening, Kate suggests he watch the television while she makes supper. A short while later, he walks back into the kitchen.

"These television presenters are a little like the interrogators in Stalin's time," he jokes. "I just watched your John Major squirm. Interviewed by a Jeremy someone...?"

"Ah, that would be Jeremy Paxman," Kate fills him in, with a smile of acknowledgement.

"It's so good to see this," Valentin says. "To see how they draw these politicians of yours out and listen to different perspectives. How they don't treat the politicians with deference but really question and challenge them."

As the next day dawns, Valentin tells Kate he wants to go off on his own and discover more about London while she makes some phone calls for her charity.

Shortly after he returns in the afternoon, the doorbell rings. Kate goes to the door.

"Tom!" Kate is pleased to see him. Simon stands behind him.

"He's been great. He's helped me hang the paintings for the new exhibition at the gallery. And, of course, he has been studying very hard," he adds, "so I hope you will carry on the good work with him."

"Of course," Kate replies, affronted. She is aware that Valentin has come up behind her.

"Tom, this is Valentin. Valentin, this is Simon, my ex-husband," Kate introduces them. The two men exchange looks and shake hands. "Come on now, Tom, let's get you inside," she says.

Simon hugs Tom, then turns on his heel and gets into his van, with its smartly painted 'Chisholm Fine Art' branded on its sides.

Kate watches as Valentin puts his arm around Tom's shoulder. "So, Tom, what football team do you support?"

"Arsenal!" Tom responds forcefully, and the two of them start to talk football.

"And you are in the school team?" Valentin asks.

Kate watches from the kitchen and notices that Tom's reserve begins to drop a little, though he keeps his arms folded.

Later, as they eat supper together, Kate knows that she is trying a little too hard, praising Tom's skills to Valentin, which embarrasses him.

"Oh, Mum, do stop it!" Tom raises his eyes to the ceiling.

"Which is your favourite subject at school?" Valentin asks Tom to distract him.

"History is interesting."

"I had a marvellous history teacher when I was at school," Valentin comments. "A committed communist. One of the old guard who had played a part in Stalin's times. I think of him often. He was inspiring, really influenced me and helped me to do well, well enough to go to university. But then came Afghanistan."

"What was it like?" Tom asks, his eyes big. "To fight?"

"Brutal." Valentin nods. "Recruits are treated very badly in Russia, bullied, you could say tortured. Some die as they train." A faraway look comes into Valentin's eyes. "I had a comrade who died in this way. I got through it, but it was hell, and then Afghanistan, it was cold and mountainous, with an enemy we often couldn't see."

"You must be very brave," Tom suggests.

"Not brave, Tom. You just survive. You just have this instinct to survive, to keep going. And you're a team; you rely on your comrades. There's no choice. You can't escape or get out of it, so you have to fight."

Tom goes quiet and looks serious, then takes himself up to his room.

Valentin goes off on his own again the next morning. When Kate asks him where he's going, he simply replies, "Here and there," and changes the subject.

On his return, they sit over supper in the kitchen, and he sighs.

"It is amazing to be able to walk around all day and

195

not worry whether I have my passport and documents. In Russia, if you don't have your documents on you, then you can be in trouble. You have to pay a bribe, or you get sent to the police station, get beaten up, accused of something you didn't do."

"It must be a relief," Kate agrees and walks over to him and puts her arms around his shoulders. "Perhaps you should come and live in London, then?"

He looks up at her. "Well, there is a maybe there, for sure, Kate."

Tom looks from one to the other but says nothing, then leaves the room. As he shuts the door, Valentin says, "Kate, I think I will leave that package here. It's safer here than if I carry it back to Russia, and now I should be able to store some of the information digitally, but there's sensitive evidence against Novikoff and about where the President hides his money. I don't want it getting into the wrong hands."

Kate looks at him, doubtful. "Will that put my house at any risk? I thought you were going to take it back with you?"

"No. After all, they left that calling card many weeks ago now, and they haven't tried anything, so I don't think they will see you as a threat, just as a means to get to me, perhaps."

"I don't want me or Tom put in any danger," Kate says hesitantly. "You know I support what you are doing, but I have my life here to protect."

"No, no. I won't put you in danger, don't you worry." Valentin puts his hand out to hers and squeezes it, giving her his most seductive smile. "We're good together, you and I, aren't we." It's a statement, not a question, and Kate squeezes his hand back, warmed by his words.

"But I am interested in your free press," Valentin suddenly changes the subject. "You know, the more I investigate, I don't think it is as free as you like to think?" he carries on, as they sit and eat a chicken casserole around the kitchen table.

"What do you mean?" Kate asks, as she pours him some more red wine, wondering again what information lies under the pillowcases in the drawer in her spare room and wondering whether she should insist on asking him to remove it.

"There are fingers at work that you don't see, infiltrating, manipulating."

"Well, we know that all the papers have their own specific political bias, but that is because of their ownership and the editors and sponsors who run them," she replies.

"Your people are so naive and so pampered." Valentin looks at her in a strange way. Whose side is he on?

"But Russia is turning towards the West now, surely?" she asks. "Even now Gorbachev has gone, I thought Yeltsin too wants to move away from the Cold War ways?"

"Many people in Russia prefer the old ways, you know, the socialist ways."

"But you want to run a press agency more like those who are free here in the West?"

"Yes, out of the manipulation of the Kremlin, for sure," he says. "But we want our agency to have its own political voice."

"What do you mean by that?"

"I don't think you would understand the Russian ways yet, Kate," he says enigmatically, then gets up from the table and goes to sit on the sofa, picking up today's newspaper which is lying on the rug. Kate is left to clear up.

"How is it going?" Eve asks on the phone later that evening.

"Good," Kate replies.

"When am I going to meet him?"

"I don't think you will have time. He flies back tomorrow."

"So, you have kept him from me on purpose, I think? Don't I detect some hesitancy in your voice?" Eve probes.

"No, no, we are having a good time and he tells me he is learning a lot that he can take back to Russia for setting up his press agency."

"But something doesn't quite add up?" Eve suggests.

Kate stops and look out of the window. This is her closest friend; she deserves the truth. "No. It doesn't."

TWENTY-SIX

Russia, 1992

Getting home from the pharmacy, Anya finds a letter in the letter box in the hallway. It is on blue airmail paper, from England.

Dear Anya,

London is an extraordinary place. So many people, of so many different backgrounds from all over the world, in the shops, on the streets, a huge number of cars on the roads, nice cars, privately owned.

Kate took me into a shop, a supermarket called Sainsbury's, in Kensington. You can't imagine how much food there was – I've never seen so much in all my life. And the choice – twelve different types of bread, or eggs, cereals. Even many different brands of cleaning products. You would be amazed. And lots of health products, Sister, so your idea for a health food shop could be a good one, though I hate to admit it. It is overwhelming, when we still have so little in the shops at home.

I left Kate on a couple of days this week, told her I needed to walk the city to get a feel of the place, and I spoke to people on the street. It's not all wonderful, you know. There are those who are struggling financially here too. There is a recession. They like to present the capitalist system as if it is the only answer, but it has its problems. The strong do well but the weak, well I am not so sure, even with their welfare system.

I watch the news, scan the newspapers. See what I can learn about different perspectives, but I think they are naive in the West. They don't understand who pulls their strings. They see what they see but miss what's really happening below the surface.

I went to a restaurant my boss, Mikhail, told me about in an area called Soho. Like he said, there were some Russians there. I talked to a couple sitting at the bar. They told me how the KGB have been operating here for years, how they befriend the union leaders, left-wingers, pass information. One of them joked about how we Russians are pleased that these people in the West support CND, you know – the anti-nuclear protests – because it leaves Russia free to develop our own and get strong. He called those Brits 'useful idiots' because that is what Lenin used to say about people who are innocent and can be manipulated. It makes me look around, wonder who is standing next to me on the bus!

One thing I have learnt is that our television presenters need to get more challenging. In London the television presenters put people on the spot, ask them difficult questions. We need to do the same, you know. Expose them. I can do it on paper, through my writing, but we need to develop an ally in television.

There are those who like to think that they would like a socialist system here, but I am not convinced that they would be willing to adopt our ways unless they were forced to. They like their comfort, their supposed democracy, their freedom, their choice.

Lara would love the fashion. Short skirts. The girls are hot.

Valentin

Anya looks at the letter in amazement. How can her hot-headed brother talk of the naivety of the British and yet expose all his thoughts on paper here in the post, she wonders? He must have lost his mind. Perhaps he was drunk, or homesick.

She looks at the airmail envelope again, to see if there is any sign that it has been opened before reaching her, but she can't tell because she ripped it open before she realised how compromising his words were.

Oh, Brother, you may say that you are protecting us, but the reality is that you put us in danger when you write to us like this, she thinks, then goes to the sink, lights a match and burns the letter until it is just a pile of ash. She scrapes up the ash in her hand, walks to the bathroom and flushes it away down the toilet.

PART FOUR

1999-2001

TWENTY-SEVEN

Russia, 1999

Anya returns from her day at work feeling good. She's had her hair cut in a fringe and straightened and bought a fake-designer pair of jeans and a leather jacket at the street market.

"Hey, Lara," she calls, as she shakes off her jacket and hangs her bag on a hook on the door. "I had so many new customers in the shop today. It was brilliant."

Lara sits at the table studying. She looks up at her aunt but doesn't respond.

"Come help me tomorrow, Lara," Anya suggests.

"Must I?" Lara shrugs. "I wanted to go visit Elena tomorrow."

"Well, you can go afterwards. It's no bad thing that you learn what hard work is all about."

"I know what hard work is all about – just look at me studying!"

"Yes, but this is different. This work will give you a view of the everyday world of work, a view of what options you have when you finish your studies. We women have opportunities now that my mother and grandmother never had. We have to grasp them with both hands. This is my health food shop, Lara, my own. The one I have dreamt of creating for so many years."

"Hmmm, yes, yes, I know, Auntie." Lara looks at Anya with a bored expression. She's taller than Anya now and as beautiful as Valentin is handsome, with her long dark hair, pale skin and deep brown eyes with lashes Anya would die for. She is studying hard, planning to go to medical school.

"Anyway, Lara, you're always saying I am spending too much time at the shop these days so you can come with me, and we can spend the day there together. I have a whole lot of stock that needs opening and putting on the shelves. I shall pay you a little for your trouble."

Lara's eyes widen now. "Oh, how much would that be?"

"So now you're interested!" Anya laughs. "You young, all you want is something for nothing, or a new pair of jeans."

"Yes... and a top I've seen."

The next day they walk to Anya's shop together. The sun is shining low in the sky. Anya takes the counter and serves the customers while Lara helps to unpack bottles of vitamins and packets of protein supplements and neatly stack them on the shelves. She seems to enjoy herself.

Anya shows her how to enter prices into the cash machine and keep records. At the end of the afternoon, the two of them sit together and work out the profits from the day.

"You can go get those jeans." Anya smiles at Lara.

"Great – Elena and I can go to the shops together."

Anya puts on her jacket and locks up the shop carefully. When she gets home, she rings Valentin. It's been almost impossible to track him down in recent months, but this time she catches him on his Nokia mobile phone.

"We're beginning to make a profit," she tells him. "And Lara came and helped me in the shop today."

"You're making her into a right little capitalist?"

"She saw that hard work meant that at the end of the day she got paid enough to go buy a new pair of jeans, if that's what you mean."

"You're gloating, Anya."

"Yes, indeed I am," Anya replies and puts the phone down.

Anya, when she thinks of her brother, realises that Valentin is spending his time in increasingly sleazy company as he investigates and reports on criminal gangs, corrupt local officials, money laundering and share-dealing. He has been reporting more gun crime, as rival gangs fight for territory and profit, and tells her that Moscow is literally hotting up with the sound of bullets ricocheting around the streets. He keeps lecturing her and Lara, saying that the voice of his old teacher echoes in his ears, "'Fight for the Motherland, Valentin, socialism is the best system of government,' that's what he would tell me." He reminds Anya, too, of their grandfather, who lost the little he had to a fraudster, and Valentin says he wants to protect others from the same fate.

Brother and sister never agree on this. She knows he is keeping in touch with the other ringleaders from the coup against Gorbachev back in 1991, who also want to return Russia to Communism and the old ways. They dig and dive to expose the greed of those going after the rich pickings of the state organisations being sold off, but their outrage falls on deaf ears. Everyone and everything seem to be malleable to bribes in this new world. People are throwing away their Communist party cards, but the majority don't have the heart to fight these battles. The poverty and hardship has ground them down, so they have no energy left for change. It's only those closest to the men in power who can make money. *The rest of us*, Anya thinks, *have to toil away*.

"That isn't necessarily the way it is in the West," Kate had told Anya on her last visit to Russia. "Sure, you get some greedy people out to make money. But if you get it right, then capitalism can bring people out of poverty, through employment. This empowers them, gives them choices and opportunities, and the tax can pay for a better welfare state."

"You know, I don't understand what Kate is doing with Valentin," Anya tells Mama after Kate has gone back to London. "I'm fond of her, but she seems to have some blind spot where she can't see how self-centred Valentin is, that he will never give her his heart. But he still has some kind of hold over her after all these years. I guess it must be the sex!"

"Valentin enjoys London," Mama muses. "He tells me about the Russians living there, the business men, setting up in London. He has got them in his sights, he says, and it gives me the shivers. They won't like that. He'll get into trouble."

"I don't believe they are that frightened by his threats to expose them. They have so much money, they think they are Gods," Anya says.

Anya has been saving up to take Lara over to visit Kate and Tom. She doesn't know if Valentin will join them. He has been so busy that they haven't seen him for months. He moves from one place to another, hiding himself in the shadows so his targets can't find him. He can't seem to plan for next week, she reflects, let alone decide on dates to fly to London.

As Anya sits at the breakfast table a week later, she gets a call from Mama's neighbour, Maxim. Mama has collapsed. Maxim says he hasn't seen her all day and thought it unusual.

"I had to knock the door down," he tells Anya. "Then I found her, on the floor beside her bed, still conscious, but she couldn't talk. She's in the hospital now. You'd better go there."

Anya calls Valentin immediately and by some stroke of luck catches him. "Mother's ill. You need to come."

"What's up?"

"She's collapsed. She's in the hospital. Please come."

Valentin sighs at the other end of the phone. "Is it really necessary?"

"Of course, it's fucking necessary!" Anya shouts at him. "Your mother, our mother, is in hospital. You need to come to her!"

"Yes, yes," Valentin agrees grudgingly. "I will see what I can do."

"You had better do more than 'seeing what you can do', Valentin. You had better get on a train this morning and come!"

"It's not as simple as you think. Anya."

It's evening and the sky is dark. Anya sits in the hospital next to Mama, holding her limp hand in hers. She rubs her thumb gently over her mother's dry, papery skin to soothe her, looking hypnotically at the blue veins and liver spots, as her thumb traces its gentle track backwards and forwards. She is numb with the shock of seeing her brave and feisty mother unconscious and unresponsive in the hospital bed.

She is in a large ward of women, a drip, strung from an ancient and rusty hoist, inserted in her other hand. Lara sits next to Anya, but they find little to talk about. Every so often Lara gets up and tidies and strokes Mama's hair, soothing her forehead, telling her she loves her. Doctors and nurses bustle up and down the ward. There's a smell of antiseptic mixed with urine. The double doors at the far end of the ward open and Valentin walks in. He's taken off weight, his face pale, his tall frame somehow more fragile, but nonetheless, Anya can hardly look at him. Lara runs up to him and throws her arms around him.

"Papa, Papa, I haven't seen you for so long," she says, with tears in her eyes. "My babushka is really ill. She's not talking."

Valentin holds his daughter to him, hugging her tightly. "I'm sorry about your grandma," he whispers while mouthing to Anya, "what is wrong?"

Anya points to Mama's head, suggesting a stroke.

"The doctor's been. They're understaffed. Medicines have been in short supply, he said. But to be honest I am not sure what they would do for her anyway, really. It could just be time."

"Has she been talking?" Valentin asks.

Anya shakes her head, tears in her eyes. She's trying to hold herself together for Lara's sake.

Valentin finds another chair, and they all sit beside the bed. A tray of bread and soup is brought and placed beside her, but Mama is in no state to eat it, and so the three of them share some spoonfuls of the soup. Lara chats away, talking about her friends and seeming to try to smooth over the coldness that continues to shape the relationship between brother and sister.

A little later, Mama stirs. "Where am I?" she mumbles, her words almost indistinguishable.

"The hospital, Mama. You had a fall," Valentin tells her, seemingly not wanting to spell out the seriousness of her condition.

"Ah, my boy, so wonderful to see you," she says slowly, in halting words that slur together, so Anya would have found it difficult to understand them had she not heard those words so many times before.

Anya raises her eyes to the heavens. "Oh, you boys, always the favourites!" she mutters to herself.

Mama, despite her incapacity, sends Anya a sharp look, to signal that she heard her words. Then her body suddenly goes into a paroxysm of shaking, her eyes wide open, her teeth chattering.

"Doctor!" Anya shouts, running down the ward. "We need a doctor!"

Lara looks horrified at the sight of her grandmother, such an anchor in her life, now so frail and ill. "Papa!" she shouts at her father. "Do something!"

A nurse comes to the bed, but as she arrives, the shaking stops. Valentin can do nothing as Mama's body slumps in the bed in front of them, her eyes wide, her mouth frozen open but her body immobile.

"She's gone, Lara," Valentin says after a short while, putting his arm around her.

"But she can't have done." Lara's shoulders heave with sobs. "She's my babushka. She's always been here. I can't imagine life without her."

A tired-looking young doctor arrives, in a worn overall. He stands beside the bed and takes Mama's pulse, listens for a heartbeat and shakes his head.

"I'm sorry," he says. "We did expect this when we saw the state in which she came into the hospital, but it has happened faster than we thought. I am glad you were all able to see her before she died and be with her."

Anya moves towards Lara and the three hug, then sit down again in their chairs, in silence. Anya's tears flow down her cheeks as she holds Mama's hand and keeps her arm around Lara's shaking shoulders. Valentin takes charge of the formalities. When Mama's body is wheeled away down the corridor, they go back to Anya's flat. All the time Anya is berating herself for having made the sarcastic comment about boys being favourites and knowing that those were possibly the last words Mama ever heard.

"I need to go back in the morning," Valentin tells them after Anya has fixed some supper.

"You are joking me?" Anya says, looking at him.

"No, I have to go. There's a major story I am working on. It's important."

Anya sighs, giving up on him, then says quietly, "You do realise we have to arrange the funeral? And I won't have another pair of hands to help with Lara now."

"She's eighteen, Anya, nearly nineteen. She can look after herself, surely. I'm sorry," Valentin replies, his voice tense. "I can't stay, and that's that. My movements are always traced. I know I am being followed. If I come to the funeral, I would be a sitting target. We can talk now about the funeral, before I go."

"Do I have a choice?" Anya's voice is a monotone.

Lara just looks at her father, then puts her hand out for his. "I love you, Papa," she says, as if she wants to do anything to ensure she does not lose another person.

"I know," he replies.

Damn him, Anya thinks.

TWENTY-EIGHT

Russia, 1999

It's a grey day, and cold. Lara and Anya are preparing blinis and kolyva to serve when they return to the flat after Mama's funeral. How Anya wishes there was more room in her apartment. She knows there will be many of Mama's neighbours and friends who will want to come to celebrate her life. Everyone will be so squashed in the little kitchen, and the bedroom only has a small space around the bed to stand. They will have to spread into the corridor and maybe Natalya's flat.

Anya holds Lara's hand through the funeral service, and they stand close together, listening to the chanting. Lara is so upset, and both are in shock. It was all very sudden, and they have that numb feeling that seems to take over after a death, where it doesn't seem real, and somehow those left behind experience a sort of euphoria as they remember the person. Anya recalls the days after her papa died many years ago. She knows the reality will hit them after today, as the preparations for the funeral have kept them busy, and they haven't had space to stop and take in the fact that Mama has gone and will never come back.

The frescoes and icons in the church are beautiful and Jesus's face looks down on them as they pray. There's a sombre atmosphere and Anya misses Valentin not being here, her little brother who shared his childhood with her and she with him. All those shared memories of their parents, the home, the arguments, the games they played together, even though Anya was so much the older sister. Now she wants to share them with him, to talk about it all. She knows he will be grieving, even if he is so busy covering his stories, and now he's reporting on the Chechen war. Cousin Olga has come down from Moscow, but she was an only child, so there are only three from the family.

At the graveside, Anya takes a moment to reflect on Mama's life, on the struggles she must have had as a child living through the Stalinist era, her father, her grandfather, sent to a gulag and tortured. He returned a broken man and died young, so she didn't remember him. There was worse poverty and destitution then than there has been in recent times. But, despite her diminutive height, Mama was a strong woman and a strong disciplinarian when they were young, or rather, she was with Anya. Valentin could get away with anything.

Anya is the first to throw some branches of fir on the coffin, then Lara, and Olga, followed by the others gathered there who throw soil into the pit, until the

Orthodox priest brings the service to a close and they make their way back towards Anya's apartment. As they walk across the grass of the graveyard, Anya notices a man leaning against a tree, smoking. He is bald and is wearing a dark blue coat, the collar turned up against the cold. She doesn't recognise him, and there is something about him that sends an alarm through her body. Could he have been waiting to see if Valentin would come?

As they reach the gate, Anya looks back and sees that he is still there; his sturdy frame has shifted around to allow his eyes to follow the progress of the little group. She feels chilled as she remembers the raid on her flat all those years ago and wonders what this could mean. She hurries Lara out of the gates.

There is very little room for everyone in Anya's apartment, and she is glad that Olga brought some food so that they don't run out. People exchange words of love and celebration for Mama as they drink vodka from any glass or cup Anya has managed to dig out of her cupboards. A glass is kept on the side, covered with black bread in Mama's memory. There is warmth in the room, a sense of consolation through their shared grief and friendship.

As people are beginning to take their leave, Anya realises that she hasn't seen Lara for a while, so she moves around the crowded room and into the tiny corridor to try to find her. Guests tell Anya that they have seen her but not for a while. She panics and pushes between people fearing that Lara may have become ill. She tries the bathroom door. It's locked. She knocks gently.

"Lara? Lara? Are you in there?"

A muffled voice replies with a faint yes.

"Please unlock the door, my little bluebell. Let me give you a hug," Anya whispers.

She hears the door unlock and finds Lara, her face pale and streaked with tears, her eyes red. Anya takes her into her arms, and Lara gulps for breath as the sobs heave through her slim young body.

"Are your levels low, my darling? Do you need sugar?"

"No, I am OK, Auntie. I've checked. I just can't believe I shall never see my babushka again. She's always been there for me, and when you're at work she's here in the kitchen with me, telling me stories, helping me with my studies, playing cards, keeping me company. I feel so alone without her."

Anya understands, yet can't help feeling just a tiny bit offended by this as she says, "I am here, sweet Lara. I am here."

She nods, but Anya knows that she does not give her the comfort that Mama gave her, and she knows also, though she hasn't said so, that she had so hoped that her father would turn up for the funeral today and that she misses him. She can't possibly understand how risky it would have been for him to come, which Anya is now beginning to understand better herself. Lara knows little about the kind of journalism in which he is involved or the dangers it presents to him, and potentially to them both.

Anya hugs her until she feels her tears cease, as they do eventually. Lara washes her face in the basin, and Anya tidies her dark waves of hair with her fingers, pulling it into a ponytail with a small band. Lara gives her aunt a weak smile.

"Thanks, Auntie," she whispers as she kisses her cheek.

They return to the gathering and talk to Mama's friends, thanking them for coming. Olga has to leave to catch a train back to Moscow. She tells Anya that she hasn't heard from Valentin for years, though enjoyed his company on the guided tour of British literary enthusiasts all that time ago. Anya grudgingly makes excuses for him, explaining that he is very busy in his work. Olga nods, kisses her cousin, and Lara, and waves goodbye.

Anya turns back to the kitchen, and sees for a moment the image of her mother there, a comforting figure sitting at her table, but the next moment, a neighbour jolts her from the memory to sympathise, and reality returns.

Later, when everyone has gone, Lara and Anya clear up the dishes. Anya washes and Lara dries, placing the crockery and glass on the kitchen table, then they both turn and put the items back in the cupboards.

They are exhausted as they prepare for bed, drained of both emotion and physical energy. Lara falls straight into a deep sleep.

Before Anya gets into bed herself, she locks the front door, putting the bolts at the top and bottom firmly across into position. She has become more complacent about their safety in recent months. Now she hopes she shall be able to sleep, worrying about the stranger at the funeral. She feels a gaping hole in her life now her mother has gone.

In Moscow, Valentin walks away from the building in which he and Mikhail have been working. As he turns the corner, a tall figure steps out of the alley in front of him, barring his path.

"I'll take that laptop now," the man says, his mouth sneering. Instantly, Valentin recognises him as the security guard with green eyes that he had met all those years ago during his visit to Gorbachev's dacha in the Crimea when he was covering the coup.

"No, you won't!" Valentin clings to the laptop case, but suddenly he's in the grip of someone behind him, holding him around the neck in a stranglehold.

"If you want to live, you will give us that laptop," a coarse voice speaks into his ear. "What's another journalist dead on the street?" The man tightens his grip on Valentin's throat until he can't breathe. He lets go of the laptop case. Immediately, the man holding him throws him down onto the street.

Valentin hits his head on a lamp post as he falls. Pulling himself up again, he looks around but sees the two men disappear into a side road and out of sight, then loses consciousness.

TWENTY-NINE

Russia, 2000

It's a cold January day when Kate boards her plane to Moscow. It's been many months since her previous visit, and she is looking forward to seeing Valentin. Email is easing their communication, but she can't wait to see him in person.

As the plane takes off, Kate's mind is taken back to her times with him. He has made short trips to London developing his network of newshounds, as he calls them, professional and amateur, setting up a network of journalists reporting back to him and Mikhail. On those trips he also interviewed people working for the Russians now based in London. The men themselves would give him no time, but he managed to talk to some of their lackeys and to the Brits who were providing services to them, including Eve.

It's big business now, the Russians in London. Londongrad, they call it. Eve's consultancy is busy designing and renovating houses in London and the suburbs, transforming them into luxury mansions. There are plenty of businesses, large and small, who want to milk the millions that are coming out of Russia, too.

Kate smiles as she thinks how Valentin puts on the charm, and little do his interviewees know that he is storing up information that will damage them when he pulls it all together into a major article, always anonymously. He constantly moves from place to place, changing his mobile number, and is maddeningly difficult to contact. She accepts that perhaps that is what makes her long for him. He's always just out of reach.

Kate has now nailed down two big Russian donors for her charity, too. They like to be seen to be philanthropic as it gives them an entry into the hierarchy of London circles, the House of Lords, politicians and senior executives. They send their children to the best private schools and, chameleon-like, endeavour to be accepted into UK society.

Eve's Grigory has given the charity a huge amount of money, which, when invested, will provide it with an annual income, allowing Kate and the trustees to continue to run the maternity home, with on-call obstetricians, midwives, neo-natal specialists and anaesthetists. The first couple of years were tricky as they renovated the old house and recruited staff, but Kate was always terrified that the money would run out and they would be forced to close. Now, with the donation of the house, and a large sum invested to create interest from Grigory, she can feel pretty secure that the annual costs will be covered so, unless the roof caves in, the home and the charity are OK for now.

Lunch is served, and Kate notices a mother and baby across the aisle. The mother is breastfeeding the small infant, who is struggling and waving his little hands around. It reminds her of the beautiful moments she has already experienced with the mothers and babies in the maternity home, and she's thrilled with how Elizabeth and Chris have designed the place to provide a peaceful environment. Eve has donated her time and effort to help with the finishing touches. So far there have been no tragedies or mistakes, thank heaven, with Dev overseeing the clinical side, though Kate realises they cannot be complacent.

The day before her flight, Freddie and Kate met with Edward Babbington, who continues to hover on the edge of donating, playing power games. He pretends not to hear the information Kate gives him. He only hears it when Freddie speaks to him. This appalled and upset her at the beginning, but she has learnt to put her own feelings aside for the sake of the charity, and Freddie has brought him close to signing away a large donation. Kate is hopeful this might happen while she's in Moscow.

Edward is always brusque, always difficult to deal with, and yet he does have an invaluable eye for the detail and how to make it all work. It's only when they tick all his boxes that he will be willing to sign the cheque. Kate has now learnt from Annabel that they have a mentally and physically disabled son themselves living in a care home, as a result of a difficult birth some eighteen years ago. Edward refuses to talk about it.

As the plane touches down in Moscow, Kate feels the excitement run through her body. It always gives her a thrill to be in Russia. There's a magic to the place, the history, the people. Valentin is pleased that the new man in power wants to restore the Soviet Union, to bring Ukraine and the other states back into the fold. Kate doesn't trust him. He's a KGB man, clever, a strategist, and she experiences an uncomfortable feeling when she looks at his face.

The taxi passes by the Kremlin walls, the familiar green rooftops and onion domes. People are looking smarter every time, she notices; there are more cars on the roads, but the old elegance and mystery of Moscow remain. They pull up at the Metropol Hotel and she checks in and goes to her room. Valentin said he would be busy until the evening, so she walks the streets all afternoon, in a mixed state of nostalgia and excitement, wondering how she can have been in love, in lust, obsessed, with this man for ten whole years.

As she walks around, though, she sees that, despite the new shops, there do not seem to be many people actually shopping. She knows that average wages are still very low after the economic crisis of 1998 and reflects that Russia still feels like a country trying to come to terms with itself and its history. *Is this me too?* she wonders. *Never quite sure who I am, or how I have got to this place in my life?*

She goes back to her room, which looks over the back streets. She remembers the very basic accommodation of the Rossiya in 1990 and is glad to be in the comfort of the Metropol now. She bathes and changes for supper.

At seven o'clock Kate goes down to reception and sits on one of the sofas near the revolving doors. He's late. *Groundhog Day*, she thinks, wondering why she is so often waiting for him, waiting on him, whiling away the anxious hours. She hates herself for it. Then he walks through the door. He's wearing a hat and a black coat, with the collar up, but she would recognise him anywhere. All these years later, he's thirty-six years old now, his beauty still shocks her.

"Shall we go and eat?" he asks, his voice low and slow in her ear as he holds her to him.

"Or maybe later?" she whispers, pressing her body to his, longing to be close, to be a part of him.

He chuckles and they walk, in silence, to the lift and up to her room. The moment the bedroom door shuts, their hands move over one another's bodies in a frenzy of desire.

"What's that bruise?" She recoils as she sees a black-blue stain on his back.

"Oh, nothing. I just fell." He shrugs off her question. "Here." He pulls her to him, and they come together.

The temperature has dropped when they eventually walk out of the Metropol to a nearby restaurant for supper. They talk of Valentin's work, of the new regime.

"Who's paying you, now that you are no longer working for the paper?"

"We have some sponsors. I can't tell you too much about them, Kate. They want to remain anonymous, but there are a group of people who are anxious to expose the truth of life here in Russia. So much has changed in the last ten years, you know. We lost the Union, then we moved into this state where anything goes, where deals are done, and there is no transparency, where the average person has little power to influence events but has to pay their taxes while the powerful few just get richer."

"So, you aren't very popular in those circles, I imagine?"

"No, but it's worth the risk," he says. "It's what I have to do. It's in my blood."

"Along with a strong streak of stubbornness?" she teases him. He shrugs.

"It's necessary. But don't you worry about me. I know what I am doing."

"But what you have told me of the bombs in the Moscow apartments sounds horrific. And you're saying it could have been the Kremlin wanting to impress on people that they will have a strong new leader?"

"Shh. Not so loud," Valentin whispers forcefully. Kate looks around but can see no one who looks suspicious or seems to be watching. "Yes, it was horrific, Kate. Three hundred people killed, over a thousand injured."

After the meal, they walk the streets together. It's dark and the cold air is bitter. As they approach the hotel, there is the sound of screeching brakes at the traffic lights just behind them. They turn to see the figure of an elderly woman step out into the icy road on a pedestrian crossing. Suddenly everything goes into slow motion as Kate watches the car hit her and fling her across the road, then speed on. The woman lies on her back, her legs, in thick beige woollen stockings, akimbo, the contents of a shopping bag strewn across the street, blood running from the back of her head onto the snow-packed tarmac.

"We must go and help her!" Kate says urgently to Valentin, starting to run towards her. He grabs Kate's arm and pulls her back.

"Stop!" he says between gritted teeth. "We can't get involved."

"What do you mean? She's lying there. We could call an ambulance."

"No!" his face contorts in anger. "I said no, Kate. Walk on back to the hotel."

"Why? Nobody seems to be helping her or taking any notice of her."

"It's not our problem. If we make it our problem, I shall be an open target for arrest. The police here trump up charges against you for no reason, just so they can demand a bribe to release you again. They will suggest we had something to do with it, and I can't afford to get into trouble or for any of them to start investigating me."

"Surely," she repeats in disbelief, "we could just call for an ambulance?"

"No, they would have our mobile numbers on their records. We can't afford to let that happen. It's Moscow, not London, Kate. I know what I am talking about," Valentin says coldly as he frogmarches her back towards the Metropol.

Kate's teeth are chattering, and her hands shake as they return to the hotel. He leaves her at the door. The passion of the evening has dissipated, and she feels sick.

Dazed, she walks back up to her room, all the excitement and anticipation of this visit drained from her body. She feels she is in an alien country, a place where there are no laws, no police to be trusted. She has known about the corruption in the police force back home but has always felt that she could assume most coppers on the beat were trustworthy and has always told Tom the same. But here she is suddenly aware that everything works through extortion. She crawls into bed, still shivering, pulls the bedclothes over her head and tries to forget the image of the old lady lying on the roadway.

THIRTY

Russia, 2000

Valentin has told Kate that he is preoccupied with an investigation and has suggested she visit Anya and Lara for a couple of nights. Kate is pleased to leave Moscow and get on the train to Orel the next morning.

The shock of Valentin's response to the old lady lying in the road still kicks around Kate's mind and body, the idea that he could be so indifferent to the woman's pain triggers more of the doubts she has been having about him. Yet, she tells herself, she doesn't know the country, nor the police, so cannot make a judgement. One has to manage situations differently in another country, another culture, she reflects, yet her emotional brain recoils from the brutality of leaving an injured person on the street for fear of some kind of backlash. *I am just an innocent abroad*, she thinks.

As the train leaves the station, Kate puts her head back against the backrest and watches the countryside pass by, her memories travelling back to the literary group, her first meeting with Valentin, to meeting Harry, Margot and Mike, and how her life has changed since that time, how Russia's history has gone through turmoil and transformation too. She feels somehow bound up in this history.

As the train ploughs its way through open farmland, she sees mothers bent over, working in the snowy fields while a child kicks its boots in the frozen mud close by, just as she had in 1990. She wonders what Tom is doing at home, with Simon, whether they are going to a football match, or maybe a rugby match at Twickenham. She notices that little jealous vibe run through her as she thinks of the male bonding activities they enjoy together now Tom is nearly seventeen. The thought of Tom leaving home leaves a hole in her stomach. She can't imagine living alone. What will her life be like then?

Arriving into Orel station, Kate pulls her small case behind her as she walks along the platform and makes her way towards a taxi. She is in a more heightened state of anxiety after the visit to Moscow. She suspects that the taxi driver charges her more than he should for the journey to Anya's flat. But she feels she has no choice but to pay him, even though he drives so fast, weaving his way through traffic along Orel's crowded roads, that she's convinced that she, or some unfortunate pedestrian, might die. There's no safety belt, so she clutches the seat as they skid around corners or brake fiercely to a halt at traffic lights.

He stops the cab in front of a tall, grey, concrete block. She pays him and looks up at floor after floor of small square windows, checking her notes. She rings the buzzer to Anya's flat. After a few minutes she hears her voice. "*Privyet?*"

"Hello!" Kate calls, berating herself for not becoming more fluent in Russian. "It's Kate. Can you let me in?"

Anya buzzes the door release and Kate walks into a dark hallway. The stone tiles are a dirty polished brown, the walls the colour of urine. It feels cold and unwelcoming, and Kate wonders whether Anya really wants her to come and stay, or whether Valentin bullied her into it, in order to give himself more time on his article. But there isn't anything she can do about that right now, and she pulls the suitcase slowly up the stairs.

Anya is standing in the hallway to greet her.

"Kate," she says warmly, taking Kate into her plump arms. Anya looks a little older, her dark, wavy hair showing more signs of grey. They are about the same height and age, but Kate still feels younger, fitter, luckier. "Good to see you. Come, in," Anya welcomes Kate into her flat. It is tiny, and Kate wonders where she is to sleep, looking around the small kitchen, its old pine table cluttered with crockery, the windowsills crowded with green plants, and noticing the bedroom with its two single beds drawn close together.

"Put," Anya indicates Kate's suitcase and points to the bedroom.

"Thank you," Kate says and puts the case down on one of the beds, wondering how the three of them are to sleep in an apartment with only two beds.

"Tea?" Anya asks, pulling a lock of grey-flecked hair from over her brown eyes and tucking it behind her ear.

"Yes, please. It is so good to see you, Anya. How is Lara? Is she coming home?"

"Lara? Yes. Studying now, home later." Her words come out haltingly in broken English. Kate notices that she's more fashionably dressed these days, in jeans and a navy jumper, yet she senses that she is fragile.

"She sad." Anya looks at Kate. "Mama. She died, recent. You know?"

"No!" Kate exclaims. "I didn't know that. Valentin never told me. Oh, Anya, I am so sorry. She wasn't old, was she?"

Tears come to Anya's eyes. Kate wraps her arms around her shoulders. She feels Anya's soft body as her face buries in her neck. *How could Valentin not have told me about his mother's death*? she wonders.

After a short time, Anya pulls away, rubs her eyes and pulls a handkerchief out of her skirt pocket to blow her nose.

"Sorry," she says. "Was sudden. Lara, very sad. She very loved her babushka."

Kate nods. It brings her back to her own father's death, the emptiness that followed, an emptiness inside as much as an emptiness in the house.

Anya turns and hands Kate a cup of pale tea. They sit down together at the table. "Valentin, not here. Busy. Moscow."

"Yes, I saw him. He's writing a major article, he told me." Kate wonders why she always feels the need to make some kind of excuse for him.

Anya shrugs. "What more important than daughter? Lara? Or Mama? He didn't come to funeral."

Kate doesn't know what to say to this, and they sit in a silence where she feels both of them are trying to grapple with the enigma that is Anya's brother.

"Diabetes. You know, difficult to manage. Worry, worry, for Lara, for me," Anya says suddenly, rubbing her forehead with her hand, as if it's all too much for her. "No sleep, too high, too low. She's a woman now and she... she push me away."

"Ah yes," Kate replies, connecting to her own feelings of caring for a teenager. "Tom is the same. He wants to be independent, go with his own friends. I am boring for him now!"

Anya laughs. "Yes." she nods in strong agreement. "Lara, out, always. No talk, angry, if I worry."

"Yes, I can imagine. It's bad enough being a parent without having the added concern of her health on top of all those everyday worries!" Kate sympathises. "And now beginning to be responsible for herself must be hard."

"Yes. Won't listen. She know best, like all teenagers!"

They sit in silence, reflecting, for a while.

"Walk?" Anya asks after they finish their tea.

"That would be lovely," Kate agrees.

Lara is home when they return. Kate is taken aback by her beauty. She's taller than both Anya and Kate and looks so like Valentin, her deep brown eyes, dark hair, pale skin. She welcomes Kate politely, in good English, though Kate does not get the impression she is totally enthusiastic about her visit.

Lara and Kate sit at the table while Anya serves a stew of chicken and vegetables. Lara asks Kate about London, and it seems she is keen to come and visit.

"You would love it," Kate tells her. "And Tom would love to meet you. We must plan your trip this weekend."

"That would be great," she says, her eyes lighting with enthusiasm.

They eat in silence for a while and then Lara suddenly says, "I think maybe I saw my mother today, Auntie."

Anya stops still, the fork that was about to enter her mouth, hovering in mid-air. She goes pale. "Really? Where? How you know?"

They speak in English for Kate's sake. She knows that Anya can understand more than she can speak.

"I wanted to ask her if she was Yulia, but I just kept looking at her. She's pretty. I've been asking around. She had a child with her, maybe six years old. Maybe she's married now."

Kate watches Anya's face crumple. She puts her fork back onto her plate, food uneaten.

"Why didn't she want to know me after I was born? Why was it only you who would look after me, Auntie?"

"So young," Anya explains, grudgingly. "Not able. Have told you before." Then mutters something in Russian, and Lara gives her a defiant look and shrugs her shoulders.

Kate looks at the girl and her aunt and wonders how hard it has been for Anya to take care of her niece. It is difficult to bring up a child alone, especially if that child is not your own.

"I might look Yulia up. Check if it's her," Lara says in English, in a slightly hostile voice. Then she gets up, puts her plate in the sink and says, "I'm going out with Elena now. I'll stay with her overnight."

With that she puts on her coat, waves to the two women from the doorway and is gone. Anya sits still at the table, shaking her head back and forth.

"Her mother," she says, "no want Lara as baby. Only fifteen." Anya shrugs. "Valentin, he no want her. I took her. Beautiful girl."

"Yes," Kate agrees softly. There's a pause.

"Now I worry. I always worry!" Anya gives a self-deprecating laugh. "Boys."

Kate looks at her questioningly.

"They stupid."

"Well not all of them," Kate replies, thinking of Tom. "She's very beautiful, Anya. She will find a loving boy soon, I am sure."

"Yes. Hope so." Anya nods.

Kate helps her tidy up and dry as Anya washes the plates. She's tired but feels awkward about saying she would like to go to bed as she doesn't understand yet how they are to sleep.

Eventually, Anya points to the bed and gesticulates that she will go next door to sleep.

"I go there," she points to the front door. "My friend, Natalya," she explains. "You, stay."

Kate is relieved that they are not to sleep together – pillow to pillow, in the small bedroom – and smiles to acknowledge she has understood.

"How kind of you, Anya. I shall be very comfortable."

"Tomorrow," Anya says, smiling suddenly, "I show you my shop. Health food."

As she leaves, she demonstrates to Kate that she must lock up after her.

"It's important," Anya impresses on her, and Kate feels a shiver of disquiet slice through her so turns the key in the lock after her and draws the bolts across at the top and bottom of the battered wooden door.

She closes the bedroom door behind her, settles into the small bed and hopes to get some sleep.

THIRTY-ONE

Russia, 2000

Anya's health food shop stands on a corner in a midway suburb of Orel. Anya unlocks the door and bustles around, showing Kate the vitamins and powders, the cereals and supplements. Everything is in perfect order. Although Anya struggles with her weight, she tells Kate that she keeps herself fit and eats as nutritious a diet as she can afford for herself and Lara.

Kate gives her a hug. "This is fantastic, Anya. A real symbol of feminist power and enterprise in your culture. Well done!"

"Has been difficult," Anya raises her brown eyes to the ceiling as she talks, "getting rubles. Bank no like women. How you say, patro… patronise?"

Kate nods. "Yes, patronise. I know. It happens in the UK too. I guess, people are getting used to private enterprise here, but the banks tend to be traditional, patriarchal."

"Yes," she says, and Kate can see from her tired face that it has all been an uphill struggle, but the achievement is one of great pride. "Is my baby." And Kate knows what she means as it mirrors her own experience with the maternity home, which has been running almost four years now. It was a difficult start, finding the right staff, encouraging people to sponsor it, but the pride Kate feels with every baby that is born safely is enormous. And she feels each birth is a gift to William's memory.

They part as Kate makes her way back to the railway station.

"When will you and Lara come over and visit London?" Kate asks as she kisses Anya goodbye.

"Autumn? Flights cheaper?"

"Yes, they should be cheaper after schools go back. Lara is studying?"

"Da, she go medical school. Is good job."

"Excellent, you come to London in September and stay with me. I will show you both the city. You will love it."

Anya smiles. "Something, look forward to, after all my hard work. But Valentin, I worry," she confides. "Determined to write about bad men. Dangerous men."

"I know. It's good work, though, Anya. I admire him for this."

"But now, this new president, I have bad feeling. Can't explain."

"We have to trust that Valentin knows what he is doing, Anya, don't we?"

She just shrugs. "I wonder, how will world be, for Lara? I worry."

"We always worry about our children, Anya. It's natural."

"But she not my child. She find her mama. What mean for me?"

Kate pauses, understanding that Anya feels her role in Lara's life is a tenuous one.

"Anya, you have been her mama, for all these years. She won't forget that. She's a wonderful girl. It is natural that she is curious about her biological mother, but I can't believe she will forget all that you have done for her."

"Hope not, Kate." Anya puts her hand out to Kate's, and there are tears in her eyes.

"A wise man once said to me to live in trust and not to live in fear," Kate tells her. "That way you can enjoy your days, and if something goes wrong, you will be stronger, more able to manage it. And if it goes right then you won't have wasted your days worrying about something that never happens."

"I like that." Anya smiles a watery smile. She looks at her watch. "You, train."

Anya walks Kate to the next street where there is a bus to the train station.

It's dark when Kate reaches Moscow. She gets a taxi from the train station back to the Metropol and is given the same room. There's no news from Valentin. He has kept changing his mobile number and Kate can't get through to him.

Eventually, she feels so hungry that she goes down to

the reception area and looks around. There's no sign of him, so she walks through the double doors at the side of the hotel to see if she can see him on the street. She's greeted by a blast of cold air, and she wraps her arms around herself, looking up and down the street. The pavements are busy, but there is no sign of Valentin.

She sighs and goes back inside to the hotel restaurant. The waiter shows her to a table and gives her the menu. Although she's hungry, she has no great appetite for any of the dishes but orders some fish. She looks around the elegant room under its stained-glass ceiling.

There are very few people eating, but she notices a young couple sitting at a nearby table. They look like the new Moscow rich. The girl is expensively dressed, and her partner is wearing a rather shiny Italian suit, his dark hair slicked back. They constantly touch and kiss; the woman tosses her long dyed-blonde hair backwards and forwards and stretches her slim legs out into the room, for effect. It makes Kate conscious of the empty chair beside her.

As she leaves the restaurant and walks towards the lift, she feels a tap on her shoulder.

"Kate, I'm sorry." Valentin slides in beside her, like a shadow. *How many times do I have to hear him say that?* Kate wonders to herself. He's dressed in black and has the hood of his jacket pulled well down over his head, so he is almost unrecognisable. "I got held up."

Kate feels awkward. His appearance is sinister, and she doesn't want to show him that she is upset that he hasn't been in contact. "No problem," she says, as lightly as possible.

"Have you enjoyed your dinner?"

"Not particularly. Do you want to eat something?"

"No. I've already eaten, in fact. Can we go to your room?" He keeps his head down all the time he is talking.

A dull, heavy feeling enters Kate's stomach, as the same old scene plays out, and she tries to overcome her disappointment.

"I'm not sure," she says, as coldly as she can fathom.

"Please, Kate," he says urgently. "I will explain."

"OK."

"I will go up by the stairs first and wait for you," Valentin says, and he slips away before Kate can speak.

When she reaches her floor, she can't see Valentin, but once she opens the door to her room, he suddenly appears beside her and slides through the gap and into the darkness.

Kate shuts the door and turns the light on. Valentin stands against the wall, his breathing is short, and he pushes his hood back off his face so she can see the pallor of his skin, his eyes wide.

"I have been trailed all day. I think I gave him the slip this evening, but I am not sure." He stops for a moment. "I wasn't honest with you the other night. My bruises are because I was robbed. They stole my laptop again – it keeps happening. I encrypt the files and save them where I can, but they keep finding me."

"Oh, how horrible." Kate moves towards him, with concern.

"It's nothing." He moves away. "I have all my files backed up, but it's Novikoff's son. He's out to kill me, I think."

"That's not 'nothing'," Kate protests. "Drink?" she asks, going towards the minibar where she has stored the bottle of vodka she bought for their times together. He nods. She pours them both a shot and hands him the glass. They sit down on the sofa and place the glasses down on the low coffee table.

"What's happening?" she asks him, unnerved, as she considers that if he is being shadowed then he is drawing attention towards her too.

Kate watches him as his body takes on a restlessness she has noticed before when he talks of his work.

"I have to educate people about what's going on here," he says. "There's Chechnya, you know, I mentioned to you, the bombings, there's the money that has been going to Yeltsin's network and, you know, Yeltsin banned the Communist party in Russia, banned all its activities. Such a bad move. Yeltsin has been worse than Gorbachev. Gorbachev sucked up to the West; Yeltsin has created lawlessness. Dog eat dog. Then there's Igor Novikoff, as I said – he's responsible for arranging the assassination now, I know, of the wives of two of his enemies, and maybe another. He enjoys terrorising his enemies. I know it was him, but he gets away with it because he's a friend of the President."

Kate watches him, noticing how the enthusiasm for the story seems to override any compassion he may have for the victims of these crimes.

"So, it's the joy of the chase for you?" she quizzes him.

"Pah, Kate, I am exposing these people!" He stands up and paces the room. "Yes, it's a great story, but it will bring justice, can't you see?"

"I can see that, but it frightens me when you speak of murder with seemingly little care for those who died, especially when it is wives, maybe mothers leaving children."

"You don't get me!" He is angry now. "I have to stay objective. I am a journalist. I have to investigate the truth. I can't be too soppy about the facts, or I wouldn't be able to do my job. Can't you see that?"

Kate bows her head to acknowledge what he is saying. Suddenly he comes to sit close beside her and takes her hand, his eyes looking deep into hers, a passion, a fire in them that lights up his whole face.

"I will expose these evil people, Kate. I will. My reports can go around the world now, with the internet, you see? I was for the new President, you know, at first. He wants to bring the Soviet Union back together, like I do, but I was wrong about him. He is not a socialist, not communist, he is out to make his money. Him and his favourite oligarchs out for power while the poor people have to fend for themselves. The truth is what matters. Can you see that?"

His rage is infectious. She feels his fervour; it traces through his body beside her, his leg now next to hers, her hand in his strong grip. She is caught in his flames, yet fearful of him, fearful for him. He moves forward towards her and his lips touch hers. He takes a sip of vodka, turns her head to his and, as he kisses her, the vodka slides from his mouth to hers, the heat of the alcohol hitting her throat like an explosion. She is alight as he lifts her in his arms and takes her to the bed, his need exciting her to a point where nothing else matters.

Later, as she turns over in bed to touch him, her hand slides across an empty space.

"I've fallen for it all again!" she scolds herself and tries to sleep.

As dawn breaks, she takes a bath, dresses and goes down to breakfast, wondering what she should do with her day. Returning to her room after she's eaten, she feels a pang of homesickness and sends a text to Tom. She endeavours to sound purposeful and happy and writes that she hopes he is having a good time with his dad.

She visits St Basil's Cathedral and says a prayer for Tom, Eve and for her mother. There's a small group of Orthodox monks singing in a side chapel, and she listens, captivated, to their sombre chanting and deep bass voices.

It's cold and raining when she walks back across Red Square. She returns to the hotel to see if Valentin has returned or left a message. There is no text or call on her mobile, and the girl on the reception desk is cold, unsmiling. Nothing. No message. No call. It's no surprise, but she can't help feeling the disappointment.

At a loss, she goes up to her room to rest, but the maid is cleaning it. She wanders back down to the streets, then returns, reads her book and falls asleep. Eventually, at around six o'clock in the evening, there's a knock on the door. Valentin. She lets him in.

"You disappeared," she says accusingly. He looks puzzled.

"What d'you expect? I told you I have to write, Kate. And here I am, and I have brought us a picnic."

She feels churlish that she should have imagined she could stand in the way of him writing his reports, which have far greater world import, she thinks, than him spending time with her. He unpacks some rather soggy-looking parcels of food, and they sit down on the sofa and eat.

"Anya is worried," Kate says. "Lara thinks she has met her real mother."

He looks startled. "Really? Yulia?"

"Yes. And Lara was going to try to bump into her again. It's made Anya feel vulnerable, maybe rejected."

"Anya, she is always feeling rejected, vulnerable, burdened. It's her way, all her life. The martyr."

"But, Valentin, she has been a mother to Lara. You must understand that she could feel threatened by Lara finding her real mother?"

He just shrugs. "Anya makes everyone feel bad, feel guilty. She made her own choices. There's nothing I can do about it. Lara will do what Lara will do."

"But you are her father. You have some influence," Kate argues. "You didn't even tell me when your mother died, when Lara lost her grandmother—"

"Stop nagging me, Kate," Valentin interrupts angrily. "I have more important things to do."

"More important than family, your daughter?" she challenges him.

"You can talk, Kate. You are here, not with your son."

Words die on Kate's lips, and she sits and eats the fruit kissel he has brought. There's an expression of impatience on his face, and they sit in silence for a moment, then he shakes his shoulders and turns to her.

"We had a good time last night, yes?"

Kate nods, but the passion has gone.

"We have magical moments together." His voice goes soft, deep. "We shall have more, believe me. I will come to

London again."

Kate looks at him and doesn't know how she feels.

"Now, I must go. You have a safe flight back, and I shall stay in touch." He stands up and puts his anorak back on. He kneels down in front of her. "It's a busy time, Kate. Forgive me, but I must go."

He lets himself out of the room.

The next day, when she returns to the warmth of her house in Notting Hill, Kate sees the voicemail light is flashing. She picks it up. Six messages. But when she presses playback there is silence, followed only by a series of clicks. She stands beside her desk for a moment, ruminating, then goes to the window and turns on the outside lights and looks out on her garden. Nothing moves but the breeze.

THIRTY-TWO

England, 2000

Kate busies herself planning two fundraising events to raise money for the maternity home. Eve's client Grigory is being very helpful, putting Kate in contact with other Russians who may be willing to contribute funds. The first big event is at the Savoy Hotel.

"I'm really nervous," she confesses to Eve one evening, as they eat risotto in Kate's kitchen.

"Yes, it's a big event to pull together, but you're used to it. You know what you're doing. You've done it so often for other clients. It's bound to be great," Eve comforts her.

"Let's hope we get lots of money."

"From what I see of the Russians in London, I suspect they will be very generous."

Kate picks up their plates and takes them to the sink, rinsing and loading them into the dishwasher, then pulls two yoghurts from the fridge, with some fresh raspberries. She pours them both another glass of white wine.

"I'm still worried about Anya," Kate says, biting her lip. "She was feeling really disconcerted about Lara finding her birth mother, Yulia. She thought she would be pushed aside. I told her that she had basically been Lara's mother all these years, and I couldn't imagine Lara would be so unkind as to sideline her now."

Eve sighs. "I hope not. I had a friend at uni – you may have met her, Bella? She was adopted as a child. She found her birth mother many years later, while we were studying, and her adoptive mother was very put out and threatened. Bella found it really difficult to meet her biological mother – there was a lot of anger between them. Bella accused her of abandoning her, and the mother wasn't that happy at having been found. It was really complicated and, ultimately, rather sad, as Bella had upset her adoptive mother and never made a relationship with her birth mother."

"Well, biological mothers can be difficult enough!" Kate sighs. "Mum's really frail now, but she can still somehow get her hands on some booze and then she goes wild. She's trouble when she's in rehab, and she's trouble when she's home with a carer. I can't win or relax."

"Yes, indeed, families can be so bloody bewildering," Eve agrees. "I'm quite grateful to my mum and dad for having died young and not been any worry for me. I'm also not sure I would have had it in me to be a parent – I suspect I am too selfish. I like my creature comforts."

"Well, Anya certainly hasn't many creature comforts, that's for sure. The trouble is, Lara is just going through that stage of pushing away from her anyway. You know, asserting her independence. I feel it with Tom too – I am just boring old Mum these days. He's applying for universities. He wants to read physics. He's taking it for A level, but it is like another language to me, and he is very much in his own world, spending time with friends at weekends and busy in his books in the evenings. We chat over suppers, but he's moving away from me."

"It is natural, Kate. Shows you have done a good job as a mum."

"I know, but it hurts, and I am frightened about the future alone. What will it be like? He's getting closer to Simon, talks of spending more time with him now. He says Simon is good at explaining the theories behind his course. I don't understand how or why as Simon did a fine art degree, but he tells me they have interesting conversations. I try not to feel rejected by this, try to comfort myself that it is natural for father and son to grow closer as the boy becomes a man."

"It is, Kate. Totally natural. Let him go; focus on your work, the charity; and for God's sake find a nice man here in London and stop fantasising about bloody Valentin!"

"OK, OK." Kate puts her hands in the air. "You know, I have to say, Eve, you are looking a million dollars! Your Russian clients have really made a difference to your life, haven't they?" Kate looks at her friend, her black bob shiny, wearing a black and silver Japanese designer outfit that is loose and relaxed but perfectly shows off her tall, slim frame.

"It has really been a life-changer, yes."

"I feel like a country bumpkin." Kate laughs as she kisses Eve's cheek, remembering how she had always felt like the also-ran in the shadow of her glamorous friend when they went to teenage parties.

"Rubbish," Eve protests. "How can you say that when you are the one who has just come back from being ravished in Russia?" She takes a drink of her wine. "But you're not the only one about to be alone. Willow is going to need to be put down." Tears come to Eve's eyes as she says this.

"Oh, Eve, what's wrong with her?"

"A great fat tumour in her stomach. I shall miss her horribly."

"I'm so sorry." Kate puts her hand on top of her friend's as she gets an image of Tom playing with Willow, Eve's golden retriever. "That's a real bummer. They're part of the family, aren't they, and she's been such a companion to you."

Eve nods, unable to speak. They sit in silence for a few minutes.

"Anyway," she says eventually, "I don't want her to suffer, and she has been whimpering so plaintively it's been ghastly. I know that when Charley died, I held him in my arms while the vet gave him a sedative, and he fell asleep, then a few moments later he had the final injection and just went limp in my arms, and that was it, a great bundle of fluffy spaniel left at peace. It was dignified, compassionate and loving – it's what I would want for my own death."

"Yes, me too," Kate agrees. "Animals get a better time than we do, I think."

Eve nods in agreement.

"So, Kate, spill the beans, how was Russia, really? I haven't been able to catch up properly since you got back."

"It's ridiculous, Eve, I see the guy and all my good intentions of finishing it fly out of the window. I'm excited by what he is doing, you know, reporting on corrupt individuals and events, and when he tells me about it, he gets so passionate, and then the passion is infectious. And marvellous. But the next minute he is off on his project."

"But you said you needed the space this gives you to run your life here, didn't you? And he must feel something for you. Otherwise, why does he keep in touch? He finds you attractive, that is for sure, and with the internet, he has access to more Russians in the UK, plenty of sources of information now. So, he must have some place in his heart for you, surely?"

"Well, a pretty strange place, I think. And I can't believe there isn't another woman, maybe several other women."

"You probably have to put that thought aside and really focus, like I endlessly suggest, on finding someone here. Anyway, what do you two talk about?"

Kate stops to think. "Loads of things – his investigations, a little about Anya and Lara, the Russians in London, English media, where Russia is going now."

"He still pumps you for information?"

"Yes," Kate says slowly. "I like to be helpful. He's fascinated by the Russians who have come to London, who they are, what they're doing, where they live, where their money is."

Eve's head bows slowly up and down as she listens, her expression reflective. Then she seems to shake some thought out of her mind, and she raises her glass to sip the wine.

"And his money? Does he ever ask you to fund him?"

Kate is silent. She can't bring herself to tell her friend how she has funded all their times together.

"I do still worry that he is tagging you along," Eve goes on, "keeping you on a string in case he needs you some time. Like keeping that stuff he does in your spare room. I mean surely that isn't necessary now? With the internet he can keep files wherever he likes. It has to be that he wants to feel he has some hold over you, some part of him in your home?"

"I don't know. He's had his laptop stolen several times." Kate pauses and takes a breath. "So, who's the latest lover in your life, Eve?" she asks, changing the focus.

"An Italian. He's a furniture designer I met through a project we are doing. You know, it's like that scene in *A Fish Called Wanda* where I faint with excitement every time he says 'Spaghetti Bolognese' or 'Pizza Romana'…"

They laugh together at the memory of the film, and Kate envies her the way she seems to be able to keep so cool about her love affairs.

"My, that risotto was delicious, thanks." Eve licks her lips and puts down her fork.

"Good. Now, how is Grigory getting on with inviting people to our fundraising?"

"Well, there are six guys coming along who he says will give you money for the home, so we are on a roll."

"Great, and we have the usual execs and aristos coming too, and a couple of celebs. Mike has been a brilliant contact."

"Sorry about giving you a hard time about going to Moscow all those years ago," Eve says. "Mike is great, even if I am not at all sure about Valentin."

"You have always been the voice of my conscience. Don't forget, too, that Margot has been incredible at getting the branding of the charity and spreading the word through her agency."

"Did you hear from Harry?" Eve asks.

Kate puckers her face. "He did ring last week. Wants to meet up for dinner."

"Have you been working with that coach I mentioned?"

"Yes, she has been helpful in getting me to shape the charity and work out fundraising events."

"It's the inner you that concerns me. You've got major events coming up, Kate. You need to get a grip, work on yourself and what you want for your life."

Kate looks at her, unsure what to say. "I thought I was," she replies feebly.

"You are. You have achieved so much, and you should have more confidence when you consider the maternity home, the events you have organised, the fact that Tom is doing well and off to uni later this year. But you go off to that bloody man Valentin in Russia and you are like a leaf in the wind." Eve takes Kate by the shoulders and looks into her eyes, with some frustration. "You remember what the stoics say – be like a tree. The more the wind blows, the stronger a tree's roots become. Feel that strength, the roots firmly in the ground yet the trunk flexible enough to bend a little when life events change. You know what I mean?"

"OK," Kate agrees. "I shall work on that, I promise!"

THIRTY-THREE

England, 2000

The room looks amazing. The Savoy has done Kate proud. The tables glitter with sparkling glasses and polished cutlery. There is a three-piece orchestra playing in one corner and a stage set for slides, the presentation and for the auction later, to raise money. Kate's hands are slightly clammy, and her heart races as she busies herself with final details for the fundraising evening and gives the waiting staff instructions of when to serve dishes and when to allow time for presentations. The charity auction will be after dessert.

Kate has bought a Chinese-style patterned black and red silk dress for the occasion, and it feels soft and delicate against her skin. She looks around the room and spots Margot discussing something with the auctioneer. Margot's firm has designed the programmes and banners for tonight, and they look wonderful. Eve, looking like elegance itself in a stunning long black halter-neck dress, is beginning to greet guests as they arrive through the door. *We're a great team*, Kate thinks, *like Charlie's Angels*, then turns towards the door.

Mike and his wife arrive, bringing with them several senior managers from his investment bank. Kate has found it a joy to maintain the relationship with him over all these years. He is such a warm and generous man. He kisses Margot on both cheeks, and the waiters give him and his party glasses of champagne.

He is followed by Simon, with his new girlfriend, Jane, with Tom trailing behind them. Simon looks a little uncomfortable as he greets Kate. Tom kisses her and asks, "Is Grandma coming?"

"No, I don't think she can manage this kind of event now," Kate explains. Just at the moment that Simon looks as if he is about to comment on her mother's condition, Eve approaches and draws him, Tom and Jane away to meet the others. Kate blesses her quietly.

Edward and Annabel Babbington arrive. He shakes Kate's hand, squeezing it so hard it hurts. Annabel winks at her and whispers, "Well done, girl," as they are whisked into the crowd by Eve. Kate is a little disappointed that Harry hasn't changed his mind and accepted the invitation. Their last dinner together went the way of the others and they got no closer. But he has given a generous donation.

Crowds begin to push through the doors now, the men handsome and elegant in dinner jackets and bow ties, the women in swirling evening dresses. A couple of pop stars and their wives, models, an earl, and Kate becomes aware of Eve being surrounded by a group of lavishly dressed and quite rowdy people, tall women and men drinking champagne, and, not far away from them, standing close by, but beside the wall, bodyguards in dark suits. The Russian contingent.

Kate walks up and greets Grigory, whom she has met many times before, and he introduces her to the friends and colleagues he has brought with him. Boris, a suave-looking young man with a stunning-looking wife or girlfriend, a rather short, paunchy-looking fellow with dark stubble around his chin, called Vladimir; there's Dmitry, Nikolai and then, however hard Kate tries to keep up, she loses touch with the unfamiliar names. Her mind is darting around as she spots people she knows from the maternity home, the nursing staff, Dev and a couple of his consultant colleagues, the manager, the midwives, so she excuses herself and rushes over to greet them before calling everyone to attention and asking them to take their seats.

People study the table plans, and it takes some time for them to find their places and sit down. The noise level rises as conversations start to echo around the room. Kate sits on a table with the trustees, Freddie by Kate's side to give her confidence. The chair, Margaret Steerforth, is to give the main speech, and after the first course, the master of ceremonies from the Savoy calls everyone to attention so that Margaret can take the microphone.

She summarises the proceedings of the trust and outlines some of the financial details. She receives a rousing applause at the end. Kate can't eat anything as she shall be up to give her presentation next, after the main course. And then the moment comes, and she walks up onto the stage to the microphone, in front of all these people, important people, wealthy, successful people. She remembers to take a moment to centre herself, to ensure that the room is silent, their attention on her, to focus on feeling confident about the message she wants to communicate.

Then she starts, outlining the history of the maternity home, shows slides of the building before it was converted, the progress of the plans and architecture, thanks those who have already donated so generously. She explains her reasons for founding it, brings up the little photo of William and, in the briefest of details, describes how she doesn't want other women to have the experience that she did. She catches Simon's eye as she talks, and he smiles at her and bows his head a little in support and acknowledgement. Tom is looking shy but proud. He looks so young in his rather oversized dinner jacket but very handsome, too, becoming more like Simon every day.

Kate goes on to show the slides of the first babies, the staff and the plans for the future and thanks all those who keep everything functioning. And phew, she's at the end of her talk and, somehow, she has got through it without stumbling, without crying, and has made the points she wanted to make, and even included a few jokes that made them laugh. Applause fills the room, and she walks back to her table, relieved and happy.

After dessert the auctioneer takes the microphone. He is amusing and motivational. People have donated many gifts, designer outfits, holiday homes, jewels and more, and the auction begins. The figures being thrown around are out of all Kate's expectations, £25,000 for a small handbag, £100,000 for a silk trouser suit, then suddenly there's £500,000 for a holiday, and jewels, days out. She can't believe what she is hearing and sees that Eve is looking delighted at her table of Russians, who are raising their hands over and over. The charity raises over £2 million, an amazing sum.

After this, the whole evening is rather a blur of sensations and emotions for Kate, and she doesn't feel she's talking properly to anyone, just having short snippets of conversations. Simon and Tom come up and congratulate her. Simon takes her in his arms and gives her a huge hug, with real warmth and a slight break in his voice, as he tells her William's memory has been honoured in all that she has done. Tom pats her on the back. She notices that he has drunk a little too much, his long arms not quite coordinating, as she squeezes his hand.

People start to move around the room and make their farewells. Eve and Grigory come up to her. He is smiling his big smile. "Kate," he says in that wonderful Russian voice that immediately takes Kate back to Moscow, "amazing job! Well done."

"Well, I have you to thank, Grigory. I can't tell you how grateful I am."

As he talks, Kate notices a man standing just behind him. He's mid-height, grey-haired with icy-blue eyes, and has a broad face with some grey stubble on his chin. He steps forward and puts his large hand out to shake hers.

"Ms Kate Chisholm," he says in a loud and rather harsh voice. "I introduce myself, friend of Nikolai here. My name is Igor Novikoff."

Kate's heart goes cold, and words dry on her lips. She looks at him and there is unconcealed horror in her eyes as she hears his name.

"I have heard so much about you," he says. "I am sure we shall be in closer touch now." He's holding her hand in a hard grip, looking her straight in the eye. With this, he releases her suddenly and waves towards a mean-faced younger man, dark-haired, with a scar across his cheek.

"And this is my son. In the business with me."

Then they both walk away, a wiry henchman with distinctive green eyes beside them.

Kate stands paralysed for a moment.

She continues to shake the hands of the final guests, as if on automatic, and then walks directly over to Eve.

"What the hell was Igor Novikoff doing here tonight?" she asks her. "I didn't notice his name on the guest list." Eve turns to look at Kate, with a confused expression.

"Igor? He only replied last night. Why shouldn't he be here? He's bought a property in Mayfair. I am giving him a proposal to convert it. In fact, we have just started the work." She looks genuinely surprised at Kate's anger.

Kate sits down on a nearby chair, shaking.

"But, Eve, it was his men who held us up in Gorky Park all those years ago with Valentin, Anya and Lara, the man Valentin is investigating. He's an evil man. He's murdered people, defrauded people. You name it, he has done it."

"Oh God, I didn't connect the two, Kate. I am so sorry. I wasn't keen on him, but one of my other clients, Nikolai, introduced us, so I thought he was OK."

"All the President's men…" Kate murmurs, the celebratory

feeling of the evening disappearing in a flash. Then she looks at Eve. "How on earth do we extricate ourselves from this mess?"

THIRTY-FOUR

England, 2000

The days after the Savoy fundraiser prove challenging for Kate. She is on edge after meeting Igor Novikoff, and the sight of his son has alarmed her even more. She is delighted that so much money has poured into the charity, and yet there is a dark question mark running through her mind about the source of the money. To add to her concerns, Edward Babbington, who has finally become a trustee, is grilling her about where the funds have come from.

"We don't want any money from criminals or gangsters," he repeatedly tells her.

She feels out of her depth, and now Valentin has emailed and asked her to get Eve to copy Igor Novikoff's bank statements and accounts when she is in his house supervising the renovation. She feels thoroughly uncomfortable about this, although she is aware that Eve is becoming equally concerned about the background of some of her clients and yet needs them for the success of her consultancy.

As the summer draws to a close, Tom is preparing to pack up his room to go to university. Kate doesn't like to watch or play any part in this but has arranged for Anya and Lara to come to stay just before he leaves.

Tom and Kate go to Heathrow to collect them and, as they appear through the doors to Arrivals, Lara runs up to Kate in her excitement, dragging her case behind her.

"Meet Tom," Kate says, proud of her handsome son.

Lara smiles and greets him in excellent English. They start walking towards the car. Tom grabs the cases and puts them in the boot of Kate's black Audi. He insists that Anya sits in the front. Tom and Lara chat easily in the back. Lara babbles away excitedly and jumps out of the car when they reach Notting Hill.

"Oh, what pretty houses," she exclaims at the row of red-brick terraced Victorian houses and both she and Anya are bowled over by Kate's home.

"Beautiful," Anya comments. "So big! You seen my little place!"

"Ah, different ways of life, Anya. But each beautiful in its own way," Kate tells her.

She shows them up to the spare room where she has separated the twin beds, and Anya is delighted that it looks over the pretty little garden at the back.

Later, they walk around Notting Hill, and Kate promises to show them the film with Hugh Grant.

"Not sure I understand anything!" Anya says when this is suggested.

"Yes, you will, Auntie. I shall translate for you," Lara offers.

Tom and Lara walk behind the two women and seem to find one another easy company. Kate is relieved she doesn't detect any kind of physical attraction between them as she feared this could prove complicated.

"Where Valentin? You seen him?" Anya asks.

Kate turns to her, surprised. "He's here in London. He sometimes stays in North London, with another colleague. Setting up his network of reporters. Didn't you know?"

"We not seen him. Months." Anya shakes her head.

"There are many Russians in London now, Anya. Valentin is still following Novikoff – the man whose men attacked us in the park all those years ago. Novikoff and his son are renovating a house in London."

"Oh, and they, how do you say, raided my apartment too." Kate looks surprised.

"Valentin didn't tell me that," Kate says, looking puzzled.

"Was frightening. Took papers. Made mess. Long time ago."

"Ah, Anya, that must have been nasty. Valentin thinks that was Novikoff?" Kate commiserates with curiosity.

"Yes, Novikoff local to Orel then. Now Moscow, London…"

"Oh dear." Kate turns away a little as she speaks. "Hopefully Valentin will come and see you both. I never know where he is or what he's doing, but I do know that he likes being in London because he doesn't have to keep his documents with him every day."

Anya laughs. "Yes, I understand!"

"Mum, I'm going to take Lara to a pub. We'll be back later," Tom calls.

"Lovely. Take good care of her."

"Of course." Tom raises his eyes to the sky.

"And, Anya, did Lara contact her mother? Yulia?" Kate asks when they have gone.

Anya sighs as they walk back into Kate's house. "Yes. Not good. She very young. Very beautiful, 'cool', they say. I…" she hesitates, "I feel old. Useless. The old auntie."

"I'm sure Lara doesn't feel that. She seems very affectionate with you."

"Ah yes, here, she OK. But Yulia pushing for Lara to live with her. Has small child. Lara babysit."

"Will Lara have her own flat soon?"

"No. Can't afford. Medical studies. Wants to be doctor. Study long time," Anya explains.

"I'm sure everything will work itself out in the end, Anya," Kate says as she prepares some supper, and they chat of other things. They hear the front door open, and Tom and Lara return. Her cheeks are pink, and her eyes are sparkling with excitement.

"London is wonderful, and we went to a real English pub, Auntie!" She hugs Anya, and they all settle down for supper.

The next day, Kate takes her guests around London. In the evening, after they have eaten supper, the doorbell goes. Tom walks to the door and opens it. There is Valentin.

Tom greets him. Kate notices Anya watching the exchange. She knows there is a coldness in Tom's voice that Anya will pick up. Valentin walks into the hall, dressed in jeans and a leather jacket, looking more mature and perhaps even more handsome than when he was young. He opens his arms wide and walks towards Lara, whose face lights up as she sees him.

"Papa!" Lara reaches up to give him kisses. Valentin walks towards Anya and puts his arms around her shoulders.

"Anya, my dear sister, lovely to see you," he says to her. Anya squeezes his hand and half pushes him away at the same time.

"So," Anya says, as they make themselves comfortable in the sitting room, "tell me all about what you've been doing. We haven't heard from you for weeks."

"Things are going really well, Anya. We have built up a good network of individuals, not all journalists, who tell us what they hear, what they see, in bars, *cafés*, at political meetings, in business meetings here and in Russia. We seek out what might be underneath the surface, what might be brewing beneath the main headlines, then publish it online."

"Isn't that dangerous, Valentin?" Anya thought of her late mother's fears for him.

"Well, the authorities at the Kremlin and their cronies are not so happy. They don't like us exposing the organised crime, corruption, prostitution rings, drug rings, all those things I have spoken to you about before – how government bodies are parcelling out benefits to their friends and families. We have so much information now and plenty on the President himself."

"And have you had these reports published in Russia?" Anya asks.

"Some of them, but we have to be careful. We have been threatened, as you know. That's why Mikhail, my ex-boss – you remember, he is my partner now – wanted us to set up an agency here in London so that we are safer to publish our investigations without fear of being killed on some Moscow street."

"So how will it work?"

"We have networks of colleagues and associates now, across the world. Mikhail is staying in Moscow to support the network there. He doesn't speak much English, his kids are in school, so it made sense for me to come to London. The internet has really helped us build contacts. People who agree with our political viewpoint." Valentin looks proud as he tells his older sister of his achievements.

"And what of the President?"

"Ah, he hides his percentage of the deals he makes in the bank accounts of his cronies so that they cannot be traced back to the Kremlin. Or so he thinks. But we know about his dachas and yachts. He behaves like a Mafia boss."

"Does this agency of yours have a name?" Anya struggles to sound positive while her heart is contracting in fear at what her brother is doing.

Valentin laughs. "We worked on this with our English friends here. We have called it 'Gabintcell'."

"What? That's a complicated name, isn't it?" Kate joins in the response.

Valentin nods. "Yes, it is rather, but it comes from 'gab', e.g. the gift of the gab as my English colleague tells me, and gab is also talking about things, then 'intcell' is the idea of cells of people, groups talking with one another sharing 'intel', e.g. intelligence."

"Hmm, well that makes some kind of sense, and I guess there isn't another press agency with that name!" Kate responds with a smile.

"No," Valentin laughs, "and I think we like what it stands for."

"I think it sounds dangerous," Anya exclaims loudly.

"Well, you would. You're just like Mama. But we have to take risks to achieve justice. And London isn't the same as Moscow."

Anya bites her lip, watching him. She feels unable to string enough words together to make an intelligent comment in English and also remembers how Valentin always takes over a conversation with the power of his physical energy. She notices that Kate, while seemingly admiring, is on edge, and that Tom is very quiet. He has a sullen expression on his face.

Kate and Valentin go to make coffee in the kitchen and Anya overhears Kate say to him, "I wish you wouldn't ask these things of us, of me, of Eve."

THIRTY-FIVE

England, 2000

This isn't my fight, Kate admonishes herself, as she walks home from an event she has run for a law firm. Her heart is racing as she thinks of asking Eve to steal or copy papers at Igor Novikoff's house. *My fight is here, keeping my events business on course, ensuring that the charity has sufficient funds, making Tom's and my life happy enough. Why do I find myself so unable to say no to Valentin?*

As she returns home, she delights in having the house to herself now that Anya and Lara have returned to Moscow. She settles down to relax on the sofa with a book but, almost immediately, the phone rings and she has to get up and walk into her study.

"Hello?"

There is silence and then a click. Nothing. This has happened to her several times recently. She makes a mental note to mention it to Valentin, and as she thinks of this, the front doorbell rings and he is standing there, a red rose in his hand. He walks in and gives Kate the rose, taking her into his arms and pressing her close to him. She feels the breadth of his chest against her, his desire rippling through his body into hers. They haven't made love for several days, with Anya and Lara staying, but she pushes him away.

"Come on, Kate," he says, grasping her around the waist. "We only have a short time. I want you; don't deny me," and he kisses her longingly. Kate allows herself to follow him upstairs and goes through the motions but all the while thinking to herself, *what on earth am I doing? He is asking me to put my best friend in danger.*

Later, as Valentin makes coffee in the kitchen, Tom returns and grunts hello as they stand by the worktop.

As Valentin moves towards the front door to leave, he stops and looks at Kate, hissing forcefully in her ear, "Have you asked Eve yet? To get the papers for me?"

Kate hesitates. "No," she replies.

A dark expression clouds over his face. "I need this information, Kate," he says urgently. "I have told you so, many times now. Eve is the only one with access to Igor's house."

There is displeasure in his voice. Kate resents it but feels cowed by it, and she lets him out of the door.

Eve and Kate meet at a café in Kensington the next morning. Eve is glamorous as always in a camel coat and dark boots. They kiss and order cappuccinos and a pastry each.

"How are you?" she asks. "Have your Russian contingent enjoyed themselves?"

"Yes, absolutely," Kate replies. Inside her there is a heavy sense of dread at what she has to ask her friend. "We went to *Swan Lake* on their last night," she continues. "It was so poignant. Valentin told me about how they played the music from *Swan Lake* during the coup against Gorbachev in 1991. I hadn't realised the significance of this ballet in Russian history before, but apparently it has been played on their television screens at various moments in history when things were not well, when those in charge didn't want the population to have access to news. A delaying tactic, if you will. Valentin wanted the coup to succeed, so it has negative associations for him, but the audience at Covent Garden lapped it up."

"That sounds very special. I'm sure Anya and Lara enjoyed it. You have been very generous to them, Kate."

"They did love it. I think the production blew their minds. The staging was superb, and the principal dancer playing Prince Siegfried is Russian and flew like a bird across the stage. Lara was amazed."

Kate looks around the room for a moment, aware of how many foreign voices she is hearing on the streets of London these days. It is exciting and is transforming the city. There are new cafés and restaurants opening up all the time with varieties of food from all around the world.

"Eve, I need to ask you again," Kate lowers her voice, girding herself to ask the unaskable, "is there any way that you can get copies of Igor Novikoff's accounts and bank statements?"

Eve looks irritated. "How can you ask me this, Kate? You know how impossible it is. It could land me in enormous trouble if I betray the trust of a client."

"I know. But Igor is a really bad man, Eve. And his son is worse. We know that."

Eve takes a deep breath and pauses. She looks as if she is in pain, conflicted. "I know. I sense it too, and you have told me what has happened to you, and to Anya. But that makes it all the riskier, plus he is a client, and he knows so many of my other clients. This is my business, my livelihood, and I am doing good work for these people. If I got found out, it could ruin my consultancy forever."

Kate hesitates, feeling for her friend, then ploughs on, "Yes, but sometimes we have to do what is right, don't we? I am also in jeopardy because it could be that the Russians who have donated to the charity will also take umbrage if they find out, because they know that you and I are friends. But Igor should not get away with fraud, theft, murder, should he? And hopefully he will never find out."

Eve shakes her head, biting her lip, and sits in silence for a while. "Come with me then, Kate," she says suddenly, in a challenging tone. "Now. To his house. It's just up the road. I can pretend to measure up something in his study. You look at his desk and take photos. We can pretend you are taking photos of the room for my designs."

Kate freezes. She knows it is cowardly but it is one thing to ask Eve to do it, and that is bad enough, but to have to do this herself terrifies her. Yet she can hardly refuse when it is Kate herself demanding that Eve put herself at risk. "Bloody Valentin," she mutters under her breath, then says, "oh God, yes, OK then. It scares me stiff, but of course I should do this with you."

Eve nods, calls the waitress for the bill, and they throw their coins into the saucer, put their coats on, and Eve strides out of the café with deliberation. Kate follows, her footsteps feeling like lead as she drags them towards Igor's house, a huge white stucco affair, with pillars on either side of the large, shiny, black door.

"It's bulletproof," Eve whispers as she stands at the door and rings the bell. Kate raises her eyebrows. It's just a hint of what this man is all about.

The door is opened by a huge, bald man, dressed all in black. There is a gun holster over his shoulder, and he makes no effort to hide it. Eve tells him she needs to measure and take photos in Igor's study. The man shrugs and lets her in. He has seen her before many times.

The two women walk into the study, a large booklined room with a high ceiling and a massive chandelier dangling over his enormous mahogany desk, the desk of a man who needs to look big in front of others. On it are stacks of folders and files, pens, a coffee cup still full of dark liquid.

"The one thing about Igor is that he is not organised. I don't understand why he doesn't get himself a better secretary, but I think he is screwing the young girl who works for him at the moment. That's probably where he is now, upstairs with her, fucking," Eve says softly. "She's absolutely hopeless, but she's tall and thin, with the longest legs in history, and always wears the shortest skirts and lowest tops, and I can see him slavering over her as she moves around the room."

Kate listens, horrified to hear that this man might

actually be in the house at the moment. "Let's get on with it," she whispers back.

Eve nods. "Here, take this," handing her a small camera. "You look around his desk, and I shall pretend to measure up the rest of the room. He does want me to do a makeover at some stage, but I can't imagine why, as it looks amazing already, doesn't it."

It does. Lush, plush, over-the-top luxury. Kate takes Eve's neat Olympus camera and stands at the desk. She picks up the folder at the top. Of course, the trouble she has omitted to consider is the fact that most of it is in Russian, so she hasn't a clue what it says. She looks through a few folders to get a sense of the material she is dealing with, then comes to some invoices, some in Russian, some in English.

She quickly takes photos of the top ones and moves on. She finds it hard to believe that he would keep his bank statements open on his desk so investigates the bottom drawer. It's locked. Kate ferrets around in the top drawer and, to her relief, tinged with fear, underneath a pile of papers, she finds a key that fits. Rifling through the disorganised papers, stored higgledy-piggledy, she crouches on the floor beside the desk trying to make sense of the documents. Eve busies herself around the room taking measurements of the windows, shelves, doorways, and writing them ostentatiously on a large pad so that anyone coming into the room will see what she is doing.

Kate's hands are shaking and her heart pumping as she comes across some pages that look like bank statements. She hastily photographs what she can see, still mind-blown that they should be seemingly so easy to find. She searches below and finds some letters and invoices. She doesn't know why but she feels they could be important, even though she can't read the language, so she photographs as many as she can.

"Kate, stop! There's someone just outside the door," Eve gasps in a hushed voice. Kate freezes, then bundles up the papers she has been photographing and shoves them back in the drawer, secreting the camera in her handbag.

The door opens and Kate stands up, trying to look as calm as she can. Igor Novikoff stands in the doorway, a stocky figure in a checked shirt open at the neck and baggy beige trousers. A frown crosses his face as he sees them.

"Eve," he says in a creepily charming voice. "I wasn't expecting you today?"

"No, Igor, I was passing and just wanted to measure up to get new designs for your study. As Kate was with me, she has been helping me. You've met before, haven't you?"

He frowns. "Yes," he says slowly, and he pauses, his hands in his pockets and his eyes surveying the room. "I didn't know you worked with Eve?" he addresses Kate. Kate finds no words to answer him, and he continues, "Hmm, well you finish off now. OK. Now!"

Kate starts to walk around the desk, towards the door, and suddenly realises she still has the key to the bottom drawer in her hand and wonders how to put it back in the top drawer without him seeing. But he is standing in the doorway watching them, so there is no way she can do this. She slips it into the pocket of her coat, as deftly as she can, and walks around the desk.

Novikoff doesn't move, blocking their exit. Eve and Kate stand before him like two schoolgirls facing their head teacher, although Kate knows that he is capable of far more evil than any teacher she has ever known. He scrutinises them silently, without moving, and Kate begins to wonder whether he will ever let them out. Then, eventually, he removes his hand from the door frame and lets them pass.

"Nice to see you again, Ms Chisholm," he puffs into Kate's ear as she passes him. Then, as they reach the front door, he asks, "And how is your nice friend Mr Kotov these days?"

Kate doesn't know how to answer so hurries out of the front door, pretending she hasn't heard him. She is aware that he follows them to the top of the steps and stands watching as they walk away down the street, the key burning a hole in Kate's pocket.

THIRTY-SIX

England, 2000

Kate calls up Valentin as soon as she gets back to the house. "I've got what you needed." He comes immediately and, as they stand in the hall, she passes him the camera, but he will not take Novikoff's key.

"I will put it with the other envelopes upstairs," he tells her. "I may need it another time. Igor may not even notice it's missing."

"I am sure he will. He terrifies me and I hate keeping this stuff of yours upstairs. I just don't understand why you don't find somewhere else to keep these things, especially now you have another place in London," Kate asks him, looking up, but he's running up her stairs without answering. When he comes down, she continues, "Valentin, listen to me, you keep saying it's safe but—"

"Bye, I've got to go. I return to Russia now," he

interrupts, giving her a perfunctory kiss. "You've done good work. Thank you."

"I have my plane ticket booked to come over to Moscow soon, remember," she says, wishing he had been the one to say he was looking forward to seeing her in Russia again.

"Yes, of course," Valentin speaks quickly, looking at his watch.

"But please, what's in the information I have upstairs?" She follows him to the front door.

"I keep telling you! It's better you don't know, Kate. Just take care of it so if they – Novikoff or the FSB – raid my room or take my laptop again, at least I know there are copies here. It's crucial. For the world. Tell Eve I'll get her camera back to her."

She tries to grab his arm to stop him but he simply says, "I must go," and turns and leaves. She's left standing in the hallway, acknowledging that he has again dismissed her concerns.

Tom is packing up to catch the train to Durham. The rain beats against the windscreen as Kate drives him up to King's Cross.

"Don't come into the station, Mum" he insists. "Just drop me here in the forecourt. I can go by myself from there."

She hesitates but accepts his suggestion and kisses his stubbly cheek as he moves to get out of the car.

"Keep in touch, Tom," she says and hears a slightly desperate tone in her voice.

"I will, Ma. Bye!" And she watches his back as he turns

and walks away into the station, pulling his large case behind him, without a look back at her. Tears run down her face as she recalls what good companions they have been these years, even if she has been busy with the charity conferences and the occasional trip to Russia, and Tom with his studying. As a traffic warden comes towards her, notebook in hand, Kate wipes her eyes, blows her nose, starts the car and heads back towards Notting Hill.

The house feels desolate as she lets herself in. She surveys the detritus of their breakfast, left on the table from the morning, and clears up the cereal packets, puts the bowls in the dishwasher and washes out the teapot.

Then she walks into Tom's room and sits on his bed. She's surrounded here by all his books and posters, his guitar sitting propped against his wardrobe, clothes on the floor. Kate picks up each item slowly, gently, sniffing it to capture his scent, the scent that is part of her life, her being. She forces herself to throw everything into the laundry basket and lug it down the stairs to the washing machine. It's the beginning of the next part of her life, and she knows she's going to have to get used to it.

The evening after Tom has left, Kate makes herself go on a dating website. She scrolls through photos and puffed-up biographies of various men. She's not hopeful as she finds them dull in comparison to the adrenalin current that runs through her body even now when she thinks of Valentin. She has had no news of him, which makes the longing all the more intense. She can only presume he returned safely to Russia.

Seeking to fill her time, she drives down to the maternity home the next day and is delighted to meet a mother who has just given birth to twins. The happiness on the face of the young woman is tangible, and she expresses her relief to be able to stay in the home for a few days so as to acclimatise herself to managing the babies. She's a single mother, her own family living in Sri Lanka, so she is feeling very alone as her husband left her recently. Kate is glad that she can offer the girl peace and support.

As she walks around the building, looking at mums breastfeeding their babies in quiet corners, the scent of aromatic candles filling the air, she feels content that she has done a good job. She stands and looks out at the rich green lawns, the trees turning colour for the autumn, and remembers the challenges of the last few years in creating this space, the voice of her mother's doubts. Edward Babbington's pessimism still echoes in her ears. "I've done it," she says to herself. "So far, so good."

She spends the afternoon talking to the clinical and admin staff, checking the kitchens and ensuring that the menus offer healthy food. As she looks around, she is deeply aware that she could not have done any of this without Edith Carter's legacy, nor without the donations of the Russian network in London and her own support team of friends and colleagues.

As she makes herself supper that night, the phone rings. There is no one there when she answers, just a click. She realises she forgot to ask Valentin about these calls. She hopes he will be in touch soon so they can talk about it, but she hasn't heard from him since he collected Eve's camera. She has presumed that the calls are deliberate and designed to unsettle her.

When the phone rings again a few minutes later, Kate stops, not sure what to do, but thinking it could be Tom, she answers it, hesitantly.

"Kate, Edward Babbington here." His voice sounds so harsh in her vulnerable mood. "We have to have a trustees meeting to discuss the donations and check that we are all on the same page, that there is no hint of money laundering."

"Yes, yes, I agree, Edward." Kate jumps to his attention. "I'll send an email out with a suggested date."

"It needs to be soon. Next week. Especially in view of tonight's news."

"What news?" Kate asks. She hasn't had the radio on as she had been listening to Bach's cello suites to soothe her.

"That fellow who came to the Savoy dinner, Nikolai. He's been found dead. Looks like poisoning."

THIRTY-SEVEN

Russia, 2000

"I'm going out to see Mama... I mean Yulia," Lara hastily corrects herself as she calls to Anya.

"Oh, I thought we were going to have supper together tonight?" Anya replies.

"No, she needs me to babysit for a while, and I won't be back. I have to study at the hospital later, so I shall stay over." Lara kisses her aunt quickly on the cheek, then buttons up her blue wool coat and goes out of the door.

Anya looks around her. The apartment feels both cramped, after her visit to Kate's London home, and yet empty, and she wonders how her life will change now that Lara is so independent. She still needs support, Anya thinks to herself, for her diabetes, to make sure she doesn't get pulled into circles of friends who persuade her to drink too much or forget her condition. Anya worries all the time about her but is helpless to play any more part as Lara wants to be in control of her own health now. Anya can see that she needs to move the focus of her concerns more towards herself and her shop.

As she potters around the kitchen, the doorbell rings from the street. Anya presses the intercom. It's Valentin. His voice sounds different, almost unintelligible. What is he doing here? She thought he was in London. She buzzes him in.

A few minutes later he is standing at her door, his head covered in a hood, his shoulders hunched as if he is fending off the wind.

"Valentin, what are you doing here?" Anya asks. He pushes past her into the kitchen.

"Shut the door!" he commands in an urgent whisper. Anya does as she's told, and as she looks around, she sees that his face is bleeding, his right eye bulging and bloody.

"Valentin! What happened?"

"They're after me," he says bitterly, as he sits down on a chair at the kitchen table.

"Who?"

"I don't know, Anya," he says irritably, as if it's her fault, as if she has asked a stupid question. "It could be Igor Novikoff, or it could be the FSB. I don't know – they're all in it together. But I was jumped on as I walked out of the airport in Moscow this morning. I came back as soon as Kate gave me photographs she took in Novikoff's house. I got the first flight out of London. But someone was following me. Someone knew. They beat me, but I fought back and managed to get away and catch a train here. I have business to do here in Orel. And I told you my army training would come in useful. I fool them every time."

"Did they take anything?"

"Yes, my laptop. Yet again. I'm getting used to this now, and everything is backed up. And I held on to the most important thing." He pulls Eve's black camera out of his pocket. "I have bought another laptop on the way here."

Anya doesn't ask for any more information. She doesn't want to know. She turns and pulls a bowl out of the kitchen cupboard, walks to the sink and fills it with warm water and a little salt. She takes a kitchen cloth from the drawer beside the sink and dips it into the bowl. Gingerly, gently, she washes his eye with the soothing water and washes the cut on his cheek.

"Oh, Brother, what have you got yourself into?" she asks, missing their mother, wondering how to protect him.

"I have evidence, Anya, evidence that Novikoff has murdered seven people now, defrauded others of their money, stashed his money in foreign bank accounts, in London, Panama. He needs to be exposed for what he is," Valentin tells her, with fury in his voice.

"But, Valentin, is it worth being beaten up for, maybe dying for? You know that if he has murdered others, he could murder you." Anya puts her hands on his broad shoulders and massages them.

"Someone has to do it, Anya. That is the role of the investigative reporter. We are here to tell the truth where and when we can. And I have information on the President too. They're in it together."

Anya catches her breath as she thinks of the implications of this. They sit silently side by side at the table for a while. There's a small chopping board in front of her with half-sliced onions and carrots, a leg of chicken, the supper she was about to make for herself and Lara.

"You want to eat something?" she asks him, ruffling his hair. He is her little brother again, needing her protection.

"That would be good, thanks. And I need to stay here tonight, maybe for a few days."

It isn't a question. He looks up at Anya with his deep brown eyes, bruises turning purple as they speak, and her heart sinks. He is the last person she wants to be staying in her tiny flat, but how can she say no to him?

"We hardly have room for two of us, let alone three," she says feebly.

"I'll sleep on the floor of the kitchen. I just need to stay, Anya. You're my sister. Family. Who else can I turn to?"

And so Anya nods and, when Lara returns unexpectedly early after supper, she gives her father a huge hug, and her face lights up with delight at the thought of him staying with them. She fusses over his wounds and treats him like a long-lost hero.

"You can have my bed, Papa. I shall sleep on the floor between you and Auntie. It will be like camping."

Suddenly, the room that had felt so empty a short time before feels very full again, and Anya finds herself longing for the space that just a few moments ago she had hated. Somehow, they all manage to get a reasonable night's sleep, tucked in like sardines in the small bedroom. Lara goes to medical school and Valentin stays to work on his article.

Anya has a busy time at the health shop the next morning and puts a notice in the street to remind her regular customers of special offers. She enjoys welcoming people in and chatting about their health, the supplements they might need, the food they are eating.

She makes her way home at the end of the day and finds Valentin in the kitchen. He is angry, she can see, as soon as she walks through the door.

"Fucking police. In London I had got used to not having to take my documents out with me every time I walked around. More fool me. Of course, as soon as I am back here in Orel, I forget them, and I get stopped. '*Documenti!*' they say. They push me up against a wall. I had my hands in my pockets. 'Pleased to see me?' One of them pushes up close to me, filthy brute, chewing gum in my face, saliva dribbling from his mouth. I didn't have my fucking papers, but I did have some dollars. 'Let me give you something to show my respect for you,' I say to them obsequiously. Of course, he wanted more, so I had to give him all the dollars I had, around $200, then they let me go. The pigs," he spits out the word.

Anya looks at him, this brother of hers who is always causing trouble. "Who else is in all this with you?" she asks.

"Mikhail, my colleague from the old days at the newspaper. He is nervous, thinks they're getting too close. He is planning to try to get to Istanbul; he has a cousin there. He will get his wife and kids out after him."

"If he is worried, then surely you should be too? It wasn't sensible to return to Russia or to come here to Orel," Anya challenges him.

He shrugs dismissively. "No one saw me come here. They tried, but I shook them off after they attacked me. I know they didn't follow me out of the airport complex; I was too quick for them. I reckon I am as safe as I can be here for now. I need to get the report typed up online and circulate it. Then I can go back to Moscow. I have enough evidence now. I need the kitchen table, Anya. Can you go next door? Maybe to Natalya's flat for a while so I can concentrate?"

Anya resents his request. It's her apartment, small as it is, and he is taking it over. It is typical of him, always expecting to get exactly what he wants. But she has no words, and a few minutes later, she knocks on Natalya's door and asks if she can watch her television with her.

When Anya returns to her flat later, she finds Valentin has gone. No sign of him, but his laptop and papers are strewn all over the table. Anya curses. He might have tidied it all up. She doesn't dare touch it and feels her hands could catch fire just from being close to his business.

She's tired so she gets undressed and takes a shower. The water is cool; she can't get it hot. There's always a problem with the boiler. She shivers but feels refreshed as she steps out. Then she hears someone rustling around in the kitchen.

"Valentin?" she calls, but there is no answer. She's puzzled. "Valentin? Lara?" Again, no response. Now she freezes, wrapping the towel around her. She doesn't know whether to go out and see who it is, or whether to stay hidden in the shower room.

She hears grunting, shuffling of papers, footsteps thudding around her kitchen, footsteps she does not recognise.

"Who's there?" Her voice sounds feeble and seems to make no difference to the activities outside the door. Her temper is raised now – how dare someone walk around her place without her permission. She unlocks the bathroom door to peer around the door frame and sees a large man in a black balaclava. He is grabbing Valentin's papers and laptop, and she sees him move to the bedroom and find more papers hidden under Valentin's mattress. He is working fast, not making any effort to be silent. She is transfixed, can find nothing to say, and just watches while he puts everything into a khaki green holdall, zips it up and makes his way to the door. Noticing Anya, he stops for a second.

"You can't take that!" She finally manages to get the words out.

"Who says? You?" He looks at her derisively, spits on the floor and exits.

THIRTY-EIGHT

Russia, 2000

It's late, and Valentin hasn't returned. Lara has called to say she is staying with Yulia tonight to babysit her son. Anya is relieved and doesn't tell her about the intruder. But she can't stop shivering. She bolts the door then goes to bed and wraps the blankets around her. Her teeth are chattering, and she keeps having flashbacks of the man in the kitchen.

Eventually, she falls asleep and is woken a short time later by a soft knocking on the front door. She lies there still, unsure what to do, then puts her dressing gown on and tiptoes as silently as possible to the door, cursing the creaky floorboard.

"Anya!" She hears Valentin's whisper the other side of the door. "Anya, let me in."

Anya unbolts the door. Valentin is standing on the

other side, white as a sheet, his cuts and black eye still looking hideous and painful. He slips in and she shuts the door. He surveys the scene in the kitchen, the place where his laptop and papers had been. Now there is nothing.

"Did you clear it all away?" he says accusingly.

"No. There was a man." Anya's teeth start chattering again, and it is hard for her to get the words out. "I was in the shower. I heard him in here. I was terrified."

"But what happened? How could you have let him take away my laptop and papers, Anya!" He is screaming at her now. "You know how crucial they are to my work!"

She takes a deep breath and says very quietly and calmly, "I did not 'let him' take away your laptop or papers. I had no choice. I was in the shower. I had no clothes on. This man somehow entered my flat – *my* flat you notice – without breaking down the door. I don't know how. Did you give a key to anyone? He was a large man. I was alone. What did you want me to do – fight him? And where on earth have you been all this time?"

Valentin stops pacing the room, pauses and looks at his sister. "No, I'm sorry Anya. Of course not." He comes over to her and puts his arms around her shoulders. "There was nothing you could do."

"How did he get in if he didn't have to break the door?"

"I don't know, do I. He must have got hold of a key from the caretaker or something. You didn't have the bolts on, did you?"

"No, of course not, because I thought you or Lara might come back to the flat. Anyway, you assured me that you were such a brilliant soldier and no one was trailing you."

Valentin bows his head. She's not sure whether he's embarrassed.

"I'll make you some tea. I need to make a call, Anya. Do you want to go back to bed?"

"I'm not going to sleep now," Anya replies.

She goes back to bed, though, just to get warm. He brings her some tea. "This should calm your nerves."

"Where were you all this time?" she repeats, but he doesn't answer, just turns and leaves the room.

She hears him next door, talking on the phone to his old friend, Lev. He was in Afghanistan with him. Anya hears him tell Lev that he must get out of Russia. Her heart sinks. She shall be left behind here, with bad men watching her, following her.

About an hour later, she hears the doorbell go. Valentin buzzes someone in and then a few minutes later opens the flat door. Anya climbs out of bed to see what is happening. She sees the two men hug. Lev is shorter than Valentin, with close cropped hair like an American soldier, a cigarette in his mouth. He has black shadows of a beard around his chin.

Valentin and Lev talk in low voices in the kitchen. Anya tries to hear what they are saying as she sits on the end of her bed. She hears the words Finland... passport... dollars... car... She watches as Lev pulls a camera out of his bag and takes a photograph of Valentin against the white kitchen wall.

"I've processed those photos you gave me," Lev tells Valentin. "I will get them to you." Then he takes his leave and, when he is at the door, he turns and puts his hand inside his jacket. He pulls out a gun. "Here," he says to

Valentin. "Take it."

"Really?" Valentin asks, and Anya sees Lev nod.

"If they have already traced what you know, then you are a dead man. You remember how to use it?" Lev asks.

"I haven't held one of these since our days in Afghanistan."

"It's like riding a bicycle, Valentin. You will know how to use it if you need to," Lev says and hurries out of the door. "See you downstairs in a couple of hours."

Anya hears him run down the stairs. Valentin comes back into the bedroom.

"I have to go, Anya. I have to get back to Moscow first, to pick up some things. I have copies of some of my investigations there. Lev will find me a car to take me to Moscow and on to Finland. He's getting me a passport tonight. I'm not sure what I shall do when I get to Finland, but I shall probably try to get back to Kate's house in London and lie quiet for a while. I can't fly straight there because they'll be looking for me at the airport."

Anya heaves a large sigh. It feels as if she is emptying all the air in her body.

"What kind of mess have you got yourself into? Got us into?" She looks at him, exhausted. "I worry about Kate and Tom too…"

"It's worth it, Anya. I must expose Novikoff. He's close to the President, so that means he has links to the FSB. I haven't a chance if I stay in Russia. And he isn't the only bastard screwing our country. But I don't get the impression that Novikoff wants to get on the wrong side of the law in the UK. I guess he wants that escape route."

Spontaneously, Anya gets up, goes to him and hugs

him. "My little brother, you have bitten off more than you can chew this time, I think."

He accepts her embrace, and she can feel his body slump under her hold, feel the fatigue that is draining his system.

"You go to bed now. I shall let myself out in a little while. I'll have to be very quiet. Lev will meet me in the square around the corner, then I shall have to go to the fountain and a car will pick me up. I'm not sure if it will be tonight or tomorrow night. I'll have to hide in the boot, probably. Once I reach Finland, hopefully I shall be safe. I'll try to get word to you, and to Lara."

"May God be with you, Valentin." Anya kisses the top of his head, the sensation of his thick hair brushing against her lips.

She goes back to bed, but she can't sleep. She's wound up like a spring.

THIRTY-NINE

Russia, 2000

It's nearly dawn when Valentin makes his way to Lev's basement room, leaving Anya to sleep. Lev gives Valentin a hard look as he lets him in. Valentin is tired and unshaven, holding a small bag, ready for his journey.

"You're a liability." Lev sighs. "All this ferreting around in the dirt of our leaders will get you nowhere but buried. I don't know why you do it."

Valentin shrugs. "I can't stop now, Lev. I have so much information. People in the West need to understand."

"But you can't do anything about it, can you, Valentin? It's too big for you. Be careful, just retreat now while you can."

"Honestly you wouldn't say that if you knew the extent of the propaganda and influence that the Kremlin guys are filtering through. Their aim is to disrupt and destabilise the US and Europe. That won't do any of us any good."

"I can get you to Finland but no further. You have to make your own way from there. Have you somewhere to stay in London?" Lev asks.

"Yes, I have a friend there."

Lev raises his eyebrows with a wry smile. "There's always a woman!"

Lev brews them both a strong coffee and tells Valentin that he will have to wait until the following night now to make the journey. He tells him to get some more sleep while he busies himself with the documents. Valentin lies down on the scruffy sofa and is asleep in seconds.

Valentin sleeps fitfully on and off as the next day dawns. When he wakes, he sees Lev meticulously creating his documents. He scuffs the papers to make them look old and used, then hands them to Valentin.

"Your name is Yuri Baranov. You must memorise all the details in case you are stopped. They took your old documents, so they shouldn't have any great suspicion about you, unless the FSB have circulated your photo, which they may well have done, so keep your hood up when you can." Valentin takes the documents and flicks through them.

"The car's waiting for you outside," Lev tells him the next night, around midnight. "Good luck."

Valentin lets himself out and sees a battered grey car waiting for him across the street by the fountain. The driver, a skinny man of about fifty with grey hair, gets out.

"Here I am," Valentin tells the driver.

"Andrey," the man growls to introduce himself. "Have you got the money?"

"I gave Lev the money," Valentin tells him.

"Ha, no, that was just the deposit," he sneers. "$500 and I will get you to Moscow, then Finland. Cheap at the price."

This represents almost all the money Valentin has available. He hasn't a clue what he will do once he crosses the Finnish border. But he has little choice.

He pulls the rubles out of his pocket. "Here."

"No dollars?"

"No," Valentin lies. He has to keep these for his transfer to London.

Andrey sighs and seems unsure what to do next but eventually gets into the car and counts the notes, while Valentin continues to pull himself into the shadows of a doorway. Every second matters, and the man seems to take forever. Eventually, Andrey climbs out of the car and opens the back door for Valentin.

"OK," he grunts and lifts up the back seat to show a hidden compartment below. He shoves Valentin down into the cramped, dark space.

"How do I breathe?"

Andrey kicks to point to a small mesh grill in the floor of the car.

"Won't I get exhaust fumes?"

"Take it or leave it." The man shrugs.

Unwillingly, Valentin climbs in and watches as the seat base closes above him, leaving him scrunched up in the dark. An acrid smell of exhaust, oil and other undefinable chemicals make it hard to breathe.

It's a long way to Finland, and before that he has to get to his Moscow room to collect his research papers, without being seen. Is it all worth it, he wonders for a second, this endless running?

From the cold confinement of his hidden compartment near the chassis of the battered Lada, Valentin can sense the driver, Andrey, brake and park. He hears Andrey open his door quietly, leaving it on the latch so as not to disturb the sleeping neighbours, then walk to the back passenger door. He undoes the catch above Valentin's head, lifting up the back seats, and helps Valentin to extricate himself from the mesh cage below, in which he had been travelling, curled up like a foetus. Valentin pulls his long legs out and manoeuvres himself onto the darkness of the pavement. He hesitates. Then, as an afterthought, he grabs his laptop from the car, not wanting to leave it with Andrey, and quickly slides into the shadows at the back entrance to his apartment block. He lets himself in.

Once in the hallway, he starts to climb the dimly lit stairs. The grey light of dawn seeps through the landing window. He stops for a moment, leaning his back against the wall, exhausted, cursing the fact that there is no lift in the apartment block. The laptop is heavy on his shoulder, but he's grateful that his old army colleague Lev has sourced it for him after his last was stolen. Reaching the fifth floor, he puts the laptop down beside his front door. Flicking his dark hair from his eyes, he pulls the key from his trouser pocket but, as he fits it in the lock, the door swings open. He stiffens.

Silently, he inches himself through the wooden door, his body taut. He pushes open the kitchen door to his right with his foot, then the bathroom door. No sign of anyone. The small studio room, that doubles as a workspace and bedroom, is ahead of him, and he suddenly sees a flicker of light. He backs himself against the wall, his heart pounding. What to do, run, or risk being killed?

Taking control of himself, he pulls his body up to his full height, feeling his strength as he does so. *Remember, Valentin, you were a soldier, you fought in Afghanistan*, he thinks to himself. *You can tackle this.*

As he moves forward, a man, short, stocky in a black anorak, barges like a streak through the door, throwing Valentin back against the wall so hard that he bangs his head. The man runs down the short hallway and out onto the landing. It takes Valentin a moment to right himself, then he chases after him, but the man is quick as a bullet, already several floors below on the stairs and out of sight.

Valentin follows, jumping over the banisters to the next landing. He wants to see the man's face, be sure he would recognise him, but he is out of practice. Those army days were many years ago now and the intruder has vanished out of the apartment block and halfway down the street by the time Valentin reaches the door. He sighs, gasping for breath. He'll never catch him now.

Wearily he runs up the stairs for a second time. He knows Andrey won't wait for long. At his doorway, he stops to collect his laptop. It's gone. He and Lev had spent most of the night downloading his articles and research. All gone. Again. He punches the wall in fury.

"How could I have been so stupid?" he curses himself, but he didn't know Andrey, couldn't trust him, so he couldn't have left it in the car.

He runs to his desk in the studio and sees that the drawers have been rifled. His research papers are everywhere. He's worked hard to hide away in recent months, to move from one place to another, but they have found him again. Taken everything. He gathers up what he can, but he can't afford to keep Andrey waiting. His fellow journalist, Alina, had been shot outside her apartment block last month. He knows he could be the next target. His mind works fast. He reaches for his mobile phone and dials London.

"Kate," he whispers her name with urgency, "I need your help."

FORTY

Russia, 2000

Valentin aches from the top of his spine down to his tailbone as the car bumps along the road. His long body is forced into a foetal position, his neck bent over, his hands almost in prayer. He has managed to sleep for about an hour, exhausted from his exploits the night before.

There's no cushioning for his bones. The car's suspension lifts Valentin into the air on every turn, his skull crushed against the steel of the chassis. Andrey takes no heed of his hidden cargo as he accelerates hard towards the border.

Valentin can tell they are travelling fast, the engine of the old car straining on hills as they leave Moscow and head north. The road slips away beneath the mesh vent, cold air tinged with fumes passing into Valentin's cramped compartment.

Doubts fill his mind, questioning what he will do when he reaches Finland, how he will find his way to London with little cash. The fire for his *exposés* still burns in his belly. Taxpayers' money stolen, the hard-earned rubles of people so poor they could hardly feed their children. But he knows he will be tortured, or killed, if he is caught. A vision of the notorious Lefortovo Prison flits before his eyes. He has heard of the brutality carried out in the outbuildings of these detention centres, of the cells where lights are left on continuously, where sewage spews all over the floor, of beatings and torture. In the darkness of the car journey, his mind runs riot.

After a while he can tell they are in the countryside. The roads are long and straight. Then the car slows, and he can hear Andrey shout to someone. Valentin freezes, then realises that Andrey has simply stopped at a garage for fuel. He longs to get out, to relieve his bladder, to stretch and breathe but realises he has not worked out a system to signal his needs to Andrey. He stays still until they are on the road again and then starts knocking on the side of the compartment with his knuckles.

There seems initially to be no response to his needs, so he raps harder and eventually he can feel the car slow down again. It feels as if they are crossing from the road onto a grassy track. He can see mud and earth beneath him and understands that Andrey is taking the car into some wooded area.

As they stop, Andrey opens the door to the compartment and helps Valentin out. Valentin can hardly move. His body feels paralysed from being in the same position for so long. He hobbles out and sees that they have parked on a track in a forest, some distance from the road. He relieves himself against a tree, then collapses on the ground, allowing his body gradually to unfold along the long grass beneath the trees. He stretches his hands above his head, points his toes, rolls from side to side, then eases himself back into a stand.

Andrey lights a cigarette. The two men lean against the tree. They both know it is safer not to talk. The less Andrey knows about his 'package', the safer he will be, and the safer Valentin too, should Andrey ever get questioned.

After about ten minutes, Andrey signals with his head that Valentin should return to his compartment, and they set off again. Hour after hour passes in agony until Valentin realises they have reached the Finnish border. He can hear the guards questioning Andrey, can hear dogs barking in the distance. Andrey's voice sounds calm and gruff. The guards on the Russian side shout at him to get out of the car to show his documents. There's silence for a few minutes, and Valentin lies as still as he can.

Then he hears one of the guards raise his voice to Andrey and demand to inspect the car. "Open the boot," he shouts. "Open the doors... open the bonnet," and Andrey obeys their commands, quietly doing exactly as he is told. Valentin is suddenly aware of a torch being shone under the car and holds his breath. The guards kick the tyres and bumpers until eventually they have to accept that they can find nothing untoward, and Andrey is waved on through to the Finnish border. Here the guards are calm and matter of fact. Valentin can hear Andrey pass them his papers again and, eventually, after about five minutes, the car starts to move once more. Valentin shuts his eyes and breathes a sigh of relief. He is free.

A few minutes later, he feels the car brake and turn off the road. "Out," says Andrey, opening the compartment again.

"Where are we?" Valentin asks. All he can see in the darkness is forest, silhouetted against the night sky.

"Finland," Andrey mutters. "This is it."

"But we're in the middle of nowhere," Valentin argues. "You can't leave me here – it could be miles to the nearest town."

"I am paid to take you to the border," Andrey replies. "That's what I have done. That's it." With this he turns and climbs back into the car without a second look.

Valentin runs to open the door. He tries to pull Andrey out of the driving seat, but he is too slow. Andrey accelerates as the door swings shut and Valentin is left standing. He clutches his backpack and looks around him, a sinking feeling in his stomach. He is tired, cold, thirsty and hungry, but all he can see around him are trees and darkness.

FORTY-ONE

Russia, 2000

It's a sunny November day in Orel. Anya has not heard from Valentin since he left. The air is crisp as she takes a bus to her health food shop. As she steps onto the pavement outside her shop, she notices three armed policemen in black combat gear standing beside a line of yellow tape that blocks off the doorway to the shop.

She gets the key out of her handbag and signals to one of the policemen. "I need to open up the shop. What's happening? Has there been a burglary? Did the alarm go off?"

The policeman looks at her and immediately takes her by the arm, dragging her towards him.

"You can't go in there. You have to come with us," he says in a gruff voice.

"Why? What do you mean?" Anya can feel the adrenalin pumping around her system.

"You're under arrest. You come with us," he repeats as one of the other police officers takes her other arm, almost lifting her off her feet.

"This must be a mistake. I have done nothing wrong. Who are you?" She raises her voice, hoping that someone passing nearby will hear her and come to her aid, but she sees pedestrians keeping their eyes down, or in a fixed stare ahead of them, others crossing to the other side of the road. They know well enough not to mix with armed police.

"We're the FDCS, the drug unit. Get in the car, now." He pulls her wrists behind her and cuffs them.

"But there are no illegal drugs here. We follow all the rules, the regulations. You must know that I do. I have done nothing wrong," Anya repeats, her voice catching in her throat as she begins to panic.

"Get in!" the officer commands, this time more forcefully, pushing her into the black car that is parked outside the shop. Anya hits her head as she lands ungraciously with a thump on the floor in the back of the car, her skirt rucked up over her thighs by the strength of the push. The jolt brings tears to her eyes.

"I need to ring my niece," she tells them. She sits on the back seat next to the third officer, a thin young man who looks uneasy as he sits beside her.

"No phone calls," the first officer says and lights a cigarette.

"But I must phone my niece," Anya repeats. "She's a student, she lives with me and needs to know where I am."

"No phone calls," the policeman replies curtly, blowing tobacco smoke towards Anya's face as he speaks.

She sits scrunched in the back seat. The three

policemen talk and laugh, smirking at her as they share crude jokes that she can understand.

They drive her to a red-brick building with large green gates. It is near the shopping centre, and she can see people going about their everyday lives, shopping and talking. It feels as if, just a few metres away, they are living some parallel life where everything is normal, and in here, in this car, nothing is normal.

Two of the police officers pull Anya out of the car. Their hands hurt her arms as they hold her. They lead her through a hallway that reminds her of scenes from Bosch's painting, *The Last Judgement*. A throng of police are manhandling drunks, addicts and pale, fearful-looking people, pushing and barging past them. Anya is taken to a small room in the basement and left there. They lock the door behind them as they leave.

The walls are pale green, smeared with dirt and damp. There's a wooden desk with iron legs and two iron chairs with plastic seats. Her mobile phone has been taken away as she entered the police station. She is offered no food or water, and she's thirsty.

Anya sits and waits. No one comes. She hears sounds outside in the corridors, people shouting, some screams. She bangs on the door. She needs the toilet. She wants to find out what is happening. She becomes uncomfortable and has to walk up and down to take her mind off the need to empty her bladder.

Eventually, after what felt like forever, a man dressed in a shiny blue suit comes in and hands her a paper, detailing the charges against her. She looks at the form and can't seem to read it properly.

"What is this about?" she asks him, confused. Her mind isn't working well.

"You don't have a licence to sell opiates," he says in a monotone.

"I don't sell opiates," Anya replies, shocked.

"You sell a lemon herbal supplement for sleep. It has been recategorised as an illegal drug."

"You know that isn't true," she exclaims. "I have traded legally for five years. I have always abided by every regulation. This is completely unjust." Anya can't believe what she is hearing; it must be a mistake.

"We shall be keeping you in detention. You will be given clothes."

"But I must let my niece, Lara, know. She's at medical school. She lives with me. I am her guardian. She is diabetic. She has no one else," Anya argues, her voice breaking.

"No phone calls," the man says coldly. "This is the end of this conversation."

"But she will be worried about me... and my health shop. There's no one to run it. I have put so much work into building it up—"

"No calls!" he interrupts her angrily.

"But you can't do this to me..." Anya feels she is rambling incoherently, her words falling on deaf ears.

"Quiet. Sit down!" he shouts.

She sits on the chair. Her brain can't compute what is happening. Nothing makes sense. A short time later, a female police officer comes into the room.

"Clothes off!" she barks.

"No!" Anya screams. "This can't be happening to me. I have done nothing wrong."

The woman steps forward and starts to manhandle her, undoing her shirt. "Clothes off! Now!"

Anya's hands tremble so much she can hardly undo her buttons. She has to remove every item of clothing. She's told to bend over and is strip-searched before being handed some prison clothing. The woman then hands her over to two policemen, who are waiting outside the door. They bundle her along the corridor and into a van outside.

She arrives, after some time, at what seems to be another detention centre, outside the city. They push her into a dark cell with two other women. There is one small window high on the wall, and she is struck by the smell of drains. She feels her whole identity has been removed. No one knows her; no one knows where she is. There is no one to tell Lara or to check her levels with her. Valentin will be far away in Finland or London. She hasn't heard from him since he left her flat the night Lev came round, but she knows her arrest has more to do with him than her.

She falls onto the hard iron bed cursing, "Valentin, you bastard. What have you done?"

FORTY-TWO

Russia, 2000

Anya wakes the next morning to a cold, grey light seeping through the dirty patch of window in the cell. The woman in the bunk above her is snoring loudly, the other whimpering in her sleep. The window is built too high up in the wall for Anya to be able to see anything but sky. She shivers, crossing her arms around her for warmth and comfort. She knows she shall have to use the bucket again soon but is putting it off for as long as she can hold out. It feels like the ultimate degradation.

She lies on her back and tries to calm her mind, just watching the clouds move past the tiny panes of the window. Her thoughts are racing, and her body feels as if it has been plugged into an electrical socket. Every part of her is alert, fearful, unbelieving.

Suddenly, a guard in a mud-brown uniform bangs open the door with a clang.

"You!" he shouts at Anya. "Get up! You come with me."

She jumps up, hitting her head on the bunk above as she rises. She is trembling and now wishes she had used the bucket earlier as she realises that she has to use it before she goes with him. She asks him to turn away, but he doesn't, so she sits on the bucket, face to the wall, eyes shut, then, as she finishes, she stands and straightens her crumpled prison clothes. There's nowhere to wash. She hasn't slept well and hasn't eaten for twenty-four hours. She tries to pull her hair into some kind of order with her fingers.

"Where am I going? Are you releasing me?"

"Follow me!"

Anya finds herself walking along an ill-lit corridor. There are doors on both sides and eventually the guard opens one and pushes her in. There is a table and two chairs, nothing else, in a room with bare white walls. Her heart chills. An interrogation.

She sits down, and the guard disappears. She can't stop shivering. Time passes. There is nothing to do but wait and try to keep her mind from panic.

Eventually, the door opens, and two men come in, one in a suit and the other in the same muddy uniform as the earlier guard.

"So, Miss Kotov, you have been selling illegal drugs," the suit says.

"I have not. You have changed the rules. You have recategorised products that are perfectly safe, not illegal. You have not informed me of this change in advance, so I have not broken any law. You should release me as you have arrested me in error," Anya states, heatedly, taken aback by her own forcefulness.

"I would be careful what you accuse us of, if I were you." His voice is a monotone of ice.

"Have you informed my niece where I am?" Anya asks as firmly as she can. He ignores her.

"We have enough evidence to keep you in prison for several years," he continues.

"You can't do that!" she protests. "What evidence?"

"If you help us, we help you. You tell us where your brother Valentin is, and maybe we help you."

She sits back in her chair. The air goes out of her lungs. Him. It is all about him.

"I don't know. I hardly ever hear from him, even though I am looking after his daughter."

"I am not sure you are telling us the truth, Miss Kotov." The man's voice becomes more menacing. "We have evidence that you have seen him recently."

"I don't know where he is, I'm telling you."

"He is an enemy of the state, and if you are his accomplice, then you are implicated too." The suited man leans towards her across the desk, his eyes cold, his finger pointing at her.

"He's a journalist," she pleads. "He's not an enemy of the state. That's nonsense."

"You don't get to tell us we're talking nonsense, understand?" and the guard beside her suddenly slaps her face. She shrieks in shock and pain.

"I am just running a shop. I am not my brother's keeper. I don't know what he is doing."

"I don't believe you."

"Listen, he is my brother. I love him. I am as anxious about him, to know where he is, as you are. But I don't know if he is in Orel, Moscow or London. All I care about is that you tell my niece Lara where I am. Please."

Her words are met with silence. The suited interviewer gives a nod to the guard, who comes over to her, grabs the tops of her arms and pulls her out of her chair. He wrenches her round, taking her breath away, and pushes her towards the door.

"I'll see you again," are the words she hears as she is pushed into the corridor and taken back to the cell.

The next few days pass in a blur. She is questioned, blindfolded, slapped, searched. Anya can't get her mind to think straight. Nothing seems real, and she frets about Lara. She knows she is nearly an adult now, but she will be worried and does still rely on her for money and care.

The women who share her cell are unfriendly, unhelpful. One is in for drugs, the other for prostitution. Anya feels lost. She has nothing here that is hers, no part of her old life to demonstrate to people who she is. She feels exhausted; her skin is dry and papery. The cell has rats running around, and the stench of sewers disgusts her. She has had diarrhoea for the last two days and feels weak but keeps reminding herself that she must keep strong.

It's mid-morning, and the women prepare to go out into the yard for a walk. A female guard comes in and takes hold of Anya's arm.

"You're coming with me!" she baulks at her. *Oh no, not again*, Anya thinks. *Now what?*

She hardly has the energy to get up off her bunk but rises and walks along the corridor, with a sense of dread as to whether they will hurt her even more.

"Let's try again," the man in the suit says, a sense of threat in his voice.

"I have told you that Valentin is probably out of the country – what more can I say? I want a lawyer."

"If you tell us where he is, give us an address, then we shall let you out," he sneers.

"I don't know where he is. I haven't heard from him, have I. I've been stuck in here and I have no phone."

"I don't believe you don't know a contact that he might link up with?" As he says this, the guard puts a hood over her face and grabs her wrists behind her.

"I don't know! Why can't you believe me?" She collapses, feeling faint.

"We'll find him," the man assures her.

"Fine," she mutters. Right now, she is ready to give up trying to protect Valentin, but she does want to protect Kate and Tom. As the guard's hands are tight around her neck, she blacks out.

FORTY-THREE

England, 2000

Edward Babbington gives Kate a hard time at the trustee meeting. Edward, Freddie and the other trustees are freaked out about Nikolai's death. The newspapers are reporting that it was a heart attack, but the rumour is that he was poisoned. Grigory has told Eve that he thinks it is something called Novichok, which apparently kills off the nerve cells one by one and then disappears from the body so that it won't show up at a post-mortem.

"OK, I see that this needs careful investigation, Edward," Kate agrees. "But not all Russians are evil, and not all Russian billionaires are money-launderers. I believe Eve's client, Grigory, is a good man. And a generous man."

"We need to check them all out, Kate," Edward insists. "I shall arrange for all the records to be audited and ensure that everything is in order. We can't risk any discrepancies."

Kate nods. She still frets about Novikoff's key and the papers or files that Valentin has left in her spare room. She wonders whether the phone calls of heavy breathing she keeps getting are anything to do with him, whether Novikoff is playing with her, wanting to frighten her? Or whether he might be planning something worse, some kind of revenge? But surely he would have acted by now?

"We're so lucky that Novikoff doesn't seem to have said anything about us going into his study that day to any of my other clients," Eve tells her on the phone when Kate rings to let off steam after the trustee meeting. "I wonder if he could be fearful that it could reflect badly on him?"

"You mean that others could get a whiff of what he's up to if he shares the information that two English women have been snooping around his desk?"

"Well, it would sound pretty ridiculous to most people, wouldn't it? And people would surely wonder what on earth we were doing, and why," Eve argues. "Anyway, it's a great relief that he doesn't seem to have spooked anyone as I haven't lost any clients as a result. Except him, of course, and good riddance."

"Yes, good riddance," Kate agrees. But the menace that Igor presents lingers like a bad dream in her psyche. "I still feel bad, though, about asking you to go into his house for Valentin, Eve. It was asking too much and putting Valentin's needs before yours, I can see that now."

"It was a big ask and I did resent it, for sure," Eve says slowly. "But I don't want to work for a crook and if he has done wrong then he should get his comeuppance, so don't worry about it."

"Kate, you can relax a little," Freddie says on the phone the following Friday. "The investment house has confirmed that, as we thought, the donors met their money laundering requirements. Also, our auditors and systems passed through the Charity Commission regulations. But there are question marks over one or two of the new donors, and we shall learn a little more in a few weeks."

"Thank God for that." Kate heaves a sigh of relief. "I knew Grigory was a good chap. Do you know, it makes me so happy when I visit the home and see those contented mums and babies in their peaceful surroundings, none of the usual clatter of hospital life. Quiet, calm and good care."

"Yes, indeed, thank God," Freddie agrees. "Speak soon." He puts the phone down.

Yes, my little William, we did it, thinks Kate. I did it for you.

Kate is looking forward to Tom coming home for the Christmas holidays, to treating him to good food and comfort after his student accommodation in Durham. Before that she is heading to Moscow for a brief visit. She had planned the trip for some time, and before all the latest events. She hasn't heard from Valentin and is getting no answer from Anya's phone either but presumes that Valentin is doing his usual hiding act and that Anya is probably busy. She is excited though nervous about a little more adventure and is sure she shall track them down in one place or another.

The last few weeks since Tom left for university have been hectic, pacifying the trustees, another fundraising evening to organise, this time out at Windsor, and keeping her life going. Her mother has had another setback and the visiting carer had to call the police when she became uncontrollable. Kate knows that she will have to put her in a secure home soon but is fearful of the cost. She wishes she had a sibling with whom to share the problems.

This evening she's tired and, after supper, she relaxes to Debussy, some of her favourite piano pieces. She lays her head back on the cushion and closes her eyes.

She falls asleep listening to the music but is woken by the telephone.

"Is that Mrs Kate Chisholm?" a voice asks.

"Yes, speaking," she answers hesitantly. She doesn't recognise the voice.

"This is the Foreign Office. My name is Dennis Thompson. You don't know me, but I am ringing to advise you that we do not believe it is advisable for you to travel to Moscow on Tuesday."

Kate is taken aback. How do the Foreign Office know that she is travelling to Moscow anyway?

"I don't understand. What do you mean?"

"I can't tell you much over the telephone, but you should know that the Russian authorities have been seeking Mr Valentin Kotov. They know, as we do, that you know him."

"But why does that impact my visit?"

"Let me just say, Ms Chisholm, that his sister, Anya Kotov, has been arrested. As I said earlier, we do not believe it advisable for you to travel to Russia at this time."

"Anya, arrested? What for?"

"We don't have that information, I am afraid."

"How have you discovered this information or found me, my telephone number?"

"It's what we are here for, to protect our citizens. Please do take heed. We shall be back in touch should we feel the need." He puts the phone down.

Kate is lost for words. Do they check everyone who flies to Russia? She thought the Cold War was over. She had no idea that they knew who she was. Could it be a scam? She wishes she had asked this Dennis Thompson for more details of who he really was, his title, his role, how she can contact him. Too late now. Looking at her phone, she sees No Caller ID.

She walks into the kitchen and makes herself a cup of tea, then wanders out into the garden. It is a cool winter's evening. She feels the breeze on her cheeks. She looks at the fallen leaves on the path and makes a note that she must sweep them up. The berries on the holly tree brighten the scene, and it comforts her to think of cutting a branch for the Christmas pudding with Tom in a few weeks' time.

But she needs to make a decision. Should she take notice of this call or go to Moscow anyway? She's shocked to hear that Anya is in prison. What on earth could she have done to get herself arrested? He didn't say whether she was still in custody. She berates herself for not asking him more about that, or what is happening to Lara if Anya is in trouble? And Valentin? Her mind is like a whirlpool of questions. The man only said that the Russian authorities were 'seeking Valentin'. Another journalist got shot last week in Moscow, which just shows how dangerous it is to get on the wrong side of either the government or dodgy individuals, or both. And she knows all too well that it isn't just the journalist who is at risk; their families and colleagues can get on the wrong side of the law simply by association. Kate paces up and down as the thoughts and doubts fly through her head.

When none of the numbers she has for Valentin are responding, she comes to the conclusion that she should take Dennis Thompson's advice. She goes to her desk and phones her travel agent, leaving a message to cancel her flight. She will ring them to confirm in the morning. Then she sends a fax to the Hotel Metropol and cancels her booking. She wonders whether her travel insurance will cover this and how she shall explain it to them, questioning whether this gives her grounds to get her money back.

She phones Eve and tells her all about it. Eve is shocked.

"That bloody man Valentin. How many times have I told you to let him go, that he is no good for you? Do you ever listen?"

"I know. But he is doing vital work there."

"God if I hear you say that one more time I shall scream! And for goodness' sake, Kate, as you have told me before, this is his fight, not yours," Eve butts in.

"OK, and now, if Anya has been arrested, I am really worried about what this means for us."

"God!" Eve gasps. "This must be about Igor Novikoff, mustn't it? He's a mate of the President, isn't he, so I guess it could be a conspiracy to shut Valentin up. Perhaps we shouldn't even be talking about it on the phone. I feel we are in some John le Carré film, Kate. It's frightening."

"Yes, I really worry about being watched, maybe the phone being bugged. Has Igor gone back to Moscow now?"

"I don't know. As you know, he stopped the contract after you and I went to his house that day. We didn't get any more work from him. He paid the money, thank heaven, and I haven't heard anything from him since."

Kate pauses and breathes heavily. "I feel out of my depth in all this, Eve."

"Yes, me too. Grigory is such a gentleman, but some of the others are scary, with their bodyguards and armoured cars. I don't think I shall do any more work for them. I must look for new clients," Eve muses, "but I can't imagine how I shall ever be able to bring in the income they have given me. You should be careful about who you take money from, too, for your charity. We can have a concerted effort together to widen our network in other directions."

"Yes, that would be a huge relief, wouldn't it," Kate agrees. "I want to do business with people I can really trust, and I don't feel safe in all this. I'm feeling really stupid and naive. So so out of my depth."

"Let me think about it," Eve says, in her more calm and comforting voice. "I'll call you back tomorrow."

Kate puts the phone down and walks into the kitchen. She pours herself a glass of red wine and wanders into the sitting room. She puts her glass down while she pulls the curtains, then sits and scrolls through the channels to find a soap to watch on the television. She wants to feel cosy, like none of this has happened. The thought of Anya in some Russian prison gives her the shivers.

A few nights later, at the end of the day when Kate would have flown to Moscow, she turns the television and lights off in the sitting room and starts to go up the stairs to bed. As she is halfway up, there is a knock on the front door, then the doorbell goes. She stops on the stairs and wonders whether to answer it or ignore it and go to bed. She turns and creeps down the stairs and stands in the hall and listens. Nothing. Nothing but the pounding of her heart.

She's about to turn around and go back upstairs when she hears the knock again. She tiptoes closer, wondering if she can get any glimpse of the person on the other side of the door through the stained-glass window. There's a shadow.

"Kate!" She hears a whispered sound. "Kate."

It's Valentin. She goes to the door and opens it slowly. He pushes her back and hurries into the hall, quickly shutting the door behind him. He's in a black anorak with the hood covering his head. She can see his chin, and it is unshaven. He pushes the hood back and she sees his gaunt and bruised face and recoils.

"What's happened to you? You look a wreck," she exclaims.

Valentin lifts a rucksack off his back and puts it down in the hall, then takes off his jacket as if he assumes he will stay. His hair is long, unwashed, tangled; the growth of beard on his chin is a mess, and he smells stale. Kate pushes him away as he tries to kiss her.

"Tell me what's happened. I hear Anya has been arrested? Valentin, you must explain what is going on. But first go and have a shower."

Valentin uses the downstairs shower room to clean up while Kate makes him a coffee and warms up some frozen soup from the freezer. She closes the blinds in the kitchen.

"I had to get out of Russia. They came after me, beat me up, stole my laptop, papers. Again!"

"Who are 'they'?" Kate asks.

"I'm not sure. They could be FSB, or Kremlin men. Or maybe Novikoff's own men. I just don't know. Either way they want to shut me up, if not kill me."

"Where have you been then?"

"I got a lift to Finland. It was horrible. I had to hide in a box under the back seat of this car that my old army colleague Lev organised. I paid $500 to the man, but he literally took me to the Finnish border and dumped me in a forest. I had to find my way from village to village on foot. It's been freezing, and I only had a small amount of money left after paying the driver, so I had to keep that for food and water. I've been living like a tramp, Kate."

He looks at her, as if expecting sympathy, but she can't feel anything for him. She looks at him with horror, wondering who he is and what she was drawn to, and she feels guilty, too, that as soon as he is in real trouble, she is disgusted by him. It doesn't feel very Christian of her, but her priority, she realises, is her own security, and Tom's. She knows now only too well that Valentin has become a liability in their lives.

"I don't know where Anya is. I didn't know she was in prison." Valentin shrugs off the thought. "They must have made up some charge against her, but I know her better than that. She would never get on the wrong side of the law, so I suspect they arrested her because they wanted to get at me."

Kate is silent. Everything he is saying fills her with terror that the Foreign Office know that she is on some watchlist because of him.

"OK, I am sorry, Kate, I have messed up, messed you around, not been what you wanted. We always knew it would be like that, from the beginning, didn't we? But there's a strong connection between us, I can feel it." His voice has a pleading tone, and it repulses her. His neediness is mixed up with images of when he has hurt her, not turned up, walked away. She feels used.

"Can I stay?" he asks and moves forward and pulls her to him.

"Stop!" she shouts. He clamps his hand over her mouth.

"Shh," he whispers urgently. "Please, Kate, please let me stay."

She feels cold, a nothingness in her heart. She looks at him and pauses.

"You can stay tonight, in the spare room, but you must go tomorrow. I had a call from our Foreign Office today. They know about me, about you. We're being watched."

Kate can see from his face that this is no surprise. So why has he put her in more danger by coming here tonight, she thinks.

"Thanks," he says and turns around and goes up to the spare room and shuts the door without another word. She stands at the bottom of the stairs, numb.

Kate is in the kitchen early the morning after. She didn't sleep a wink and feels exhausted and anxious. She heard Valentin moving around in the spare room during the night and locked her door. She didn't want any more embarrassment or to have to reject him again, and was relieved that he didn't try to come in.

"I need money," he says as he walks in the door, not even a 'good morning'. "Can you lend me some? I need to try to turn this situation around."

"I'll see how much I have in my wallet," Kate replies and picks up her handbag and counts out some notes. She had been to the bank the day before. "I have £200. You can have that."

"Can't you walk down to the tube and get some more out of the cash machine?" he wheedles. Kate feels angry now he is being pushy.

"No. I want you gone, Valentin. You are a liability."

"I need the money!" he says angrily, looming over her.

She steps back, stunned by his aggression, then summons up her courage and says clearly, "I am not giving you any more than that because I don't have it, and I don't want to go out of the door and possibly be followed as I go to get cash and bring it here or wherever. I don't want you to come back here ever again, do you understand?"

"You bitch!" He suddenly slaps her face. She staggers back and sits down, stunned by the pain. He grabs the notes from her wallet, runs to the back door and lets himself out, slamming it behind him.

FORTY-FOUR

Russia, 2000

Anya doesn't know one day from the next but can see from the rays of winter sun coming through the skylight that it is a sunny morning. Her body aches all over. She longs for her old life, for the business she has worked so hard to create, for the warmth of her little kitchen, for Lara. Her cellmate tells her, a cigarette dangling from her mouth, that it's unlikely she shall get out for five years, maybe ten. Her prime. She'll lose everything.

A different guard enters the room as she sits on the side of the bed.

"You! You go to court today," he says to her.

Anya's heart leaps, a chance of justice, of freedom. But what to do? She looks like a mad woman; her hair is dry and too long – it straggles all over her face. She has no way to tidy herself up or make herself look normal. How can anyone possibly take her seriously, she panics.

The guard pulls her hands in front of her and handcuffs her wrists, and she follows him upstairs. He pushes her into a van. The steel bench feels like ice beneath her. The temperature has dropped overnight, and the vehicle must have been kept outside. She blows on her fingers and tries to tuck them between her thighs to warm them up, though the handcuffs chafe against her legs.

There are two windows in the double doors at the back of the van. Both are barred but through them she can see familiar sites of Orel, shops, parks, the buildings and squares she knows so well. They are reminders of her old life, a time when her days had been normal and fairly predictable. But this is Russia, and she now realises that nothing is predictable.

She recognises the roads through the back window of the van as it makes its way through the oblast region of the city. It hurtles along the road, horn blasting at the traffic, lurching around corners. Anya tries to hold on to the bench to stop herself being thrown against the metal sides, but the handcuffs make her unwieldy.

She wants to bang on the windows and shout to the people on the street to help her, to explain that she is being kidnapped by the police, arrested by mistake, and that they should come to her rescue, but the guard sits opposite her, his cold eyes watching her every movement.

They arrive in front of a grey concrete building, its windows framed in white. There's a red porch over the entrance. Anya is pushed and pulled through some grey-blue double doors, down a corridor and into the courtroom. She catches a glimpse of the male judge. He is elderly, his face has a weary expression, his eyes pale and tired. She's hopeful that he will see that this whole episode is a mistake, that he will grant her bail. She doesn't want to think of the statistics that her cellmates have so gleefully told her, that 99% of women charged in Russia receive guilty pleas. This wouldn't, couldn't, happen to her, surely, she worries. *After all, I am a professional woman, running my own legitimate business now. I am well respected.*

"Where is my niece?" Anya blurts out as they lead her past the judge into the court cage where she, as the accused, has to stand. "Does she know where I am now? Have you told her? Made sure she is all right?"

"That's not the business of this court," the judge replies. His voice is slow, measured, but not unkind. She feels he is choosing his words carefully, and she realises that his life is not a simple one either. No one in Russia has a simple life. Everyone is prey to bribes, trumped-up charges, whoever they are. Everything he says and does in the court will be recorded. If he puts a step wrong, a word wrong, he will end up in a similar position to her.

Anya feels weak from lack of nutritious food, from the cold and discomfort of the cell life.

"Can I have a glass of water?" she asks. The judge nods and a uniformed attendant leaves the room and returns with a smeary plastic glass and some water. She drinks it in noisy gulps.

The prosecution reads out the accusations. They claim that she has been trading a herbal medicine categorised as an opiate, that she has abused licence restrictions and failed to pay her taxes for two years.

None of this is true. How can they concoct such a story, and why? *I am a no one*, she thinks, *and my business is tiny. I can't believe they don't know where Valentin is. This must just be revenge. Igor Novikoff could have arranged all this, or one of Valentin's other investigative reports has annoyed someone else.* Anya wrings her hands as she thinks of her brother.

"This woman is a criminal. She should not be considered for bail," the prosecution lawyer finishes.

"I'm not!" Anya shouts, but she's aware that if she loses her calm, they will just assume she is mad, so the words die on her lips.

The judge listens, nods and looks down at his desk. Anya holds her breath, her fingernails pressing into the palms of each hand. The moments tick by, and she prays to a God she is not sure exists, that he will grant her bail.

Eventually, after what seems like a lifetime, the judge coughs and clears his throat. He repeats the words of the prosecution and tells her that bail will not be granted. She's to return to prison for an indefinite period while they look into the case further.

"No!" Anya calls. "You can't do this to me! I have done nothing wrong..." But she breaks down in tears and can't get the last words out.

The courtroom guards, dressed in black uniforms with black Cossack hats, open the cage and pull her out. They drag her down the long corridor to the entrance. Back in the van, the world looks grey; her stomach is churning; and her mind circles in disbelief. She stares once more out of the van windows. This time she sees that she is being driven out of Orel, down long roads she doesn't recognise. She tries to calculate where they are going, but all she is getting is glimpses of roads, traffic, churches and shops, and she can't place any of them now.

Then eventually the van stops, and she hears a clatter of locks being undone. They go through some large metal gates where the driver calls her name to the guards, then stops to chat for a few moments and exchanges cigarettes with the gatekeeper while she sits there freezing. Finally, he gets back into the van and moves on, pulling up in front of a dirty grey concrete building with dark windows. Anya assumes she must be arriving at a different prison but has no clue where she is. The watchtower looms above them, and she can see floodlights breaking through the low, dark cloud and scanning the ground. Everywhere she looks there are bars, high walls and barbed wire.

She is taken through the building to a room on the ground floor and strip-searched again. She feels less than human now and completely powerless.

"In here!" someone shouts, and she finds herself in a tiny dingy cell. This time she is alone. There's a metal bed, thin mattress and a filthy toilet. She sees rat droppings on the concrete floor. A glimmer of light comes in from a window high above her bed. Night is falling. A perfect sliver of half moon is rising against the black of the descending night. She looks at the new moon and thinks of Lara looking at the same moon, and it gives her a little comfort.

She lies down, exhausted, and weeps, then closes her eyes to try to shut out the world.

FORTY-FIVE

England, 2000

"I have been so stupid. Was it all for vanity? Vanity that such a man would find me attractive, and vanity that I was somehow supporting him, through my own misguided idea that he was doing something of value to humanity. Perhaps he was, but in doing so, he was hurting all those who were closest to him, wasn't he?" Kate exclaims to Eve. Tears stream down her cheeks, and she wrings her hands, unable to find any peace.

"Realistically, Kate, he probably was using you," Eve tells her as they sit in Kate's kitchen. "But he did find you attractive, and that made you feel good. You were lonely after your divorce and a bit lost, I think. And he may indeed be doing some good for humanity. Plus, he didn't interfere so much in your life that you didn't manage to build a successful charity, as well as keep yourself and Tom fed and watered through your events business. So don't beat yourself up too much. Just don't ever, and I mean ever, see that man again. Move on. There's nothing you can do about the past. It's the present you need to focus on."

"It's as if I have had a blindfold on all these years. I hear that they describe women in dysfunctional or abusive relationships like a frog put into cool water that is warmed up over time until, all of a sudden, the water gets so hot they can't stand it and jump out. That's what it feels like for me, for sure. But, Eve, how on earth has it taken me so long to wake up? And what do I do now? Tom's coming home this weekend for the Christmas holidays," Kate says, with some desperation in her voice.

"I've been thinking about that," Eve says, "and I think I might have a solution."

"Really? What?"

"I think you need to get out of your house for a while. As you say, people may know where you are, whether they are KGB, FSB, Novikoff's men, or whatever. So, I have a client whose flat I am doing up, and I can arrange for you to go and stay there. They aren't living there yet, they're waiting for some Italian marble to arrive for the bathroom, but it is perfectly habitable and will tide you over until you can find out more from the police, or the FO, as to how to protect yourself."

"Where is it, this flat?" Kate asks.

"I will tell you later. Let's meet again this evening when we finish work," Eve suggests.

"Great," Kate says. "Thanks, Eve, you're a real friend."

"Love you," Eve says, and they hug.

They meet that evening at a wine bar in the City. It's a cold evening, but dry. Eve's assistant has texted Kate the address. The bar is full of men in suits, talking loudly and drinking beer. *There must be a rugby match*, Kate thinks, as she watches them congregate around a television screen, or maybe this is the way they unwind every night. Kate puts her coat lapel up around her ears as she enters and tries to drown out the noise of shouting and drinking. She walks around the large area of tables trying to spot Eve. She hasn't arrived yet so Kate finds a table by a window and waits for her friend.

Eventually, Kate spots her scurrying along the pavement towards the door. She has put her hood up, as if she is trying not to be seen, but she can't help but look elegant whatever she does, her slim ankles showing in expensive shoes.

Kate waves to her as she enters and signals that she should get them both a drink on her way over. Eve goes to the bar and brings over a bottle of Pinot Noir and two glasses.

"It's cold out there!" she exclaims.

"Yes, and it's noisy in here!" Kate counters.

"I thought that might be a good thing. We don't want to go somewhere quiet and be overheard, do we?"

"You're getting good at this clandestine stuff, Eve."

"One of us has to!" she says ironically.

"Ho, ho," Kate replies woodenly, and they chat about their day, and Eve listens as Kate tells her more about Valentin's visit the night before, his journey from Finland, the fact that Anya has been arrested.

"I can't believe all this is happening, and I can't bear

to think of Anya in some Russian prison, Eve," Kate says, shivering.

"What we have to do is to make sure you don't end up there with her. And I am serious. You know how the Russians work, putting pressure on family members, colleagues, friends. You could be next. Bloody good thing that guy from the FO rang and warned you off your trip."

"Yes," Kate concedes. "So, what are you suggesting for Tom and me?"

"It's a flat in Limehouse, in an old warehouse. I am in the process of converting it for an Italian executive—"

"That Italian who was your lover?" Kate interrupts.

"No, one of his colleagues. This one is married, so it's hands off as far as I am concerned," Eve says firmly.

"That's good. I agree."

"Anyway, he and his wife are in Italy. They live near Rome. They haven't moved in yet and want everything to be shipshape before they do. We can't do any more until we get the marble and a few other things we have ordered, so I asked if you and Tom could rent it from him over the Christmas period. I said that you had experienced a major leak in your house and needed to move out. He said yes, and it's a peppercorn rent."

"Fantastic, thanks Eve." Kate feels a great sense of relief and yet conflicted. "I fear Tom is going to be really fed up about this. He told me last week that he is really looking forward to being in his own bed, his own room, and with his old friends in nearby streets. I feel bad because he didn't take a gap year, so he's one of the youngest in his department, and I wanted to give him a really good Christmas break."

Eve nods, quietly, pausing while she thinks. "I agree, that's going to be difficult, and explaining all this to him is going to be tough, too. But you have to do it, Kate, and I think you should move in tomorrow. I have the key. Come and sleep at my place tonight; we can pick up your stuff in the morning, using my car, and I can come and settle you in."

Kate's head feels discombobulated, with all these plans being made around her. She doesn't feel in control of her life anymore.

"Mum, this is ridiculous! For fuck's sake! I don't want to live anywhere else over Christmas. It's Christmas, for God's sake, we have a tree, presents, all the cosy rituals. It won't be the same in some flat miles away from my mates and from Dad." Tom is furious when Kate explains the plan to him on the phone.

"I'll be able to explain a little more when I see you, but I think we have to do this, I'm afraid. I don't think we have a choice." Kate tries to sound convinced.

"If this is all to do with that bloody Russian bloke, I shall kill him!" Tom hangs up, and Kate mutters to herself, "You may not have to. Someone else might do that for you."

The flat in Limehouse is large and done in Eve's exquisite minimalist style. There are two bedrooms with en-suite bathrooms and a huge open area of kitchen, dining and sitting room with a high vaulted ceiling. The kitchen has all the latest Italian-designed equipment. Neither of the bathrooms has been converted yet, but they are operative, if not smart.

"I think you should stay here for the Christmas holidays, you know, the next four weeks, then try to get more information from the FO, or the Russian Embassy, or the police, about Valentin's whereabouts and hope that your life can revert to normality again when he has sorted out his affairs." Eve sounds so sure of herself, and Kate feels like a child being told by a parent how to live, which doesn't feel too bad to her as she feels in such a mess and is finding it difficult to make decisions for herself.

She hugs Eve. "Thanks, darling. You're my rock, and this is beautiful and will be even more amazing when you have put the finishing touches to it."

"It is rather superb, isn't it," Eve agrees, as she surveys her own handiwork. "Now, I have to go off to work. You settle down. I think you should work from here now, not go back to Notting Hill until January."

A couple of days later, Kate meets Tom at King's Cross. He walks down the platform with his arm around a pretty blonde girl.

"Mum, meet Marianne," he says. Kate shakes the young girl's hand. She has beautiful blue eyes and a gentle smile. She is a little taller than him.

"Pleased to meet you," Marianne says. "Well, I'll be off, Tom. See you later, in that pub in Ladbroke Grove, then." She kisses his cheek and walks across the station concourse on her way towards the tube.

"She looks nice," Kate remarks to Tom as they walk down to the car park. He grunts.

"Yeah, she is," he says. "So where are we going? And why?"

As Kate drives through the Christmas traffic to Limehouse, she explains to him what has happened and why they need to be careful.

"I knew it. That fucking man Valentin. He's always been trouble, Ma, drawing you into one thing or another."

"Yes, I accept that I have got myself into a frightening situation and am out of my depth," Kate agrees. "But he is doing good work, Tom, writing articles, investigating corruption. I admire his efforts and have wanted to help him."

"But he's put you in danger. And Anya. And Lara. It's appalling that Anya's in prison! Poor Lara must be so worried."

"I know." Kate turns to him. He is looking vulnerable, his face surrounded by his thick hair that has grown during the university term, his chin covered by a shadow of stubble. He looks half boy, half man. "I am sorry, Tom. I'll make it up to you."

"How?" he seethes. "I had all these plans for these holidays, parties, seeing mates, Marianne. I'll bloody do what I like, whatever you say! I can't sit at home with you all these weeks."

"I think you will have to, Tom, until I get more information from the police or the Foreign Office. I'll do that as fast as I can."

"I'm going to meet Marianne tonight, whatever happens, at the pub in Ladbroke Grove. You can't fucking stop me doing that."

Kate sighs. "Well, OK, but you absolutely must not go back to our house. Promise?"

"Hm," he says through gritted teeth, in what could be taken as an affirmative.

Despite his moans, Tom is impressed with the apartment when Kate shows him. He dumps his things in the spare bedroom and wanders around, inspecting what Eve has created.

"Pretty good!" he exclaims approvingly. "Eve's done a great job. I guess if you have to stay somewhere, this place isn't bad! But I'm absolutely not going to be confined to barracks over this time. I just refuse—"

"Please, Tom..." Kate tries to explain but he walks out of the room and then shouts that he is off to meet Marianne.

"Bye!" she hears his voice defiant across the spacious room as he slams the front door.

Kate sits and tries to work out how the television remote works. It is all the latest high tech, and she fiddles with the various buttons, her hands still shaking from the shock of recent events. She doesn't know what she is doing but eventually she presses a button that gets her the BBC, and she watches a crime thriller. It's not the best thing for her to see, she decides later, with men creeping out of dark shadows, and the odd body, but it mostly keeps her mind off her own problems.

She goes to sleep around eleven o'clock, and hopes that Tom will be home soon, as the pubs close and he will have to get the Central Line and the DLR over to Limehouse station from Notting Hill.

She sleeps fitfully, and each time she wakes, she goes into Tom's bedroom to check whether he has returned home. Nothing.

By nine o'clock the next morning, he still isn't back. Kate calls his mobile. It goes straight to voicemail.

FORTY-SIX

England, 2000

Valentin works his way through the back streets of London up to the room of a fellow journalist, Alexei, in Kentish Town.

"Valentin!" he exclaims. "I wasn't expecting you. Where have you been?"

"No, I wasn't expecting to be here either. I was mugged. My laptop stolen when I got back to Moscow. My apartment raided. I guess the FSB or Novikoff. I had to get out, go to Finland. I guess whoever raided there, and my sister's flat in Orel, must have all our contacts now and the details of the investigations we've been working on. I don't think it will be long before someone catches up with me again."

Alexei goes pale. "And the rest of us too, then."

"Yes. We need to go underground again immediately. Tell the others not to answer calls from anyone they don't know and be careful about opening their doors or clicking email links."

Alexei bites his lip. "Bugger. I thought we had begun to set up something really good here."

"We have. And we can continue, but we need to reset all emails, ISP and encrypted services. Get new phones. Don't warn the others until you have done that. We've had enough journalists killed by these monsters. We don't want more. You have money don't you? I have none."

"Yes," he replies. "Should we tell the UK police? After all, we are doing legitimate work here in London. Just reporting facts."

Valentin sits down on Alexei's bed. "No. I just don't know how much we can trust them. Could they pull us in for anything we have done?"

"I don't think so. We are an agency of individuals. Journalists investigating facts. We have links around the world, just a few here in the UK. People are just trolling through data and sifting out the facts of situations. I don't see what part of that is breaking the rules."

"Treading on toes, maybe? Perhaps putting their government in compromising situations with their foreign counterparts occasionally. There isn't anything exactly illegal about that. You know London better than I do, Alexei, what do you think?"

Alexei says nothing. He just shakes his head as he tries to work out what to do.

"I'm going down to a call box to phone Mikhail in Moscow. I've been thinking that he needs to make sure he has destroyed all the information about us and leave Russia."

"Do you think he can act fast enough? Destroy all our files?" Alexei asks. "He won't want to leave Maya or the children, Valentin. We're fucked."

"He may have to leave Russia. He knows that. We've always known that. He has a relative in Istanbul. He has to get out before they kill him."

"I'm going to go back to Kate's house later and get that data I left there." Valentin sighs in exhaustion. "They are bound to search her house now. The trouble is I don't know who 'they' are. But it's probably Novikoff who's arranged for my sister to be arrested. He wants to shut me up but there are certainly others who don't like what we have exposed."

Valentin gets news later that night that Mikhail has taken a flight to Turkey. His wife Maya doesn't understand where he has gone and rings Valentin to find out what is happening. He can't give her any information as it could compromise her position were she to be interrogated. He tries to console her, assuring her that Mikhail is bound to be in touch as soon as he is able, as soon as he feels it safe to call for her.

In the depth of the night, in a basement cellar in North London, Tom wakes to find his hands tied. The last thing he remembers is that he had gone back to the house in Notting Hill to collect some clothes to wear for the party. He had left Marianne at the pub, thinking he would only be ten minutes. Just as he was opening the front door, he had felt a massive club on the head. He can't remember anything else. He doesn't know where Marianne is, or whether she is safe.

He looks around. The room is dark, and he is lying on a dirty rug on a brick floor. He moans. His head aches.

"So, you have woken up at last" he hears a voice with a Russian accent come from what seems like the other side of the room. Tom tries to turn to see who is speaking. In the darkness of the room, he sees a tall, thin, figure leaning against a door.

"Yes," Tom replies. "Who are you, and what do you think you're doing?"

"You don't honestly think I'm going to answer that, do you," the man sneers. "I'm the one who asks the questions here, don't forget."

Tom doesn't reply, scared that he could say something to let his fear show through.

"Your mum's little lover – Valentin Kotov – where is he?"

"I don't know, and I don't care," Tom replies, genuinely.

"Ah, but you must have some idea when she saw him. He's in London; we know that. He would have contacted her."

"I repeat, I don't know, and I don't care. How many more times do I have to say it? He can die for all I care. He's been nothing but trouble."

The man moves forward and kicks Tom's leg.

"Stop that," Tom winces and shouts, "I don't know where he is. Believe me, if I did, I would tell you because it's no skin off my nose if you get hold of him and do your worst. There's no love lost there. My mum's better off without him."

The man squats down beside Tom, his green eyes piercing through the dim light into Tom's. "Say that again," the man says. "Tell me where Valentin is."

"I don't know!" Tom shouts into his face. "I don't know. I don't care. You can kill him, and if I knew where he was,

I would tell you."

"OK, maybe I believe you." He paused. "So, where's your mum?"

Tom's heart almost stops. "I don't know the address. She's staying with a friend," he lies.

The man is silent, then sniggers. "Now, that I don't believe." He kicks Tom again, but harder.

Tom yelps. "Stop it! That hurts."

"So funny, that. It's an odd thing, but you're going to get hurt until you tell us where your mum is."

"I know she doesn't know where Valentin is. She told me."

"Hmm, that's as may be," says the man menacingly, giving Tom's shin another hard kick, "but I'd rather ask her that myself. So where is she?"

FORTY-SEVEN

England, 2000

There's no news from Tom. Kate has heard nothing since he waved goodbye to her in the flat to say he was meeting Marianne in Ladbroke Grove. She girds her loins and rings Simon to explain what has happened and why they had to move out of Notting Hill. His voice is as cold as ice as he tells her that he will go to Notting Hill and check out the house, then phone the police if he can't track Tom down. He has a key.

The confidence that the last few years has endowed in her slips away when she hears Simon's voice upbraiding her for her foolishness, for putting their son in danger.

She waits at the flat, speaking to Eve on the phone, pacing up and down, until Eve tells her to put the phone down in case Simon is trying to call. The minutes drag like years.

An hour later, the mobile beeps. It's a text from Simon: 'No sign of Tom, but he has obviously been at the house. The back door open, his backpack in the hallway. Did you leave it open?'.

Oh God. 'No, of course I didn't', Kate texts back. 'Any sign of damage, or theft?'.

There's another long delay, during which she imagines all kinds of scenarios where Tom is murdered, kidnapped, beaten up. She tries to calm herself that there may be a simple explanation to it all, that perhaps he came back to the house with Marianne, they were drunk, left the back door open.

Her phone rings. It's Simon. "Kate, we must go to the police. Things don't feel right here. The bush between your house and your neighbour's looks like it's taken a pounding. And your spare room was a mess – have you been tidying it up or something? There was laundry, sheets and pillowcases all over the carpet and the drawers open and empty."

"No, I haven't been tidying. Someone must have come in looking for something," Kate says, thinking of Valentin's stuffed jiffy bags under the pillowcases.

I've tried Tom's number over and over, but there's no reply," Simon continues. "It just goes straight to voicemail."

"OK," Kate says in a small voice. "I don't know whether I should leave here or not?"

"Stay," he commands. "Stay until I have spoken to the police, explained the situation and all you have told me. I'll call you back."

She collapses onto the chair by the window, both resentful yet comforted that Simon is taking charge. She looks out on the river, bargaining with God to bring her son home safely.

Hours later, the doorbell rings. Kate goes to the telephone on the wall, unsure how to beep people in.

"It's Simon, let me up."

With a shaking hand she pushes a couple of buttons and finally there is a buzzing noise that sounds as if it is opening the door below. Simon appears at the inner door with two men. Kate welcomes them in. They introduce themselves as Special Branch officers.

"We have explained to your husband—"

"Ex-husband!" Simon reminds them irritably.

"That we want to investigate the whereabouts of your son. His mobile was left at your house…"

Kate gasps and looks at Simon. "You didn't tell me that!"

"There was no point in frightening you," he says shortly.

"Anyway, we were able to trace the phone numbers of his friends and contact them to discover whether they had seen him. They hadn't. So, we must trace him. We haven't managed to get hold of his girlfriend, Marianne, yet, but will keep trying. We have reason to believe that Valentin Kotov also went to your home last night, that he may have forced open the back door, but your neighbour also says that they were woken up by noises and a large black Mercedes SUV outside your house. We think it may have been a gang to pick up Kotov…"

"Well, we are not at all concerned about Kotov. He gets what he deserves," Simon says angrily. "It's our son we are worried about."

"I realise that. We're doing all that we can to trace him."

There's a silence in the room as Simon and Kate look at one another. Her stomach is turning as if someone has a monkey wrench and is twisting it through her gut.

"I have to go to the gallery," Simon says coldly, and Kate notices he has developed a nervous tick of rubbing his hand over his beard as he speaks. It makes a scratchy sound. "I have an important exhibition starting tomorrow. You have my contact details," he addresses the two officers.

"Yes." They both rise at once and move towards the door. "We shall contact you as soon as we get any news. Ms Chisholm, we advise that you do not go back to your Notting Hill house now. It is a potential crime scene. Do you have someone who can be with you?"

"I'll call my friend Eve," Kate replies.

And all of a sudden, they are gone, and Kate is left standing, looking out of the window at the clouds scudding by, the odd tourist boat on the river. She can't imagine what she is supposed to do with herself.

Eve brings over some supper, but Kate is not hungry. She has a large glass of gin and tonic, but nothing soothes the anxiety as to where Tom is. She tries to do some work, organising the catering for the next fundraiser, but simply can't concentrate.

"I just want to go to sleep and wake up to hear he is OK, Eve," she pines.

"Yes, I know," Eve says. She loves Tom too. "Why don't you take a Zopiclone? I've got a spare. Go to sleep. I shall stay here with you tonight."

Kate nods, incapable of making any fuss or argument, incapable of thinking straight.

The sleeping pill does its trick, and she gets six hours' sleep. The sun is shining a wintry light in through the window as she wakes. Eve is standing in the doorway to her room in a white towelling robe.

"I heard from Simon," she says.

"What?" Kate shoots up in bed.

"That the police believe that Valentin may have been taken back to Russia. CCTV at Heathrow showed three men going through boarding, two men on either side of someone who seemed to have been unwell. They were propping him up. No doubt they all had false papers, but they are pretty sure that it is Valentin as they did identify the two men on either side of him as Novikoff's men."

"Oh my God. They're evil. What on earth have they done with Tom?"

Eve shakes her head. "I'm afraid there's no news of him yet." She turns her back and Kate hears her go to the kitchen, the espresso machine hisses and splutters, and she comes back with a mug of strong black coffee. "Here," she says, handing it to Kate. "You drink this, then have a nice relaxing bath to calm yourself. I'm in touch with Simon, and he is keeping tabs on the police activity. At least with Valentin going back to Russia, potentially, that should take the heat off you, I would have thought."

"Oh, I hope so," Kate says. "But where is Tom? Why are they keeping him if they now have Valentin? Oh, Eve, I can't lose him. He's my only son. I can't lose another child." Kate breaks down crying. "And if they have gone back to Russia, is there anyone here supervising Tom?"

she continues between sobs. "They may have just left him in some awful place, and no one will be there for him, no food, no water, no escape. Just forgotten…"

"Don't let your imagination run away with you, Kate. I'm sorry, but we just don't know." Eve sits on the bed next to her friend, stroking Kate's hand with her long, perfectly manicured fingers.

FORTY-EIGHT

England, 2000

Tom wakes again to find himself alone. Shadows fall from a crack of light under the doorway. The last thing he remembers is that the man who was attacking and interrogating him was called away by someone outside the basement door, shouting something in Russian. Tom can't remember what happened next, but he heard a door bang, then lost consciousness again.

He stretches. The wires chafe his ankles and wrists. He doesn't want to die alone in this room, with no one knowing where he is. He wonders if he dares to try to force the door open, wonders if he has the strength, or whether there might be a guard on the other side, and whether such a guard might have a gun.

He gradually stands up and relieves himself against the wall. He pulls up his trousers to check the bruises on his legs and decides he cannot sit and do nothing. He has to try to escape.

His wrists are tied in the front. The wire has worked its way a little loose, but he can't pull it apart. He tries to undo the wire around his ankles but fails. He struggles to his feet, shuffling to the door. The door is Victorian, with four wooden panels, but he can see that it isn't particularly sturdy. He wonders if he could push through one of them.

He starts to hammer the wood as hard as he can with his fists. It doesn't seem to make any dent in the surface. He waits, wondering whether he has drawn attention to himself. There is no sound outside. He fears he may have been abandoned.

He feels his way around the room. It's dark, and he can hardly determine anything. Then, as he moves cautiously around the back area of the room, his foot clangs against something metallic. He bends down and finds his hand around an iron bar. With a shudder, he realises that his kidnappers had probably intended to use this on him, that it could have been the weapon that knocked him out. But now it could be his saving rather than his downfall.

Clutching it with both hands, he crashes the iron bar against the weak panels of the door. It takes several attempts, and then he is able to push through one of the panels. He manoeuvres his bound arms on their side through the open gap, feeling for the doorknob. He can't believe his luck. The green-eyed man had obviously left in such a hurry that he had left the key in the lock the other side of the door. Tom strains his hands until his fingers are able to get hold of the key. He can feel splinters of wood go into his arms as he twists and turns to get a good purchase on the key. With some effort, bending his arm in various directions, he manages to clasp the key in two fingers and, eventually, he unlocks the door.

He almost falls out of the door as it opens, finding himself at the bottom of a steep set of wooden stairs. He crawls up to the top, caterpillar-style, pulling himself up with movements of his arms and shoulders and pushing with his feet when he can. Every movement is painful from where he was beaten. There's a door at the top of the stairs but it's been left half-open, and he slithers out into the hallway. Here he can see a front door with frosted-glass windows. He pulls himself to standing, then hops across the black-and-white tiles in his stockinged feet and is able to let himself out into the street. He shuffles as fast as he can along the pavement, away from the building. He has no idea where he is. He just knows he has to get as far away as he can.

It's dark. The streets are empty. It has been raining and the pavements are wet. When he is some way from the building, he stops and sits on the stone steps of a house, his clothes wet and bedraggled, his shirt smattered with bloodstains where he had cut himself breaking through the door.

Suddenly, he hears a noise behind him and sees the front door of the house open. A young girl comes out. She is dressed in high boots and a cream mackintosh. She stops to put up her umbrella and then sees him.

"Hey," she asks, fiercely. "What are you doing sitting there?"

"Sorry," Tom says. "I'm just taking a moment to get my breath. I'll be gone in a minute."

The girl comes down the stairs and looks at him inquisitively, pacified by the polite sound of his voice and words. "Are you OK? You look awful. God, your shirt's covered in blood!"

Tom pauses, wondering whether it is safe or sensible to tell her his story. She has a kind face, round cheeks and brown hair and a friendly smile on her lips. She reconnects him with a sense of normality.

"No," he says. "I'm not all right. I was mugged and had to fight my way out," deciding it's safer not to give her all the details. He doubts very much she would believe him anyway if he said he had been kidnapped by Russians. "Would you mind calling the police for me? The muggers took my mobile phone."

"Sure," she says. "Why don't you come in? My boyfriend can wait. You come and have a cup of tea, and I'll call 999."

"Thank you."

She holds him under the elbow and helps him slowly up the three steps to the front door. Once inside, the girl, who tells him her name is Sharon, points him towards a chair in the hall and shouts, "Dad! I need your help."

A short, middle-aged man in shirtsleeves and cord trousers appears from a doorway. He has grey hair and brown eyes.

"Hello there, what have we got here?" he asks of them both.

"He's been mugged, Dad. And look, his ankles and wrists are tied up. What can we do to help him? Will you try to cut the wire? I'll call the police." Sharon seems to take charge of her father.

"Sure, I'll get the bolt cutters from my toolbox. That should get through that wire OK."

"Thanks very much," Tom says, and the man goes back through the doorway into the kitchen beyond.

Tom sits there, and his body starts to shiver with delayed shock. His teeth chatter and his whole body shakes.

Sharon comes back and says, "I've called the cops. They're on their way. Oh my, you're all freezing. Let me get a blanket."

Her father returns with the bolt cutters and quickly cuts through the wire, releasing Tom's wrists. They are bruised and red. Then his ankles.

"Dad, I think you should lend him a jumper. I don't think your trousers will fit him, he's much taller than you, but he's going to die of hypothermia if we don't warm him up."

The father disappears through another doorway and then comes back with an old green jumper. He helps Tom take off his rain-soaked shirt and pushes the jumper over his head, working his arms into the sleeves as Tom is shaking too much to have control of his movements.

"I'll make a hot cup of tea," Sharon says, running into the kitchen.

The doorbell goes. "That must be the cops already!" she calls out. "Dad, let them in!"

FORTY-NINE

England, 2000

As Kate lies in a warm bath at the Limehouse flat trying to calm herself, her mobile rings. She almost slips over in her rush to answer it, trying to dry her hand on the towel before touching the phone.

"Kate?" Simon's voice is flat and cold.

"Yes, do you have news?"

"I think the police must have some news for us. They have asked me to go to your Limehouse flat. They will be there in an hour or two's time."

"Oh my God, do you think they've found Tom? Do you think he's OK?" she asks.

"Kate, I know no more than you do, so there's no point in speculation. I'm coming over. Let me in when I ring."

Kate dries herself and puts on jeans and a jumper. She combs her hair to try to make herself look less like a panicking mother. She is just putting on her watch when the doorbell goes. Eve answers it and, a few seconds later, Simon is at the door.

"Coffee?" Eve asks him.

"Have you got any whisky?" Simon's voice betrays his nerves. Eve pours them all a short slug of whisky each. They sit down together, two anxious parents waiting for news of their child. Neither of them is able to find the words to share their concern. Eve makes a little conversation but then gives up, and they sit in silence.

Then Kate's mobile rings. She hesitates for a moment, then picks it up. "Hello?" she says hesitantly, then hears her mother's voice shouting on the other end. "Mum!" she snaps. "For goodness' sake go away. I just can't cope with you now!"

She puts the phone back on the table and rests her head in her hands. The others say nothing.

It seems like forever before they hear a police siren out in the street. A car pulls up and Kate rushes to the Entryphone and buzzes them in. Minutes later, the lift door opens, and she sees Tom, standing between a male and female police officer. His hair is bedraggled, and he's wearing the old green jumper Sharon's dad lent him. Kate gasps and, in a second, intuitively detects that Tom so wants to be a man, with his father and the police watching, but as soon as he sees Kate, he runs into her arms and sobs. She holds him tight, reaching up to stroke his hair, then leads him gently into the sitting room, at which point Simon quietly walks up behind her and puts his arms around them both, hugging his son to him.

"We'll leave him in your care tonight," the detective says, "and take a fuller report in the morning. Try to get some sleep."

That night Kate is awoken by howls. They are visceral, primal sounds, and she leaps out of bed and runs to Tom's room. He is lying in a half-sleep, his body jumping around, and he's emitting terrible screams. She sits on his bed and takes his arms in a firm but gentle grip.

"Tom! Tom! Wake up, darling. You are safe, you are safe, you are safe!" she repeats quietly but clearly in his ear, over and over until he begins to wake.

He is sweating, and his hands are trembling in hers.

"Oh, my darling," Kate says as she holds him to her, stroking his hair and forehead.

"Mum," he mumbles. "Thank God. I thought I was back in that horrible dark basement with men coming at me from all sides. I couldn't get away."

"You did get away, sweetheart. You did, and you were very clever. Tomorrow maybe you tell us more about it, but for now you are safe, and Marianne is safe too. She didn't know where you'd gone. She's at her mum's house."

Kate passes him a glass of water. He looks up at her with haunted eyes, as if he can't trust that he is truly out of danger.

"We're in Limehouse, remember? There's a policeman outside here tonight, Tom. And they believe that both Valentin and his nemesis, Igor Novikoff, are back in Russia and will no longer threaten us. So, you can sleep easy, darling boy."

"It was terrifying, Mum," Tom says through gritted teeth.

"I am so sorry, Tom, so very sorry that you got wound up in all this. We will talk about it again in the morning, but please know that I never ever imagined anything like this happening to you or any of us here." Kate's gut is twisting with horror and guilt at what has happened, what could have happened, how blind she has been to the dangers.

Tom grunts. She knows she has a lot of making-up to do. Her fear is that he will never forgive her.

"Lie down, darling. I shall stay with you until you are asleep again. It's only three o'clock in the morning. You need sleep." She helps him settle on his side and sits on his bed, as she used to when he was a toddler and had a bad nightmare, and she strokes his back. Kate quietly sings the lullaby she used to sing when he was little, and within a short time, he is asleep again and sleeping more calmly.

She feels exhausted herself and, eventually, she pulls up the armchair near his bed and falls asleep there. She doesn't want to leave him alone tonight.

Simon arrives in the morning with a gentleman who introduces himself as John Wyatt, an officer from the intelligence department. Tom, Simon and Kate sit around the dining table while Wyatt assures them that he believes they are now safe to lead normal lives.

"Valentin Kotov published an article on the web a few days ago exposing this man Igor Novikoff for having been responsible for ten murders, as well as having created his wealth and power from corruption. Kotov implicated several other men in the Kremlin circle, including the President. We believe it was this article that sparked the kidnap of your son, Tom, as a way to get you to lead them to Kotov, and maybe as revenge. Kotov seems to have done a reasonable job of hiding himself over the last few months, bar the odd mugging. But they've really got him now. Novikoff's gang certainly wanted to silence Kotov, prevent him from publishing any further evidence against them. It seems he had gained access to some of the President's bank accounts. We're not sure what will happen to Kotov's colleagues in London and Moscow."

"My God!" Simon explodes, looking at Kate with fury.

"I'm sorry," Kate whispers.

"Kotov was correct, we believe, in his accusations about Novikoff. He is head of an organised crime gang, with links to the Kremlin, and we understand that he has indeed committed assassinations of his enemies in Russia. This is the first time he has carried out any kind of violent act here in the UK, so we suspect he was desperate. He's kept his head low up until now. As if he wanted to keep on the right side of the law here, not draw attention to himself. Probably wouldn't have wanted to be deported. The kidnap seems to have been rather ineptly carried out," John Wyatt tells them.

"Not from my perspective," Tom says grimly. "Nothing inept about it. They grabbed me when I got back to the house."

"But, darling, I asked you not to go home to Notting Hill, to stay at the Limehouse flat, not go out anywhere—"

"I had said I would meet Marianne, Mum," he interrupts Kate. "The last thing I wanted was to be confined in the flat for the whole of my Christmas break."

"I know, but I did ask you to, just this once." Kate sighs, half hating herself for her 'told you so' tone.

"Well, I hardly thought that you would be cavorting with criminals who would hurt me, Mum!" Tom flares up.

"I wasn't cavorting with criminals, Tom," Kate says, defensively. "Valentin is not a criminal; he is an investigative journalist. It's the people he is writing about who are the criminals."

"Yes, and his work exposing corruption has had a negative impact on all of us, hasn't it?" Simon looks at Kate accusingly.

"It must be very distressing for you all as a family. Perhaps, for now, we can focus on the events so that we can build up more of a picture and ensure this kind of thing doesn't happen again, if possible," John Wyatt suggests in measured tones. "I shall talk to your mother separately, but for now I would like to focus on your experience, Tom."

"Yes, yes," Simon agrees.

"So, Tom, tell us what happened to you, if you would," Wyatt asks, turning himself to face Tom.

"I know Mum asked me to stay in the Limehouse flat, but I really couldn't face it. I had a party that night that I had agreed to go to with my girlfriend, Marianne, and I wanted to go. So we went to the pub. We were going on to the party, but I didn't have any decent clothes, so I said I would pop back home to change and be back before she knew it. I ran back home to the house and, as I let myself in, someone hit my head. I don't remember anything after that, until I woke up in that basement room."

"We believe that Novikoff's men were probably watching your Notting Hill house. They may have taken you in an opportunistic moment – seen it as a way to get to Kotov – grabbed you and waited for Kotov. They must have thought he would come back to your house. But he was the one they really wanted, of course, and so they hung around and caught him. The neighbour heard a noise later that night, then saw a black SUV screech off," Wyatt explains.

"I hate to think what could have happened to Marianne if she'd been with me," Tom murmurs.

"Yes, that was fortunate," Simon agrees. "Hardly a good way to start your new relationship, Tom. Your mother did ask you to stay away from the house," Simon remonstrates with him.

Tom looks at his father, raises his eyes to the ceiling. "Fuck off, Dad."

"Don't worry," Wyatt replies. "Just tell us what you can remember."

"I don't remember much. I became unconscious when they hit my head. The next thing I remember was lying on this dirty rug. It felt like a brick floor. They took the hood off my head, and it was completely dark. I couldn't see a thing. And very cold, damp, a dank smell in the air as I breathed." Tom stops and takes a breath. He turns and looks at Kate.

"Someone, a man, somewhere in the room, asked me where my mother's lover was," he continues. Kate feels her ribs tighten as she hears this question and all that is insinuated within it. Simon gives her a withering look.

"I told them I didn't know and didn't care. The man said he didn't believe me, that he knew Valentin was in London. I repeated that I didn't know, couldn't give a toss, and that he could die for all I cared." Tom stops suddenly.

"Then what happened?" Wyatt coaxes him.

"He kicked me. Kicked me in the ribs," Tom says, as if he could hardly believe it even now, "then over and over in the shins. Your first aid guys bandaged me up when they came for me.

"Then the man kept asking me, 'So where is your mother now?' His mouth was right up close to my ear – it was horrible. 'You must know where she is,' he kept repeating. I told him she was staying with a friend but that I didn't know where that was."

Kate and Simon and the officers all sit quietly, waiting on his every word. Kate looks at her son and wonders how he has managed to survive this ordeal.

"Then he kicked me again in the shins several times, really hard, but there was some kind of noise outside, men's voices, and the man became distracted, I think. I lost consciousness again, and when I came to, everything was quiet. I was alone in the room."

"We believe that was the moment they discovered that one of their men had captured Kotov. It was him they were interested in, not you. Other than to get to Kotov, maybe through your mother. What did you do next?" Wyatt asks Tom.

"I started to wake up, get my act together. They'd tied my legs around the ankles, so I sort of shuffled around the room and found an old iron bar or something, it could have been a curtain pole, I'm not sure. My hands were tied in front of me, by the wrist, with some wire. It was really difficult lifting the bar, but I banged on the door with it. I was scared someone might hear me, beat me up, or have a gun, but no one came. I managed to break through a panel. I couldn't believe my luck. The guys had obviously gone off in such a hurry that they had left the key in the other side of the door. I fiddled around and was able to unlock it. I almost fell out of the door and crawled up to a hall. Everything was dusty, so I don't think the house was occupied."

Wyatt is busy making notes as Tom speaks, nodding from time to time as encouragement.

"I let myself out and hopped and shuffled along the street as fast as I could to get away from the house. It was raining. I'm afraid I didn't take the time to look at the number or the name of the road. I just wanted to get away. I couldn't untie my ankles because the wire around them was really tough.

"Eventually, I stopped, out of breath from the struggle of shuffling along, and sat on the front steps of a house. That was when Sharon came out, and she saw me, nearly tripped over me. God knows what she thought finding me bedraggled and tied up on her steps. Her dad found a bolt cutter from his toolkit and cut the wire around my wrists and ankles. It was such a relief. The rest is history because then your guys arrived."

Wyatt stops writing and looks at Tom.

"You may want to talk to someone about this experience. We have experts who can debrief you, if you would like."

"I'm fine," Tom responds brusquely.

Kate looks at him quizzically. "Really?" she asks.

FIFTY

England, 2001

Screams fill the silence of the night. Tom is having another flashback in his sleep. They're back in their home, and Kate has dragged the spare mattress into his room now and leaves it there, so she can sleep beside him. He isn't that keen on having his mum in his room, but he understands that he needs to be woken when he gets the nightmares. Kate knows all about the impact of traumatic experience. She has had nightmares for so many years now about William. She notices now that when her life goes well, she has fewer nightmares, but when she is stressed or anxious, they still return. Looking at the contorted face of her son now, as he dreams, she hopes beyond hope that Tom's mind will release these terrible memories soon.

She calms him back to sleep but can't sleep herself. She is due to talk to John Wyatt, the officer investigating Tom's kidnap, in the morning. He wants to know all that she knows about Valentin. Her mind reels around with images of the years that they have known one another, here and in Russia. Thoughts of Anya and Lara, too, and wondering how they are doing. Images of Anya in a cold Russian prison horrify her, and she worries about Lara managing her diabetes. Will she cope alone now that her aunt is in prison and her grandmother is dead?

The night seems never-ending to Kate as she worries about Tom. On top of all this, her mother has been sectioned and is in some home in South-East London, so Kate will need to visit her as soon as she can.

As the pale light of morning comes through the window, Kate creeps out of Tom's room and puts on a sombre trouser suit for the interview with John Wyatt. She feels embarrassed about her relationship with Valentin and doesn't want to look like some floozy. At the same time, there is some part of her that feels quite strong. As Eve has reminded her, she has admired Valentin's work as an investigative journalist, but she's been in denial about how Tom or she could be in danger in London. "How can I have been so stupid, so blind?" she asks herself over and over.

Eve is also horrified by the fact that her ex-client, Igor Novikoff, turned out to be such a murderer, and yet they both feel quite pleased with themselves that they provided Valentin with some ammunition for his exposé. And so, Kate walks from the tube to Vauxhall Cross feeling quite confident that she will share all she knows and be as helpful as she can be.

John Wyatt is waiting for her in reception and takes her to a small room, where she is introduced to his colleague,

Krishnan Anand. Kate sits, and Wyatt pours her a glass of water.

"So, please, Ms Chisholm, tell us what you know of Valentin Kotov. We shall tape this session, if that's OK with you?" It wasn't really a question, but she nods, then proceeds to tell them about how she met Valentin on the literary tour of Russia, how their relationship continued over the years in Russia and London. She tells them about meeting Lara and Anya, of the time they were mugged in Gorky Park, how she was happy to support Valentin in his role as an investigative reporter, respected his aim to expose corruption.

"Kotov has been a bit of an anomaly to us, too," Wyatt concedes. "At first, we wondered whether he was a Russian asset. We kept an eye on him, but he didn't seem to have connections to the KGB or FSB, or the Kremlin. In fact, although he does seem to want the Soviet Union to reintegrate, he doesn't support the kind of capitalism as practised by the Kremlin. He's more of a socialist, wants to return Russia to Communism if anything. So, he seems to have thought that by exposing bad practice within the capitalist system, he had more of a chance of convincing people that the old ways were the best."

"Yes, I got mixed messages from him," Kate admits. "I thought he wanted Russia to turn towards Europe, but I wasn't sure I'd got that right. He was hard to read; he had sudden and confusing mood swings."

"We believe he's a Marxist at heart. The articles he's written, and connections he has made, suggest that he and his network were building up anti-capitalist narratives and publishing them on the web. To influence and sew doubt and division. Not all his colleagues agreed with him, and this has set him against the President, of course, who, as Kotov does, wants the Soviet Union to return to its former glory but not to return to Communism. More likely to make himself rich, which is anathema to Kotov. So, it's not just Novikoff's men who consider Kotov to be trouble. We suspect that he gained evidence of Novikoff's part in the corruption in the Kremlin several years ago."

"Ah," Kate hesitates. "I wonder if this is what he stored at my house?"

"Quite possibly, yes. We have taken some papers from your house for investigation."

"And what about his sister? Anya?" Kate asks, agitated.

"I'm afraid there isn't much we can do about that. She is in a prison outside Orel, on a trumped-up charge as far as we can tell."

"Do you have any word about Valentin's daughter, Lara?"

"We did get word that she is at medical school. I don't have more information than that."

There's a silence while they all digest the situation and the facts they have shared.

"He was rather an amateur, really," Anand says. "A young man who took an opportunity to try to understand the West through your eyes, perhaps, then build up his own project."

Kate nods and hesitates. "I should have made more of an effort to learn Russian," Kate confesses. "I made assumptions about what he was doing, or writing, but I couldn't fully understand the articles I saw him working on." She pauses, not sure whether she dares to ask the question that hovers on her lips. "Am I in trouble?"

"We don't see that anything you have done has broken a law here. You are not the first person to fall for a Russian and, as you say, he was, in his own way, doing good work. Heaven knows what will happen to him now he is back in Russia, though." Anand's mouth twists as he insinuates that Valentin could be tortured. "He's likely to end up in prison, at the very least."

Kate's arms automatically fold around her. Although the magic snapped on their last meetings, she has memories with Valentin that she treasures. She's not the same person she was when she flew to Moscow back in 1990, that's for sure.

They see her out, and she wanders back through the London streets in a daze. What an extraordinary series of events. She feels as if she's ended up on the pages of a thriller.

The house is quiet when she returns. Tom has left her a note to say that he and Marianne are going out for the day. He adds at the bottom: 'You'll be pleased to know, Mum, that I have made an appointment with the counsellor!'.

Kate is relieved. She suspects Marianne may have helped influence this decision and is grateful. She feels sure it can help him, and it was probably what she needed to do herself all those years ago after William, but in those days, counselling was not so readily available.

She feels exhausted, goes into the kitchen and makes a cup of coffee, clearing up the mess of plates that Tom has left in the sink. Then she goes and lies on the sofa, closes her eyes and allows herself to relax. Her body feels weary right down to her soul.

She's woken a short time later by the telephone.

"Kate?"

Harry's voice sounds like an anchor in the middle of a rough sea.

"Yes, is that you, Harry? I haven't heard from you for so long. How are you?"

"Still in the land of the living," Harry's voice is warm, slow. "How are you? I've missed you, girl. Do I detect a little tiredness in your voice?"

"You always find me out, Harry. Yes, you do," and she finds her voice breaking as the emotions of the last few weeks catch up with her.

"What's up?"

"It's such a long saga, Harry. I've been very gullible, and Tom and I have had a ghastly time. It was that Russian, Valentin. Do you remember? Well, it all ended up with Tom being kidnapped—"

"My God, Kate. Tom, kidnapped? Valentin? That Russian guy we met on the tour? How horrific."

"Yes. Him. As you know, I stayed in touch with him over the years. He became an investigative journalist, focusing on exposing corruption. Of course, some of his targets live and operate here in London now, so he came over to follow them, got on the wrong side of one of them, and these guys pounced on Tom, wanted him to lead them to Valentin. Tom's traumatised by it all."

"I'm not surprised. It all sounds completely crazy, Kate. But are you OK now, both of you?" He sounds genuinely concerned.

"Yes, thanks, we are getting there, I think. Tom's fed up with me, but we are both pleased that we are safe now that Valentin, and also the men who were after him, have gone back to Russia, it seems. But I'm still trying to get the Foreign Office to find out what has happened to his sister, Anya, who got put in jail because of him. I worry about her so much."

"Investigative journalism, eh? It's a noble profession, but I seem to remember remarking to you all those years ago that it doesn't do to be a writer on the wrong side of an authoritarian regime!"

"You did indeed," Kate says ruefully. "And it's not good for anyone around them either!"

"Well at least Valentin hasn't been shot, which is the fate of some of those journalists and writers."

"Not yet, anyway, but I fear he is not in for a good time now he's back in Moscow," she points out. "I seem to remember that you also warned me to be careful who I fell in love with…!"

"I did indeed," Harry says, quite seriously. "It all sounds exhausting, and frightening, Kate."

"It has been. It's been a nightmare."

"What a mess. And it all started on that visit to Moscow back in 1990. How could we have guessed it would end up here? I never thought of Valentin as a bad man, when he was guiding us around."

"No, nor did I, and I am not sure he is a bad man. Complicated, for sure, passionate about his causes, yes, but does that make him bad? I'm just so confused about it all, to be honest," Kate says.

"I've been thinking about you often, you know." Harry's voice slows and is affectionate. "Why don't you take a break, Kate? Come down and see me for a day or two? No pressure. Just get a bit of quiet and some sea air?"

Kate hesitates. It sounds so appealing.

"I'd love to do that, but I must take care of Tom's wellbeing first. He's getting counselling, post-traumatic stuff, you know. I need to make sure he is OK first. Can I give you a call when I feel he is settled?"

"Of course," Harry agrees. "You do what you need to do, and I am here to calm your nerves when you're ready."

"Thanks. I'll call you."

FIFTY-ONE

England, 2001

Kate had been rather sceptical of the ability of counselling sessions to turn around the traumas people experience in life, but she is happy to admit that she was wrong. Over the last weeks, Tom has been visibly healing. He has fewer nightmares, is less tetchy and stressed and seems to be taking charge of his future. The counsellor must know what he's doing – certainly John Wyatt recommended him as someone who had helped those bombed in terrorist attacks. Kate is supremely grateful.

She busies herself arranging a big conference event for Mike's investment bank. It's good money, and she's enjoying it. The last few years have provided her with a reasonable income now, and she has been able to pay back into her savings the money she took from her father's legacy so that she has something in the bank. But now she is fretting about how she will afford care for her mother, whose mind and body have been devastated by her alcoholism.

"I'm going back to uni next week," Tom announces at breakfast.

"Really? Are you sure you are ready?" Kate asks, surprised and yet relieved that he feels well enough to do so.

"Yes, I've done the six weeks counselling programme, and he says I can carry on over the phone for another six weeks, or as long as I feel the need for it, if you are willing to pay for it?"

"Of course, my sweetheart."

"Marianne says she will keep an eye on me and make sure I don't go backwards."

"You've found a good one there, haven't you? She's kind," Kate says, delighted that he has love and support.

Tom turns around. "Mum, I know this wasn't your fault, exactly. Of course, Dad thinks it was, but I can see that Valentin had a mission, and you got wound into it. The counselling has helped me see things more clearly. It wasn't easy for me, but it wasn't easy for you either, and along came this Russian glamour boy. I guess it's not surprising you were bowled over."

Kate stands and looks at her son. He looks down on her with a sweet smile. She hardly recognises him. He hugs her to him awkwardly, muttering, "Love you, Mum," then releases her and takes his plate to the dishwasher.

"I love you too, Tom, and am so proud of you. Keep in touch when you're back at uni, won't you?"

"Yeah, yeah," he says dismissively and disappears up to his room.

"Harry?"

Kate has hesitated and postponed this call many times.

"Kate."

"Can I take you up on that offer of a little sea air and comfort?" she asks tentatively.

"Of course."

She arrives at Harry's house late in the evening, after work, the next weekend. She parks her car on the gravel drive in front of his red-brick, Queen Anne house. He comes out and greets her, kissing her on both cheeks, then takes her case out of the boot and carries it inside.

He shows Kate to his spare room, a room that overlooks the sea.

"Come down when you've made yourself comfortable," he says and goes down to the kitchen below. She can hear him moving dishes around, and there is a nice smell of cooking coming up the elegant staircase.

"Ah, here, have a glass of wine," he says when she comes down to the kitchen and leads her to the conservatory to watch the sun set over the sea.

"We've known each other a long time now, Kate," he says.

"We sure have, though there have been more gaps than times together," she replies.

"Yes, but I have always felt connected to you. Wherever you were, however long the weeks without a phone call, you have been a part of my life since we first met as we boarded the plane to Moscow." His blue eyes are gentle as he looks at her and says this. She's not sure what he is feeling, what he is meaning. Ever since he read her the

Pushkin poem that day in Russia, he has managed to confuse her. *Or maybe*, she thinks, *all men confuse me, and I am unskilled at reading them?*

"These have been some extraordinary years for me," Kate ventures. "I was such a scaredy-cat when I boarded that plane. Did I tell you it was the first time I had gone abroad on my own, ever? Before I got married, I went abroad with girlfriends, and after I was married, it was always with Simon. I just didn't know how I would manage."

"I would never have known you were unsure of yourself, though. And I think now, from what you tell me, you have achieved what you wanted with your charity, and your company, haven't you?"

"I've made so many mistakes in the meantime, though, Harry. I can't believe how I put Tom in such danger."

"What would life be all about if we didn't try things and make mistakes? Dull, dull, dull. And it sounds as if he is OK now, thank heaven. I think my life here has been a doddle of provincial boredom in comparison to yours!"

"What I would give now for a life of provincial boredom." Kate laughs.

He pauses, then says, "Would you?" She sees that he is looking at her intently, and she takes a little time to answer.

"Yes, I think I would. I'm exhausted. I've had enough adventure for a lifetime."

"Well in that case, I shall give you an early supper and put you to bed." Harry stands up and goes into the kitchen, leaving her in the conservatory. Her body begins to relax as she sits and watches the light fade on the sea. The wine is calming her incessant thoughts and fears, and she's happy to sit here and do absolutely nothing.

"OK, soup's up," Harry calls a little while later. They sit over soup and shepherd's pie in his kitchen, listening to the waves lapping against the shore outside.

"I feel I am beginning to breathe easy again," Kate says. "If I ever did. In fact, I am not sure that I did ever breathe easy, but it feels like I could now."

"Good." Harry smiles warmly at her. "Do you know, the minute I met you, I knew we would be friends for life?"

Kate pauses for a moment, reflecting, and then says, "Yes, I know what you mean. Shaking hands as we boarded the plane, you telling me there were no lemons in Moscow! That was a moment of connection," she agrees, smiling at him.

"Ah yes, I remember it well," he quips from the line in *Gigi*. "I'm not a particularly spiritual man, but I do think that there is sometimes a spark that seems to carry from one person to another in that first instant of meeting. You know, meeting a gaze across a crowded room. It's like a recognition, as if one has met before, or as if one's soul, for want of a better word, knows there is something meaningful in the relationship, for better or worse."

"I know what you mean. The trouble is, I had that feeling with Valentin, the moment I met him, and he looked at me with those dark Russian eyes of his—"

"I don't want to hear any more of that, thank you, Kate," Harry interrupts her, with a hint of irritation. "That was surely 'for worse.'"

"Yep, I agree. Yet I don't totally regret it."

"Enough. I don't want to hear about him, Kate. He has messed up your and Tom's life enough. I don't need him to invade ours."

She looks at Harry and sees that he is genuinely disturbed by her mention of Valentin. It seems to knock him backwards, and it reminds her of their earlier meetings or phone calls where he had come towards her, then retreated. Rather like a knight on a chess board.

"I'm sorry. That was insensitive of me. Thank you, Harry, for this invitation. It's just what I need," she says in a more conciliatory and affectionate way, to pacify him.

He looks up from putting the dishes in the dishwasher and smiles, the lines around his blue eyes crinkling.

"It's my privilege."

Kate wakes late the next morning. Spring sunlight flickers across the oak floorboards of Harry's spare bedroom. The seagulls call across the water. She sits up and watches the waves, the clouds scudding across the sky. She breathes deeply, and her shoulders relax.

Harry knocks on the door with a mug of tea. He sits on the side of the bed.

"We can have a lazy day," he says. "Take a bath, and I'll make some breakfast."

Kate lies in the warm bed, drinking the tea from a homemade pottery mug. She feels so comfortable in the folds of the white cotton sheets. She dozes and then gets up and runs herself a scented bath. When she goes down to the kitchen, she seems to be alone, so she wanders around the ground floor of the house. There's a large hallway, a dining room close to the kitchen, Harry's study with papers stacked on his desk and a large sitting room.

She hears Harry return.

"I just biked into the village to get the papers," he explains. "A boiled egg?"

"Yes please." They settle in peaceful companionship, eating breakfast, reading the papers, commenting occasionally on the articles they're reading.

After a walk, Harry suggests they listen to some music. They go to the living room. From the window, Kate can see the lawn sloping down towards the sea. Harry puts on a CD, and music fills the room. They sit next to one another on the sofa, and Kate starts to tell him about Tom and Marianne. Harry puts his hand on hers.

"Shh, dear Kate," he says. "Just listen. No need to speak. Allow the music to play around you. My grandmother taught me the gift of silence, of paying full attention to music. She told me off, when I was staying with her as a teenager, for always having music on in the background and talking over it. 'Just be with it, Harry,' she'd say, 'give way to it.'"

And so Kate does. Her breathing slows, and she lets go of the need to speak or amuse him. She just soaks in the notes as she looks around the room. Pale yellow walls, cream silk curtains, long Queen Anne sash windows on three sides. The piano notes of Beethoven's 'Emperor' Concerto seem to dance and echo around the cornice of the room. She lies back on the sofa, tucks her feet under Harry's legs and absorbs the harmonies. As the notes cease, she opens her eyes, to see Harry watching her.

"There," he says. "Wasn't that beautiful?"

Kate feels at home, as if she can just be herself, no acting or putting on airs. Looking out at the calm sea beyond the window, she feels at peace for the first time in many months.

"You will stay again tonight, won't you?" Harry asks.

FIFTY-TWO

England, 2001

"Hi, Mum. How's things?" Tom's voice sounds chirpy.

"Good, thanks. Have just run the conference for Mike's investment bank, and it went really well, so I am thrilled. The last few weeks have been good. And how about you?"

Kate's delighted to hear his voice but detects that there's something he's going to tell her, or wants to tell her, and she is anxious, just in case it is something she doesn't want to hear.

"Yeah, term's going well. And, Mum…"

"Yes?"

"Just wanted to say that Marianne and I are going skiing with Dad next break."

"That's exciting," Kate says, hoping that her voice doesn't betray the disappointment she is feeling that he won't be coming home to her.

"Yes, Marianne has been before, but it will be my first time. I'm really excited."

"Great, where are you going?"

"Austria. For two weeks, so I won't be home much, just for a couple of days before we go."

"I'm delighted for you, Tom," Kate tells him, wishing she didn't feel jealous that Simon was treating them to this lovely holiday.

"Good. OK, Mum. Just wanted to let you know. Bye."

The house suddenly feels empty, and Kate allows herself just to sit and look out on the garden, reminiscing on all the changes she has experienced since moving to Notting Hill.

As she makes herself a cup of tea, the phone rings.

"John Wyatt here," the voice says. "We have news of Valentin Kotov."

"Oh, good. Is he OK?" Kate asks.

"We have had confirmation that the ground staff of Aeroflot did report that one of the passengers on that flight was ill. It's in the log. It's taken us a while to confirm this. That person was listed as having two companions who were looking after him. They must have had forged papers as the name Kotov was not mentioned, but we are pretty sure it was him."

"Do you know what happened after he arrived in Russia?"

"It hasn't been confirmed yet, but I'm afraid we think he was transported to a prison east of Moscow."

"Oh dear." Despite everything, Kate hates to think of him being harmed.

"We can't tell you more than this. We have no further news of his sister, either. But we shall update you, of course, should we get more information."

"Thank you," Kate says, with a heavy heart.

Kate takes herself out for a walk in Kensington Gardens, then walks across the Serpentine and wanders aimlessly along, looking at the young mothers and their babies, remembering Tom when he was young, knowing she must accept that those days are gone. She must shape her own life now.

She is seeing Harry often, walking, talking, going to the theatre. She had wanted to take it slowly, and it was three months before they eventually made love. She feels so comfortable in his company. There are no fireworks but a steady companionship, and she feels it is turning into love. She wonders why she has spent so many years seeking thrills and adventure when being in this quiet space with Harry is so enjoyable. His daughter, Isabelle, is a delight, too, pregnant with her first child.

Time passes gently then one morning as they sit over breakfast in Notting Hill Harry suddenly says, "Your house or mine?"

"What do you mean?" Kate asks. "For the weekend?"

"No, girl, for us to live together!"

"Oh…" Kate is taken aback. "Is that a good idea?"

He looks puzzled. "Why wouldn't it be?"

"Well, I don't know. We've been getting along so well, I didn't think anything needed to change, really," she replies, rather feebly.

"But I want to spend more time with you," he says,

with a slightly pleading look in his eye. "I want to wake up with you every morning rather than just occasional mornings, kiss you goodnight every night."

Kate listens and says nothing. She's worked so hard for this home and for her independence. She's not at all sure about giving it up.

"Why not my house for weekdays and yours for weekends?" she suggests.

He shakes his head. "It's too confusing. I can't manage that. I like to know where things are. I like to be able to walk around my house as if I were blind and know that I could find everything I needed, even if all the lights had fused."

Kate laughs and shakes her head at him. "A stick in the mud, then!"

"Absolutely," he agrees.

"Well, if that is the case then it has to be your house, doesn't it, but I shall keep my house here. Maybe get a lodger to pay the bills."

Harry gets up from the table and comes around behind her, places his hands on her shoulders and kisses the top of her head.

"That sounds perfect."

Kate loves being by the sea. She hadn't wanted to leave the warm elegance that she had created in Notting Hill, but now that she's here, with Harry, she's loving her life. She has brought enough of her own precious books so that she doesn't feel bereft. And her photos and albums. Those are the things she cares about most.

The weeks have whizzed by. She feels very much at home here and with Harry. She drives down to the maternity home several times a month and runs events. It seems possible to continue her projects despite moving away geographically.

It's a beautiful evening as she and Harry go for a walk along the beach, weaving in and out of the cliffs. The air is still when, out of the blue, Harry says, "Shall we marry?"

She stops and looks at him, checking whether he is serious.

"I don't think we need to, do we?" she says carefully. "We know we love one another and are committed to one another. I don't see the need, at our age, to marry again, do you?"

"That doesn't sound very romantic, Kate," he complains.

"No, I know. I'm sorry. But I've been there once before. So have you. All this ''til death us do part' thing, it didn't bring either of us happiness or certainty. I am very happy the way we are. But anyway, if you are grumbling about me not being romantic, then you should have got down on your knee, shouldn't you, instead of suddenly asking me the question out of the blue, with no warning," she teases him.

"Ah, you mean, just to get rejected?"

"Yes, exactly!" she replies, as they laugh together.

He stops walking, draws her to him and kisses her lips.

"I love your independence, Kate. The way you stand on your own feet."

"And mess things up?" she questions.

"Well, yes, because that makes me feel better about messing things up. So, of course I love it when you mess things up."

"Perhaps we should get a dog?" Kate suggests, not

knowing where that suggestion came from.

"What, instead of getting married?"

"Yes, it's much simpler. No party, no wedding."

"You'd rather have a puppy pee all over the carpet than a fancy reception somewhere then?"

"Definitely."

"Well, if you are into avoiding commitment on the relationship front, I can assure you that a dog is a far greater commitment. Totally incapable of looking after itself, looks at you with great guilt-laden eyes that tell you you're never doing enough for it. Farts, demands food and walks. Are you sure you wouldn't prefer to marry me?" Harry jests.

"Sure. A dog it is," Kate replies.

The golden retriever puppy is heaven. They christen her Blondie. She provides them with endless entertainment and mess. As the year ends, Kate has never felt so happy and relaxed.

"Let's cancel that dinner party tomorrow," Harry says to her as she returns from walking Blondie.

"Why?" she asks him, confused. Then notices he looks rather pale.

"Are you feeling OK? What's up?"

"Nothing. Just a bit of indigestion. But I don't feel I have the energy to make lots of conversation, that's all."

"OK," Kate agrees. "I shall give them a call and explain we can't make it."

She starts to go out of the room, then turns around. She sees him sitting in his favourite armchair and notices that he has already closed his eyes.

"Are you sure you're OK?"

PART FIVE

2002-03

FIFTY-THREE

Russia, 2002

Anya walks through the prison gates in a daze. Two years have gone by since she first arrived. She's been to hell and back and feels only half-human. Her rights, and her dignity, have been stolen. She's lost several kilos in weight, which she thinks perhaps isn't a bad thing, but her skin is dry, and her hair has fallen out in clumps over the last few months. Who will want her now, she wonders. She has come to hate the idea of spending the rest of her life alone.

The brightness of the daylight blinds her. A prison bus takes her to the centre of Orel, and she climbs out. She finds she's a few blocks away from her old flat. She doesn't know what has happened, whether someone else has moved in now, as her rental payments would have dried up when nothing was going into her account. She doubts the landlord would have kept the place for her, as no one knew when she would be released or, indeed, whether she would ever be back.

She walks slowly and tentatively along the street. She hardly dares to get to her front door because she doesn't want to know the truth. But eventually she's there and rings her own bell. Nothing. She rings it again and again. No reply. At least, maybe, that means there is no one else living there. That's her hope, anyway.

Then she rings Natalya's door. The buzzer goes and she drags herself up the stairs. Natalya opens the door when Anya knocks. Natalya is looking tall, slim and fit, so much younger than Anya feels herself, although they are the same age. Natalya looks puzzled at first, then, with a frown, asks, "Anya? Is it you? It is, isn't it!" and she takes Anya into a warm hug. "Ah, my Anya, it's so wonderful to see you. Come in, come in. How are you?"

Anya falls into her embrace, tears running down both their cheeks. It's the first human warmth she has felt in years.

"Ah, my darling, come and sit down." Natalya takes her hand and leads her into the small sitting room. Anya sits down in a comfortable chair. She can hardly remember what it feels like to have the softness of upholstery beneath her.

"I'll make you a tea," Natalya says and busies herself, then comes and kneels in front of Anya as she drinks. She strokes her arm.

"Talk to me," she urges Anya.

"Where's Lara?" Anya whispers the question, not wanting bad news. "I have heard nothing all this time, although I asked over and over again."

"Relax," Natalya tells her. "She is living with her

boyfriend. He's a doctor whom she met at medical school. Now they both work at the same hospital. She's fine. And her mother, Yulia, has been helpful and supportive."

"Oh, what a relief." Anya finds herself convulsed in sobs and even grateful now that Yulia has been a presence in her life. "Is she far away?"

"No, they live near the hospital. He's a nice young man and, of course, being medical, he supports the care of her diabetes. She's looking beautiful and happy, though of course she has been desperately worried about you. And Valentin. She was told that neither of you were allowed visits or letters."

"Have you heard news of Valentin?"

"Only that he's in prison. It doesn't sound as if he will be out for a long time." Natalya sighs. "The story is that he was about to leak some more dirt on the President."

"I feel so cross with him, Natalya. He put us all in danger."

"Yes, he did. But he's your brother. Lara's father. You could try to see if you are allowed to visit or discover if there's any way you can help him get out, perhaps?"

"Right now, I don't have the strength, but maybe one day I shall, yes." Anya sips her tea and begins to feel a little restored. "What happened to my flat?"

"The landlord had to get another tenant in there, I'm afraid. But I think he will possibly try to give it back to you or find you another place. He's kept asking after you. He knows you're a good tenant, and he's none too keen on the authorities who put you away."

"Thanks, Natalya. I don't know what has happened to my shop, either?"

"No, I don't know the legal position, but it's boarded up. You'll have to ask when you feel ready."

Natalya fills her cup and brings her some bread and honey.

"Now," she says, "tell me all about what happened, please, because I just don't know why you suddenly disappeared."

Anya tells her of the arrest, the charges against her, the court case, how unbelievable it all was.

"It's completely destroyed any trust I had in the legal system here, Natalya. How can we live like this? Where we could be picked up off the street any time for doing nothing?"

"It's frightening, I agree," Natalya replies. "Especially as this really had nothing to do with you but everything to do with Valentin. They just wanted you to tell them where he was, and what he was up to, presumably?"

"Yes, and I didn't know. I certainly didn't know where he was, because the bastard had to leave Russia, go to Finland, maybe go to England. I was worried about Kate and Tom too."

Natalya listens, holding her hand.

"I had thought, Natalya," Anya continues, "that our country would be free after 1990, but in the end, there is no freedom. We cannot say or do what we like. It's like living in a marriage with an abusive husband who controls everything we do, everything we say."

"Look, you can stay here tonight," Natalya says. "And for as long as it takes to get settled. Have a shower and a good sleep. I'll lend you some clothes, so you begin to feel like a woman again. Then tomorrow you can call the landlord and see what he can do for you."

"Thanks, Natalya, you're a great friend." Anya gives Natalya a hug. "I don't know whether there's any money in my bank. I haven't known what life is like on the outside. The news that Lara is alive and well is the best news ever."

After a bath, Anya uses Natalya's phone to call Lara. Lara almost collapses when she hears her aunt's voice. They talk for an hour, sharing stories and love. Lara says she will come to Natalya's flat after her shift tomorrow.

"Have you heard from your father, my kitten?" Anya asks.

"No," Lara hesitates at the other end of the line, "but I did hear through a contact that he isn't in a good state. They have sent in a doctor several times. I don't know when he will be released, if ever."

"I know," Anya replies. "I don't like to think about it. It was bad enough for me, but for him it will be ten times worse. He is counted as an enemy of the state, or enemy of the people, or whatever they like to say. They won't make life easy for him. Have you tried to visit?"

"Yes. I tried, but I'm not allowed. He isn't allowed any visitors. But do you know, Auntie, I've discovered he had a son in Moscow, with another woman. Perhaps that's why he didn't have time for us?"

"I didn't know that." Anya is shocked but not totally surprised by this news. "At least you are alive, Lara. Can I meet your boyfriend? Natalya tells me he is kind."

"He's lovely, Auntie. He looked after me when you disappeared. And Yulia too, you know. She's been great. But Konstantin is special – I became ill during one of my lectures, had a low. I was so worried about you. The tutor took me to a department of the hospital and there was Konstantin. You'll love him. He balanced up my levels and one thing led to another. We fell in love. I couldn't stay in the flat because I didn't have the money for the rent, and Konstantin said I could live with him. I'm OK, Auntie. I promise."

"That's wonderful news." Anya sighs with relief. "It makes me feel that perhaps I can get my life back bit by bit, as long as you are well and happy."

"I am."

FIFTY-FOUR

England, 2002

It's a big evening. Everything is set and ready. Kate has a major fundraiser charity event at the Natural History Museum. Harry's coming down by train later to join her for it.

Eve is helping with the arrangements.

"Where's Harry?" she asks.

"He's seeing the doctor. He just rang to say that he is at the hospital now, having a scan. He'll join us later. In the meantime, I reassured him that you would be here with me, supporting me."

"Fair enough," says Eve. "Is he OK?" Eve stops and looks at Kate with concern.

"I'm not sure, to be honest. I think he has been keeping things from me. You know what men are like, they hate anything medical, anything that reminds them they are mortal!"

"True." Eve looks at her. "He's a good man but then I've been telling you that for years! I hope he's OK. Tonight, though, we shall have some fun. Dress up in our glam dresses together. Like we did when we were teenagers."

"Yes, and the wonderful news is that I just had word from Anya. She's out of prison, and Lara is safe too, living with a doctor at the hospital where she's studying medicine. Anya doesn't say much, but it's such a relief not to wake up thinking about her in some horrible jail."

"That's great news!" Eve says. "Something more to celebrate tonight."

Kate is happy to be with Eve, though there is a dark shadow somewhere in her stomach, worrying about Harry.

They both change for the evening at Kate's house in Notting Hill, laughing and helping one another put on their make-up and do their hair, like old times. Kate's lodger, Pete, is amused by them and compliments them as they leave for the evening. They get a cab and walk into the museum feeling good. The room is full of people, and Kate is happy that they have managed to replace many of their Russian donors with others, as well as some corporate donors. Grigory is here, though, and Kate and Eve are both very fond of him. "Not all Russians are bad," Kate tells everyone. And Eve's Italian designer, who seems to have become quite an item in her life, greets her effusively.

Harry arrives halfway through the second course. He looks pale as he comes in the room but handsome in his dinner jacket and bow tie. He comes over to Kate and gives her a kiss.

"Darling girl, this looks splendid."

"Yes, I'm thrilled that we have so many generous people here. Edward and Freddie are over there, why don't you go and say hello?"

"I think I'll just sit quietly here, thanks, sweetheart."

And Harry sits down at their table and pours himself a glass of water. Kate doesn't want to ask him about his results in the midst of a social occasion, so she forces herself to leave him and continue the rounds of talking to people and thanking them for their generosity.

As the evening comes to an end, Harry asks if they can go home.

"Sure," Kate says. "Shall we walk? It's a beautiful night."

"No, can we get a taxi?"

"Of course."

They make awkward conversation in the taxi, knowing that something of import needs to be shared. Kate doesn't want to know what it is. She has a foreboding.

When they get home, they sit in the sitting room. Kate gives Harry a camomile tea. He takes her hand in his.

"It's cancer," he says, kissing her fingertips.

"How can they be sure?" Kate argues, not wanting it to be true.

"I haven't been completely straight with you, I'm afraid. I have been having a series of tests over the last few weeks. I didn't want to worry you, but I could sense something wasn't right. And now I know."

"What sort of cancer?"

"Pancreas. But it's spread. All over the place, bloody thing! Bloody nuisance!" Harry tries to smile and make light of it, but Kate leans forward and holds him to her with all her might, as if that will keep him alive.

"Oh God. How horribly unfair," she whispers in his ear, caressing him, kissing his cheek.

"Yes, it feels like that, doesn't it? But why not me? Ultimately. I am just a human, and if it can happen to one person, then it can happen to me, can't it."

"That's all very well. You can be logical and philosophical, darling Harry. But it feels unfair." Her tears fall into his hair, the blond now streaked with grey, and slide down the back of his neck.

"Will they do chemo?"

"No," he replies.

"Why not?"

"Because there's no guarantee it would work. It's spread to my spine with secondaries. I don't want to go through all that or put Isabelle through it, or you. I've decided to let it run its course. Without treatment. Just with pain relief."

"But you could have discussed that with me, Harry," Kate says indignantly.

"No, because I knew what you would say. I knew that you would want me to try every single kind of treatment available, all the chemo, the clinical trials and anything else. But, my darling Kate, I don't want to do that. I can't face it. I can't face going backwards and forwards to some hospital, potentially just to get a few more weeks of life. I would rather we enjoyed an ordinary, and precious, time together living our lives without all that."

Kate is speechless. It had been such a wonderful evening at the Natural History Museum, where she felt so happy and proud. She wasn't expecting it to end like this, nor his attitude towards it. But she looks into his eyes and sees his resolve. She understands what he is saying, and her love for him is strong. She tells him she shall support him through the times ahead.

They sit together quietly and then go to bed.

Getting back to the countryside, Kate parks the car in the drive and helps Harry out. She notices that she still thinks of it as his house. They are greeted by Blondie, who has been looked after by Meg, Harry's cleaner.

"She's been very good," Meg tells them, giving Harry a quizzical look as he walks slowly into the kitchen and brushes Blondie away from him as she jumps up.

They walk into the conservatory and sit quietly, watching the sea. Today it is almost silver, and the horizon between the sky and water is invisible.

"That view of endless silver sea seems like a metaphor," Kate remarks. "Of no boundaries, no difference between sky and water, just an invisible energy between life and death. You'll never be far away from me, in liminal space. That's what that sea is telling me."

He takes her hand, and she rests her head on his shoulder.

"Yes," he says, "I shall always be with you, wherever I am. I just wish I hadn't dawdled so long in bringing you into my life. I so wanted you to find your own way, without the confusion of me in the middle. You were divorcing Simon, sorting out your future, and I didn't want to complicate it, plus I was terrified of getting hurt. Then you got hooked on bloody Valentin, and I didn't even believe I stood a chance. Now I regret it. All that time we could have been together. There was always the connection between us."

Kate looks at him and understands. *What a generous man*, she thinks now.

"Yes, there was always that connection," she echoes, "it's like that warm thread of love you spoke about outside the monastery at Zagorsk that day. Do you remember? The kind of love that burns quietly, like your Aga. But I was so lost when I first met you. I hadn't a clue who I was or which way was up. I've decided none of us gain even the tiniest bit of real wisdom until we are at least forty years old, and I certainly didn't have any!"

"No," he says quietly, "perhaps everything has its time and has to evolve in its own way."

"And what's the point in regrets, my darling?" Kate says as she kisses his cheek.

A few days later, they share a simple vegetable soup for supper. He's very weak now and can only manage a few mouthfuls.

"I've been thinking about Shakespeare today." He takes a battered copy of the *Collected Works* from the sideboard next to him and reads:

"That time of year thou mayst in me behold
When yellow leaves, or none, or few, do hang
Upon those boughs which shake against the cold,
Bare ruin'd choirs, where late the sweet birds sang.
In me thou see'st the twilight of such day
As after sunset fadeth in the west,
Which by and by black night doth take away,
Death's second self, that seals up all in rest.
In me thou see'st the glowing of such fire

That on the ashes of his youth doth lie,
As the death-bed whereon it must expire,
Consum'd with that which it was nourish'd by.
This thou perceiv'st, which makes thy love more strong,
To love that well which thou must leave ere long."[3]

"That's 'Sonnet 73'," he says. "The title is 'That time of year thou mayst in me behold'. It seemed appropriate for this phase of our lives."

"It's beautiful," she tells him.

That evening, as they lie in bed, Harry takes her hand.

"I've been such a fool," he says. "So hopeless at expressing myself. I knew from the moment I saw you that I loved you, but I've screwed it up, over and over again. And now it's too late. I have wasted so much time – yours and mine."

"You have always been there, in your own way," she replies quietly. "And you didn't approach me, because you wanted me to find my feet alone. That was so kind of you, so thoughtful. And I did."

"Yes, you did," he agrees. "And it's wonderful to see that you have lived this time to the full and become, I think, the woman you wanted to be. If there's one thing I hope Isabelle learns from me now," he continues, "it is to stop and listen to the stories we tell ourselves and to check them out. I kept assuming that your affection was elsewhere, but I didn't take the time to check it out. And I didn't have the guts to express my own feelings, for fear of rejection. But 'nothing ventured nothing gained' is an old saying that still contains

---

3   'Sonnet 73', William Shakespeare

its wisdom, and I can't remember who said or wrote it, but I read a phrase about honesty taking us to the edge of the precipice where falling could lead to pain but might otherwise lead to love. Have you heard that?"

Kate takes his hand and kisses it. "No, I haven't, but it makes sense to me. I was preoccupied, Harry, for a long time. Bloody obsessed with this crazy selfish Russian who thought he was saving the world and didn't mind how much havoc that played with those who loved him. His family, his friends. I was hooked in some kind of alternative universe. And then the whole paradigm shifted, and I saw him for what he was, for the pain he had put me through all these years, and Anya and Lara. The pain my obsession had put Tom through and how it had kept you away. I'm the one who should be sorry, dear Harry."

She stands up and settles the pillow behind his head.

"I think you need to rest now, Harry. We can't change the past, can't change what we did or felt. That's where we are at, and it wastes these precious moments to regret them. But it's good to make amends where one can and now to live each precious moment that we have together."

Harry rests his head back on the pillow; his eyes close; and his hand releases its intense grip on hers. She sits beside him for a long time as he sleeps a morphine-induced slumber, a well of emotion inside her.

"I shan't live to see my grandchild, Kate. Give him a kiss from me," Harry says a while later, almost in his sleep.

"I shall," she assures him.

Kate texts Tom: 'I love you. I fear we don't have long. Are you able to come and be with me? I could really do with a hug.'

Harry lies, pale and emaciated, next to her. Tom and Isabelle are downstairs preparing some food. Kate holds Harry's hand, though his grip is weak. His breathing is laboured. The end will come soon, and she knows that it will release him from this pain and discomfort.

"Do you remember this?" he says softly, and with all the effort of mind and body that it takes him, he recites Pushkin's poem:

> "*A magic moment I remember:*
> *I raised my eyes and you were there,*
> *A fleeting vision, the quintessence*
> *Of all that's beautiful and rare*
> *I pray to mute despair and anguish,*
> *To vain the pursuits the world esteems,*
> *Long did I hear your soothing accents,*
> *Long did your features haunt my dreams.*
> *Time passed. A rebel storm-blast scattered*
> *The reveries that once were mine*
> *And I forgot your soothing accents,*
> *Your features gracefully divine.*
> *In dark days of enforced retirement*
> *I gazed upon grey skies above*
> *With no ideals to inspire me*
> *No one to cry for, live for, love.*
> *Then came a moment of renaissance,*
> *I looked up – you again are there*
> *A fleeting vision, the quintessence*
> *Of all that's beautiful and rare.*"[4]

---

4   Alexander Pushkin, 1799–1837, 'A Magic Moment I Remember'

The words come out slowly, haltingly. He has to stop and gain his breath between sentences. Tears run down Kate's cheeks. "Yes, of course I do remember."

"Well, that's you, my darling Kate. Beautiful and rare. And do you know what?"

"No," she whispers, hardly able to find words.

"You'll be all right. You're strong – you can start a new life, a different life. I believe in you and have been so lucky to spend time with you."

"I wanted to live that life with you, Harry, not alone."

"I know, my sweet girl. Me too, believe me, but I also do know that you can do it alone. Some can't, but you can."

She looks down at his pale face, his gentle smiling blue eyes that have a translucence as the life fades from him.

"Yes," the word escapes with her breath. "Don't you worry about me. And don't forget, like it or not, that you will always be with me here, in my heart," she whispers. And as she looks out of the window she remembers how, all those years ago in Moscow, her Scottish friend Gillian had told her that love can be found in many different places, from friends, nature, a pet, or even from a stranger's smile. She would not be alone.

After the funeral, Kate spends time in the country house to recover. One morning she finds the courage to start to carefully pack up Harry's clothes to give to charity. As she folds his shirts, her laptop, sitting on the dressing table, pings. She glances over and sees an email from Anya. 'I just heard that Valentin has been transferred to the Matrosskaya Tishina Detention Centre. It has a terrible reputation'.

Kate feels sorry for him and hates to think of him suffering. But in that moment, as she takes in the knowledge that Valentin is imprisoned, she is aware that as the lock on his cell snaps shut, the snare that has held her captive for so long is finally broken.

ACKNOWLEDGEMENTS

I would like to thank the members of my creative writing group at the Avenue Club, Kew, and particularly our wonderful tutor, Harriet Grace, for getting me started on this project and for their encouragement throughout the many edits and changes.

I would also like to thank those who have given me excellent editorial advice and helped me shape the narrative – Adrienne Dines, Claire Dyer and David Haviland. Beth Archer, Jonathan White and all those at Troubador for their professional support.

Members of my book club, Rupert Bowen, Dulce Merritt, and Robin Byron who have also been helpful in reading early versions and commenting on where I could improve, as has my dear sister, Sarah, and my close friend Penny Corke, and Sandy Adamson for proof reading.

To friends and family far and wide who have given me encouragement, and Susanne Groom who gave me some helpful references.

Marilyn Peachey for filling me in on the challenges and joys of fundraising for a charity.

My brother Richard for his love and support.

My sons Rupert and Oli who are always my cheerleaders when I begin to doubt myself, and I am eternally grateful for their belief in me.

And for Daniel, whose short life I shall never forget.

ABOUT THE AUTHOR

Helen Whitten is an established author, blogger and prize-winning poet. She is the winner of the Elmbridge Literary Festival Adult Poetry Prize 2021 and 2014 and the Winchester Writers' Festival Poetry Prize 2013. Her first collection of poetry, *The Alchemist's Box* was published by Morgan's Eye Press in 2015.

She read history as a mature student at King's College, London and has written six non-fiction books on the subject of personal and professional development and cognitive-behavioural coaching. During her career as a business coach she travelled extensively, including two visits to Russia.

She lives in Kew. **No Lemons in Moscow** is her first novel.

Thinking Aloud blog site: www.helenwhitten.com

This book is printed on paper from sustainable sources managed under the Forest Stewardship Council (FSC) scheme.

It has been printed in the UK to reduce transportation miles and their impact upon the environment.

For every new title that Matador publishes, we plant a tree to offset CO_2, partnering with the More Trees scheme.

For more about how Matador offsets its environmental impact, see www.troubador.co.uk/about/